TERMINAL POINT

ALSO BY K. M. RUIZ

Mind Storm

TERMINAL POINT

K. M. Ruiz

THOMAS DUNNE BOOKS
ST. MARTIN'S PRESS
NEW YORK

THOMAS DUNNE BOOKS.
An imprint of St. Martin's Press.

TERMINAL POINT. Copyright © 2012 by Katrina M. Ruiz. All rights reserved. Printed in the United States of America. For information, address St. Martin's Press, 175 Fifth Avenue, New York, N.Y. 10010.

www.thomasdunnebooks.com
www.stmartins.com

ISBN 978-0-312-68155-5

First Edition: June 2012

10 9 8 7 6 5 4 3 2 1

For Kelly Weingart, because you've always been a brilliant friend.
This one is for you.

PART ONE

DEPRIVATION

SESSION DATE: 2128.05.07
LOCATION: Institute of Psionics Research
CLEARANCE ID: Dr. Amy Bennett
SUBJECT: 2581
FILE NUMBER: 418

She is young, only a child, bent over the table and coloring furiously. The wires attached to her hands, arms, back, and head shake with the motion. The crayon she is rubbing down to nothing is red, the black one tossed away. The paper she is using is covered with a shapeless picture. It's the only color in the white room, save for the yellow dress she wears.

The doctor sits across from her and touches a finger to the waxy residue on the large drawing paper. "Is this how you see the world?"

"This is how the world is now," Aisling says, pushing a trailing wire out of the way.

"You could change that," the doctor says. Her hand beneath the table is shaking. "You could tell us how to stop the wars."

"No, I can't."

"You are being a very selfish little girl, Aisling."

The girl looks up, her bleached-out violet eyes wide and unblinking as the EEG and supporting machines she is connected to whine shrilly behind her. "Am I in trouble?"

"Not if you help us. Not if you save us."

When Aisling speaks, she sounds mournful. "I can't do that."

[ONE]

They flew east into Bellsund, the arctic waters below mostly free of ice floes. The group of shuttles descended into the Van Mijenfjord beneath the government's security grid, light from the midnight sun shining down on their wings. They stayed locked in tight formation, all nine following a route uploaded on another continent. The whine of the engines echoed eerily across the vast emptiness of the island they were approaching.

The Van Mijenfjord began to narrow after the first forty or so kilometers, the lack of airspace noticeable, but not dangerous. Skimming above the still arctic waters between ragged shorelines, the shuttles sped toward their destination.

Sveagruva was a mining settlement abandoned long ago, located some distance from the head of the Van Mijenfjord. A dilapidated airfield sat at its edge, where the nine shuttles finally came to ground, landing gear sliding dangerously on uneven terrain. Less than half a kilometer away were the remnants of Sveagruva, the dormitories and the supply center long since iced over and eaten away by the elements.

The shuttles switched to standby mode, only their environmental systems running at full. Inside Alpha shuttle, the pilot leaned back in her seat and looked at her navigator.

"Well?" Matron asked. "Now what?"

Lucas Serca didn't answer. He stared out the forward windshield, dark blue eyes red from burst capillaries. Bruises pressed beneath his eyes and dried blood clung to the skin of his face, his ears, his neck. As a Class I triad psion, Lucas possessed one of the most powerful minds born in this generation, and it was killing him.

"Lucas."

"We need a day," Lucas finally said, glancing at the leader of the scavengers. "Can the shuttles' stealth systems handle that?"

Matron pressed her lips together, brow furrowing. The exhaustion on her dark face was impossible to miss. "They got us here, so they should be good for it. Let me check with Novak, since he was the only one jacked into the system."

Lucas levered himself out of the seat, his lean frame rigid with pain. "You do that."

He stumbled back into the cargo bay. It was warmer in the main guts of the shuttle than on the flight deck. Lucas leaned his back against the cool metal of the hatch, letting it hold him up as he surveyed their passengers.

Threnody Corwin, a Class III electrokinetic, was pale-faced and sitting up, a vast improvement from the beginning of this trip, when she couldn't even breathe on her own. Wrapped in several thermal blankets, the former Stryker was carefully peeling off blackened skin from one hand, revealing healed pink flesh beneath the damage. She was still hooked up to an IV and trauma kit, her blue eyes glassy, but she no longer looked mostly dead.

Sitting beside her, one hand gently pressed to the back of her neck, was Jason Garret. The only Class 0 microtelekinetic in existence wasn't looking at either of them. Jason's attention was focused on where his partner, Kerr MacDougal, sat slouched in a seat against the bulkhead beside Quinton Martinez. Both men were unconscious with exhaustion. The IVs hooked to their arms were almost empty and would need to be replaced soon.

"Should you be moving?" Lucas asked.

"Felt the landing," Threnody rasped. "Jason took off my restraints."

"She's doing better than she was even an hour ago," Jason said. "Though she still has a long way to go."

Lucas studied Jason. The microtelekinetic looked better than the rest of them, but that didn't mean he wasn't in pain. Jason's power now let him work on the subatomic level, let him manipulate DNA in order to heal, to create. It's what he was doing right now, still leaning on the nanites in

Threnody's body to help heal her since he didn't trust his new strength alone yet.

Jason's upgraded Classification didn't come without cost. His mind had been violated by Lucas's youngest sister, Kristen Serca, a dysfunctional Class III empath, in order to give him access to his full power. The psychic bond Jason once shared with Kerr was severed after Kristen broke his nearly impenetrable natal shields. Lucas permanently reset the bond into Quinton, and the link between the pair was still raw. It had saved Jason's life, yes, but at what felt like the cost of Quinton's.

"We make it?" Jason asked in a low voice. He moved his head a little, tipping it back until he exposed his throat. Lucas could see the rise and fall of his Adam's apple as the older man swallowed.

"To Sveagruva, yes," Lucas said. His English accent got thicker with every word he spoke, exhaustion heavy in his voice. Lucas shoved himself away from the hatch tiredly.

Jason frowned, blinking slowly as he turned his head to look at Lucas. "Thought it was supposed to be Longyearbyen? Those were the coordinates you uploaded."

"We'll get there soon enough. In a day or so." Lucas crossed over to where his sisters sat slumped together on the other side of the cargo bay. "We need a day to recover."

"We need more time than that."

Lucas said nothing as he looked down at Samantha and Kristen. Of the three siblings, Kristen came away from the fighting in Buffalo with the least amount of damage, not surprising when one considered her default damaged state. Most psions tried to keep insanity at bay; Kristen reveled in it. His sixteen-year-old sister destroyed the minds of others in her search for a balance she would never find. Kristen's dysfunction made her dangerous, yet also powerful. Even at full strength, Lucas was hard-pressed to keep her in check. Kristen was the only person who could have broken Jason's formidable mental shields and survived. If they were lucky, maybe she had learned how to build sanity out of Jason's neural pattern.

Lucas wasn't going to hold his breath.

Reaching out with a steady hand, Lucas stroked his fingers over Samantha's tangled blond hair, cradling her head. The eighteen-year-old

Class II telepath didn't stir at his touch, her mind a mess that Lucas didn't bother to reach for. He could feel her wounds through his shields, those she sustained at his hands and also at her own. When Samantha severed the bond she once shared with her twin and Lucas's brother, Gideon, it nearly broke her. Lucas didn't attempt to heal her mind. She knew how to fix herself.

"Why didn't you take your brother?" Jason asked. "If you're saving your family from your father, why not save them all?"

"Aisling has no use for Gideon," Lucas said as he pulled his hand away from Samantha. He returned to the center row of seats where Jason and Threnody sat.

"What about you?"

"Family ties mean little to Sercas and their Warhounds."

"I find that hard to believe after you dragged your sisters into this mess."

Lucas laughed, a dry, hacking sound. "They chose the lesser evil. That's all. We don't love each other. We don't even like each other. They're going to need to be reminded that this course of action is the right one, or the minute we turn our backs they'll try to kill us."

"Your family is really fucked-up."

"Says the man who was leashed and collared like a dog not even a month ago."

"I still had people I could rely on," Jason countered as he lifted his other hand to press it against Threnody's sternum beneath the blanket. His careful, gentle touch was at odds with the raw anger in his voice. "I still had Kerr."

The loss was still too recent for the emotion to just be swept aside. Lucas didn't need to be an empath to understand that the twist to Jason's voice was fury, grief, and pain.

"You know, Lucas, I could probably kill you right now," Jason said, his eyes locked on Threnody's face.

"I may be suffering from psi shock, but trust me when I say I'd survive whatever you tried to throw at me. Then I'd have to mindwipe you, and there goes all my hard work," Lucas said evenly. "How is Threnody?"

"I'm not a psi surgeon."

"No. You're something better."

Jason didn't argue. It was the truth, whether he liked it or not. He sucked in air around his teeth, looking for a balance he wasn't sure he would ever get back. It was different, reaching for his telekinesis now that nothing held it back. The depth of his power, the strength, was frightening. He could no longer trust his control or any of his childhood training in the Strykers Syndicate. Most of that training didn't apply, not when he had the power to see the atomic makeup of cells. Channels he never knew existed were now accessible, areas of his mind geared to see the world on a completely different level all synced up now.

Maybe telekinetics who attained Class V strength and could teleport had the potential to become what he was now. Jason didn't know. All he knew was that he didn't want to be the only person who could do this.

Jason tapped into the wealth of power in his mind and let it pour out of him. He slipped through Threnody's skin down to her bones. An echo of her damage crawled across his own nerves, countless pinpricks of heat and sudden scar tissue that was being absorbed back into her body at an accelerated rate. The new nerve endings created through cellular regeneration were going to take time to rewire, even with Jason able to control the nanites.

"Ow," Threnody said, grimacing. "That feels—weird."

"Does it hurt?" Jason asked, gaze blank.

"Not exactly." Threnody frowned, feeling the muscles in her face move stiffly. She peeled skin over the top of her finger and tossed it away. "It feels like my insides are being moved around."

"I had the nanites target your organs first. I think they're still working on them." Jason adjusted the placement of his hands. "The reason you lived long enough for me to help you was due to your electrokinesis. You'd be dead if you were any other kind of psion."

"That makes me feel so much better. Really." She flexed her fingers carefully. "How did you fix me without a biotank?"

"Take a wild guess."

The lightning strike that seared through Threnody's body and jump-started the power plant back in the sprawl of Buffalo had fried her entire body. When Quinton finally found her, he hadn't been sure she was even alive, but her electrokinesis had preserved her brain and central nervous system from total destruction. It shut down her body, then shocked it back to life over and over again, a dangerous cycle that her system had struggled to overcome. Only when Lucas arrived to keep her heart beating to a steady rhythm with his telekinesis did Threnody start to stabilize.

Jason did the rest. He was still doing the rest.

The amount of power Jason carried now left him seeing the world—literally—through new eyes. His optic nerves shifted through spectrums of vision that should have been impossible for any human or psion to process without biomodifications. It made him nauseous, especially when magnification was thrown into the mix, allowing him to see the microscopic with the naked eye.

The nanites were doing their job. Threnody was alive and healing. For now, that was enough.

Jason carefully pulled his power out of her body, letting every last cell and nanite go, until he could no longer even visualize the layers of skin cells and capillaries that made up his eyelids. His head felt heavy. He watched as Lucas changed out Threnody's IV bag. The soft, constant beeping of her cardiac rhythm was almost lulling.

Jason shifted his focus to Lucas, sinking his power into the younger man's body. It showed Jason the dark spots in Lucas where trauma had left ugly pools of damage beneath his skin.

"I can feel you," Lucas said as he finished securing the IV bag. "Get your power off me. Now."

"You've got bleeding in your brain."

"I'm handling it."

"Not well enough. That subdural hematoma isn't going to fix itself. Let me do something about it."

"You finally get full access to your power and suddenly you think you can do the impossible."

Jason arched an eyebrow as he pushed himself to his feet. "That *is* why you were after me, right?"

"I'm not the only one," Lucas said as he went to toss the used bag in the head's disposal system. "Not anymore."

Jason grimaced. "Nathan."

Nathan Serca, the oldest psion alive at the age of fifty-one, was a Class

I triad psion that Lucas rivaled in power, if not cruelty. Lucas's father had no equal when it came to cruelty.

Lucas came back out, nodding at Jason's answer. "And every last War-hound at his disposal, so remember to read as human on the mental grid, at least until the launch, or you'll get us all killed."

Unlike Warhounds, Strykers were never taught how to match their psi signature to a human's, reading as human on the mental grid, that vast psychic plane of the world's thoughts. But Jason wasn't a Stryker anymore, and Lucas had taught him how to shield on the flight over, lit-erally dumping the information straight into Jason's mind and letting the microtelekinetic sort through the overload on his own. There hadn't been time for subtlety, but Jason still got his shielding right.

Jason looked over his shoulder at Samantha and Kristen. Three of Nathan's children were turning their backs on their heritage, but Jason still didn't trust them. One of the founding families of the society that survived the Border Wars, the Serca Syndicate they owned was well-known for its forays into politics and government-restricted sciences. Ge-netic manipulation and segregation were just the beginning. The Sercas were the ones to force the Fifth Generation Act on the world, beginning the long cleanup of tainted and mutated human genetics. The Act went hand in hand with another Serca creation, the Registry, a list of people whose genetic makeup was clean and utterly human. The Sercas had placed themselves on top of the list, though they were far from human.

The Sercas had freedom and they wanted to remake humanity on Mars Colony, with themselves ruling atop society. The World Court and their chosen elite contemporaries were planning to inherit what the world's ancestors had left them—Mars Colony. They dreamed of a uto-pia and a chance to start over. Caught in between were the Strykers, psion slaves bound to a paramilitary company, who only wanted to save what was left of the world and their own skins. The whole mess of false fronts and alliances was the reason why they were here, on Spitsbergen, follow-ing Lucas. Jason owed him for more than just removing the neurotracker that was once grafted to his brain, but that knowledge was a bitter pill to swallow.

"Sit down," Jason said flatly. "Let me fix you."

Lucas seemed amused by Jason's temerity. "Do you honestly think Nathan hasn't inflicted worse on me before? I'll be fine."

"Don't compare me to Nathan." Jason scowled, but his gaze held steady. "I'm not going to kill you. Now sit the fuck down and let me take a look at your brain. We still need you, Lucas. Even I know that."

"How altruistic of you."

"Just take a damn seat."

"You should listen to him," Threnody said. "He does okay work for being such an obnoxious pain in the ass."

"I'll take that as a compliment because I'm not arguing with someone in your current state." Jason eyed her. "You should lie down, Threnody."

With Jason's help, Threnody once again stretched out on the row of seats that was her berth, wrapped securely in thermal blankets and modified harness straps to keep her stable. Once Jason saw to Threnody, he headed over to Lucas, picking up a hypospray half-full of nanites from a case as he moved through the cargo bay. They couldn't afford weakness, and all of them were damaged in some way. Recovery was going to be slow for some, quicker for others, but even Jason knew that if they wanted to survive what was coming, they would need Lucas at full strength.

"Get the bleeding stopped," Lucas said as he sat down beside Samantha and let Jason inject him in the throat with a dosage of nanites. "The rest will keep."

Jason braced himself over Lucas with one hand, his other curving carefully over the left side of Lucas's skull, pale blond hair beneath his fingers a dirty mess. Jason closed his eyes, bent his head, and let his power seep into Lucas's skull. Down through the blood-brain barrier, down to the dura mater, into the brain itself with its swollen tear, just a few centimeters long. Jason could feel where Lucas had picked at it telekinetically, struggling to ease the pressure there with a power that couldn't compete with the one Jason now wielded.

"Messy," Jason muttered.

"I don't need your opinion on how I keep myself alive."

Jason dug his fingernails into Lucas's scalp. "Be still."

Jason saw capillaries and cell structure, flash images of hemoglobin and plasma, as he worked through nanites to carefully reattach torn capillaries. Blood flow returned and the swollen tension in the cells around the area began to fade. Jason spread his microtelekinesis through Lucas's skull, helping the nanites chase down stray blood cells that were shifting into clots and teleporting them out of Lucas's body. Tiny drops of red splattered intermittently to the shuttle's deck until Jason was certain he'd done enough to ensure that Lucas wouldn't keel over and die from an aneurysm right when they needed him most.

Jason retracted his power, opening his eyes. The layers in the world wavered and it took effort to fix his vision. He wondered if he would ever get used to this, to the way he could see things, feel things, through his power.

"I never wanted to be this."

"This is what you were born to be," Lucas said, satisfaction curling through his voice. "I'm not the only one the world needs."

Jason's answer to that was a twisted smile that reminded Lucas of Kristen. Lucas found little comfort in the expression. They stared at each other for a moment, the only sounds in the cargo bay the quiet hum of the environmental system and everyone's soft breathing.

"You're awake" came Matron's rough voice a few seconds later. She stood in the open hatch with her arms crossed over her chest, tapping her foot. "Get your ass up here, Jason. Novak needs some help with the hack."

Jason straightened up, but didn't move. Lucas smiled tightly at him. "Go."

"All right." Jason left the cargo bay for the flight deck.

"How come you're the only one not bleeding out their eyes?" Matron asked as he took over the navigator's seat.

Jason reached for a wire embedded in the controls. "I don't know."

His fingers brushed over faint flecks of blood on the console, his power momentarily slipping free of his control. It seeped into the blood, and the only DNA he could identify in the fluid was Lucas's. He grimaced, clenching down hard on his control.

The world looked, and felt, strange.

It always would.

[TWO]

The seed bank is going to be difficult to get into," Lucas said. He studied the map on his datapad that showed the surrounding terrain of Longyearbyen and the airfield a kilometer away. A bright red dot identified where the Svalbard Global Seed and Gene Bank was located. "It's going to have layers of security, and the first layer we're going to have to take down is the one that breathes."

"Distraction? Make it a two-group feint, but only one group goes in and the rest draws their fire?" Threnody said, rubbing at her mouth and scratching at her skin. "Everyone's going to have to pull their weight and we're all in crap condition, but we could try a head-on attack. Or maybe something more subtle might work?"

"We don't have time for subtle."

Quinton prodded at his teeth with his tongue. They weren't broken. Neither were the bones in his face or the ones in his arms. The scattered burns on his hands resulting from his being a Class III pyrokinetic were gone, as were the biotubes. All he felt was their absence when he pressed his fingers down over skin and muscle. The tips of his middle fingers and thumbs no longer had the thin plating of metal needed to spark natural gas into fire. For the first time since being extracted from a cartel drug lord's training camp as a child by Strykers, Quinton's arms were wholly flesh and bone.

"I'm going to need something more than a lighter if you're hoping to work my power into your plan," Quinton said, raising his head to look at Lucas. "I'd do better with a gun."

"We've got grenades if you need to make fire," Matron said, staring down at a list of supplies on her datapad. "Otherwise, I've got guns, but they won't be military grade. Lost most of those when the rest of my shut-

14

tles blew getting out of Buffalo. You'll be shooting with bullets, not energy darts."

"I can work with that."

Everyone in Alpha shuttle was awake and huddled in the cargo bay, pretending the chrono wasn't ticking away seconds that they needed. Lucas rubbed at his forehead, unable to get rid of the ache building there. "I don't care which weapon you use. This part is going to be a straightforward hit-and-run."

"You can't have my scavengers for your suicide run," Matron said. "I only have enough left to pilot the shuttles and you need them for that."

Lucas waved aside her worries. "When we arrive in Longyearbyen, we'll need to make sure none of the quads manage to send out a signal for help. I wouldn't put it past Nathan to have Warhounds up there."

"He placed two teams there last month," Samantha said. "We'll be dealing with both psions and humans."

"And none of us can even stand up straight," Threnody said. "Great planning, Lucas."

"I kept you alive," he reminded her.

Threnody shrugged, the motion a little stiff. She was wearing an insulated skinsuit beneath her clothes now like everyone else, but still looked as if a good wind would knock her over. Ten hours since landing and Jason had already worked on her twice more. She was healing at a pace that outstripped the regular cellular rate, but was on par with a biotank. It was a tiring process, for both her and Jason.

"I won't be any good at shielding," Kerr said, his teal eyes bloodshot. He cleared his throat, words riding a heavy Scottish accent. "You'd do better to put me on offense. I can handle a few quick and dirty strikes. I can't hold up any shields right now but my own."

"What about your empathy?" Jason asked.

"If you want an empath, use Kristen."

Kerr was a dual psion with Class II telepathy and Class IX empathy and was worn down like everyone else. His empathic power was newfound, but nowhere near Kristen's level. The younger girl graced him with a teeth-baring grin. Her dark blue eyes had lost some of their sick silver sheen with the dubious onset of borrowed sanity.

"Is that admiration you're feeling?" Kristen asked.

"Hardly."

Jason eyed Kristen contemplatively. "If we can get her inside, she'll get everyone else outside for us. We can handle the quads and Warhounds better if we can see them rather than wondering if they're trying to call for reinforcements. It'll be a bloodbath, and we can't let the fight get drawn out, but the odds are in our favor if we keep the element of surprise."

"They're in our favor even if we don't," Lucas said. "We aren't failing here."

"Do we know how many targets there are?" Threnody said, scratching at peeling skin on the underside of her jaw. She couldn't seem to sit still. "Any previous reconnaissance records to extrapolate off of?"

"The World Court posts five quads up here at any given shift," Samantha said. "Regular check-in happens at oh six hundred every day."

"So we hit them ten minutes after. Plenty of leeway for them to finish checking in, and we've got hours after that to break into the seed bank. What's the terrain like?"

"The ruins are overrun with sparse vegetation, but there are a few buildings that the government has taken care of. It'll be a clearer line of sight than what we had when we fought in the bunkers," Lucas said. "The mountain isn't habitable and they've got a weapons system surrounding it for defense. It'll be cold, but no major radiation risk."

Threnody nodded, brow furrowed. "Our best bet is to drop down right on top of them. We'll have to go in shooting, so to speak."

"That's a brilliant way to die," Samantha said. "We're all burned-out. How do you expect us to function when our range is so limited?"

"Do you have a better idea? No? Then shut up until you can give us something useful."

Samantha glared at Lucas. "Are you going to let her talk to me like that?"

"Yes" came his calm reply. "I am. You've never organized a plan of attack on this scale. You only led them on Nathan's orders. Threnody is better at this than you are."

Samantha abruptly stood and went to the only place for privacy in the shuttle—the head. The door closed behind her with a faint hiss and she locked it. Leaning against the sink, she took in a deep breath and struggled to calm her nerves. With slightly shaking hands, she turned the cold water on and used a little to wash her face and ease her dry eyes.

Her skin itched everywhere the acid rain had touched it back in Buffalo. That annoyance would fade, given time. The swirling nausea in her gut would probably stay with her for a little while longer. Pressing a fist to her middle, Samantha stared at herself in the tiny mirror above the sink and gave her reflection a smile that was more snarl than anything else.

The door to the head slid open.

"That was locked," Samantha said flatly.

"I know the override," Lucas said. "Are you regretting your decision already?"

"Sercas don't do regrets."

"Glad to see you've kept the arrogance." Lucas stepped inside and let the door slide shut. His presence made the space feel even smaller.

Samantha turned her head fractionally to keep him in her sights. "What else did you let me keep?" she demanded, voice harsh. "Sanity, obviously, but you function like Nathan at your most basic level, Lucas. You use people the same way he does. You're just better at rationing our lives."

Lucas pinched the bridge of his nose, eyes half-lidded as he gazed at her. "You're alive. Be grateful."

"You haven't given me a reason to be."

Lucas smiled. It was the only warning she got. Lucas's hand wrapped around her throat too fast for her to block, then he was slamming her head against the mirror. Samantha choked on a scream, biting it back. The edge of the sink bruised her hip. Lucas had a death grip on her throat.

Agony ripped through her skull. "I won't beg for you."

"I don't want you to beg," Lucas said. "I want you to work with me. If we're going to survive at all, I need you on my side, Sam."

"My mind should be my own."

"You're a Serca. Your mind belongs to whoever inherits the Syndicate."

"Gideon won't accept me after what I did."

The loss still hit like a sucker punch, that emptiness in her mind where her twin once resided through their bond. It was as if she still had a body, just no vital organs to make it live; a hole at the bottom of her mind with no way to fill it.

Lucas eased his grip, letting her go. Samantha shoved him away, putting as much distance between them as she could. It wasn't enough to make her feel safe. She curled her hands over the edge of the sink and glared at him. Lucas didn't seem bothered by her animosity.

"You knew when I ripped apart your mind in Buffalo that you had no other options but this, but me," Lucas said, flicking his fingers at his chest. "I expect you to obey, Sam."

She raised her chin, defiance in every line of her body even as she licked her lips. "And if I don't?"

"Then Kris can change your mind for me. Or at least your loyalty."

"She was always yours, wasn't she?" Samantha said, remembering those moments in Buffalo when Lucas spoke through their youngest sibling.

Lucas nodded. "Always."

"How did Nathan never know?"

"If Nathan fears anything other than death, it's insanity. He feared losing himself in hers. I never did." Lucas shrugged. "Kris was the perfect tool. I wielded her as needed."

"And me?"

"I needed you sane and I need you to be on my side. I saved your mind over the years because I can't do what needs to be done alone."

"What if I refuse?"

"We've gone down that road many times before. It never ends well when you choose Nathan over me." Lucas's gaze was steady. "There's too much at stake, Sam. We both know that. Surviving this fight starts here."

She looked away, seeing their reflections in the mirror. They were both a mess, but still alike in their resolve.

"What's in it for me?" Samantha said.

"Your life and the ability to live it in a changed world."

"Never knew you were such a humanitarian."

"We aren't human, Sam." Lucas passed his hand over the control panel to open the door at his back. The sound of everyone else's conversation filtered inside. "I won't be anything less than what Aisling promised."

"And that would be?"

Lucas didn't answer as he stepped out, but she didn't need him to. If the Sercas had one thing in common, it was their belief in themselves and what they could accomplish. Samantha lifted a hand to scratch off a tiny flake of dried blood she had missed in her washing. She flicked it off her finger, wondering how much blood she would end up losing to reach her brother's goal.

[THREE]

AUGUST 2379
LONGYEARBYEN, NORWAY

ongyearbyen lay north of the arctic circle, a frozen graveyard of a time when almost every last coastline in the world had communities thriving with people, even a tiny, wintery archipelago. Currently, the town center was surrounded by buildings eaten away by the cold and disuse, time having made inroads on a place only twenty people inhabited on any given day. Richard Cuellas had spent the past five years on sentry duty in the far north, drinking his way through gallons of coffee and whiskey. It was a lucrative, if boring, post.

Richard was one of those who didn't mind the isolation, along with the rest of the people assigned with him in the north. Up here at the top of the world, there was space to stretch out, land that wouldn't kill you if you stayed too long in one place, and air that smelled better than in any other place on earth. Their mission was to monitor bioscanners and a security grid that encompassed a quarter of the island. The computers could do this well enough on their own, but the government still required a human mind to interpret the data that ran across the vidscreens.

Sipping at steaming black coffee, Richard tilted his chair back on two legs, balancing there as he called up the log for the past ten hours. It was shift change, and despite its being a post where nothing ever happened, they stuck to protocol. The government expected full protection of what was buried in the ice and volcanic rock of Plataberget. Neither he nor his compatriots knew what was so important up here, and they weren't stupid enough to ask. Their mission was to guard Spitsbergen. In the entire time that the government had manned the island—250 years and counting—no unauthorized person had ever set foot on it.

That morning, the long-standing record was broken when Richard saw the image of a civilian girl on one of the security feeds in a place she shouldn't be.

Choking on his coffee, he let his chair fall back to the floor and swore as some of the hot liquid splashed over his bare fingers. He set the cup aside and reached for the controls to magnify the security feed, but the girl had disappeared. Richard swore again, wondering if the madness that came from being cut off from society was finally getting to him after five years of duty. He commed the rest of his quad.

"Graham, get your ass up here, I need a second sign-off," Richard said as he leaned forward and squinted at all the various angles he could call up on the security feed.

He found no sign of the girl, and replays of the feed didn't show him a damn thing. It was as if she'd never been there. Five seconds was a long time for it to be a glitch, and he knew for a fact that the last shipment of entertainment bodies had all been dumped in the water a month ago. It wasn't some government-supplied whore.

The door behind him slid open a few minutes later. Richard looked over his shoulder at the man who came into the control room, his second-in-command, bundled up against the cold. The environmental system kept the place warm, but heat could stand up against the elements for only so long before the arctic chill seeped into everything.

"I'm on break," Graham said irritably.

"Yeah, and I don't care." Richard stabbed a finger at the vidscreens. "Got a glitch. Security feed showed some blond-haired girl outside."

Graham frowned and leaned over the console to bring the feed up in a quick loop, showing him every angle of their tiny settlement. All he saw was barren land and decrepit houses that were once part of the ancient town. The airfield a kilometer away was empty and the waters of Isfjorden were placid against the icy shore.

"You drink too much at last night's poker game, Rick?" Graham asked as he let the security feed revert to its default circulation mode.

Richard scowled at him. "Do I fucking look hungover? Do a recon of the area with the others. I want it cleared by a live report."

"You're kidding, right?" Graham laughed. "Hell, there's no one up here but us."

"If there's no one here, it shouldn't take you long to confirm that fact, right? Now get out there."

"Asshole."

Graham left the control room. Richard didn't doubt that the other man would follow orders, but Graham was a lazy son of a bitch who'd been packing on weight over the past two years. He'd take his sweet time getting it done.

Sometime later, Richard could see Graham and some of the other soldiers posted up here wandering around outside on the security feed—along with a shuttle that dropped down out of vertical, coming within camera range nearly on top of the small outpost. Richard didn't recognize the make, and it was completely off schedule. He flipped open the plastic cover that protected the emergency button and slammed his hand down on it to trigger the alarm. The piercing sound nearly ruptured his eardrum, catching everyone's attention in the connected buildings.

"We've got a breach!" Richard yelled into the system's local comm frequency before moving to switch it into an outgoing uplink.

The press of a gun barrel to the back of his head made him freeze.

"No bioware net." The voice sounded young, her words riding on a soft laugh. "They should have given you one. Hands up. Turn around."

Richard complied. He came face-to-face with a tall, thin teenage girl who smiled wide enough to show all her teeth. Her bony face was dominated by gleaming dark blue eyes, and her smile made Richard's skin crawl. The girl stared at Richard over the barrel of her gun, and Richard thought about reaching for his own weapon, but he couldn't remember why he needed it. Standing there, breath coming in rapid bursts, he tried to remember his duty, but it was difficult to think around the fear flooding his body.

"Who—," Richard choked out, one hand clutching at his chest. His heart was beating so fast it felt as if it were going to beat right out of his body.

She lowered the gun, smile still in place. *"What."*

Scared to death wasn't how Richard wanted to die, but Kristen didn't give him a choice. She dug her power into his emotions, twisting them beyond anything he'd felt before. Fear, yes, but also pain, both of which incited panic. The body could be made to feel anything, and what Kristen made Richard feel stripped him of all control. His heart burst seconds later, the sound a muffled pop in his chest.

Kristen pulled the body off the chair. Taking the dead man's place, she spun around a few times in the chair before finally settling down to face the monitors. The security feed was framed in every vidscreen, showing her the entire outpost. Empathically, she could sense everyone's position, and she put faces to psi signatures using the security system.

Outside in the cold morning air, Threnody's body was already regretting this plan of action. Breathing heavily, she took shelter behind a crumbling foundation wall slick with moss, teeth clenched against the pain she was feeling.

Stay low, Quinton said through the psi link. It was a tenuous connection, all that Lucas could provide. *I've got your back.*

He lay on top of the shuttle, teleported there by Jason and spared the heat from the fuselage by a thin telekinetic shield. Rifle in hand, aiming through the sight scope, Quinton shot once to get a read on the air current, purposefully missing his oncoming target, watching where the bullet hit to check wind speed and distance. He adjusted the angle of his rifle slightly, curled his finger over the trigger, and pulled it between one breath and the next.

The soldier was thrown backward to the ground, blood spraying out of his chest as the bullet hit home.

Go, Quinton told Threnody. *I don't see anyone in that hallway.*

She scrambled to her feet, throwing herself forward, eyes on the door the soldier had come out of. Threnody skidded inside, glancing up at the security feed embedded in the wall.

I'm your eye in the sky, Kristen said cheerfully into her mind on the psi link. *Two soldiers coming your way at fifty meters and closing, second inter-section down the hall. One is a Warhound.*

Class? Threnody said.

That would be telling.

Lucas, your sister is a rude little shit.

That Warhound is a Class VI telekinetic, Lucas said. *You'll have to handle what she throws at you, Threnody. I can't get to you yet. And, Kris?*

Yes? Kristen said.

Don't piss me off.

All that filtered down the psi link from the girl was a sense of sullen discontent. Threnody kept running, using her teeth to pull the glove off one hand. The buildings here were old and patched, metal threaded through the structures everywhere. Threnody took a chance and fell to her knees as the footsteps got louder. She slammed one hand against the metal wall, looking for a conduit, and brought her gun up to bear right as two people came hurtling around the corner.

Bullets cut through the air over her head. She felt telekinetic pressure on her bruised ribs, but her power was already arcing up into their bodies. Threnody's vision tunneled out, a roaring sound filling her ears. For one long moment, she didn't know if she was even breathing, then a sharp pain spiked through one side of her face. Spiked harder on the other. She blinked, vision coming back to her in time to see Jason's hand descending for another slap. She made a wordless noise and he stopped in midmotion.

Threnody was lying on her back, staring up into Jason's face, his hazel eyes wide and worried. He let out a harsh breath. "Shit, Thren, don't go undoing all my hard work."

It was strange hearing the familial diminutive of her name come out of his mouth. Threnody struggled to sit up. Jason helped her out, bracing her with one arm behind her back as she caught her breath. "My hand."

Jason looked down at the limb in question, finding red lines spanning across her skin like circuit wires. "Nerve damage. Guess you aren't as healed as I thought you were. I think you might have fried the nanites in your veins, too."

"Wonderful." Threnody grimaced. "Help me up."

Jason got Threnody to her feet. She checked her gun and they got moving again. The faint mutter in the back of their minds was everyone else's conversation on the psi link as they cut through the outpost section by section. Overlaid across that was Kristen's heavy, intense presence that was blocking the Warhounds' ability to teleport away or telepathically get a warning out. Her psionic interference scratched against their shields. Kristen didn't care about harming the Strykers if it meant the humans died, and Lucas was too busy right now to make her see reason. Kristen's help was needed but it was difficult on their end to deal with it.

The sound of an explosion nearby pulled them up short. "That came from outside," Threnody said.

Was that us or them? Jason sent out along the psi link.

Us, Quinton answered. *Samantha just blew up part of a building. We've got fire.*

Joining the fray?

No. I'm staying put.

"We need to get to the control room," Jason said as they started moving again. *Kerr, sitrep.*

You aren't feeling the headache I am, came Kerr's pained reply. *Remaining Warhounds are in merge. Lucas and I are picking their minds apart, but I'd rather put a bullet in their brains.*

And the quads? Threnody asked.

None in your section. Go knock some sense into Kristen and tell her to stop biting at my shields.

Kerr's mental voice faded. Threnody and Jason were still methodically careful on their way to the control room, but Kerr was right. They didn't find any more quads on their way to Kristen's position, and she greeted their arrival with a soft and raspy "All clear."

Jason hauled Kristen out of the chair and took her place. She immediately draped herself over the back of it. Threnody eyed the girl, keeping a finger on the trigger guard of her gun.

"Maybe you should go find your brother," Jason said as he yanked connecting wires from the console and plugged them into the neuroports in his arms and wrists. "I don't like having you at my back."

"I know," Kristen said. "It's why I'm staying."

"I'm not leaving," Threnody said evenly.

Jason switched on his inspecs, data rolling across his vision, merging with the hologrids that snapped into the air. "I remember your psi signature from a few years ago, Kristen. Every Stryker died trying to get close to you. No one managed a solid ident."

"You wouldn't have," Kristen said. "We Sercas are supposed to be human, remember?"

Jason shrugged his opinion of that. "You've fooled the world. Don't expect anyone to be happy about that."

"You Strykers never are. You should see the faces of the ones we keep when they meet with old teammates. So many tears. So sad."

"What are you talking about?"

"We retrieve select Strykers for our own purposes and make them loyal to us. We can make them forget where they came from, but we can't make those they left behind forget who they lost." Kristen stood up on her tiptoes to peer over the seat at Jason. "Your rank and file keep secrets better when dead."

Her empathy rolled through them, brushing up against their shields, but went no further than that. Lucas's previous warning was enough to make Kristen stay her hand this time, just not her mouth. Pointedly, neither Threnody nor Jason engaged her in that conversation.

Jason set to work breaking through encrypted software, inspecs streaming data over his sight. Lucas arrived several minutes later, looking tired and tense. He pried Kristen off the chair and pitched her toward the hallway.

"Go back to the shuttle, Kris," Lucas said, not watching to see if she left.

"Maybe you should go with her," Threnody said. "Make sure she doesn't try to kill everyone else."

"Kris knows what will happen if she tries."

"You're in no condition to stop her."

"Doesn't mean I won't." Lucas gave Threnody a hard smile before addressing Jason. "Give me an update."

"That damn mountain is surrounded by artillery," Jason said as he moved his hands through the hologrid, searching out leads for the hack. "Most of it is still active."

"I want you to keep anything from coming online when we get up there," Lucas said. "That's all we need."

"It's going to take a while. The security up there runs on a different system than the one we hacked flying in."

"You've got two hours."

Jason grimaced. "I doubt I can do it in two. It already took us a day to fly to this island and hack the outer security. This is going to take longer."

"We have less than twenty-four hours to finish this. I'm moving everyone to the airfield that services Longyearbyen. I want you to set up five days' worth of future communications to be sent out during the required status check-in time. The quads up here had a standard security code. I'm sure you can falsify it."

Lucas left and Threnody followed after him. Jason started hacking into everything the government had built up in Longyearbyen. Novak couldn't help him with this, the scavenger having burned through most of the wiring in his brain and body already. Jason knew the feeling, knew the heat of burned wires before they cooled, the tiny surges making sections of his body go numb. He wasn't looking forward to going through that again.

Two hours later, Jason had to resign himself to the inevitable: he wasn't going to meet Lucas's timetable. Jason rubbed at his eyes, inspecs bright against the darkness. "Shit."

He was tired. Staring at command windows and the framework of a security grid he had no hope of breaking would exhaust anyone.

Right on schedule, Lucas commed him. "Finished?"

"I finished the communications you wanted, but we've got a problem."

"That's not what I want to hear."

"I managed to hack the security feed around here earlier only because it was tied into the same system Novak hacked on our flight over the Atlantic. I got lucky with the artillery, but I can't hack this last system, Lucas. It's completely separate, half of it is tied into biometrics on-site, and I'd need a week, at minimum, to build a back door."

The comm hummed softly with static. Jason winced as Lucas implanted an image directly into his mind for a visual. "Get back here."

Jason extracted himself from the hack and closed out before teleporting back to the shuttles sitting on the airfield a kilometer away. Alpha shuttle had its cargo doors open, metal ramp digging into the dirt. Lucas was standing at the edge of the ramp, bright blots of red dripping from his nose to the metal beneath his feet. Lucas might not have been hemorrhaging anymore, but nosebleeds were common while suffering through psi shock. Jason was surprised the younger man was capable of walking, much less pulling off an attack on a government outpost.

Shaking his head, Jason jerked his thumb over his shoulder in the direction of Longyearbyen. "Security grid for the island is set. The artillery on the mountain is dormant now, but the security system tied into the seed bank is something else."

Lucas wiped at the blood dripping from his nose, flicking it off his fingertips. "If we jacked Novak into the hack?"

"He's burned through all his neuroports."

"We could strip new ones onto different nerves and modify the ones in his brain."

Jason stiffened. "That will kill him."

"Most likely." Lucas turned his head to stare south at the flat-topped, small mountain that rose into the sky nearby. It was mostly white near the peak, the rest dark rock and dull green moss. "If you can't hack it, we only have one option."

Lucas headed back into the shuttle, Jason on his heels. Matron and Kerr were huddled near some of the cold-storage units, with Samantha and Kristen sitting nearby, watching them. Jason didn't see Threnody or Quinton.

"Did you scan the terrain?" Lucas asked Matron as they got closer.

"This place don't get tectonic shift like other continents," Matron said, glancing up from the readouts on the unit's control screen. "That road is stable enough, but I wouldn't want to land a shuttle on it. Lucky for you, two of the shuttles that survived are carrying the gravlifts. We'll be able to transfer whatever Jason can't teleport."

"I take it I'm the stevedore," Jason said with a heavy sigh.

Matron smiled at him, showing a line of metal teeth. "You know you're worth more than that, so stop complaining."

"Is the hack finished?" Kerr said.

Jason shook his head. "No."

"Then how the hell are we getting inside that mountain?"

"Better question would be how are we doing it without tipping off the government?" Matron said.

"They won't know what's happened up here until it's too late," Lucas said, heading for the flight deck.

"You sure about that?"

"We'll be in Antarctica by then."

"We'll be *where*?" Jason said. "What the hell, Lucas? You want to go from polar day to polar night? There are other places in the world we can go to ground that are less extreme."

"And that's exactly where the government would think we'd go, except we won't be in Norway, Greenland, or Canada. There's no other place to match the Arctic except the south pole. Antarctica wasn't worth the trouble for the government to excavate after the Border Wars, which means they won't be searching for us there." Lucas glanced over his shoulder at them as he palmed open the hatch to the flight deck. "The seeds need to be kept frozen. These shuttles won't run forever."

Matron snorted. "Tell me about it. We're gonna have to refuel somewhere between here and there. Hope you've got a place in mind."

"Just stick to the plan and don't ask questions, Matron. You'll live."

"You keep saying that. I keep not believing it."

Lucas ignored her in favor of Quinton's sharp gaze. "I need Threnody."

"No." Quinton stood up from the navigator's seat. Threnody was curled up in the pilot's seat, seemingly asleep, but at the sound of Lucas's voice, she opened her eyes. She looked worse than she had before the fight.

"You don't have a choice."

Quinton put himself between her and Lucas. "She can't handle whatever it is you need her to do."

"She survived a focused lightning strike. She can survive this. Move."

Quinton's fist smashed against Lucas's jaw hard enough to knock the other man on his ass. Pain stabbed through Lucas's skull from the blow, blood trickling over his tongue from where he bit it. Black dots edged his vision, telepathy slip-sliding against his shaky shields. Lucas sucked in a deep breath, taking a few seconds to anchor his shields before anything else. Then he propped himself up on one elbow and glared at Quinton.

"You're starting to annoy me, Stryker."

"Quinton," Threnody called out, pushing herself out of the seat. "Lucas—*don't*."

Telekinesis yanked Quinton forward, slamming him onto the deck beside Lucas with enough force to knock him briefly unconscious. Lucas used those few seconds to roll over until he was crouched over Quinton, hands on either side of the pyrokinetic's head.

Wake up.

The older man's eyes jerked open as that harsh mental order stabbed into his mind. Blood dripped out of Lucas's nose, falling onto Quinton's cheek.

"Still a bloody telepath, even with psi shock," Lucas said, voice low and flat as he moved one hand to Quinton's throat. "I'm not powerless here."

"Fuck you," Quinton forced out between lips that barely moved, telekinesis holding him down.

"We don't have time for a hack. Threnody is the only one who can get us into the seed bank. And she will. You don't get a say in the matter."

Lucas pressed his hand down hard against Quinton's throat, feeling the ridges of the other man's trachea roll against his palm. Quinton choked from the pressure, incapable of fighting back.

Cool, shaking fingers pressed against the back of Lucas's neck. He felt a faint, warning electric tingle against his skin. "Let him go, Lucas."

Be grateful Aisling needs your life, Lucas said into Threnody's and Quinton's minds. *I would eradicate you if given the choice, Quinton.*

Lucas stood up, his telekinesis shifting off the other man. Quinton dragged in a ragged breath of air, shoving himself to a sitting position. Lucas bared his teeth at Threnody around a split lip. "Ladies first."

Threnody shook her head and walked away from him. Quinton got to his feet and followed Threnody to the cargo ramp. Lucas tracked their movement, watching as Quinton supported Threnody with a care he showed no one else.

"Matron," Lucas said. "Pick half your crew to come with us up the mountain. The rest can stay here and organize the shuttles for loading."

"You psions up to the task?" Matron said, eyeing them.

"Worry about your own people."

Matron knew better than to argue and took herself out of the shuttle, yelling for Everett and Novak. Lucas focused his attention on his sisters and the other two Strykers as Quinton and Threnody argued in whispers near the cargo ramp.

"Let's go," Lucas said.

"Are you sure about this?" Kerr asked, glancing from Lucas to Threnody. "If all she's doing is frying the system, won't that trigger an alarm somewhere?"

"The alarm would have to reroute through the outpost first, and Jason has done enough damage that it won't get very far. No one outside of the highest reaches of the government knows about this place, and the government is busy dealing with the mess in Buffalo," Lucas said. "The Strykers were never informed of this location, so a teleport can't happen. The World Court won't send a team by shuttle until it's too late and we'll be long gone by then. It's still a calculated risk, but we're taking it."

"And is using Threnody up a calculated risk?" Quinton asked harshly.

"We're all taking a risk here," Threnody said. "Let it go, Quin."

Jason shook his head. "I don't know if I can save Threnody again, Lucas. My first few attempts apparently didn't take."

"Keep her breathing until we reach Antarctica, that's all I need," Lucas said. "I've got someone there who can help if it comes down to it."

Surprise flickered over Jason's face. "Don't tell me you've got black-market surgeons stashed all over the world?"

"When I find useful people, I keep them."

"I've always liked your collections," Kristen said as she skipped past them for the cargo ramp. Everyone followed her outside.

Matron and ten of her scavengers were busy hauling three gravlifts off two shuttles. The machines were capable of carrying heavy loads on the flatbed, with lifts that could deposit the cargo on any given surface. Their max was half a ton, and they would be utilized as much as Jason's telekinesis.

"These are good," Matron called out to Lucas as she hauled herself up into one of the gravlift control seats. "No damage on the flight out."

"You know how much of whatever's in those vaults you want to load?" Everett asked as he climbed onto another gravlift. He sported a quick-heal patch over his left temple, having taken a minor beating on the flight out of Buffalo.

"Half or more of everything the World Court is hiding in there," Lucas said.

"Yeah, you better hope we've got room."

"If we don't, you stay behind." Lucas climbed up onto the flatbed behind Matron and settled in for the ride. "Your scavengers need a refresher course on how to take orders."

Matron glanced at him over her shoulder. "I lost more'n half my crew getting your ass out of the fire back in Buffalo. Leave them alone."

The Strykers and Lucas's sisters climbed up onto the flatbed, finding handholds along the edges where straps were coiled into shallow recesses. Kerr helped Quinton get Threnody on board, the two men working in silence to steady her and help her get comfortable. When they were ready, Matron started the gravlift and steered away from the airfield to the rarely used road.

The incline wasn't that steep, and the long, winding road seemed stable. The wedge of metal sticking out of the mountainside was covered in moss and seemed like part of the landscape. When they reached the level part of the road, they passed by the remnants of an old-fashioned gate off to one side, the rusted metal still visible. Up ahead, the dirt road curved until it cut parallel to the entrance of the metal wedge. The gravlifts were locked into a hovering line behind Matron's lead when they arrived, the engines a soft hum in the chilly air.

A faded logo could be seen on the side of the metal wedge: The Svalbard Global Seed and Gene Bank.

"Why can't we teleport inside?" Everett said as everyone started to climb off the gravlifts.

"Teleporting requires a visual," Kerr said as he watched Quinton and Jason help Threnody get her feet on the ground. To his eyes, she wasn't looking too steady on her legs. "You can't teleport to some place you've never been, not unless you want to end up embedded in a solid object."

Lucas took a careful step forward, letting the rusted support ramp that linked the road and the entrance take his weight. The metal creaked, the sound a grating echo in their ears, but it held. He assumed the government had replaced it a few times over the years. Lucas looked over his shoulder. "Threnody."

"Front and center, yeah, I know," she said.

Quinton had her by the elbow as they walked across the ramp slowly, trying not to jar her too much. Jason was right behind them while everyone else waited on the road. Threnody leaned heavily against Quinton, staring at the control panel.

She swallowed thickly. "I don't know if I can do this. I don't know if I'll be fast enough."

"I can have Kris turn off the pain," Lucas said.

"No. I'll lose myself that way."

"Then I'll anchor you."

Stepping forward, Lucas carefully pressed one fingertip against her temple. Threnody flinched from the pressure, skin still sensitive. She needed a biotank, but he didn't have one here to put her in. Lucas closed his eyes and concentrated on pulling his telepathy together. He hadn't lied about his ability to recover. That still didn't mean it was easy. Psi shock made it difficult to focus, and Threnody's mind was disturbingly quiet when he dipped into it.

We fixed your body, but I forgot about your mind in the aftermath, Lucas said, his words ghosting over the shadow of her thoughts. *I wasn't in any shape to fix it.*

Meaning?

You blocked out a good chunk of what happened in Buffalo and your mind is still reorganizing those memories.

Psions don't forget.

This isn't you forgetting. It's you rebuilding. We just need you to do it faster. I think if you have those memories as a template, you'll know how far you can push your power.

He bypassed her shields, coiling his telepathy around the pulse of her personality, thoughts, and memories buried deep beneath the shock of trauma that still lingered. He dragged Threnody's mind into full awareness, steadying her as she reconnected with the memories of her fight at the power plant.

The pain wasn't something Lucas could block, and it drew a ragged sound from her, like an animal's. Quinton closed his eyes, holding himself perfectly still even though he obviously wanted to shield her from Lucas's implacable drive and their current desperate need.

"Thren," Quinton whispered.

She didn't seem to hear him, face screwed up in pain, hunching in on herself when she should have been resting in Alpha shuttle.

Threnody, Lucas said. *The doors.*

She remembered lightning. He felt the protest in her thoughts, in some distant, primal memory that came from the mind knowing the limits of the body, but she was a Stryker and Threnody knew how to follow orders. She knew the cost of disobedience. She was here with Lucas because of it.

Blue eyes cracked open, dark with pain. Breathing harshly, she lifted one hand to the panel. Faint sparks popped around her fingers, tiny electric lines emerging from her skin. She was mere centimeters away from touching it when she stopped, hand curled like a claw.

"It's not enough," she panted. "I don't have enough power in me to do this."

"You will," Jason said.

Threnody's breath came in shallow, painful gasps as she pressed her hand against the control panel. Threnody was a Class III electrokinetic, and her power was the only option in light of the failed hack. Electricity sparked along the tips of her fingers. The surge she was readying wouldn't be enough to do the damage they needed to fry the system before the alarm triggered.

Jason fixed that. Fixed her.

He saw how her nerves were still a mess, synapses unable to talk correctly to each other, electrical impulses dying before they bridged the distance between nerves. He let his power bleed into her body. The connection was there, her body knew it, she just couldn't find it on her own.

Microtelekinesis coursed through her instantly. The shock of the shutdown and reboot lasted for half a millisecond, if that. The results were all that mattered. Threnody's power snapped together inside her body, her baseline stabilizing. Electricity ripped through her limbs and out of her skin, surging through the control terminal with a blinding burst, the same way it had surged through Jin Li in Buffalo.

Jason and Lucas withdrew their power. Quinton was the only one holding Threnody up as she shuddered through the aftereffects.

The doors jerked in their casing, unlocking. Lucas telekinetically pulled them apart, breaking through decades of built-up ice and debris. Cold, stale air filtered out of a place no one had walked into since the government's SkyFarms Inc. agricultural towers first went online in the last major cities.

Lucas strode into the ancient seed bank and didn't look back.

[FOUR]

AUGUST 2379
THE HAGUE, THE NETHERLANDS

The ache in Ciari Treiva's gut had nothing to do with nerves or emotion.

It was a physical reminder, one the Class III empath hadn't fixed before leaving Toronto. It grounded her in a way she knew nothing else could. As the officer in charge (OIC) of the Strykers Syndicate, it was imperative that Ciari maintain her health. Like every other Stryker, she didn't own her body—the government did. And what better way to prove that ownership than to appoint a psion as the liaison between the government and the Strykers Syndicate?

"This is not going well," Keiko Nishimoto said. The Class II telekinetic and chief operating officer (COO) for the Strykers Syndicate kept a sharp eye on the set of quads stationed in the hallway with them. "We've been waiting for hours."

"The morning session for citizens comes before our punishment," Ciari said quietly. "Erik likes having an audience."

Keiko ducked her head, hiding her grimace from the security cameras embedded in the walls. She had teleported Ciari to The Hague as ordered. They'd been told to wait outside the courtroom doors in the Peace Palace, which held the International Court of Justice, called the World Court by most people on the planet.

To be kept waiting after the rush to arrive wasn't a surprise, simply annoying. They had no right to argue about anything, not when the neurotrackers implanted in their brains could kill them so easily. Every Stryker who didn't die in the field or from overuse of his or her power died with the flip of a switch, victim of a government termination order. Perhaps the wait was psychological on the part of the World Court, but the two Strykers accepted it as part of the job. The government's dogs, as they were so often called, could do nothing but obey.

They weren't the only ones going about their business in the hallway. Aides, lobbyists, and politicians walked the halls, most of them hurrying past the two women without a second glance. Most humans, registered and unregistered, didn't trust psions. Too many people had died at the hands of rogue psions since the Border Wars ended for trust to ever be more than political lip service.

Despite their disease and danger, psions were useful, lucrative, and rare enough in the world's surviving gene pool that the government kept them around for business and security reasons. Contracts brokered with the Strykers Syndicate pulled in a lot of money, and the government wasn't willing to give up a ready source of income.

The World Court beat obedience into their dogs. The failure of government indoctrination and the escape of formerly subordinate Strykers were the reasons why Ciari was here.

The door to the courtroom finally opened an hour later and a legal clerk stepped into the hallway. "The World Court will hear your case."

He didn't look at them. Out of fear or disrespect, Ciari didn't know. Probably both. The Peace Palace was owned and operated by humans, by the only government that had survived the Border Wars. Psion power, unless explicitly permitted by the World Court, was illegal here. Bioware nets spanned the brains of all the politicians and registered humans who could afford the technology, constantly monitoring for outside manipulation. Any deviation from the baseline resulted in psion deaths. When it came down to it, though, the World Court didn't need an excuse to kill their dogs.

Ciari and Keiko stood, tugged their uniforms straight, and walked into the public courtroom. The grand, rectangular place had old wood paneling and stained-glass windows that had survived the relentless bombings. Ancient, beautiful crystal chandeliers hung from the ceiling. The rows of seats between the door and the long bench set high on a raised dais beneath the windows were full. So was the balcony that extended halfway into the room.

Open session, Ciari thought as she and Keiko walked down the center aisle. *This won't end well.*

They came to a stop between the tables of opposing parties at the front of the courtroom; both were empty. Arrayed before them along the judicial bench were fifteen seats filled by the most powerful humans on the planet. The occupant of the center seat was the only one who mattered to Ciari.

Erik Gervais, president and justice of the World Court, stared at her. Ciari met his gaze without blinking. The faint narrowing of his brown eyes showed annoyance, but only to her. Erik had built his life around political aspirations that required him to be unreadable for the sake of legal neutrality. But the government was never truly neutral, especially when it came to their dogs. Years of reading the microexpressions of bureaucrats and politicians had saved Ciari's life many times where psion power would have gotten her killed instantly. She wondered if that skill would be enough this time.

"Sirs," Ciari said, dipping her head in rote respect to the fifteen judges before her. Keiko did the same.

The crowd around them wasn't completely silent. Registered humans, the elite of society, shifted in their seats. The rustling of personal items and the soft buzz of cameras from reporters sitting in the press box filled the air like static.

"Are you prepared to give your report?" Erik said.

"Yes, sir."

"Then begin your statement. If we like what we hear, we might be persuaded to show leniency."

Ciari didn't blink at the threat. It meant nothing to her. She lived with a death switch in her brain; words were merely sound.

"A month ago, we lost four Strykers in the Slums of the Angels. They were in pursuit of a rogue psion targeted for retrieval. We believe the target took them. When we carried out your orders to terminate the Strykers, the results from the neurotrackers were inconclusive. The baselines spiked as human on the security grid through bioscanners." Ciari paused for a moment, letting the information sink in. "We have no witnesses to the events in the Slums. Human bodies were eventually retrieved from Russia with the missing neurotrackers. When that same target from the Slums appeared in Buffalo, I initiated a full-scale field transfer of Stryker teams to deal with the threat."

"You've had two years to retrieve or terminate this rogue psion," Anchali said. The vice president of the World Court was its oldest member and one of its shrewdest. "Transferring that many Strykers to Buffalo was a mismanagement of resources and a failure on your part."

Ciari met her gaze as calmly as she had Erik's. "Other rogue psions were on the ground in Buffalo aside from the target. I felt it prudent to take action against them."

She was careful to refrain from numbers, from names. The public knew about rogue psions. They didn't know about Warhounds unless one believed in the stories downloaded into pirate streams. Truth could be found in those conspiracy theories, even if most people didn't have all the facts.

"So you initiated a full-scale field transfer, taking Strykers off prior contracts and sending them to Buffalo without authorization?"

"It wouldn't be in anyone's best interest if the target slipped away during such a blatant attack on the government," Ciari said. "My orders are to protect. We did."

"And yet, the target still escaped," Erik said.

There was no way out of the punishment she could hear in Erik's voice. Ciari could never admit that she knew the identity of that seemingly unknown target. All Strykers who held the OIC position and those of the company's highest officer ranks obeyed a hidden law, and it had nothing to do with human legal wrangling. The Silence Law gave and took, but above all, it saved. Some might argue that the cost was too high, but Ciari never had.

Despite everything that was going on, she wouldn't betray her people. Her life wasn't worth theirs. She stayed silent.

Erik leaned forward slightly and rested both hands flat against the old wooden tabletop. "You are not justifying your case, Ciari. Silence is not an acceptable defense."

She could have spoken for days straight and it wouldn't have mattered. The judgment had been decided prior to her being summoned before the bench. This was merely a formality and a showcase of control.

"We announced the presence of rogue psions in the city as required by law," Ciari said. "It served to explain the large numbers of Strykers on the ground and resulted in the deactivation of the electrical grid. We thought the reduction in power would help us flush out and corner the target."

Travis Athe raised a single finger. "It didn't."

Ciari shook her head. "No, sir."

"How could you think that frightening human citizens was a good idea?"

"We acted in accordance with the laws in order to save them."

"That is debatable."

"Is this a debate, sir?"

"You overstep yourself, Ciari. Much as you overstepped yourself in Buffalo."

"We did what we thought was correct in the face of rogue psions and an unknown threat. We only ever had the well-being of humans in our thoughts."

It was a lie, they all knew it, but one every Stryker learned to tell.

"Your actions produced failures that resulted in this mess," Erik said. "That is unacceptable."

Ciari couldn't argue that statement. "We did what we could with the information we had. It was my decision."

"Do you stand behind your decision?"

Ciari looked him straight in the eye. "Yes."

In a world full of deadzones and toxic gene pools, with a population barely at a million and a quarter strong, Erik created order with the strike of a gavel. The World Court's efforts over the years had resulted in hundreds of secretly built space shuttles waiting to be filled in the Paris Basin, poised to leave the planet for a distant promised land. Earth meant nothing to the elite descendants of those who survived the Border Wars and managed to clean up their DNA by the fifth generation and join the Registry.

Erik embodied that mind-set, as did everyone else seated in judgment before her. This fact hadn't changed in all the decades the World Court had been in power.

"You've been such a model psion to those beneath you in the Strykers Syndicate over the past eleven years, Ciari," Erik said.

"I train my people as you require me to, sir."

"And therein lies the issue. They are not yours. They have never belonged to you. We own them, as we own you."

Ciari expected the pain, the flip of that switch. For one crystalline moment, she thought she could feel the hum of the neurotracker implanted in the back of her head as it processed the order for punishment. Perhaps she did, but it was drowned out by the searing agony that burned through her brain, pressing against the interior of her skull and spiking down her nerves.

She screamed when it became too much, too hot, knowing that to hold it all in would just drag it out longer. The sound of her voice echoed in her ears. It was the only thing she heard, the only thing that made any sense as she writhed on the floor, both hands clutching her head, incapable of making the pain stop. When it became too much, when it seemed as if the agony were too big for her skin to contain, Ciari clung to the self-inflicted pain in her gut to differentiate between the real world and the threat of insanity that began to crawl through her mind.

I want, Ciari thought through the fiery feeling of having her brain torn apart. *I want you—*

She tasted blood on her tongue, smelled metal all along the inside of her nose and mouth. She swallowed air and couldn't breathe, her nerves following the dictates of a machine and not her own body.

It went on and on and on.

[FIVE]

What the hell is *Cinnamomum verum*?" Kerr said. He held up a silvery foil packet to the fluorescent lights bolted to the ceiling of the vault, squinting at the faded text printed over the front of the packet.

Jason telekinetically added another box of seed packets and clear glass vials to the top of a pile. The entire stack teetered precariously near the entrance to the storage vault they were ransacking. "Hell if I know."

"Cinnamon," Kristen piped up from where she had climbed one of the storage racks and was methodically handing boxes down to a scavenger for loading. When he didn't move fast enough for her tastes, she dropped the boxes on the floor. "Spice out of Sri Lanka."

"Right," Quinton said as he hefted a box onto a gravlift. "What's Sri Lanka?"

"It was an island country in the Indian Ocean. Rising sea levels swallowed half of it. The Border Wars destroyed the rest."

"Huh." Kerr turned the packet in his hands from side to side, wondering what the seeds would look like. "Guess whoever built this place had the right idea. You know, I never did believe those conspiracy theories on the pirate streams about the government hiding supplies. Wonder if anything else they talk about is true."

"Most of those people are dissidents repeating false information," Lucas said. "They don't know any better."

Quinton eyed him. "You said most. What about the rest?"

Lucas smiled slightly, but his only answer to Quinton's curiosity was "You don't need to worry about the rest."

"If we can't trust government history, and pirate streams don't have the entire truth, how do you know all this stuff?" Jason said, warily eyeing Kristen where she clung to a metal shelf.

"Government history is fairly accurate," Lucas said as he entered information into his datapad. "But only if you sit on the World Court or know how to pry it out of the server farm that handles the data traffic for The Hague."

"Why didn't the governments from before the Border Wars use what was up here to save their people? The terraforming machines alone could have saved billions," Kerr said.

"Who would have gotten the right to use them first? Third-world countries? First? In the face of declining resources, overpopulation, and environmental change, the ruling classes thought Mars was the better option for them, just not for everyone."

Kerr shook his head and put the packet back into the box. He resealed it before handing it to the nearest scavenger. He reached for another one, ignoring the twinge of sore muscles all across his back and down his arms. Everyone was past the point of exhaustion, but they kept going. The only person excused from doing heavy lifting was Threnody. She was back in Alpha shuttle, sleeping off the exhaustion of opening the seed bank. Jason checked up on her once every hour or so. She hadn't woken up yet and wasn't getting any better.

The temperature in the three storage vaults was set at -18 degrees Celsius and needed to remain that cold to keep everything viable. They methodically worked their way through each of the vaults, taking half of everything: seeds, cell lines, DNA samples, frozen embryos, and everything else in the inventory. Aside from the boxes of seeds, the frozen zoo would hopefully repopulate empty continents and oceans one day through cloning. None of them expected they would live to see that miracle.

Lucas wanted more than what they were stealing, but two days was all they could risk on Spitsbergen; one day of recovery, one day of work. Then it would take hours to fly to Antarctica. The environmental systems on the shuttles had been prepped at a near-freezing temperature to handle the cargo. Each was equipped with a limited amount of cold-storage units, and they had to factor in space for the disassembled terraforming machines, but not all the stolen goods would fit in cold storage.

Looking up from his datapad, Lucas nodded to Jason. "This stack is ready. Get it out of here."

"Right," Jason said. He wrapped his telekinesis around the stack of boxes and teleported out. Appearing outside a shuttle in the marked-off arrival zone, Jason waved tiredly at Everett as the other man came down the ramp.

"How many more?" Everett said as he eyed the pile that Jason had brought out.

"We're barely halfway done," Jason said. "You can expect two more loaded gravlifts in about fifteen minutes."

Everett frowned. "We're full up on three of the shuttles already, and one of the shuttles needs to carry the terraforming machines."

"Lucas needs to check if those are still in working order. It's been a few hundred years since they were taken apart and stored."

"Tell him to hurry it up then. We need to know in order to calculate volume and weight."

Jason shrugged and teleported away, carrying Everett's concerns with him. Lucas didn't even look up from the datapad in his hands as Jason finished reporting. "Everything will fit. If we need to make space for the weight, we'll leave people behind."

Jason stared at him. "You said we couldn't risk leaving any evidence of our passage."

"No one will think to look for bodies in the water. Get back to transporting these things to the shuttles. Matron has a stack ready for you in the second vault."

Jason left. He knew better than to argue with the man who still had an iron grip on their lives.

It took hours of nonstop cataloguing, transferring, and pure grunt work to get the job done. Seeds were infinitesimal in weight, but with the amount they were transporting, it quickly added up. Toward the end, they ripped open boxes, taking just one or two packets of the remaining seeds, or just one vial of DNA, one stored embryo. For the more important items—such as algae and countless tree seeds and grains—the amounts were never reduced.

Only when the last cargo door closed and everyone was settled in for the flight did Lucas strap himself into the navigator's seat in Alpha shuttle. Matron was piloting again, and Threnody was laid out between them, unconscious and liable to remain that way for hours. The flight deck was set at a higher temperature to accommodate her.

Matron yawned through the preflight procedure. After the fifth yawn, she picked up a hypospray nearby and pressed it against her throat, dosing herself with a shot of adrenaline. A minute or so later, Lucas could feel the engines start up through the soles of his boots.

"Didn't think we'd make it this far," Matron said as she settled her hands on the stick and activated the vertical takeoff and landing.

"Get us in the air," Lucas said.

Matron did as she was told in silence, launching the shuttle and feeling the weight of the cargo in the jerk of the stick. They had a heavy load in the shuttle's belly, one more precious than anything her scavengers had ever discovered in the broken, abandoned cities of America. For all the credit that the government issued, for all the elite perks that one could have by gaining entrance into the Registry, clean DNA wasn't worth anything compared to what nine shuttles ferried out of Spitsbergen one late-August morning.

Behind them, its doors shut but not locked, the Svalbard Global Seed and Gene Bank was just as silent, just as cold as it had been for centuries.

They flew north, climbing over the Arctic Ocean, heading for the Pacific. The midnight sun guided their way, a constant bright circle beyond the clouds.

PART TWO
COGNIZANCE

SESSION DATE: 2128.03.18
LOCATION: Institute of Psionics Research
CLEARANCE ID: Dr. Amy Bennett
SUBJECT: 2581
FILE NUMBER: 251

The doctor watches Aisling play with a deck of cards. The child's small hands spread the plain, white rectangles across the table in a shapeless mess. She picks cards at random and lays them before her in a line.

"You never ask how I do it," Aisling says as she pushes the cards together. "Why?"

"Would you tell us if we did?" the doctor replies.

The girl tucks a piece of dark hair behind one small ear, studying the cards. "No."

"That's why, Aisling."

"But you're a doctor. Doctors should ask questions."

"We do."

"Not the right ones." Aisling smiles as she flips over a card, revealing a crimson red square on its face and nothing else. "Pick a card, any card. I can tell you the future."

"Would it be the right one?" The doctor leans forward to catch the child's gaze with her own. "Would you help us survive?"

Aisling flips more cards over, one at a time, until a line of shapes and symbols lie before her. She picks a card seemingly at random, holding it up beside her bleached-out violet eyes, the color of the shape a deep, dark blue. "My brother has eyes like this."

"Where is Matthew, Aisling?"

Aisling scoots the card as far across the table as her small arm will stretch. "You can't have him."

[SIX]

Beneath the Peace Palace lay a city of underground tunnels and bunkers. Its protective warrens once housed thousands of people during the Border Wars and still held their descendants today. The most well-guarded bunkers were reserved for those who served on the World Court. The business of ruling, however, was always conducted aboveground.

Sharra Gervais was blond-haired, blue-eyed, and gorgeous, human down to her very registered DNA. She was Erik's wife, his perfect piece of femininity; a woman who spent the majority of her time raising a daughter that he rarely saw or interacted with unless for a public event. The world press adored those family moments; Sharra hated the lie she was living. But she knew her role and played it well, portraying the good wife the world expected her to be. She sat in the area reserved for the families of those serving on the World Court, hands clasped in her lap, looking at her husband as he stood before the cameras of the world press.

He still wore his robes of office, the black synthfabric soaking up the glare from the cameras. Beneath the robe, Sharra knew he wore a perfectly tailored business suit in charcoal gray and pinstripes, the crisp whiteness of his hidden shirt a match for her dress. She smoothed her hands over the synthfabric resting against her thighs. White was such an expensive color to keep clean.

"I admire your husband's resolve when it comes to the safety of society," Fatima Omar said softly. The much younger woman sitting to Sharra's left wore a far less fashionable outfit, one that covered nearly every centimeter of her body. The long skirt and blouse were modestly cut, her hijab a demure black with little adornment save for a tiny amount of embroidery along the edges. Her husband, Mohammad, was a justice who stood in solid support of Erik.

"Yes," Sharra said absently, her attention focused on the spectacle before her. The reporters took up much of the area inside the renovated pressroom, with its small stage and guarded section for families and dignitaries who didn't merit a place before the microphones of the world press.

"—cannot condone what happened in Buffalo," Erik said. "The families of those who lost their lives during the cowardly attacks by rogue psions will be compensated, as is the law. The Strykers Syndicate is reviewing how they organize and initiate their missions. This will not happen again. Punishment has been administered to those responsible for the break in the chain of command."

Killing dogs makes people happy, Sharra thought, feeling the corner of her mouth tick minutely upward. *But it doesn't solve the problem, Erik.*

Politics wasn't her place, so she kept her opinion to herself as she always did. Sharra understood society's fear of psions better than most, but she also knew that psions were a cog that couldn't easily be replaced. The Strykers Syndicate kept rogue psions in check, but they also kept Sharra in couture fashion, clean food and water. Selling soldiers to the highest bidder under strict contractual terms had made those who sat on the World Court very, very wealthy over the years. Slavery was profitable, even if certain people considered it immoral. Sharra wasn't religious in the least, though she made a good show of bowing her head in prayer every Sunday.

"The Strykers Syndicate is well under our control. There is no need to fear government psions when science has produced ways to keep them in check," Erik said, gesturing faintly toward his head and the bioware net everyone knew was wrapped around his brain. "Society has nothing to fear from them."

Of course not. Sharra had to bite down on her bottom lip to keep from grimacing. *Oh, Erik, you are such a fool.*

She loved him, or thought she did. More and more as the years passed, she began to believe it was the idea of love that she adored, not the man she had married when she was young and incapable of seeing the loneliness that came with marrying a man of his social standing. They both kept secrets, and the one true thing they shared now was their daughter. Dinner needed to be scheduled in advance. Sleep was preferable to sex.

She regretted. It was an odd feeling.

Before her, the reporters were beginning to ask questions, and Sharra realized she had missed much of Erik's calculated apology in favor of her own thoughts. She already knew the gist of it. Being the wife of the most powerful human in the world had its perks.

Sharra gave a good show for the news when it was all over, standing beside her husband and smiling proudly at him. Only when they were in the back hallways of the Peace Palace, where the judges separated into their fractious little groups and went their separate ways, did Sharra speak.

"How is killing the OIC of the Strykers Syndicate conducive to everything we've worked for?" Sharra said, her voice a low hiss as they walked back to Erik's office. Behind them trailed a quad for security, the four soldiers keeping an eye on their charges.

Erik shot her a steely look. "Ciari Treiva isn't dead."

"She might as well be after what you put her through."

"Is that compassion for a dog I hear coming out of your mouth?"

"Hardly" was her clipped response. "You know exactly what I'm talking about."

Sharra bit back the rest of her argument until they were within the confines of his office and the jamming sequence for privacy was activated. She tossed her small purse on his desk in a fit of pique.

"What have I said when it comes to speaking in public of things you know nothing about?" Erik asked in a cold voice as he went behind his desk.

"For our daughter's sake, I'll pretend you didn't just say that," Sharra snapped as she headed for his bar.

"Starting early today, I see."

Sharra uncorked a bottle of merlot and poured herself a glass of the expensive drink until the red liquid reached the thin crystal rim. "Not early enough."

"Don't get drunk. I don't want you to make a mess of your clothes."

Sharra took a long swallow of her wine before she toasted him with bitterness on her tongue. "You know me so well, husband."

"I know your vices," Erik said as he unsealed his robes. Draping the clothing over the back of his leather chair, Erik sat down and studied his wife. "I mean it, Sharra. The world press is camped out everywhere right now and the last thing I need to deal with is you falling down drunk."

"I would think you'd be more worried about the problem with the missing psions than how I can embarrass you."

"I don't need your attitude right now."

She shrugged elegantly, every centimeter the supposedly perfect woman he had married. She'd come to her alcoholism late, needing something to drown out the pain and regret she lived with. "I can't decide if it's stress that's making you act so heavy-handed or merely the lack of sleep. Since you haven't slept in our bed in over a week, I'll assume it's the latter."

"I'm not cheating on you."

"I know you're not." Sharra took another sip of her wine, choking it down along with the laughter that threatened to pass her lips. "You're too busy setting up the launch and burning out our enslaved protectors to find someone else to fuck."

"I am doing this for our daughter. I am doing this for you. For *us*."

If he were a better man, if she were a less cynical woman, she might have believed him. Except Sharra knew otherwise, knew secrets of his business associates that he had no concept of. She scraped her teeth over the edge of the glass and drank down more wine, one arm crossed over her chest. "Honestly, Erik. For a judge, you're a terrible liar."

The flash of anger in his eyes told her she'd hit a nerve. Like any man, Erik took pride in his work and his ability to wield power. She watched him get to his feet and approach her, a hard expression on his face. Sharra held on to her wineglass, a flimsy barrier between them.

"I'm not the one who refuses to believe I have a problem," he said, voice low and flat as he stared at his wife over her glass.

Sharra licked a wet film off her teeth and smiled at him, mouth tinted red. "I am aware of my faults."

In the entire time they were married, he had never hit her. But some days, Sharra thought abuse would be preferable to this war of words.

"I don't have time to pander to your pathetic needs," Erik said, the tension between them almost painful. "Drink your wine, drink the whole damn bottle, but you don't leave my office until you're sober. Kindly shut your mouth and stay out of my way while I prepare for my next meeting."

"So it's the good, silent wife you want," Sharra murmured, licking her lips. "Darling, why didn't you say so?"

Her mockery made his temper rise higher, but Erik had already spent too much emotion this morning debriefing a woman he considered beneath him to expend any more on his wife. Sharra pressed a finger to his mouth, watching as he jerked back, as if he couldn't stand her touch. Her own mouth twisted into a thin, brittle smile.

"For our daughter's sake, I won't make a fool of you," Sharra promised.

Lillian was the one good thing she'd ever done with her life, and Erik was a decent father to the five-year-old child that she loved. The same could not be said for how he felt about his wife. Their private lives went much like this of late, fighting with every ounce of spite they had over everything.

Erik took Sharra at her word and retreated to his desk. She remained by the wet bar and steadily drank her way through the bottle of wine. She opened up a second one right before Erik left, smiling at the disgust in his eyes.

Sharra set the wine bottle aside after she was certain he wouldn't return and went to his desk. She grabbed her purse, pulling out an unmarked data chip as she sat down. Erik's terminal was wide-open for use, trust between them something carved deep into his mind, beyond the capacity of his bioware net to detect. Psionic interference perpetuated by the Sercas had worked wonders on his mind all those years ago. She still hated the results, though there were days she loved them. Loved him.

Their anniversary was coming up, the beginning of December. Erik had promised her the stars this year.

"I would rather have nothing," Sharra said softly, thinking of her daughter and what they would suffer through after the launch. The inevitability of a contract with Nathan she could not rationally escape.

She jacked in the data chip and uploaded the program meticulously created to bypass the World Court's security. Sharra knew her place. It wasn't by her husband's side.

She got up to pour herself another glass of wine.

[SEVEN]

AUGUST 2379
TORONTO, CANADA

The crack of displaced air from a teleport caused Jael Dawson, chief medical officer (CMO) for the Strykers Syndicate, to jerk her head up.

"Jael! Ciari needs you!" Keiko shouted.

Jael was already moving, having been on standby since being notified by a nurse that Ciari and Keiko were on the news streams. Keiko was crouched worriedly over Ciari's still form on the arrival platform. Jael swore, her thin, black dreads swinging around her face as she ran to aid them.

"Get me a gurney," Jael snapped to one of the nurses. "And prep OR three."

They had been dealing with the fallout of Buffalo for hours, even before Ciari was ordered to The Hague. The medical level was full of wounded, dying, and dead Strykers, with a handful still unaccounted for. Teams who hadn't been transferred to Buffalo for the initial fight now hunted for the missing in bunkers of that city, looking for bodies. Jael hated retrieval.

She knelt beside Ciari, dropping several layers of her mental shields to see what kind of mess she had to deal with. The Class III telepath swore loudly as the mental trauma of a mind raked through physical torture battered against her own. Jael, the best psi surgeon in the Syndicate, wrapped telepathic shields around Ciari's mind to try to stabilize her.

"We need to move her," Jael said, glancing up at the crew of medical personnel that swarmed around them. "Let's go, people, we don't have much time."

Keiko telekinetically lifted Ciari off the floor of the medical level's arrival room and onto the hover-gurney. Ciari's face was streaked with blood and tears, her lips bitten through and teeth flecked with pink-tinged saliva. Her eyes roved beneath her eyelids. When Jael brushed against Ciari's mind, all she got was a tidal wave of emotion. Jael flinched.

"The OR," Jael said. *"Now."*

Everyone rushed to obey, the medics and nurses working to stabilize Ciari's physical form as they hurried to the operating room. Keiko followed in their wake, the telekinetic pale-faced and angry, a futile emotion, Jael thought.

Don't die on me now, Ciari, Jael thought grimly as she let her crew pull the hover-gurney into the operating room. *We still need you.*

Jael thought for a moment of a time just hours ago when she'd had Ciari on her operating table for a different sort of procedure. Shaking aside that memory, Jael spared a moment to look over at Keiko, the telekinetic standing just outside the tiny sterilization room. "Do you need medical attention?"

"No," Keiko said, voice tight. "They didn't touch me."

Jael nodded. "Then wait outside. I've got work to do."

The door slid shut and Jael continued through to the operating room. She still had to scrub in, standing shoulder to shoulder with some of her nurses and assistants. For all that this was psi surgery, a physical operation was involved as well.

"Marguerite," Jael said. "Deal with the bleeding. I'll deal with her mind."

Jael's second-in-command nodded and began barking orders. A nurse cut off Ciari's uniform, another hooked her to an IV and other machines to monitor her vital signs. Electrodes were adhered to her skull, pulling up Ciari's chaotic mental readings on an EEG machine and overlaying it with the baseline in her medical records. Jael closed her eyes against the organized chaos of the operating room as she curled a hand around Ciari's own lax one. She dropped all but a single mental shield and sank her telepathic power into Ciari's traumatized mind.

A maelstrom of agony greeted her on the mental grid, jagged edges cutting into her own mind, psionic pain bleeding through her power. Jael worked to hold on to her own sense of self. She let a little of the pain seep in, needing to know where it stemmed from. The brain was a link between the body and the mind. The neurotracker that every Stryker carried was capable of doing enough damage that sometimes death would have been the preferable option.

Jael focused her power, splitting it through the burned-out pieces of Ciari's psyche. She went deep, letting herself be drawn into the other woman's subconscious mind. Jael knew that Marguerite would be putting Ciari under with as many drugs as her battered body could handle. Consciousness would be a slippery thing to grasp right now, and sometimes healing worked better as a suggestion than as an order. Sometimes it didn't.

Ciari, Jael said, piecing together the woman's shattered sense of control one thought, one heartbeat, at a time. *I need you to turn off the pain.*

Raw emotion flowed over her, no control in the response. Jael struggled to find an answer in a sensory overload where words weren't even an afterthought, but simply forgotten.

Turn it off.

Of all the psions, empaths were the best at altering how they felt pain. It was nerves and tissue, mind over matter, the concept of pain, of an ache that could carefully be denied. Jael used every bit of her power and concentration to guide Ciari into changing how her body felt, so it would change how her mind felt. It was almost a relief when the pain switched off, that all-encompassing drag on Jael's mind disappearing.

"ICP at twenty-one mm's," Jael heard a nurse say. "Scans are showing possible brain herniation, definite epidural hematoma."

"Prep for decompressive craniectomy," Marguerite ordered. "Map out placement of the neurotracker for the operation. We can't take any chances with her."

The hum of a laser saw was a hideous background noise. Conversation was reduced to medical jargon that only a tiny part of Jael's mind bothered to translate. Jael felt Ciari's mind dip sharply beneath hers, sliding away. She gripped the cold hand tighter, a physical anchor point for the one on the mental grid.

No, Jael said, holding tight to the other woman's frayed thoughts. *You don't get to leave us yet.*

They didn't like each other; never really had. They were trained to handle different tasks, to reach different goals. Ciari led Strykers into harm's way; Jael pulled them out. The only thing they had in common was that they actually gave a damn for their fellow Strykers. In this instance, Ciari was just another patient who needed Jael.

With Marguerite handling the physical operation and Jael refusing to let Ciari's mind die, they managed to keep her alive. This took several long hours and the results could be summed up in a single sentence.

"She's breathing," Jael informed Keiko and Aidan Turner, the Stryker Syndicate's chief administrative officer (CAO), outside the recovery room. "On her own. Consider it a miracle. The neurotracker did a lot of damage."

"Erik meant to kill her," Keiko said, looking through the observation window at the still form surrounded by machines and nurses. "Travis Athe wanted her alive. He managed to get a majority vote to spare her life. They appointed me Acting OIC until Ciari recovers."

Jael's mouth twisted. "Travis doesn't have a compassionate bone in his body. Why would he spare Ciari?"

"I don't know."

Possibly because the launch is so close, they can't risk the upheaval appointing a new OIC would cause, Aidan said, the Class IV telepath drawing both women into a psi link.

Keiko's Acting OIC, Jael pointed out.

They can risk me being in the public eye during Ciari's absence, but they made it very clear it was to be temporary, Keiko said. *They need her for the launch.*

Did they give you a time frame for when I'm supposed to have Ciari standing on her own two feet and not in a coma?

Aidan winced at that announcement. *Be honest, Jael. What are her odds?*

Jael crossed her arms, stepping out of the way of a nurse. The nurse, used to the silent, gesture-filled conversations that happened between 'path-oriented psions, ignored them. *She's in no pain, but only because I was able to get her to turn off part of her mind.*

What?

Her system was in overload because of the neurotracker. She's going to need a biotank and regeneration of most, if not all, of her central nervous system. We have her hooked up to an external monitor that's sending impulses directly into her brain to ensure her major bodily functions still continue to work. Jael spread her hands in a helpless gesture, grimacing. *I've got her telepathically anchored, but there's no guarantee she'll want to live. There may very well be damage to her body, to her brain, that we can't treat.*

Erik had his finger on that kill switch for a full five minutes, Keiko said softly, the look in her brown eyes bleak and hateful.

I still sensed coherency in her subconscious mind during the surgery, Jael said.

What about her conscious *mind?*

Jael was silent on that, and Keiko let out a harsh little laugh. "So it's like that."

"It's not like anything." Jael ran a hand through her dreads, pulling the mass away from her face. She sighed tiredly. "I'll keep you apprised of her condition, Keiko. We're setting up a biotank and will transfer her to it immediately once the swelling in her brain has gone down."

"Every six hours. I mean it, Jael. We have to be able to tell the World Court how she's progressing."

Jael didn't argue.

"Keep me updated as well," Aidan said. "What about the Strykers that were in Buffalo?"

Jael knew he wasn't asking about their condition. Less than half the Strykers that were in Buffalo survived. Those that did had all gone through a tiny, discreet mindwipe performed by Jael herself, their memories of seeing Lucas Serca and his siblings on the field erased. The Sercas weren't supposed to be anything other than human, and the high-ranking officers of the Strykers Syndicate were obligated to keep that secret, even at the cost of their own lives.

"They're recovering," Jael said, voice mild. "From everything."

It was enough of an assurance, and the three parted ways. Jael should have gone to her office, where she had space to think that wasn't full of people dying either beneath her hands or beneath her mind. Instead, she detoured into a lab that only had two approved biometric signatures for entry. This, Jael's personal research space, had been used by many CMOs over generations. Jael stepped inside and approached the work area in the back, where an opaque, cylindrical machine sat, surrounded by monitors.

It was securely attached to the countertop, with all readings on the tiny control screen positive and green. Jael checked the numbers, looking for anything out of the ordinary that could possibly harm the growing embryo housed inside the gestational unit. This was going to become a standard part of her routine, a deviation she never foresaw. Caring for Ciari's unborn child could arguably be considered her most important job at the moment.

She grabbed a stool, dragged it over, and reached for the datapad that lay abandoned near the gestational unit. The screen came alive at her touch, and Jael scrolled through the information. It was all preliminary lab work and reports that would need tremendous fleshing out. She wondered if it was worth it to even try. They had a month, maybe less, before everyone died, either by a kill switch, riots, or starvation. She wondered if this was how their ancestors felt during the Border Wars, that five-year span of nuclear hell that gave birth to their current lives; trapped in a situation that had no easy way out.

Stay with us, Jael thought down the psi link that tied her to Ciari for medical purposes as she looked critically at the program decoding a genome. *We still need you. Your baby will need you.*

[EIGHT]

New Zealand had tried to avoid the conflicts of old, but the shifting tides of war brought Australia's destruction to it just the same. Now it was two long, barren islands, the iron and asphalt skeletons of its cities touched only by the wind and the sea. At the very southern point of the South Island, Invercargill was just a shell.

The silence was shattered by what was left of a rusted metal door on an old river-port warehouse being torn off its hinges and telekinetically hurled down the street. All the broken warehouse windows meant the air inside was as cold and dry as it was outside.

"This way," Lucas said.

He ran past Jason, expecting the others to follow. Jason didn't hesitate in following his lead. Behind them ran Quinton, Threnody cradled protectively in his arms. She was barely responsive, her comalike state the entire reason why they had fallen off course and detoured here. The last two hours had been hellish, with her intermittently suffering through seizures and Jason unable to stop it.

"Is that what I think it is?" Jason asked. "How did you get it here?"

"I don't care so long as it works," Quinton said in a tight voice as he skidded to a halt, eyes flickering across the biotank. "Tell me it works, Lucas."

"I would have risked a teleport to Antarctica that would ruin my own recovery if it didn't," Lucas said without looking up from the control terminals. Wires snaked across the floor to a portable generator. Tubes connected a small storage tank to the holding tank through a pressure system that whined loudly as everything came online.

"How did you know to store this here? And the fuel?" Jason said as he wiped dust and grime off the biotank's top seal with his uniform sleeve.

60

"How do you think?"

No one mentioned Aisling, the child whose orders Lucas was follow-ing, but her name hung heavy between them anyway. They should have hit Antarctica already, but they'd taken the long route south across the Pacific Ocean, flying over an expanse of gray, acidic water and arriving here. They were stopping in New Zealand only because they couldn't risk Threnody's life any longer. Her health since unlocking the seed bank had only gotten worse over the hours. Staying the course meant los-ing her, and Lucas wasn't going to risk that. They needed a refuel any-way, and Matron was handling that out on the street.

These three had a life to save.

Lucas dealt with the biotank while Jason and Quinton worked to strip Threnody of the blanket she was wrapped in and her clothes. Quinton carefully removed the IV lines sticking out from the back of her hands. He pulled a long hypo out of the bag Jason was carrying and ripped the plastic seal off it with his teeth. Jason carefully turned Threnody onto her stomach with his telekinesis, letting her hover a few centimeters off the ground.

"Hold her steady," Quinton said as he spanned one hand over the jut of Threnody's hip, lining up the hypo against the bone. They didn't have time to administer a sedative, and no one was sure how she would react to the drug in the state she was in.

Jason held her still as gently as he could. Quinton jammed his thumb down on the release button, feeling resistance as the longer, thicker needle of the hypospray pierced Threnody's bone to extract a stem-cell-packed marrow sample.

Quinton passed the hypo to Lucas once it was full. Lucas slid it into the receiver tube attached to the storage tank that held nanites and the regen-therapy fluid integral to biotanks. Mixed together, the concoction would accelerate the healing capabilities of cells in the human body. With a hard stab of his thumb, Lucas depressed Threnody's marrow into the tube, letting the nanites get a preread on her DNA. Clear, viscous fluid was already pumping into the holding tank for oxygenation.

"I hope this works," Jason said as he struggled to find a viable vein in first one of her arms, then the other. The empty tubing floated in the air by way of telekinesis. They didn't have a sterility field here, so Jason was improvising, trying to keep the tube off the ground and free of contamination. "I hope—*shit!*"

He flipped her from her side onto her back so suddenly that Quinton didn't have time to let go of her wrist. His fingers snagged on the needle in her vein, dislodging it with bloody results. Her skin tore, so did the vein, and blood leaked from the wound.

"Jason," Quinton snarled, head snapping up.

"She's not breathing," Jason said, holding one hand down over Threnody's chest. "She's not *breathing*."

Which meant her heart wasn't beating.

Quinton felt the burn in the back of his mind through their bond as Jason accessed his microtelekinesis. Bright spots filled Quinton's vision, obscuring Threnody. He fumbled for the gauze in Jason's bag, working to clean up the mess her hand and wrist had become and reset the needle.

Jason sank his power into her chest, wrapped it around her heart, and started up a cardiac rhythm. He used his own as a baseline, nearly breaking her ribs from the inside out as he struggled to keep her from dying.

"Lucas, you need to move faster," Quinton yelled over his shoulder. "She's crashing!"

"This can't be rushed" was Lucas's only answer.

"God fucking damn it." Jason's pupils were dilated as he stared blankly down at Threnody. "Okay, I've got her. I've got her."

Quinton pressed two fingers to Threnody's throat, searching out a pulse that was too erratic for his liking. "Slow it down, Jays."

Jason sucked in a deep breath. "I'm trying."

"Try harder."

"The biotank is ready," Lucas said seconds later, voice taut. "Bring her."

The machine's side panels slid far enough apart for Jason to telekinetically lower Threnody inside. He held her down as the thick fluid flowed over her, sliding up her nose, into her mouth, down her throat, drowning her. Even unconscious, Jason could feel her struggling as he telekinetically attached the tubing to the sides of the tank. Lucas tapped in another command, and seconds later a heavy, gray stream of nanites mixed with the regen-therapy fluid began to flow through the tubing into Threnody's body. Dozens of sealed wires extended from the sides of the tank, pressing against her skin to monitor her vitals.

Lucas came around to Jason's side, carrying a handful of wires. He peeled the tape off the tiny electrodes, sticking them to Jason's temples and his chest. A second set of vitals showed up on another screen; Jason's baseline. It eerily matched Threnody's.

Quinton stared at the jagged moving lines representing two heartbeats. "Jason?"

"I've got her," Jason said, sounding distant.

"He's in deep," Lucas said, eyeing Jason critically. "He caught her in time, so maybe this will work."

"Maybe?" Quinton said.

"We're going to be stuck here for a few days, and Jason is going to need to be awake for the entire process." Lucas glanced over his shoulder. "Find me a shot of Adrenalin."

Quinton went for their bags. "You think he can handle it? He dosed himself pretty heavily with that stuff back in Buffalo."

"If he passes out, she dies."

Quinton came back with not one dose of Adrenalin, but a dozen.

Lucas pressed the hypospray against Jason's throat and administered the dose. Jason shuddered, leaning heavily against the biotank. Lucas helped him sit down, back to the machine. He was pale-faced and breathing quickly, sweat beading along his brow.

"Jason?" Quinton said, closing his eyes against the sudden pull at the back of his mind.

"I've got her," Jason repeated like a mantra. "I've got her."

A biotank could force cellular regeneration to happen faster than the human body could do so alone, building off a patient's own stem cells through the persistence of nanites. With enough time and training, Jason might one day accomplish the same on his own in minutes, not hours or days, but he still didn't know what he was capable of. As things stood, he was barely holding Threnody together, his power slip-sliding through cellular levels, chasing after nanites. He tried to recall through remembered agony what he had done on the flight out of Buffalo. Jason forced himself to concentrate on the shape of Threnody's cells to get a feel for her DNA and build off the genetic blueprint of her body.

Quinton looked at Jason, feeling the other man's power pulling at the back of his mind through the permanent bond they shared. He winced at what felt like an itch on the inside of his skull and tried to ignore it. Quinton pressed his hand against the dusty, dirty plasglass and didn't take his eyes off Threnody.

[NINE]

SEPTEMBER 2379
INVERCARGILL, NEW ZEALAND

She took a breath.
Then another. Deeper.
It was cold; wet.
Fluid was in her lungs. In her mouth.

Threnody cracked open her eyes to a world made of light. Fractured light, seen through the heavy, curved plasglass of a biotank and the thick, undulating fluid that breathed for her. She closed her eyes. Opened them again. The world didn't change.

Shadows moved around her outside the biotank. She could hear the soft, constant beeping of a monitor, the sound deep and distant through the fluid. She tried to move her hand, felt her fingers get tangled in tiny wires, so many attached to the length of her body. They didn't hurt.

She did.

Who am I?

Go to sleep, someone answered. The voice was clear, accented, sounding like those who hailed from London. Stretched in a way she felt in her bones. In her nerves.

Who am I?

Threnody Corwin. Now go to sleep. We aren't finished.

She was dragged under by waves of water and light, a riptide of power that took her to the depths of the ocean. Which was impossible, for this wasn't any ocean found in the world.

She slept.

When she regained consciousness, it was to cold air blowing across bare skin and pressure in her chest. She struggled to cough up the thick fluid in her lungs and replace it with oxygen. Strong arms held her steady, a deep, familiar voice filling her ears and not her mind.

"That's it, Thren," Quinton said. "Like that. Keep coughing. It's almost all out."

His skin was dark against her own, his grip solid as she heaved and jerked in his support, coughing out every last minuscule bit of the perfluorocarbons that she didn't remember swallowing.

"Hate this part," Threnody rasped as her body shuddered through the motions.

"I know. You're almost there."

When she was breathing air and not fluid, he picked her up from the cold metal floor and carried her to a portable sterilization tent. The plastic walls smelled too sharp in her nose. She thought she could taste it. Wires were stuck to her skin, in her veins, dangling like long-dead vines made of plastic and metal.

"Ready?" a voice asked.

She opened her eyes, watched as Jason came into blurry focus at the entrance to the small tent.

"Ready," Quinton answered for the both of them.

Jason sealed the inner layer shut, then the outer. The soft hiss of the sterilization process starting up echoed in her ears, vaporizing the viscous fluid sticking to her body. Threnody held one hand close to her face, struggling to focus. Her hand shook, but with no spastic jerk to the movement of her muscles. Just exhaustion, nothing more complicated than that.

"Should be dead," Threnody murmured, letting her head drop onto Quinton's shoulder. Gravity pulled her hand down, arm swinging in the air.

"Go to sleep, Thren," Quinton said, voice rough.

"Did we make it inside the seed bank?"

"Yeah." He swallowed. "Yeah, we made it."

She took a breath, felt air flow into her lungs; sterile and cold. Unconsciousness took her once more. When Threnody woke again, she was lying on a flight deck, wrapped in thermal blankets and clean clothes. It was silent, and the person watching over her this time wasn't Quinton.

"Where are we?" she asked, her voice dry, tongue sticking to the roof of her mouth.

Lucas looked up from the datapad in his hands and whatever report he was familiarizing himself with. The bruise from when Quinton had punched him in the mouth was gone. "New Zealand."

Threnody's eyebrows drew together in confusion, thin creases lining her forehead. "I thought—the Arctic?"

"Mm." Lucas set aside the datapad. "You've been unconscious since frying the seed-bank doors."

"How long?"

"We spent two days in the Arctic. It took half another day to get down here with everything we stole, and we've been here for almost two days since we landed so Jason could work on you. You weren't going to make it to Antarctica, so we took a detour."

"Antarctica," she echoed, fingers curling against her palms. Her skin felt new and it itched, but the burning pain she remembered from the power plant and the seed bank was gone. Threnody sucked in a deep breath, her mind unfolding those memories easily enough. "I feel like I should be dead."

"You don't die here."

"Here is relative."

Lucas smiled at her, the look full of some twisted understanding, as if he knew what secrets she kept. He probably did.

Threnody pushed at the blankets until she was free of them and could sit up, putting her back against the bulkhead. A faint twinge from her right hand made her look down. A small bruise surrounded the entrance point of the IV there. She eyed the tubing that connected her to the mostly empty bag hanging off the pilot's seat.

"So we succeeded in the Arctic. Did everyone make it off Spitsbergen?"

"I love that you distrust me so thoroughly. It's refreshing, to say the least."

Threnody gave Lucas a cool look, blue eyes slightly narrowed. Her black hair was a tangled mess, she needed a shower, and she had no idea what had transpired between the Arctic and now. She wanted answers. "If you're not going to tell me what's going on, I'll find someone who will."

Lucas got to his feet, looking down at her. "Who else would have the answers you need?"

Threnody curled her hands around her knees and glared. "Just give me what I want, Lucas. You already have my support. You don't need me to beg."

"It's so interesting when you do." Lucas shrugged his ambivalence and ran a hand through his pale blond hair. "We didn't leave anyone behind, if that's what you're worried about. None of our people, at least."

"Have our actions been discovered yet?"

"The government isn't going to announce what happened on a news stream. If they haven't discovered the discrepancy by now, then they will within the next twenty-four hours. We can't confirm where they stand right now without risking our position and that's not something I'll do."

Threnody had more questions, but Lucas was already leaving. Before the hatch closed, Quinton stepped inside, scowling faintly at Lucas's back.

Threnody glanced at Quinton, taking stock of how he moved, need-ing to assure herself that he was all right. Then his attention was on her, some of the worry leaving his brown eyes. She swallowed a sudden surge of relief as Quinton knelt beside her. She dimly recalled moments from her time in the biotank that made no sense to her. Dreams, maybe. Or possibly nightmares. But always, always, he was there.

"Brought you another insulated skinsuit," Quinton said as he set the pile near her knees. "You'll need it where we're going."

"Antarctica, I know. Lucas told me we're still heading there." She slid the IV out of her hand and reached for the skinsuit. "Thank you."

Quinton moved to sit in the navigator's seat. It was habit to take care of each other, the only family they'd had for years. There had never been anything sexual between them, and privacy wasn't something they had ever received. They lost their right to it the moment the neurotrackers were grafted to their brains. When you fought in the crowded streets of dying cities and along the boundaries of deadzones, privacy was a luxury you weren't allowed.

When she finished dressing, Threnody carefully stood. Quinton knew better than to help her, but from the way he held himself, she knew he would catch her if she fell.

The biotank had regenerated her nervous system, fixing the massive, self-inflicted damage she'd caused while fighting Jin Li at the power plant, and the further damage from pushing herself in the Arctic. It couldn't do anything about exhaustion. She stared at her palms and fingers, at the healed flesh that felt too new. Taking a deep breath, Threnody accessed her power and tried not to flinch as it sizzled through her nerves with a new sharpness.

Blue electricity crawled across the skin of her hands, dancing over her fingernails. It sputtered and sparked, tiny lines of power that was all her. It made her a little dizzy, but she had no other way to discover if she could still function as a psion.

A warm hand curved over her elbow, holding her steady as she absorbed that power back into her body. Still a Class III electrokinetic. Still everything she was born to be. Jin Li tried, but he hadn't been able to take that from her.

"Everything working right?" Quinton asked.

"Yeah," she said, even if it wasn't really true. Threnody felt his fingers tighten on her arm. She didn't fight when he pulled her into a hard hug.

"You pull that shit again, I'll kick your goddamn ass."

Threnody let out a strangled little laugh, turning her face against his neck and giving herself a moment—one fucking moment—to be human.

It was a minute or two before they separated. Threnody ran both hands through her hair, irritated when her fingers caught on tangled knots. "Heard we got the seeds and everything else that was on Spitsbergen. Half of it, at least."

Quinton nodded, rubbed at the back of his head, wincing. "Yeah. We got it. Jays did a lot of the heavy lifting both there and here. He's sleeping it off now."

Threnody froze when she heard that familial diminutive come out of Quinton's mouth. Only Kerr had ever been allowed to use it. She thought back to the fight at the outpost in Longyearbyen, the name Jason had called her in that hallway. She and Quinton had spent too many years living in each other's personal space for her not to know when something was wrong.

"Quinton? You've never called Jason by that name before."

He looked away from her, out the windshield over her left shoulder. His silence was unnerving. Threnody sighed and framed his face with hands that shook only slightly, forcing Quinton to look at her.

"Lucas wasn't very forthcoming with details," she said. "Did something else happen in the seed bank? Tell me what I need to know."

The Strykers mind-set would take years to break, years they didn't have. She was in charge, he would always see their partnership that way. When Threnody gave an order, she, like Lucas, expected to be obeyed.

"It didn't happen in the seed bank," Quinton said.

Threnody steeled herself for his report, knowing she wasn't going to like it. "What didn't happen?"

"You were dying. I didn't want to lose you, so I made a deal with Lucas." He pulled her hands away, putting distance between them. "Gideon Serca broke my arms at the power plant. Broke my face. I think he would have broken every last bone in my body if Samantha hadn't stopped him. I wasn't in any condition to save you back in Buffalo."

Threnody's gaze dropped to his hands. She ran her fingers over his forearm, feeling only muscle and not the ridges of biotubes. "Lucas keeps saying that he needs me. He would have saved me anyway without you asking him to."

"It's more than that. It has to do with Kristen."

"I know she's dysfunctional," Threnody said. "I don't know what she does in order to gain sanity. Quinton, what are you saying?"

"She broke Jason's shields. She was the only one who could. His natal shields are completely gone. That's why he was able to save you."

"I assumed it was Lucas's doing, that he found some way to merge with Jason."

"No, it was Kristen. Because of her, Jason's finally got his secondary shields and full access to his power. He—" Quinton broke off, voice cracking a bit.

Threnody didn't even know she was reaching for him until her hand was gripping his shoulder. "Quinton. What happened?"

"You were dying," he said, struggling to speak. "Jason's mind was opening up to all that power. He's a Class 0 now, Thren. Lucas was right. Microtelekinesis all the fucking way, but it was too much. His mind needed more room, which he didn't have."

"The bond," Threnody guessed. "With Kerr."

"Kerr isn't a 'kinetic-oriented psion," Quinton said very, very softly. "He couldn't handle the overload. Their brain patterns wouldn't match."

She stared up into his face, a curious rushing sound filling her ears. "No."

"Lucas made the connection. He took the bond out of Kerr and put it in my mind. It's permanent." Quinton gave her a careful, broken smile as he brushed his knuckles over her cheek. "You lived."

Threnody didn't know what to say. She opened her mouth; closed it again. Shaking her head, she finally found her voice. "I would never have asked that of you. Ever."

"You weren't in any condition to argue."

"Consider yourself lucky." Threnody took in a deep breath and straightened her shoulders, hiding the pain with long practice. "Jason and I need to have a talk."

Quinton blinked at her, startled into laughter. "Even with Jason having all that power, I'd put my credit on you."

The hatch slid open and Matron stepped inside, the older woman eyeing Threnody. "So you're finally awake. You missed all the fun."

"I doubt that," Threnody said.

Matron jerked her thumb over her shoulder. "Go strap in. We're launching in five and I don't need you underfoot."

Quinton put a hand on Threnody's shoulder and guided her out of the flight deck, back into the cold of the cargo bay.

[TEN]

Dawn broke over London, late-summer sunlight piercing through a haze of thin, gray clouds. The air was hot and muggy, the breeze coming from the north only marginally cooler. The people who called the winding, ruined streets home were beginning to wake up and start another day while those who worked the night went to ground. People lived in cycles and this was only one of many.

Main city towers spanned both sides of the polluted deluge that was the Thames River, with others spread out around them. Clustered in the central zone, with foundations anchored deep into the ground, the city towers were covered in hologrids, with adverts that scrolled down their sides. The Serca Syndicate called a main city tower home, and Nathan Serca sat with his back to the view from his office. He'd seen it all before and was more interested in what his own CMO had to say.

Victoria Montoya, a Class III telepath, hadn't slept much in the past few days and it showed in the stiff way she carried herself, the way stress lined her eyes and mouth.

"We lost forty-nine Warhounds in Buffalo," Victoria reported, studying her datapad. "Of the total, Jin Li Zhang was the most critical loss. Fifty-two other Warhounds are currently off the active-duty roster and under medical care ranging from a few days to a few weeks. Most won't be ready for immediate field missions. That's almost a sixth of our total ranks. We still don't know the location of your daughters."

Nathan's expression didn't change as Victoria tallied up their losses. He already knew the few major ones, the losses that involved his children; these numbers made it all worse. His fury at the betrayal of his children was difficult to hide, but he was adept at censoring himself. Nathan was supposed to be human, but as a Class I triad psion, he had more than enough power at his disposal to change an adversary's mind. He rarely used his powers, choosing instead to act through subordinates in order to extend his life span. It was how he'd survived to reach fifty-one when most psions were lucky to reach thirty.

"And my son?" Nathan leaned back in his chair and curled his hands over the armrests. "What about Gideon?"

His youngest son was the only successor he had left. Lucas defected first. Now, with Samantha gone, her absence would cause problems Nathan had never thought he'd have to deal with. She'd been taking on public duties for two years, and her disappearance wouldn't go unnoticed. Kristen had been kept hidden away, never even put into the Registry. The continuing loss of his chosen successors would, however, be impossible to hide.

"Gideon is stable," Victoria said after a moment's hesitation. "Physically, he wasn't hurt that badly. Mentally? It's been rough."

Stable wasn't enough. Nathan required a functioning heir. "Fix his mind, Victoria. I need Gideon conscious for a mission while I attend a scheduled meeting with the Syndicate's subsidiaries."

Going into that meeting alone would raise questions, but it couldn't be helped. Nathan didn't have the time or the tools to cut his way past two dozen bioware nets in a day and alter minds, even with help. Psionic interference would tip too many people off, and at this juncture that was the very last thing he needed.

"When does the meeting take place?" Victoria asked.

"The end of next week unless circumstances dictate otherwise. I'm sending Gideon out before then."

Victoria managed to hide most of her wince, the only sign being a faint tic at the left side of her mouth. It was a difficult task, but she could accomplish it if she disregarded her own health in favor of Nathan's son's. She would, because she, like everyone else in the Warhound ranks, knew that the Serca family was the only thing standing between them and government enslavement.

"He'll be ready," Victoria said, staking her life on that promise.

"Excellent. Now, what of the Strykers that were seen with Lucas? Do we have any eyewitness reports?"

Victoria consulted her notes. "Gideon's memories are intact. He tortured a pyrokinetic Stryker inside the power plant. The electrokinetic partnered with that Stryker was seen entering the power plant, but her condition is unknown. We think she may have been involved with Jin Li's death and with what happened to the electrical grid. The telepath was merged with Lucas and no one saw the telekinetic."

"Do we have any information of what may have caused the near breaking of the mental grid?"

"No." Victoria glanced up. "Sir, do you have any thoughts on the matter?"

Nathan drummed his fingers once against the armrests of his chair, gazing past her. "During her fight in the Slums, Samantha discovered that a Stryker still had intact natal shields, but could use his power."

Victoria's expression became incredulous. "That's impossible. Natal shields always fall within the first two to three years after birth so we can access our powers. If they don't fall, we can't access our powers. That is a documented fact, sir."

"Apparently not for this particular Stryker. Our records indicate that Jason Garret is a Class V telekinetic who can teleport. We can add to them that he has intact natal shields. The question we're left with is what would happen if those shields fell? What are they holding back?"

"Do you think it was him, sir?"

Nathan had been thinking about the question endlessly since Buffalo started running at full power. "I think it's a possibility."

"Will we be looking into it?"

"I will be." Nathan dismissed her with a wave of his hand. "Go finish your work on Gideon."

Victoria left, the door sliding shut behind her. Nathan allowed himself a moment of personal, frustrated bitterness at the position his children had put him in. He hadn't wanted more than one child, but Marcheline had ordered him to create more. His mother died years ago, and Nathan felt he could blame her for this mess. Fighting his own family right now was a distraction he didn't need, not when the only thing that should be occupying his attention was the scheduled launch. Nathan refused to let his ancestors' plan wither and die all because of a few spoiled children who refused to learn their place.

Except their rebellion was undermining his control.

How had Lucas discovered and kept hidden a psion of such incredible strength? Nathan had been in and out of Lucas's mind for years. Lucas shouldn't have been capable of deceit. If the Warhound ranks had a traitor, however inconceivable the thought, then Nathan knew he would never find the person. Like Nathan and all Sercas before them both, Lucas would kill to keep his secrets. Nathan doubted he'd find even a memory of the traitor. Two years of searching had proven that conclusion as fact.

Nathan grimaced. Doubting his powers and his Syndicate right now would be disastrous. He needed Gideon in the field, searching out that new target. Being introduced as the new face of the Serca Syndicate would have to come later. Jin Li's death meant Nathan had a hole in the Warhound ranks that needed to be filled, and quickly. The world press kept demanding a statement from Nathan, not just his Syndicate's official publicist, on what had transpired in Buffalo. Nathan wasn't going to cave to their demands, not yet. There was a lot to do, with little time to do it in, and too few people he could trust to get it done right.

The mental grid dipped beyond his shields, a psi signature sparking bright and high far away on the psychic plane. The presence of another mind brushed against his. Nathan recognized the orderly thoughts of a psion who lacked the impression of a static human mind, which told him it wasn't a Warhound asking for a link. Nearly all Warhounds were shielded as human to some degree in order to hide. Strykers didn't have that luxury.

Aidan, Nathan acknowledged, initiating a psi link between himself and the Strykers Syndicate's third-in-command. *To what do I owe this lovely little chat?*

You already know, Aidan said, voice empty of all emotion. Nathan could still feel the ripple of the other man's mind, how it strained against his own power. *We require a meeting.*

You require? I'd rather you beg.

Nathan. Aidan paused, the pull of his mind weakening slightly as he conversed on a separate psi link with someone else. Finally, the Stryker said, *Please.*

Any other time it would have amused Nathan. Today, it only irritated him, but he had appearances to keep up. *Keiko knows what my office looks like.*

She'd been in it before, ferrying Ciari from wherever the Stryker OIC might have been, on the pretense of negotiating a contract to hide their true reasons for meeting with him. Only in The Hague, when they were in the same city together, did Nathan purposefully keep a mental feeler out, waiting to hear from her. Ciari wasn't with Keiko this time; she had Aidan. It was a mistake on her part, even if she didn't know it. She should have brought an empath.

They arrived before his desk in a teleport, and a red alert popped up at the bottom of the vidscreen. Nathan disengaged it. Security still called in.

"Sir," someone said over the uplink. "Is everything all right?"

"Only some visitors. Nothing to be concerned about."

"Sir."

The connection cut off and Nathan took in the pair's tired appearance with a keen eye. "I expected you earlier than this."

"We're under stricter monitoring by the World Court," Keiko said.

"They're a little behind the mark, don't you think?" Nathan said. "If I'm dealing with you, I suspect Ciari's closer to dead after that little stunt Erik pulled. Such an entertaining show."

"She's alive."

"And yet, she isn't here." Nathan leaned forward and turned off the vidscreen. "I know what the World Court has planned for your people, Keiko. Their salvation has always been the duty of your OIC. Did the World Court change its mind, or are you still the Acting OIC?"

Keiko lifted her chin higher. "I am."

"Congratulations. I doubt you'll live as long as Ciari did in that post." Nathan's eyes flickered from one to the other. "If the World Court knew where your true loyalties lie, they would have terminated you all. I can't have that happen before the launch."

"Strykers are excellent liars, Nathan. We have to be." Keiko paused, weighing her next words. "Things have changed since our conversation weeks ago at The Hague. You know why we're here."

"You came here hoping to bleed off more of your people into the War-hound ranks."

"Yes."

"A wasted effort." Nathan lifted a hand to forestall any argument. "I don't have time to retrieve the amount of psions you want to rescue. What you're asking for would raise the World Court's suspicion in a way I refuse to accept before the launch. That action would get you all killed via mass termination and you know it."

The World Court was ignorant of the Silence Law that secretly tied the two Syndicates together. Only the highest-ranking Strykers Syndicate officers knew that the Serca family wasn't human. Their silence on the matter guaranteed the survival of certain rank-and-file Strykers. Suicide missions handed out by the World Court were altered into Warhound retrievals by the Strykers Syndicate OIC. Those saved Strykers were then reconditioned by the Warhounds for the Serca family's own use.

Those transfers were done with utmost care, the image of Strykers fighting for their lives against the enemy needing to be upheld until they were brought under Serca control. Freedom, of a sort. No neurotracker in their brain, but they were still required to obey strict rules if they wanted to survive under the government's radar. They lived longer in the Serca Syndicate—usually.

"You still need some of us," Keiko said. She took a half step forward, Aidan staying by her side. "You need a wider gene pool than you've got."

"You are less the conniving bitch than Ciari is, so don't think you can bargain where she failed. Our partnership will be terminated at the launch," Nathan said. "You have known that since you took the post of chief operating officer for your Syndicate, Keiko."

"We've kept your family in the clear," Aidan snapped. "You owe us."

Nathan got to his feet, letting his mind weigh heavily against theirs as he approached Keiko. He smiled down at her, his expression all teeth and utter contempt. "The same can be said of you. I am, however, not completely heartless."

Keiko snorted her opinion of that.

"You have people you still want to save. I can admire that, Keiko."

"You admire nothing that doesn't happen on your orders," she said.

"True, but I can make room on the last wave of shuttles if I want. I will give those seats up only to the Strykers that I find useful."

"And those would be?"

"Every kind of psion at a Class III and higher—excluding you officers." Nathan's smile got fractionally wider. "I don't need a rebellion within my own company."

"The question is, will you keep your word?" Aidan said.

Nathan—three Class levels higher and thirty times stronger than the other man—stabbed his telepathy outward and coiled it tight around Aidan's mental shields. Aidan's defenses were good, but he couldn't prepare for Nathan's skill. Nathan might not have the years of use under his belt that other psions did, but his strength was something only Lucas could match.

"I don't like being questioned," Nathan said as he telekinetically forced Aidan to his knees, telepathy ripping through the other man's mind. "You don't rule here, Stryker."

"Let him go," Keiko demanded.

Nathan could feel her telekinesis slam against his own shields, scraping over his defenses. He sharpened his power against her, holding her back. Sharpened his telepathy until it sheared off half of Aidan's mental shields, causing the younger man to shudder, blood dripping from his nose.

"This is my only and final offer," Nathan said, twisting his power through Aidan's thoughts. "Whether or not you accept it, I still expect your silence on the matter of my family."

"So, you live and we die?" Aidan gasped out, shields caving beneath the pressure of Nathan's telepathy. "Is that it?"

"That is how it has always been. Don't fool yourself into believing otherwise. You won't live to see Mars Colony, to take part in what my family has worked to build. Even Ciari accepted that."

"No matter the amount of unregistered humans that you substitute for those who should have a berth on the *Ark*, you won't have enough to breed psions out of them," Keiko said. "Let him go. Please."

"So little faith, Keiko. You're all about filling Ciari's shoes, aren't you?"

Nathan wrenched his telepathy out of Aidan's mind, leaving behind raw mental wounds. "I'll have what I need."

Keiko's lips curled back from her teeth as she bent to help Aidan up. "Fuck you, Nathan."

The smile on Nathan's face got fractionally wider as he felt her pull back her telekinesis. "Your jealousy is showing. Find yourself an empath instead of a telepath next time. I'd have thought you learned something from Ciari other than how to argue futilely. It seems I was wrong."

Keiko swallowed her anger and the desire to strike out. It wouldn't solve anything here. "My loyalty to Ciari was never in question. Her loyalty to the Silence Law has never been in doubt. The only transgressions here are yours." Keiko's mouth twisted as she slung Aidan's arm over her shoulder. "We'll consider your offer."

"An empath, Keiko. You need one. Now get out of my office."

In an eye blink, they were gone.

Nathan returned to his desk, accessing the system again. A new download had come in last night that he needed to deal with. Sharra, given enough incentive, managed to accomplish the impossible some days. Who would have thought a human could be so much more useful than his own children?

Sharra had sent along two files. The first was confirmation of the back door now embedded in Erik's personal computer system, where the most sensitive data on the upcoming launch was stored. Nathan forwarded that to the hackers in his Syndicate, whose job it would be to monitor and retrieve information. The second download was pure data.

He initiated an uplink with the records division of the Warhounds. "Get me everything we have on the Stryker known as Jason Garret. Check Samantha Serca's reports first, then supplement it with nonduplicative files. I want it within the hour."

"Sir."

Retrievals were done at his discretion, no matter how hard Ciari had lobbied for the saving of her people in the past. Nathan could leave Earth without the psion Lucas had discovered, but he didn't want to. The explosion on the mental grid after the fight in Buffalo must have been the breaking of Jason's natal shields. Samantha's last useful act was discovering that Stryker's unique shields, but it wasn't enough to keep her alive now that she had turned traitor.

A window popped up on the vidscreen again, stating that the second download was complete. Nathan opened the file and scrolled through the latest schematics of the *Ark* that lay docked in cold space behind the moon, its decks just waiting to be filled.

[ELEVEN]

SEPTEMBER 2379
PARIS, FRANCE

The Border Wars were instigated by first-world countries, so it was no great shock when they were the first casualties. France was hit hard, situated between countries that suffered just as badly. That nation had owned a stockpile of nuclear bombs at the beginning of the five-year stretch of war, all the excuse anyone needed to attack. Retaliation was inevitable for every country on Earth, in whatever way possible. France was no different in its response, and like many countries, it was wiped off the map by the end of the Border Wars.

Deadzones still covered the European continent, areas where nuclear fallout and lingering radiation made it impossible for life to take back the land. The Paris Basin was a toxic pit, a concentrated mess of pollution and nuclear taint that no one could live in. The Seine, that ancient waterway that carved through France, was a poisonous water route that twisted through and around the ruins of the city. Massive dams that had once graced the banks downriver to hold back the Atlantic Ocean had been destroyed or eroded over time. Salt water inevitably flowed into fresh, seeping deep into dirt to mix with toxic runoff. Pools of water and crawling fog were stained an eerie green.

Paris—flooded, abandoned, and lost—stretched out before Dalia in the early-afternoon sunlight. Dalia was one of Nathan's best spies, a human capable of taking on any identity and owning it for the duration of her mission. She was unremarkable to look at, easily forgotten once she finished a job. Switching identities and appearances to gain information was her life, and Nathan owned all of them.

Squinting through the brightness of a clear, near-autumn day, Dalia scratched at the skin where the collar of her uniform rubbed against her throat. Beneath it, she wore a skinsuit specially tailored to block the lingering radiation in the Paris Basin. Her hard helmet was on the floor by her seat. People could work without a skinsuit, as bondworkers did, but the radiation levels were still high enough to damage DNA. The government's Command Center was specially shielded, but people always took precautions.

The threat of certain death and ruined DNA kept people out of France, or should have. When records of Mars Colony, with its massive enclosed habitat, made their way back into the awareness of the surviving government, getting there became the number one priority. Surviving meant more than simply clawing one's way into the Registry by any means necessary. It meant preparing to take up the mantle of a progressive society once again. The results of that effort stood before her beyond the Command Center, reflecting sunlight.

Platforms, hundreds of them, stood above the wastewater and ruins, all holding space shuttles. Running through the middle of those platforms was a long launch ramp that curved into the sky. Built by government scientists and enslaved bondworkers, shielded against lingering nuclear taint, the shuttles were waiting to be filled by those lucky enough to be in the Registry.

"Shuttle Prime, this is Command, do you copy, over," the government's head of operations said into an uplink where he stood some meters away from Dalia.

"We copy, over," the pilot said.

Dalia trained her eyes back on the vidscreen in front of her instead of the view beyond the large plasglass windows. Her role here was in operations, just one of many bodies contracted out of government-controlled scientific divisions. She'd worn her latest identity as a scientist before, just not here. Studying the vidscreen, Dalia watched the shuttle's system come online, the same information showing on other terminals.

"Weather looks like it's holding. We've got clearance for launch, over."

"Copy that, Command, over."

"Begin preflight calibration and start countdown, over."

The countdown went smoothly, months of practice simulations enabling the crew to launch on time and without difficulty. The shuttle roared down the curved ramp, thrusters burning a bright line through the sky as it launched, smoke and vapor trailing in its wake. This was one of the larger shuttles, capable of carrying three hundred people and supplies. Today, it carried only three-quarters of a full load as it fought gravity and left Earth behind, the shuttle's route rigidly plotted on the vidscreens in the command room.

The crew on that shuttle would begin the final preparations on the *Ark* for its passengers, joining the lead group who launched six months ago. Dalia watched the shuttle until it wasn't even a pinprick in the sky, the smoke trail dragged to pieces by the wind. A soft beep brought her attention back to her console, an arriving encrypted message requiring her attention. She tapped in a few commands, downloading it to a separate folder. A background filter was already running, keeping the download from being discovered by the central command system. She'd crack the file later and retrieve her new orders from Nathan. At the moment, she had other duties to perform.

"Sir," Dalia said to her supervisor. "Preparing for communications with the *Ark* in fifteen hours and counting."

She set the clock, the numbers winding down.

PART THREE
VITIATE

SESSION DATE: 2128.06.29
LOCATION: Institute of Psionics Research
CLEARANCE ID: Dr. Amy Bennett
SUBJECT: 2581
FILE NUMBER: 596

"I'm tired," Aisling says. The nurse taking a vial of her blood for testing doesn't look up.

"We're almost finished, Aisling," the doctor says from where she stands behind the nurse, watching the procedure.

The nurse pulls the needle out of the girl's arm and places a small bandage over the hole in her skin. Aisling leans her head back and stares at the doctor, wires framing her face.

"There's nothing special about my blood," she says.

The doctor waves the nurse out of the room. Only when they're alone does the doctor step closer and stare down at her small patient. "It's not your blood we want."

Aisling slowly nods, the wires swaying with the motion. "You can't see what I see, but you want to. That's why I'm here, isn't it?"

"We have records of people that don't exist and years none of us or our children will live to see because you refuse to help us."

"Everyone has their part to play." Aisling blinks rapidly, the machines changing pitch. "Right, Threnody?"

"What about us?" the doctor asks sharply.

"You're running out of time."

[TWELVE]

They flew straight into the polar night until even the ocean became impossible to make out as darkness filled the sky. They passed over the Ross Ice Shelf, shuttle lights cutting through a blackness lit only by long streaks of green. The aurora australis guided their way from time to time, a brightly glowing ribbon in the sky. Maps drawn across hologrids surrounded the navigator's seat. They showed only two points marked on the continental outline of Antarctica. Twenty minutes later, the shuttles flew over the first point, McMurdo Station an invisible ruin below. It had long since given way to the elements.

"Gonna be a tough flight the rest of the way," Matron said as she stretched in her seat. The sound of metal popping was uncomfortably loud as she rotated her arms in ways real limbs couldn't bend. Her cybernetic replacements were covered in synthskin, but these moments reminded Lucas that she wasn't all flesh and bone.

"Wind is gonna be a bitch. Here's hoping the deicing coat we put on the shuttles holds up after the Arctic." Matron glanced over at Lucas, who was in the navigator's seat. "You want to comm them or should I?"

"When we're past the mountain range," Lucas said as he continued to monitor their route. "Piggybacking off the government's satellites is easier to do farther inland."

"You're the boss."

They kept one eye on their instrumentation and the other on the dark around them. They couldn't see the Queen Alexandra Range as they approached that small subset of the Transantarctic Mountains, which spanned the frozen continent. All they could rely on was the computer as the shuttles flew over snow and ice far below.

Like the Arctic, Antarctica was relatively untouched, only two areas of the continent having been inhabited when the bombs first fell. Most of those eight hundred people had been pulled out by their respective countries at the time due to distrust. The abandonment of McMurdo led to the abandonment of the Amundsen-Scott South Pole Station as well. The domino effect meant no one should have remembered that either place ever existed, but Lucas had a knack for finding abandoned history.

Thirty minutes later, Lucas started an uplink, one with a noticeable lag in sending and receiving. "South Pole, this is Alpha shuttle leading Operation Deep Freeze, do you copy, over."

The uplink hummed for over a minute before someone answered. "Alpha shuttle, this is South Pole. We copy, over."

"We've got nine shuttles en route and our ETA is one hour, over."

"Thought you were bringing more'n that, over."

"This is all we've got. Be ready to transport, out."

Lucas cut the connection.

Matron gestured at her terminal. "Get me a route."

Lucas silently plotted her a vector, and she waved her thanks at him when he finished. Night flying was always dangerous, especially when one needed to land in unfamiliar terrain. They saw the lights of the Amundsen-Scott South Pole Station well before they arrived. The illumination wouldn't make it any easier to land on packed snow in the middle of the polar night.

The spotlights shining through the dark illuminated the improvised airfield. Tiny figures milled about near two half-buried buildings, one in the shape of the letter *E,* but with a fourth little leg added on, and the second, which looked like a dome. Bumps protruded from the icy snow, eroded foundations of buildings that no one could live in anymore. The shuttles landed in careful unison.

Matron stared through the windshield at the group making its way across the airfield. "She's grown," Matron said as she went through the postflight protocol.

"Children do that," Lucas replied. He slid the hood of his insulated skinsuit over his head, sealing the skinmask to it for protection against the dangerous cold.

The Strykers were waiting for Lucas by the cold-storage units when he finally made it into the cargo bay. From a nearby seat, Kristen yawned behind her skinmask, gleaming dark blue eyes tracking her brother's every move. Samantha sat beside her, expression ruthlessly blank. Lucas curled his fingers at his sisters in a commanding gesture, expecting them to follow him out.

The cargo door opened, letting in a blast of freezing air. Even sealed against the elements behind skinsuits and heavy clothing, it was impossible not to feel the cold. Jogging up into the shuttle, leaving wet footprints behind her, came a slim young woman. Behind the skinmask she wore, her face was as black as Matron's, her smile one of vast relief.

"Shit, Ma, took you long enough to get down here," the stranger said as she was pulled into a fierce hug by Matron.

Matron gave herself a five-second reunion before putting her only child at arm's length. "You put on weight, Zahara," Matron said with a decisive nod. "Didn't think that was possible down here."

"You'd be surprised at what the hydroponics lab can produce. None of us starved." The woman turned to face Lucas, jerking her thumb in the Strykers' direction. "They ain't scavengers."

"Like mother, like daughter," Lucas said, a hard smile pulling at his mouth.

Zahara didn't seem to mind his coldness. "You know it. But, hell, if you brought 'em, we'll work 'em." Zahara patted one of the large cold-storage units bolted to the deck. "These the precious cargo?"

"Observant as always, Zahara."

Zahara shrugged, ignoring the glare that Samantha turned on her for the familiar way she addressed Lucas. "It's what you pay me to be. We've got the dome open and snowcats ready for hauling. How much are you gonna be teleporting?"

"None of it," Lucas said, gesturing at the others. "Jason here is your telekinetic."

"For half the load," Jason said. "If that. I need a fucking break."

Zahara eyed Jason before sighing in exasperation. She crooked a finger at him. "Follow me. Let's get you a visual."

"I take it you don't need an explanation on the functions of teleportation."

"Been working with Lucas for years. I know how you telekinetics work."

Jason followed the younger woman outside, sliding through the crowd gathered at the bottom of the ramp. Matron tracked her daughter's path for a second or two before refocusing her attention on her people.

"All right, everyone. Listen up," Matron called out. "Getting out of Buffalo was worse than getting out of DC two years ago. Lost about as many people, but we don't got time to grieve right now. So choke back whatever arguments you've got and get to work. We've got cargo to shift."

Matron expected her people to obey, and she had Everett to help make them toe the line. Lucas watched her call out orders, content for the moment to let her organize the work flow. Quinton came to stand beside Threnody, watching the scavengers.

"You're not up to playing stevedore, Thren," Quinton said, glancing over at all the cargo strapped down in the shuttle.

She bristled at the implication she couldn't pull her weight. "Watch me."

"I have. You're going to undo everything we've done to keep you breathing."

"He's right," Lucas said. "You're not helping with this, Threnody. Get inside the station. Korman needs to look you over."

"Korman?" Threnody said. "That doctor with biomodifications for eyes?"

"The very same."

"I don't need to be operated on again."

"Which is good, since he's probably drunk." Lucas shrugged at Quinton's angry expression. "He'll be coherent enough to run some tests."

Quinton shook his head. "You want me to trust some goddamned drunk with Threnody's life?"

"No. I'm telling you to trust *me*. Now get to work, Quinton. Threnody? Get inside."

Lucas walked away. Kerr drifted over, giving Threnody a sympathetic look. "You can't really argue with him. He got us this far."

"Yeah," Threnody said as she started down the ramp. "Makes you wonder how much further he's going to take us before he finds a reason to discard us."

Kerr nodded. "Come on, Quinton. Let's do this."

As Threnody headed for the nearby station, Quinton and Kerr moved to join the scavengers, all of whom had separated into small groups charged with operating gravlifts and a dozen old-style cargo sleds hooked up to ancient-looking machines with flat tracks in place of wheels. They joined a work queue, adding their strength to hauling out boxes of seeds and other items, and organizing them into piles for teleportation into the dome.

The cold-storage units in every shuttle were unbolted and gravlifts used to pry them out. They were transferred onto cargo sleds, stabilized with heavy metal chains and hooks, then driven down a brightly lit icy path. Kerr rode along with the first load into the snow-covered dome. The entrance looked as if it had been carved into one side of the dome, the road they were on canting downward at a slight incline. They drove through the entrance at the bottom, the way braced by walls of ice whose weight Kerr didn't trust.

Zahara and Jason were still looking the place over, Jason needing to know the dimensions of the dome and the placement of everything inside to form a safe teleport. It looked as if various rooms had once existed inside the dome before the scavengers tore the interior apart to form an open space. Kerr jumped off the vehicle and let the scavengers start unloading the cold-storage unit.

"Are you going to be all right, Jays?" Kerr asked as he approached Jason.

"I'll be fine," Jason said as he squinted up at the geodesic ceiling. "This needs to be done. I can do it quicker than the machines."

"If you're sure."

"What, you don't trust him?" Zahara said, arms crossed over her chest.

Kerr stared her down. "This doesn't concern you."

"The hell it doesn't. The South Pole is ours, not yours."

"I'd like to see you use that argument on Lucas."

Zahara scowled, but kept quiet at the pointed reminder of who was really in charge. "You ain't worth the people we lost," she said before walking away. "Hey, Rex! That thing don't go in the damn middle of the dome. Move it to the fucking side."

"She's got a mouth on her like Matron," Jason said as he finally turned toward his partner. "Strong genes."

"There are those who would argue that conclusion," Kerr said.

Jason shrugged. "Let's get to work. The sooner we finish, the sooner we sleep."

Jason wrapped his telekinesis around the both of them, exhaustion forcing him to go slow. Beside him, Kerr watched as Jason struggled for a second to find a balance that had shifted permanently off-center. Kerr swallowed, his mind empty of the solace Jason's shields once gave him through the now-broken bond.

"You okay?"

"I don't see the world like I used to," Jason said. "It's strange."

"I can only imagine."

Jason's power finally steadied, and in the blink of an eye they appeared outside again, off to the side of the airfield so as to not arrive in the way of anything or *in* anything. They fell a few centimeters to the ground, feet hitting against hard snow.

The two separated, Kerr returning to help load up the cargo sleds and Jason moving to the nearest pile of seed boxes stacked haphazardly in the snow. Kristen was leading the work crew nearest him, and it was almost funny how the scavengers were keeping their distance from her.

"Humans are so easy to scare," Kristen said as Jason approached, her voice cheerful. "It gets boring after a while."

"I don't think Lucas would appreciate you killing anyone here," Jason said, eyeing her warily.

Kristen gave him a sly look, her mind briefly brushing against his mental shields. "Lucas doesn't like cleaning up my messes."

Jason didn't know how her damaged power functioned and wouldn't trust her, no matter what assurances Lucas made. The dysfunctional empath rarely left her victims breathing, but Jason was still alive. The mental pattern of his natal shields must have been enough to stabilize her, to show her how to build her own. He wondered how long her sanity would last.

"Stay out of my head," Jason said. He placed a hand on top of a wide stack the scavengers had created in the twenty minutes he'd been gone.

With a slow, methodical wink, Kristen answered, "Maybe."

Jason gathered his power and teleported the boxes of seeds with him to the dome, the first of many teleports. It was less weight than the cold-storage units or the various pieces of disassembled terraforming machines, which was easier for his mind to handle. He'd have to deal with the heavier items eventually.

An hour later, but what felt longer due to Jason's headache, a commotion around one of the shuttles caught his attention. Quinton was yelling instructions at scavengers as they painstakingly shifted one piece of the terraforming machines out of a shuttle's cargo hold. Jason swore under his breath and jogged over to that area, holding his power in reserve.

"You should have called me for this," Jason said.

Quinton shrugged. "You were busy with the seeds."

"Of everything we brought out of Spitsbergen, these machines are pretty fucking important." Jason took a step forward and raised his voice. "Hands off, I've got it."

Telekinesis stabilized the heavy weight of the piece, the final product something he couldn't fully envision. Lucas had the diagrams downloaded and stored in a datapad, stolen from the Arctic. The terraforming machines could be reassembled, but more would need to be built eventually. Learning to reverse engineer that technology was going to be integral to rebuilding the planet. The terraforming machines were capable of cleansing and cloning with the aid of nanites on a level that could jump-start a previously uninhabited planet such as Mars. Fixing Earth came with government interference, and in the past no one had been willing to fight it for the sake of everyone. Even now, it was anyone's guess how long the machines would last.

"Just don't drop it," Novak joked as Jason carefully settled the piece of machinery on the flatbed of the cargo sled.

"Novak, shut the hell up," Quinton said. He followed a step behind Jason, keeping an eye on the telekinetic. He didn't like the strained look on Jason's face. In the back of his mind, Quinton could feel the push and pull of power not his own, and it made him a little dizzy. He wasn't sure when the bond would settle, but he hoped it would be soon.

"You need to find yourself a sense of humor, man," Novak said.

"Give me your lighter and I'll show you what I do for fun."

Novak didn't offer it up.

With a shuddering groan of cold metal, the transfer was complete, and Novak climbed into the enclosed cab of the yellow vehicle, flat tracks rimmed with snow.

Jason bent over to rest his hands on his knees and breathe. "How many of those are left to move?"

"Two more pieces for this set," Quinton said.

"I'll move them, but I won't be able to teleport anything afterwards."

Quinton nodded and watched as Novak started the engine of the snowcat, carefully pulling out into the small road that linked the airfield to the station and the dome, joining the work caravan that was departing and returning in a steady loop. Headlights mingled with taillights while the aurora australis moved across the night sky high above them.

[THIRTEEN]

SEPTEMBER 2379

AMUNDSEN-SCOTT SOUTH POLE STATION, ANTARCTICA

D r. Isaiah Korman was a pockmarked drunk, but he could still see straight when jacked into a system. The biomodifications that had replaced his eyes shifted in his metal-lined eye sockets, their observations fed directly to his brain through neuroports. Korman took a sip from a metal flask and swallowed as he studied Threnody's test results.

"He wants the impossible. Did I say that already? You get stuck down here and you're screwed."

"Are you done yet?" Threnody said from where she sat on the metal exam table. After four hours of tests, she was done with him.

Korman rubbed a hand over his face. His fingers skimmed over the wires that cut out from his eyes and back into his skull through his temples. Half his skull was metal plating, tapering down to his spine. He seemed to have more cybernetic replacements in his body than Matron did.

"Your nervous system is intact. More than intact. If your synapses were talking to each other any louder, they'd be screaming."

Threnody scratched at her bare arm, fingernails moving around the needle stuck into the crook of her elbow. "Doesn't feel like it."

"You said he tanked you?"

"Yeah."

"Huh." Korman took another sip from his flask. "Lucas must have found an upgraded program, because you're healed. Fully functioning body. It's a damn miracle."

"I was nearly dead."

"Well, I can officially upgrade your status to living. Congratulations." Korman let out a bark of laughter that grated on Threnody's ears and toasted her with his flask. "Goddamn it, I could use a biotank like that. It fixed you faster than any of the ones I've got here. I hope Lucas brought it with him."

"It wasn't just a biotank that did this," Threnody said, splaying one hand over her knee and thinking about someone else's power in her body.

"Your psion physiology probably had something to do with it. You've all got complicated genomes. You people can take more damage than us humans and survive it."

Korman tipped his head back and poured what remained in the flask into his mouth. What was left of his skin, already blotchy, got redder. Threnody slid the needle out of her arm. She wasn't going to stay in the presence of someone intent on drinking himself to death. She got to her feet, bootheels touching the floor as the door to the small lab opened.

Lucas stepped inside, gaze moving over the two. "Korman. So glad I caught you mostly sober. Diagnosis?"

"Mostly sober?" Korman snorted and tossed his flask onto the nearby counter. "I took the nanites out of her veins. She's got no lasting damage from trauma. More like she wasn't damaged to begin with. What am I supposed to do with her?"

"Nothing." Lucas walked over to view the vidscreen, assessing the information in silence. "Interesting. Looks like all my efforts saved your life, Threnody. Care to thank me?"

"No," she said.

"Smart girl," Korman muttered. "He's worse than the damn World Court when it comes to torture. Best to keep your mouth shut."

"What's that supposed to mean?"

"The Strykers Syndicate's OIC got terminated on a worldwide news stream the other day. They left her second as Acting OIC."

Korman was telekinetically yanked out of his chair and slammed against the wall. Dangling with his feet off the ground and struggling to breathe against the pressure wrapped around his throat, he clawed uselessly at Lucas's power.

"They did *what*?" Lucas snarled.

For the first time since they'd teamed up, Threnody heard actual, real emotion in Lucas's voice, saw it on his face. Shock and fury drained all the blood from his face, the dark circles beneath his dark blue eyes standing out sharply.

Surprised, Threnody cleared her throat and said, "He can't answer if you kill him."

Abruptly, Korman fell to the floor. Threnody never saw him land, too busy staring at Lucas's shaking hands. She took in all the tiny details of how he stood before turning her head to look at Korman.

"Get out."

The doctor obeyed her in record time, stumbling out of the room and slamming the door shut behind him. Threnody walked over to lock it. Turning, she put her back to it and crossed her arms over her chest. She knew she wouldn't be able to stop Lucas from leaving the room, but judging by the way he looked right now, he wasn't going anywhere until he got himself under control.

"Is this about the Silence Law?" Threnody said, refusing to look away from Lucas's gaze.

"No," Lucas said, taking a deep, steadying breath. Some color started to return to his face. "No, it's not."

"Then why are you worried about Ciari?"

"It doesn't concern you yet."

"Yet." Threnody let out a harsh laugh before moving away from the door to stand in front of Lucas. "We are here because of your goddamn concern, Lucas. Don't lie to me."

For one brief moment, something alien filled his eyes. Alien because Threnody never thought she'd see fear inside Lucas.

"I should have taken her with us when we left Buffalo," Lucas said. "She was only in Toronto. I had time to get her down here and have Korman perform the extraction."

"Why are you worried about her?"

"She's carrying my child."

Threnody felt as if she'd been punched, all the breath leaving her lungs. Shock came first, then the sickening realization that no unborn child would be able to survive what a neurotracker could do to a human body.

"Are you joking?" Threnody said weakly, searching his face. "You're not joking."

"I need to find out what happened to Ciari." Lucas headed for the door, but Threnody's hand on his arm stopped him. "Let go."

"You can't leave the South Pole. We only just got here and Ciari's torture was days ago."

"All the more reason for me to leave."

"And do what? You're in no condition to save anyone right now." Threnody dug her fingers into his arm and moved so he had to look at her. "We need more downtime."

"You don't understand," Lucas snapped, wrenching his arm free of her grip and glaring at her. "My daughter is why I'm doing all of this."

Threnody didn't move, never broke eye contact. "And I'm doing it for everyone else. Your reasons aren't any more or less valid than my own, despite your shitty attitude. So for once, listen to me."

Lucas blinked at her, momentarily thrown off-kilter by her complete lack of obedience.

"Korman said the World Court put the Strykers Syndicate's second officer into the OIC post as *Acting* OIC," Threnody said. "They don't do that unless the OIC is still alive. Which means Keiko is running the Syndicate and Ciari is still breathing. I can't say anything about your daughter, but if Ciari's been helping you all along, betraying both the World Court and Nathan beneath the rules of the Silence Law, don't you think she would have watched out for her own unborn child?"

"Would she?"

Threnody punched him in the same spot Quinton had. Her fist made contact only because Lucas wasn't thinking straight and wasn't up to full strength. Lucas's head snapped to the side and he swore.

Threnody shook out the tension in her hand from the hit. "You goddamn bastard. After everything that Ciari's given up for you, you're really going to ask that? Fuck you, Lucas."

Lucas touched his mouth, fingers skimming over swelling tissue. She hadn't split his lip, and she had half a thought to try again to rectify that mistake.

Don't, Lucas said into her mind, but without the heat of anger.

"The OIC is a position I would never want," Threnody said after a long moment of silence. "Ciari's argued for our lives over and over again and this is the payment she gets for it. For toeing the fucking line and letting you do what needs to be done, she gets her fucking brain fried. And you think she'd risk losing her baby?"

Lucas let his hand drop away and he spat on the floor of the lab. "I need to know what happened to my daughter."

"After the clusterfuck in Buffalo, Ciari had to know she'd be summoned before the bench. She'd have time to do whatever she could to save the baby before that order came. Your daughter is most likely in Toronto. Probably in the medical level of the Strykers Syndicate."

Lucas closed his eyes, but the tension didn't leave his body. "Can you be certain that's true?"

"No, but it's the most logical place. We can't run off and find out just yet." Threnody lifted both hands to rub at her temples, feeling a headache coming on. "We need to be at full strength before we rush into things, otherwise we'll make mistakes and it'll cost us."

"Tomorrow," Lucas said after a moment. "We'll figure out what to do tomorrow."

Threnody could only agree to that compromise, and this time she didn't try to stop Lucas from leaving. He unlocked the door and pulled it open, pausing only long enough to say, "Coming?"

She followed him out.

Lucas led her to a small room barely big enough for a single bed and an old, rickety desk. "Yours," he said. "And Quinton's. I'll let you decide who gets the bed. Cafeteria is down the hall. It's cramped quarters all around, but don't worry. I'll keep an eye on my sisters."

He said it as if they were still a threat and she stared at him. "Should I be worried?"

Lucas didn't answer and started to close the door. Threnody put her hand against it, forcing him to stop. Threnody gazed at him silently for a moment before saying, "Get some rest."

Lucas closed the door. Shaking her head, Threnody went to sit on the bed, wondering if it was worth it to peel out of her skinsuit. Instead, she slid beneath a patched blanket and dozed.

Threnody woke when the door opened again, instincts too fine-tuned to ignore even the slightest of noises. She opened her eyes and watched as Quinton came into the room and switched on the light.

"I'll take the floor," he said tiredly, carrying extra blankets. "Go back to sleep, Thren."

"The cargo?"

"Safely stored." Quinton rolled the blankets out on the floor. "Still needs to be sorted. That's going to take weeks."

It was hard to believe what they had accomplished, stealing from the government for the sake of a world. She swallowed, wishing she had water. "How many seeds?"

Quinton lifted his head and looked at her. Even through his exhaustion, she could see the awe in his eyes. "Millions, Thren. Millions."

She squeezed her eyes shut, the strange feeling curling in her gut almost foreign. Hope always was.

[FOURTEEN]

Kristen found Threnody with Quinton during lunch, when Threnody was shoveling a forkful of rice and actual beans into her mouth. They had a corner table in the cafeteria with their backs to the wall, but they never saw Kristen coming. She was suddenly there across the table from them, chin propped up on her bony hands, psionic interference scratching against their shields. Her permanent smile wasn't inviting.

Threnody paused midchew, meeting Kristen's gaze with a healthy dose of wariness. The teenager used her hands to twist her blond head into a painful angle until it looked as if Kristen might snap her own neck. "Do you know what happens when Warhounds touch Sercas without our permission?" Kristen said, gleaming dark blue eyes never blinking. "We kill them."

"You touch her, I will burn you," Quinton said, reaching for the lighter in his pocket.

"An eye for an eye." Kristen dragged a finger down over her face, scratching a long line of red into her skin. "For what both of you did to my brother. It's only fair."

Quinton cast Threnody a questioning glance. Threnody shrugged and swallowed her bite of food. "We disagreed about something, so I introduced my fist to his face."

"So proud, aren't you?" Kristen laughed, raspy and amused. She stretched out her arms, let her hands slide against the edge of the table as she leaned her weight forward, catching Threnody's gaze. "How highly everyone must think of you. To waste all that time saving you. To let your hands wander like they do."

"What caused me to punch Lucas isn't your business."

That smile never changed, though the look in Kristen's eyes became predatory. "And here I thought all they beat into you dogs was obedience."

"Would we be here if that was the case?"

"You would be wherever it was Lucas needed you to be." Kristen abruptly sat back, lifting both hands to tuck strands of hair behind her ears. Her eyes became half-lidded; the smile never fading. "I can make you be whatever I want you to be."

"Kristen," a sharp voice said. "What did Lucas say about cornering people?"

Threnody looked away from Kristen, knowing that Quinton would keep the girl from going for their throats, and watched as Samantha approached their table. Even in this cramped place at the bottom of the world, Samantha still looked put-together. Built like her older brother, she was tall and thin, gorgeous enough to shine from a news stream, but that wasn't her place anymore. Samantha came to a stop behind Kristen's chair, attention on her sister and no one else.

"Sammy-girl," Kristen drawled, canting her head back to look at her sister. "Did Lucas put you in charge of holding my leash today? How boring."

A malignant pressure slid against Threnody's mental shields, saturated with negative emotion. Quinton must have felt it as well because he was getting to his feet, ready to fight. Samantha placed her hand on Kristen's head, stroking her fingers through straight blond hair. Affection almost, or so Threnody thought. Right up until Samantha gripped Kristen's hair with one hand and slammed the younger girl's head against the tabletop.

Bright red blood splattered across the cracked plastic. Kristen choked on her laughter as the low hum of conversation in the cafeteria faded. The pressure in Threnody's mind disappeared. Quinton remained standing, but didn't intervene.

"Not broken," Kristen said, even as she lifted her head and straightened her crooked nose with both hands, blood dripping down her face. Her skin was starting to swell. She pressed her teeth into the cut that split her bottom lip, sinking the edges into a faint line of red.

"Come along, Kristen," Samantha said, her gaze flicking over to the other pair at the table, gaze icy. "Lucas wants you. All of you."

Threnody picked up her fork and tapped it against her bowl. "When I'm done."

The contemplative look Samantha gave her made the hair on the back of Threnody's neck stand on end, as if the teenager were thinking about how to take her apart in the slowest way possible. "Now, Stryker."

Deliberately, Threnody took another bite. Samantha's expression became remote and Threnody could feel telepathy claw against her mental shields. The vast power of a Class II telepath flowed around her mind, digging hooks into her defenses.

I won't pretend to understand why Lucas chose you. I just know that he did, Samantha said against the outskirts of Threnody's mind. *Stand up, or I will make you. It's a process you will not enjoy.*

I thought Lucas didn't need an enforcer, Threnody said, letting her thoughts sit where the telepath could barely reach them without inciting trauma. *He's done just fine without one all these years.*

Lucas is breaking the world. I'm simply ensuring I remain on the winning side.

Your usual position, yes? Threnody arched an eyebrow and took another bite of her food. *Always second, never first? Unless we're counting your twin. How is Gideon, Samantha?*

Really now, Lucas interrupted as he telepathically put himself between Threnody's mind and Samantha's sharply focused power. *As amusing as this is, I have better things to do than fix the both of you again. We have a meeting. It starts in five minutes. None of you will be late.*

He pulled out of Threnody's mind, taking Samantha with him. The younger girl didn't seem offended at his interference, merely turned her back on Threnody and Quinton with a disdain that no one could miss. Threnody didn't take it personally as she watched the sisters leave the cafeteria, Kristen skipping ahead.

"If Lucas gives her half a chance," Threnody said quietly, "she'll kill him."

"Which one?" Quinton said.

"Take your pick."

Quinton nodded agreement. Threnody took one last bite of her food—her third bowl in the past twenty minutes—before they got up to deposit their dirty dishes in the designated area. Everything was reused down here since they had no way to bring in new supplies unless it was either flown or teleported in. The only shuttles Quinton had seen at the outpost were the nine they arrived in. Lucas had effectively trapped some of Matron's scavengers in Antarctica for over a year. It was a wonder none of them went mad during the long polar day and even worse polar night.

The two were the last into the heated room for the meeting. The only people who looked happy to see them were Jason and Kerr, though the smile Kerr gave Threnody was pained. Despite everything they'd gone through since the Slums, it was hard to reconcile the changes that had happened among the four. Blame was just as devastating as hate and they were struggling not to feel either.

Threnody wouldn't apologize for surviving. Kerr would never believe it if she did. They still stood together, shoulder to shoulder, to face what came next.

The room was cluttered with work terminals. Novak and Everett were hunched over one, muttering to themselves about issues with a hack, while Matron and Zahara watched their progress in silence. Samantha and Kristen huddled in a corner by themselves, far from where Lucas stood next to Korman with three strangers.

Threnody thought they belonged to Matron, but then the tallest man opened his mouth and her attention locked on him. "Now that we're all here, can we upload the damn program so that me and mine can get a flight off this continent?"

The man was middle-aged, with a scar like a second smile curved around his throat. Biomodifications showed in his jaw and neck, his altered voice coming through electronics. The sound was the harsh burr of a reality no one liked to be told about, familiar from a decade of riding the pirate streams that the government could never quite kill.

"In due time, Fahad," Lucas said as he studied the datapad he held. "We have other things to discuss before I let you go."

"Yeah?" Matron asked. "Like what? We got the seeds and everything else. That's what you wanted and it cost us."

"I really don't care how many people you lost, Matron. We've gone over this."

The group shifted uneasily. Matron scowled, her metal teeth scraping together. "Those were good people, Lucas."

"They weren't mine." Lucas set the datapad aside before looking up at everyone. "We're coming up on a week since Buffalo and from what I can tell, the government isn't as settled as it claims."

"Is anyone surprised about that?" Threnody said.

Lucas shrugged. "The fact that they aren't immediately beginning to transfer the people on the colony lists to Paris means we still have time to implement our plans. We need the government to break from its current course. I want them to panic."

"Breaking into the seed bank will go a long way toward meeting that goal," Jason said. "But I don't think you're stopping there."

Lucas nodded. "Fahad will be flying to Johannesburg. Evidence of the *Ark* will be uploaded on a pirate stream from Africa within twenty-four hours, but we need some lead-up time to get things sorted. We aren't risking what we're hiding by having the stream go live on the premises. Matron, you're giving up Novak for the cause. Samantha and Kristen will be in charge of that mission."

"Why don't you just shoot me before dumping me on that shuttle with your sisters?" Novak said with a scowl, jerking his head up. He ran a hand over his tattooed skull, wiping away sweat in a nervous gesture.

Lucas ignored him. "As for the rest of you, we aren't finished stealing from the government yet."

"Don't tell me they have another hidden warehouse full of supplies?" Kerr said.

"No. You Strykers have never been hidden from the public. Your former Syndicate is our next target."

"What do you want with the Strykers Syndicate?" Threnody said.

"The same thing that I got from you four—an alliance, of sorts."

"You really do like fucking with Nathan, don't you?" Samantha said. She had her fingers curled around the collar of Kristen's skinsuit, keeping the other girl close.

"I need to pass the time somehow," Lucas said. "Korman here has spent the past year working on how to program nanites in a controlled environment outside of a biotank."

Korman's expression, moved by muscle and wire, was bitter. "And by controlled environment, you mean human."

"No one misses bondworkers, Korman. They aren't worth your grief." Lucas neatly turned his attention to the next item on whatever internal schedule he was keeping. "Korman will explain what needs to be done on your end, Jason. He produced the same results you got on the shuttle with Threnody using the nanites, only this time they won't be forcing regeneration and they won't need your power."

"I'm no scientist," Jason said. "I don't even know what I did to save Threnody. And you still haven't told us what this mission is."

"You're a psion and a hacker. That is all I require of you." Lucas glanced over at Threnody. "We won't be able to extract the neurotrackers like we do in the Serca Syndicate following a retrieval. What we're doing is simply turning off the kill switch. The signal will remain active. Strykers will continue to show up on the government's security grid, but they won't die. An extraction takes time, something we don't have right now, so we had to get creative."

"Meaning what, exactly?" Threnody said.

"You built a virus," Jason guessed, looking to Lucas for confirmation. "You're going to infect the neurotrackers on a wide scale."

Lucas nodded. "They're bioware with a system that can be hacked, housed in the best biological entity this planet has ever made. The nanites Korman programmed will infect only the neurotrackers with the virus and nothing else. Every other biomodification will be spared."

"Are you sure? Nanites are tricky to program and the neurotrackers have some serious defensive programs built into them."

"My family created this technology. It's why we could unlock the neurotrackers without the government's assistance when we retrieved Strykers." Lucas shrugged. "The government has the code to fully deactivate the neurotrackers, which is different from the code that activates the kill switch for termination. My family knows both. We supply those codes every two years."

"If an encrypted password is the only thing keeping those things in

Stryker brains, why hasn't anyone tried to hack them before this?" Novak asked derisively.

Lucas gave him a cool smile. "The encrypted password for deactivation is two hundred digits long."

Jason whistled. "That would be a problem."

"Not for too much longer. The government might want the Strykers dead, but I don't."

"How are you going to administer this virus?" Quinton said. "The Strykers know we defected and they've got standing kill orders for each of us."

"There are ways around that." None of the Strykers looked as if they believed him, but Lucas didn't care. Pointing at Fahad, he said, "Get your people and your gear. Novak will fly you out of here. You will follow Samantha's orders to the letter."

"About fucking time," Fahad said, shaking his head. "One more week in this place and I'd have gone mad. Been here three months too long."

"You get used to it," Zahara said.

"To the dark, yeah. But to the cold? Never."

Fahad and his two assistants left the room, followed by Novak and Everett. Samantha leveled her brother a cool look as she let Kristen go. The empath trailed after the humans, tapping at her recently set and swollen nose with one finger.

And when we're finished? Samantha said between them alone.

I'll find you, Lucas said.

It was a threat as much as it was a promise. Samantha left without a backward glance. Matron spat on the ground in her wake.

"Your sisters ain't got your back, Lucas," Matron said.

"I have them, which is all I'm concerned about," Lucas replied. "Korman, I want you to consolidate your work on the virus-carrying nanites, then prep your operating room. Jason needs to familiarize himself with the virus, and Quinton is going to need replacements for his biotubes. Matron, go help him."

Korman and Matron left the room. Kerr looked around at everyone who remained and said, "Got something to say you didn't want anyone else to hear?"

No one missed how Lucas glanced at Threnody. Quinton sighed. "Thren, you keeping secrets again?"

"Wasn't a secret Lucas shared until last night," Threnody said.

"Is that where he got the swollen lip?" Jason asked.

"As amusing as this conversation is, we've got business to discuss," Lucas said. "Tomorrow, Jason is going to teleport Threnody and Kerr to the Strykers Syndicate and retrieve my daughter."

Jason gaped at him. "I'm going to—what?"

"You have a daughter?" Quinton said.

"She's not born yet," Threnody said calmly, the only one other than Lucas who wasn't shocked by the announcement. "Lucas, I thought we'd get more time?"

"We can't afford to stay our hand. I want my daughter, Threnody. I trust you to get her for me."

"Who's the mother?" Kerr asked.

"Ciari." All three men glared at Lucas, who only shook his head. "It didn't happen like that. I didn't rape her."

"You wouldn't need to. You'd just have to mindwipe her."

"Shockingly enough, we discussed this issue as adults."

Kerr grimaced. "Ciari got brought before the World Court. How do you even know the fetus is alive?"

Lucas touched a finger to his jaw. "As Threnody so thoroughly pointed out last night, Ciari wouldn't risk her own child. Given the chance to save her, Ciari would take it. I have to believe that."

Maybe it was the quiet way he said the words. Maybe it was the faint hint of uncertainty in Lucas's voice when he had only ever been arrogantly assured. Either way, the Strykers didn't argue. Plans weren't set in stone and even Lucas wasn't immune to chance, despite Aisling's orders.

"We won't kill fellow Strykers," Threnody said.

"You handle this mission as you like, so long as you don't return empty-handed."

"I'm going with them," Quinton said.

Lucas shook his head. "You're getting biotubes put in tonight and you'll need a bit of recovery afterward. Jason can only help so much with that."

"Then put me in a biotank. I'm not staying behind."

Threnody stepped closer to her partner, putting a hand on his shoulder. "Quinton, no. Don't argue. I'm planning this mission, so you don't have to worry about me, okay? Things will work out."

If it were Lucas pressing the issue, Quinton would have argued. With Threnody giving the order, he kept his mouth shut. Shaking his head angrily, Quinton left the lab. Threnody gave the microtelekinetic a pointed look and Jason reluctantly followed Quinton.

Then it was just the three of them. Lucas picked up his datapad. "I need to show you something."

Threnody and Kerr approached with slow steps. Lucas tapped at the datapad for a few seconds before handing it to Threnody. Kerr looked over her shoulder, both of them staring down at the screen with its listing of encrypted files and several hundred names. The one highlighted was her own. The one above hers was Lucas's. More names were listed after hers. Carefully, she tapped the icon beside her name, and a command window popped up, asking for a password.

"What is this?" Threnody said.

Lucas leaned back and braced himself against the table. "Aisling."

Both Threnody and Kerr shot Lucas identical incredulous looks. He met their stares without blinking. Weeks on the run, following where he led, told them this wasn't a joke. Lucas didn't have a sense of humor.

"What's the password?"

Lucas shrugged. "I don't have it. That's your file, Threnody. Only you can unlock it."

"What are you talking about?"

"Type in the password. You know it, whether you realize it or not."

Threnody stared down at the datapad, studying the blank command window. She raised a finger to the keypad image, but didn't touch the screen. "What if you don't like what it reveals?"

Lucas shrugged one shoulder, but the tension in his body was impossible to miss. "It doesn't matter."

"Lucas."

"Threnody. *It doesn't matter.*" When she looked up at him, he held her gaze. "I'm not going to ruin what Aisling started. Maybe someone else will, or did, but it's not going to be me, and it's not going to be here. Not this time. I'll follow what she says, like I always have. Even if I don't like it."

He gave Threnody a strained, lopsided smile. "She told me to find you and you've been a right pain in the arse, Threnody. But I'm listening."

Threnody nodded slowly, then tapped out a string of numbers that represented the date of the first time Quinton was introduced as her field partner. The first time she got someone she could call family after becoming a soldier, even if it was only in the deepest part of her mind.

It was a wild guess, but the encrypted file unlocked. Opened. Began to play.

The camera was focused on a small table in a white room, with a woman on one end and a child hooked to machines on the other. The caption pinned to a corner gave a date and a location that made Threnody swallow hard. Kerr sucked in a sharp breath. In the room, the child turned her head to stare at the camera, and the image magnified on its own until bleached-out violet eyes were staring directly at them.

"Hello, Threnody," Aisling said over the sharp whine of machines.

Threnody almost dropped the datapad, too shocked to make sense of what she held in her hands. Kerr steadied her grip with his own hand, the pair of them looking at Lucas with horror in their eyes. Lucas stared them down, his gaze unwavering.

"She'll tell you what she wants," Lucas said. "And we'll listen."

It wasn't what they expected.

That didn't mean the knowledge hurt any less or that they had the right to walk away.

[FIFTEEN]

A re we really doing this?" Jason asked. He ran a hand through his hair in frustration, shaking his head. "Are we really going to break in to the Strykers Syndicate and steal some unborn baby we can't be certain is even there?"

"I don't like it any more than you do, but it needs to be done," Kerr said. "How's Quinton?"

"He made it through the surgery without any problems. Threnody's with him right now." Jason rolled his eyes. "I told her I sped up the recovery time, but she didn't believe me."

"She believed you. She just wanted to see him for herself."

The two were in the station's small cafeteria, eating one last ration bar before they started their mission. They no longer wore skinsuits beneath their clothing. They couldn't carry any trace of their recent activities with them to Canada. They wore clothes borrowed from Matron's scavengers, all of them black, none of it traceable to a single environment. They carried no physical weapons, forced to rely on their powers alone for this mission.

The amount of downtime everyone had managed to grab wasn't enough to bring any of them up to full strength, but they were healing. Since leaving Buffalo they'd been eating as much as they could, sleeping whenever they got a chance, just trying to mentally heal enough so they wouldn't collapse under the stress. As if being forced to fight Strykers all over again wasn't stressful enough.

"For the record, I still don't like it," Jason said.

"For the record," Threnody said from behind him, "I don't care."

She sat down in a chair and Jason handed over a ration bar without asking. "How'd Quinton take being left behind?"

Threnody tore open the ration bar and took a bite. "He's not happy about it."

"You know he said he'd kill us if you came back with so much as a scratch? After all the effort I went through to boost his healing, that's the thanks I get."

"Thank you," Threnody said, the quiet sincerity in her voice impossible to miss. "I know it can't be easy to work on any of us. How are you holding up?"

"I'm hungry all the damn time and I've had more headaches since my shields came down than I did all last year. At the rate the side effects are growing, I'll need to start limiting use of my microtelekinesis if I want to live through the next few years."

"I told Lucas we needed more rest, but he's right. We're not going to get what we need until this is over, and waiting helps no one."

"Have you decided where you want to go in?" Kerr said, leaning back in his chair.

"Medical level," Threnody said.

"Logical. If Ciari took care of the baby before going in front of the World Court, then she probably had Jael do the extraction procedure."

"Her lab." Threnody kept talking around her food. "That's where the gestational unit has to be. Jael wouldn't risk leaving it unsecured where anyone could tamper with it."

"I can't teleport into her lab. That space changes all the time," Jason said.

"I know. I'll settle for the arrival room on the medical level."

"Her lab is halfway across that floor," Kerr said. "It's going to be a hard run to get there."

"I'm hoping we won't be doing a lot of fighting. It's the medical level. There's bound to be Strykers recuperating from Buffalo. I doubt they're up to our strength right now, crappy as it is, and I doubt everyone else would be willing to fight us around the injured. They don't have Jason and we're not aiming to kill anyone."

"Kind of sick of being the answer to everyone's problems," Jason said. "Kind of sick at the thought of using Strykers as human shields."

"We don't have a choice."

"I know. Briefing over?"

Threnody tossed her wrapper on the table and stood up. "Yeah. It's over."

"Quicker than the meeting yesterday. I like that."

Kerr and Jason got to their feet. Kerr pulled them both into a psi link with his telepathy even as Jason wrapped them in his telekinesis. Taking a breath, Jason visualized a place he hadn't seen in weeks but would never forget, and teleported out.

They arrived in a room that was at once familiar and not, the stark white walls of the place manned by Strykers wearing black-on-black BDUs. A telepath and telekinetic were on duty, nowhere near Kerr's or Jason's strength, but strong enough to shield against both men long enough for one to initiate an alarm.

"Let's go," Threnody said.

She jumped off the platform and ran for the door. It had locked at the first sound of the alarm, but that wasn't going to stop them. Threnody slammed her hand against the control panel, short-circuiting the door with her power. Jason wrenched it open telekinetically, and then they were in a hallway, racing past rooms that housed recuperating Strykers. Nurses, surgeons, and psi surgeons were scattered throughout the hall, none of them knowing what to make of the alarm going off. Only when they saw the three former Strykers marked for death did they figure it out.

An intense telepathic strike rammed into Threnody's mind, deflected by Kerr's shields, but she still felt the near miss reverberate through her thoughts. She stumbled, Jason grabbing for her with one hand to keep her steady.

If you kill even one Stryker, you won't leave this city tower alive, Jael snarled into their minds on a wide public 'path. *Stand down.*

Sorry, can't do that, Threnody said, letting the words sit at the very edge of her public mind for Jael to hear them. *We've got our orders.*

And we have ours.

Behind them came the crack of displaced air from a teleport, one right after the other. What felt like ropes of telekinesis wrapped around the three, searching for a way to hold them. Jason slammed his power through the foreign telekinesis and broke through easily enough, clearing their path.

Up ahead, a heavy security door blocked the way, with two Strykers standing before it. They didn't carry any guns, but they didn't have to.

The fire that burned near one teenager's hand was warning enough. He sent it in a controlled wave at them, blocking their view of the hall as it covered Jason's telekinetic shields completely.

Kerr focused his telepathy on the two Strykers. A telepathic strike cut cleanly through their shields and he knocked them unconscious. The fire faded; their problems didn't. Threnody skidded against the security door, slamming one hand on the control panel. Electricity sparked and popped beneath her palm, frying the system. Jason again telekinetically wrenched the door open.

They immediately got another faceful of fire that couldn't make it past Jason's shields. More 'path-oriented Strykers were gathering, slamming their individual powers against Kerr's shields. They weren't merged, but they didn't need to be. Against anyone else, the initial attacks would have shattered their defense. But the Strykers didn't know that Kerr's and Jason's Classifications had changed.

"We really don't have time for this," Jason said.

Threnody slammed one hand against the wall, electricity arcing outward down its length to knock several Strykers off their feet. Jason slammed his telekinesis forward, his power ripping down the hallway. It hit against bodies, knocking everyone to the ground with enough force to break bones. His power merged with Kerr's telepathic strike meant none of the Strykers in the hallway were getting up anytime soon.

Jason still wasn't used to his strength, however, and several of the Strykers he hit were slammed hard into whatever was at their back. In one case, a young teenage girl rammed her head against the corner of a nurse's desk. She left behind a splatter of blood as she slid to the floor, knocking over a few monitoring machines, and Jason skidded to a stop beside her, swearing.

"Jason!" Kerr yelled.

"Go," Jason said, even as he knelt down among unconscious and semiconscious bodies. "I'll cover you from a distance."

"Don't touch her," a Stryker said from nearby as he struggled to stand. "You've already hurt her."

"She was in our way," Jason said even as he curled his hand around the back of the girl's head, palm pressed against the bloody wound there.

Jason was still connected to the others through Kerr's psi link, providing telekinetic shielding. Jason dropped all his mental shields, letting his power flood into the girl's body. He didn't care if people could read his intentions in his thoughts. He sank quickly into a world made up of blood and bone, rushing through the soft shadows of tissue and cell shapes into the flaring network of nerves that spanned the breadth of the brain.

He could see blood pooling, black stains in his vision that looked wrong. Jason blinked, felt everything lurch around him as he focused on that buildup of blood. He'd only had a few days of practice using his power like this. It wasn't enough time for him to trust it, but he was getting better at focusing. He teleported the blood out of the girl's brain, letting it splash onto the floor in thick droplets near his knee. She would need surgery, but he'd cleared her of immediate danger.

Jason came back to himself in a rush, the world solidifying into the hard angles of standard human eyesight. The emergency alarm that still shrieked through the air was now almost drowned out by the piercing sound of a bioscanner registering off the scale. He looked down and realized a few wires had tangled around his fingers, the electrodes sticking to his skin.

He glanced at the monitor lying on the floor. One of the nurses—human, judging by her lack of uniform—was staring in shock down at it. The machine didn't recognize the psi signature. It wasn't one the nurse had ever before seen.

"Get her to Marguerite," Jason told the youth who was on his knees now, staring at Jason with an unreadable look on his face.

Jason shoved himself to his feet, reaching for Kerr through the psi link. *I need a visual.*

Kerr gave it to him. Through Kerr's eyes Jason could see the hallway where Jael's lab was located, and the crowd that braced the other two on either side. Keiko was standing shoulder to shoulder with Jael in front of the lab door. Jason teleported into that small space with blood on his hands, automatically strengthening his shields as he arrived.

Jael's mind brushed up hard against Jason's mental shields and her face went ashen. "What happened to you?"

Jason didn't answer her. Threnody did. "Get out of the way."

"You come in here like you did, attacking us, and you think you can give *us* orders?" Keiko said.

"We didn't come to hurt anyone."

"Like hell you didn't."

"No one's dead," Jason said. "Everyone who tried to stop us will live."

Jael's telepathy slid over their mental shields, not attacking. Kerr followed her touch with ease, ready to defend in an instant. Jael could feel the difference in Kerr's power, so attuned as she'd lately been to an empathic touch.

"You're an empath," Jael said, stunned.

"Barely," Kerr said.

"Your shields?"

"Stable. Which means there's no one you can pull up who can match me or Jason."

The emergency alarm was still going off, the lights up above flashing their constant warning. Threnody caught Jael's gaze. "Is Ciari alive?"

Keiko glanced at Jael; whatever telepathic conversation they had was quick. Judging by the murderous look Keiko gave her, Jael disobeyed orders when she said, "Yes. She's alive."

It was all the assurance Threnody needed. *Kerr? Do it.*

Jael's head snapped back from Kerr's attack as he ripped open her shields and pulled from her recent memories the visual of her lab in its latest state. He shared that image with Jason.

Leave me behind, Threnody said when she felt Jason's telekinesis wrap around her.

What? Jason said. *Are you kidding? Quinton will kill me.*

Just do it.

Jason was used to obeying orders, not giving them. The two teleported out, leaving Threnody alone in the hallway with Keiko holding up Jael. Threnody felt Jason's telekinetic touch pull away, leaving her unshielded and surrounded by people who were prepared to see her dead.

We have the gestational unit, Kerr said. *Good luck.*

Then he was gone and she was alone in her mind.

Threnody raised her arms in surrender. She felt Keiko's power slam into her, telekinesis bruising her body. She hit the wall with enough force to feel her ribs crack. Threnody collapsed to the floor, struggling to breathe. Invisible pressure crawled over her throat, choking her into unconsciousness.

[SIXTEEN]

SEPTEMBER 2379
AMUNDSEN-SCOTT SOUTH POLE STATION, ANTARCTICA

Well?" Lucas demanded.

"Don't rush me," Korman said curtly, carefully plugging in the last wire. The gestational unit's control board that monitored energy levels turned from the yellow of battery power to the bright blue of a solid electrical connection. Korman hummed to himself for a minute or two, the glitter from his optic replacements shifting as he studied the data. "No damage from the transfer. Everything is fine."

"Everything except the fact that you left Threnody behind," Quinton said, glaring at where Jason and Kerr stood on the other side of the lab table.

"She told me to," Jason said. "This was her mission and I wasn't going to argue her orders."

"Now you choose to obey without question?"

"Take this fight outside," Lucas said, not looking up from the readouts on his daughter's health. "Right now."

Quinton headed for the door, expecting the other two to follow. Knowing this conversation wasn't one that could be ignored, Kerr and Jason joined him out in the hallway. Without warning, Quinton grabbed Jason by the collar of his shirt and slammed him against the wall.

"What the fuck were you thinking?" he snarled into Jason's face.

Jason telekinetically shoved him away and Quinton stumbled backward. "I already told you. She wanted to stay."

"I don't care what she wanted. There's no reason for her to stay behind if you had Lucas's daughter."

"Ciari's alive," Kerr said with a shrug. "Reason enough."

Quinton glared at him. "What the hell is that supposed to mean?"

Kerr didn't seem concerned about Quinton's temper. "If Ciari's alive, then there's a chance we can reconnect with the Strykers."

"After today, I doubt that will happen," Jason said with a faint snort. He was staring at his left hand, still smeared with blood, and the expression on his face was pained. "They'll be on heightened alert after this."

Lucas pushed open the door to Korman's lab, coming into the hallway. Quinton focused his attention on Lucas. "We're getting Threnody back."

"That was never in doubt," Lucas said, letting the door shut behind him. "But I needed leverage if we're going to convince the Strykers to let us administer the nanites virus."

"So, you traded Threnody for your daughter?"

"And we'll trade their freedom for Threnody." Lucas met Quinton's glare without blinking. "I'm not leaving her behind, as you inelegantly put it. There is a reason for every single thing I do, and Threnody knows that. She knew what was required of her if Ciari still lived."

"You don't know what they'll do to her."

"I know she's still alive." Lucas tapped the side of his head. "I've got a shield wrapped around her mind, and I doubt your Syndicate officers will immediately hand Threnody over to the World Court. For one, the loyalty you Strykers have for each other is incredibly hard to break. I've mindwiped enough of your fellow Strykers after retrieval to vouch for that. For another, the World Court is going to have far greater problems to deal with than one escaped Stryker. The pirate feed goes live today."

Kerr grimaced at that news. "You're aiming to make the world riot."

"If the dregs of humanity choose to retaliate with violence after learning the truth the government's kept hidden from them, then so much the better." Lucas shrugged, as if the oncoming societal upheaval didn't bother

him in the least. "It will make it more difficult for the government to continue with the launch."

"I thought you didn't care if they made it to Mars Colony," Quinton
said. "I thought you didn't care if the government left us all behind. We
get half the seed bank, they get the *Ark* and some other planet."

"Things change," Kerr said, refusing to look at Lucas, even if he couldn't
stop thinking about what a dead precognitive child had said in some old
recorded file.

"Yes," Lucas agreed with a faint, twisted smile. "And that's what Jason
is going to be doing to my daughter."

Jason frowned. "What?"

"My daughter needs to grow up with your type of power, and you are
going to make sure that happens."

"What do you want me to do? Alter her DNA?" Jason gave Lucas a
blatantly disbelieving look. "I don't know what I'm doing with this
power, Lucas. Do you honestly want to risk an unborn child—*your* unborn child—by having me perform some act which I can't guarantee will
work?"

"Psions are born with the genetic ability to control their powers. It's
instinct that turns into conscious control. Why do you think Kerr had
such problems with his shields? Why do you think you're capable of
reading as human on the mental grid after I showed you how to do it
once? We're born into bodies that are geared towards supporting our
minds."

"That's different than me trying to apply my power to something like
this," Jason argued.

"It's worked on all of us at one point or another since we left Buffalo."

"All of you are alive. You aren't some cluster of multiplying cells."

"Which is exactly the best time to do this," Lucas said. "Her DNA is
still very malleable. Right now is the only chance you've got to make her
into what I need her to be. What *we* need her to be."

Jason glared at him. "You don't know that I can do this."

"Yes, I do." Lucas's voice was implacable, his gaze unwavering as he
stared Jason down. "And you will."

"Why? Because Aisling told you I would?"

"Jays," Kerr interrupted. "You stopped to help a fellow Stryker back on the medical level. Do you believe what you did saved her?"

Jason let out a harsh breath. "Maybe."

"That's not an answer."

Jason scrubbed a hand over his face, not looking at any of them. "Yeah, I do."

"Then you need to do this."

After a moment, Jason pushed past Lucas to walk back into the lab, letting the old door slam shut behind him.

[SEVENTEEN]

SEPTEMBER 2379
JOHANNESBURG, SOUTH AFRICA

When Africa died, it took history with it. A continent of deserts and jungles, Saharan plains and winding rivers, teeming with a biodiversity of life that spawned the human race in all its forms, it should have been worth saving. Records existed, Samantha knew, of a time when people tried. Drought, desertification, poaching, and stubborn human greed destroyed it, just as humans destroyed the rest of the world.

Too many places in Africa were bombed to ruins. Johannesburg was no different. The surface was jagged wreckage and displaced melted slag. People lived among the remains if they weren't lucky enough to live in bunkers.

Resources were provided by the government. Johannesburg only had a single SkyFarms tower, heavily guarded by the government. Combodetox water plants desalinized and filtered out toxins from the polluted Indian Ocean before the water was transported inland on maglev trains. The city limits incorporated bunkers, not sealed towers, and the skin trade was a currency most people used in some form or another alongside credit chips. Survival came with a cost and always would.

Samantha touched a finger to the dark glasses that sat on her nose. Translucent bioware woven through clear synthskin was stuck to her facial recognition points, hiding her identity from the government's security grid. Matron's stockpile of the tech was large, most of it top-notch. Samantha had to admit that Lucas's ability to find useful people was on par with Nathan's.

"Smells like lunch," Kristen said. The girl crouched in the dirt just inside the broken entrance to one of the converted ruins, watching the oblivious humans pass them by. The dilapidated building they were in leaned at a precarious angle. Since it hadn't fallen down in the last decade or so, Samantha considered the odds of its staying up to be on their side.

Johannesburg smelled of too many people living in too small of a place, with the harsh scent of toxins rolling over the flat, devastated land on the back of the wind. It was making Samantha sick.

"You only think you're hungry," Samantha said.

"It's waning, Sammy-girl." Kristen canted her head to the side, her own dark glasses sliding down her nose. "Things are falling apart."

It was a warning, plain and simple. Nathan once predicted that Kristen would never live to see the age of eighteen. Judging by how skewed Kristen's mind was, even with a borrowed framework of sanity, Samantha knew Nathan had been right.

"Come along, Kristen."

Samantha grabbed at the collar of Kristen's skinsuit. She was the only one still wearing it; everyone else wore street clothes. It made hauling her around easier and made it more difficult for Kristen to cut into her own skin.

It's a pity we can't attach bioware to it, Samantha thought absently. *Shocking her into obedience was always so much easier than having a row with her.*

Samantha hauled her unruly sister into the depths of the building where Fahad and his assistants had set up a portable work terminal with Novak's help. The media pirate was barking out orders to the men and women around him, ruthlessly running the show, as he had for so long. He gleaned rumors from conspiracy streams and paired them with hard facts from anonymous sources to create a whole picture. The government had a bounty on his head for the information he streamed to the unregistered masses, inciting riots and spreading truth the World Court could ill afford. What he was about to broadcast next would trump all his previous endeavors.

"You just gonna stand there and watch?" Novak said as Samantha put herself and Kristen against the wall, out of the way.

Samantha slid her power through Novak's mind, uncaring of the sudden pain she caused the man.

I am not my brother, Samantha said as she increased the presence of her telepathy in his thoughts to a critical degree. *Speak to me like that again, and you won't live beyond those words. Do I make myself clear?*

"Very," Novak gasped out.

Samantha released him, ignoring the faint trickle of blood that dripped out of Novak's nose. Novak turned his back on the sisters and moved out of physical, it not mental, reach. Kristen watched him retreat with a hungry look on her face. Samantha made sure she had a firm hold on her sister.

Lucas had charged them to oversee this mission with the knowledge that Johannesburg had both Warhounds and Strykers on the ground. Samantha was needed for defense, but was uncertain of her strength. Recovering from the trauma of Buffalo had taken days. For Samantha, it had meant the restructuring of her mind from the bottom up.

In Buffalo, Lucas had ripped out of her mind layers of false thoughts that had seemed real, revealing a mindwipe that had forged her into whatever Lucas needed her to be beneath Nathan's seemingly solid control. Samantha wasn't sure when Lucas had implanted this loyalty in her, she just knew it was there, that it was foreign, and she could do nothing to break it. Odd to sift through one's own mind and not recognize it. Odder still to realize that maybe it was better this way.

What she still couldn't come to terms with was the hole that had been punched in her mind where her twin once resided. Even Lucas couldn't make her forget eighteen years of living with Gideon in her head. If she was grieving for her loss, she didn't know where that grief was.

"We're ready," Fahad said, a satisfied bite to his words. "Let's get this uploaded and begin. I can't wait to see how it all goes down."

Samantha pulled Kristen to her when the girl would have followed Fahad's assistants around the portable work terminals. Hacking into the media streams took effort, but the results were always interesting. Samantha had seen the outline of what Fahad was going to report. That it would be picked up on all conspiracy and public streams meant the government wouldn't be able to keep it hidden, that the information they would be disseminating would never die.

Fahad took his place before the camera, wearing the same sort of street clothes as the rest of them, his face covered by a shapeless headscarf that was lined with bioware to hide his identity and the same sort of dark glasses Samantha wore. Technology wasn't the only detail he employed—a quick retreat was always on the table. Their bolt hole was a squeeze in the back between two collapsed walls, out into a thin alley that linked to a market square always teeming with people.

Samantha loosened her grip on Kristen's shoulder, fingers tapping against the other girl's skinny frame. *Patience.*

Novak finished uploading the program with the help of Fahad's assistants, having worked on the actual hack on the flight over to get faster access to the public streams. They were able to access the backdoor in minutes, not hours.

"We're reporting on the edge," Fahad said, altered voice coming out strong. "If you're hearing this, seeing this, then it's a reminder that the government doesn't own all of us. Here's to the fallen, to the righteous, to Allah, who guides us. The government can't control everyone, but control was never their final goal.

"The World Court has lied to everyone since the Border Wars. The Fifth Generation Act is a long-running con for the rich to buy their way into the promised land. Their hope isn't our hope. What succors them won't succor us. How many people have died, will die, for their greed? The rest of the world, if they have their way."

Fahad gestured off camera to one of his assistants. The woman tapped out a few commands into her console. Fahad continued, "This is a picture of the Paris Basin, where the capital of France once stood. As you can see, it's not all ruins and water. It's not just a deadzone, but a hidden lifeline." The picture switched to a closer magnification, rows and rows of shuttles, waiting to launch on a sleek ramp. "What you see is the government's real plan, their way off this rock to the stars.

"Leftover nukes haven't wrecked this area, no matter the lies the government tells. The truth is that our ancestors didn't own one planet—they owned *two*. A colony ship is docked near the moon waiting to ferry the government's chosen people into paradise."

Another hand wave and Samantha knew the satellite pictures of the *Ark* were being added to the mix. She could see them on the vidscreen over Novak's shoulder.

"But I tell you this, my brothers and sisters, that we—we who have bled and died for want of a better life—*we* have been betrayed, for we will not be on those shuttles. We will never see that ship."

Samantha had seen the *Ark* before, when she was a child and Nathan had shown her what was promised to them. The pixels of a stream did the colony ship no justice, the nongovernment-controlled satellite providing the pictures old and barely functioning. But it still showed the massive scale of the *Ark,* large enough to take many citizens, but not all, to a new life.

It was a new life she had dreamed of once.

"This is the proof people have died to uncover. We deserve more than the government will leave us. We deserve more than scraps and walls and beatings and graves," Fahad said, staring into the camera. "The government talks about laws and resources, as if this world was all we were left with, when they knew of some place better. They say we aren't meant for some distant alien shore. I say, who are they to destroy our future? Who in the gutters will fight for it?"

The connection cut off, the actual feed of the pirate stream barely two minutes long, but it was two minutes that would live in infamy. Samantha knew that better than most. She had played at being human for her entire life and knew exactly how the registered elite would react in the face of such a reveal. The rest of the world, those who had never met the requirements of the Fifth Generation Act, would either take the stream as truth and riot, or do nothing and keep living the only life they knew.

"It's done," Fahad said, yanking off his headscarf and glasses.

A giddy, satisfied smile sat on his face, one born of pride and anticipation. The expression turned to horror as he watched Kristen approach one of his assistants. Kristen pressed her hand to the young man's head and ripped through his mind with her empathy. The man's scream lasted only a second or two, a sound that shredded their ears before it cut off.

"Your words are useful," Kristen said as she turned her head to face the others, gleaming dark blue eyes full of malice. "You aren't. At least, not anymore."

Fahad and his people crumpled before Kristen's unwavering onslaught, the hunger for sanity driving her. Jason's shields hadn't been enough. Nothing would be. The cracks in her mind were widening, and no one could stop her descent back into insanity.

Novak put his back against the wall. Five bodies lay scattered around the area where the pirate stream played in a continuous loop. It would run until someone on the government's end managed to hack it out of existence, which he doubted they could, because the damage was done.

"I knew Lucas was gonna kill us. Matron never listens to me," Novak said, curling in on himself as he hid his face. Samantha tore her gaze from the vidscreen and the loop, to where Kristen was approaching Novak with a dreamy smile on her face.

"Don't kill that one," Samantha reminded her sister, erecting a mental shield between Kristen and Novak's mind.

"Oh, fuck, why not?" Novak asked, head jerking up, eyes wide with fear. His own or Kristen's, Samantha didn't really care.

"We needed a message people would believe in. Fahad delivered it perfectly."

"So you killed him for doing a good job?"

"We have the message. We don't need the messenger, especially not one with traitorous thoughts. Now get up," Samantha said, already stretching her telepathy through the mental grid beneath the shield of static human minds, reaching for Lucas. "Lucas still has use for you, so stop yelling. Kristen won't kill you."

Kristen's smile was wide and vicious. "Yet."

Novak closed his mouth.

Did you finish? Lucas said as he drew Samantha into a psi link, suddenly there in her thoughts.

We're done, Samantha said. *Pirate stream is running, information is uploaded, Fahad and his people are dead.*

Good. Show me the others.

Obediently, Samantha looked at Kristen and Novak. Her vision doubled, the light from the vidscreens wrapping everything in halos as Lucas stared through her eyes. Lucas's telekinesis settled over her and pulled.

In an instant, all three were gone, leaving behind corpses, the voice of a dead man, and evidence of a betrayal that society wasn't strong enough to survive intact.

"They say we aren't meant for some distant alien shore. I say, who are they to destroy our future? Who in the gutters will fight for it?"

PART FOUR
CLARITY

SESSION DATE: 2128.08.13
LOCATION: Institute of Psionics Research
CLEARANCE ID: Dr. Amy Bennett
SUBJECT: 2581
FILE NUMBER: 750

"We can find others like you," the doctor says as she stares down at her notes. "We're learning what makes you different from us. It's in your blood. In your brain."

"In my mind," Aisling concedes. "We're different."

"Not human."

"Human enough." Aisling coils a wire around one finger, never looking away from the doctor's face. "Do you want to know a secret?"

"Of course."

"It never works when those like me are free at the beginning." She raises a finger and presses it to her lips. "Shh. Don't tell anyone."

The doctor folds her hands together over the table, knuckles white. The hum of machines fills the air and echoes on the feed. "Your parents signed you over to us. Did you know that?"

"You told them to."

"Where is your brother, Aisling?"

"You can't have him." The girl smiles; a slow, precise motion beneath bleached-out violet eyes. "You asked me once to save you. This is how I do it."

[EIGHTEEN]

SEPTEMBER 2379
LONGYEARBYEN, NORWAY

The government shuttle came in from the south, flying across Spitsbergen. Four teams of quads were strapped in for the flight out of The Hague. They escorted a single man into the cold of the Arctic, a man who would have preferred to remain in Japan. For the first time since the government started security shifts after the island was rediscovered, the watch team in the north had missed their check-in.

Elion kept his attention focused on his datapad, glancing up only occasionally at the map on the hologrid to check their progress. He was a politician, not a soldier, and the utilitarian shuttle they were traveling in didn't have the first-class comforts used by elite society. The skinsuit he wore beneath his clothes itched around his joints, but was necessary considering the environment they were heading into.

What the hell could have happened up here? Elion thought to himself. *This post has never missed a check-in, not once.*

Heir to the Athe Syndicate and his father's seat on the World Court, Elion came from a family that prided itself on science over all else and survived the Border Wars because of it. Their contributions to the world that came after were needed, if highly selective. Their forays into space were key to the World Court's plans, but they would never be as highly regarded as the Serca family.

The Serca Syndicate had helped the government establish SkyFarms Inc. after the Border Wars, using forgotten technology and salvaged seeds pulled from the Svalbard Global Seed and Gene Bank. The Athe Syndicate had lost its bid on that project, and the Sercas got the bulk of the credit for those ventures, second only to the government. Elion's family was still bitter about the issue. Elion wondered if the Sercas would get the bulk of the blame this time around as well.

"How much longer?" he asked the pilot.

"ETA thirty minutes."

Less than an hour before they found answers. The communications officer had been hailing the watch team since they took to the air, and not once had he received a response. The lack of contact was worrisome, and Elion wasn't sure what to expect. He was exceptional when it came to anticipating people. He had to be if he was going to succeed his father on the World Court, but he could never have anticipated this.

The shuttle landed not in the airfield west of Longyearbyen, but on the outskirts of the small town itself. A dangerous endeavor, as the ground was uneven and untested, but they didn't have time to waste and no Strykers were contracted for this mission. Teleportation wasn't an option. Looking out the shuttle's windshield through the floodlights, Elion felt as if he were going to be sick.

One of the buildings still used by the government had been blown up, its charred remains an ugly black spot against the steel gray of the rest of the buildings. Bodies were scattered around the area, already bloated from decomposition.

"Let us go first, sir," the most senior quad member told him. Her dark eyes didn't look away from Elion's own green ones. "You should stay here."

"By all means," Elion said around a numb tongue. "I'll remain."

The shuttle's side hatch opened. It was cold outside, the chrono indicating that it was a little after midnight. Elion's sense of time was already thrown off-kilter from being teleported to the World Court out of Sapporo before being flown north. This didn't help.

He'd been hoping it was an electrical problem, a breakdown in the communication system. It was so much worse than that, Elion decided, when the quads returned twenty minutes later, their recon finished.

"Everyone's dead," the woman from before said. "Looks like the attack was quick and brutal. We only saw signs of one shuttle. Security system is a mess. We can't pull anything from it."

Elion stared at the quad blankly before taking in a deep breath. "We're going. Now. Take me to the airfield."

The pilot got the shuttle in the air again a few minutes later and headed for the nearby airfield. They landed and the quads were the first out, doing recon. They found evidence of activity, but no evidence on who might have attacked the outpost. When Elion remotely plugged in the codes to stand down the artillery turrets, he discovered they were already off-line.

Sweat broke out across his face, cold and clammy. He swallowed the taste of bile and led the quads up the winding road to his destination on the mountain. It was a hard slog, but Elion refused to slow his pace, breathing heavily as they climbed.

Getting soft, Elion thought. *I figured I could handle this.*

If the quads were surprised by the metal wedge sticking out of the mountainside, they didn't show it. The ramp that bridged the road and the doors was newly broken in some places, as if a great weight had been applied after decades of neglect. Elion slid forward on careful feet, testing its stability. The ramp creaked and groaned, sounding as if it were about to break, but it held.

The control panel was dead. A few centimeters' worth of space separated the doors.

Elion staggered forward, one shaking hand sliding through that space. "It's unlocked," he whispered. "It's *unlocked.*"

The quads helped him haul the doors open. Lights snapped on, one after the other as they stepped into the tunnel, illuminating a space recently disturbed. Elion pressed his hand against the wall for support.

"Sir?" one of the soldiers said. "Let us canvass the area for your safety."

"Iie," Elion said, the word ripping out of him.

Breathing harshly, Elion pitched himself forward, long legs eating up the distance between the entrance and the next set of doors. Like the first set, this one was unlocked; all of them were. His chest constricted with panic as they reached the first storage vault.

"Iie," Elion choked out as he stared inside. *"Iie! Masaka . . . shinjirannee!"*

Ransacked. Gone.

Boxes and packets were strewn across the floor, whole bays empty of supplies. Someone had broken into the most secret and secure place on earth and stolen half the government's most precious assets.

Elion felt sick as he shoved his way through the quads and ran to the next vault, finding the same scene. Hurrying down the rows of storage units and shelves, Elion couldn't think. His mind was a white-hot burn of panic at the realization that everything the government had worked for had become meaningless.

Behind him, one of the quads bent down to pick up a silver-foil packet from the mess near his feet. "What the hell is an *Attalea speciosa?*"

The soldier stumbled over the words, his tongue unfamiliar with the name.

"Hell if I know," a woman said as she kicked at a box.

Elion did. Oh, not the species, but he knew what were in these packets, what had been stored here and stolen, all their careful planning, all their generations' worth of work—gone.

"They're seeds," Elion said, stumbling through the remains. "They're *everything.*"

He couldn't breathe in the face of what they had lost. It didn't matter that some of the inventory remained, that they still had two-thirds of the terraforming machines. It didn't matter because someone outside the government had discovered this place.

Elion didn't know how he was going to explain this to the World Court.

[NINETEEN]

SEPTEMBER 2379
LONDON, UNITED KINGDOM

Of his ordeal in Buffalo, Gideon Serca remembered screaming wind and acid rain, a street lit by lights, and two men standing in his way. Remembered his twin and *I'm sorry* and how nothing would be the same again.

When Gideon eventually regained consciousness, he was alone in his mind. Eighteen years of his twin rummaging around in his head, a psi link between them that he thought would never be severed, had skewed his sense of the world. Samantha had carved it out to save some worth-less Stryker. Its absence felt like a bottomless pit in his mind and he hated her for that.

Victoria had done what she could to repair his mind. In saving him, she had killed herself through overuse of her telepathy. Gideon's mind contin-ued to build off Victoria's repairs. He needed aftercare, but wouldn't get it. The only person strong enough to halve the recovery time in the War-hound ranks was Nathan, and Nathan wasn't going to coddle him.

Sitting in Nathan's office, Gideon studied his father. Neither of them had spoken while they watched the pirate stream on the vidscreen. The conspiracy-mongers were out in force, downloads crashing server farms across the planet. The world press was trying to contain the information on the government's orders, but they were failing.

"How did he do it?" Gideon finally asked.

Once, Nathan would have ignored his son. He no longer had that lux-ury. Gideon was Nathan's sole remaining heir and most powerful subordi-nate. Sharing every last detail with the eighteen-year-old Class II telekinetic who would someday succeed him was now a necessity. He could no longer force Gideon to use his power more than was considered safe to survive. Nathan was going to have to find other Warhounds to take up the slack.

"You remember the Stryker with the natal shields that Lucas took with him out of the Slums?" Nathan said, his attention still riveted on the pirate stream.

"Jason Garret, yes. I've read his file."

"We're still pulling details from the fight in Buffalo out of everyone's memories. I believe that Stryker is more than just a Class V telekinetic."

"I don't know what you're talking about. I fought him in the Slums. He was only a telekinetic, and not a very good one."

It was questionable how Nathan would react to being argued with, but Gideon could no longer remain silent. He'd been third in line to this post, never expecting to hold it, not until Lucas walked away. Samantha, bare minutes older than he was, never seemed to want it, but would have taken the position if offered. If required. It was his now, as the last child Na-than had left, the last Serca that would follow Nathan into space. An heir to whatever Nathan would build out of Mars Colony and the unsuspecting humans who were seeking refuge there. Gideon was determined not to squander his chance.

"The mental grid buckled, for lack of a better description." Nathan tapped his fingers against the hard shine of his desk, command windows popping up with each precise pressure against the touch-sensitive controls of the console. "Tracking him became impossible afterwards. Lucas must have shown him how to read as human on the mental grid."

Gideon frowned. "The mental grid doesn't buckle. It can't."

"It did." Nathan coolly met Gideon's gaze. "Whatever secondary power Jason might have, its strength is off the charts. He can't be solely categorized as a Class V, or even a Class I."

"A Class I has been the highest rank handed out to psions for decades. The only Class higher is a Class 0," Gideon said. "And the only ones ever given that ranking are precognitives. You know how rare those psions are."

"In our entire history, there have only been three precogs. None of them have been dual or triad psions, and all died before the age of five. It's impossible that Jason is a precog."

"Then what do you think he is?"

"What Lucas never was."

Gideon opened his mouth, then closed it. He couldn't hide his surprise, nor the brief spurt of jealousy. Everyone knew Lucas hadn't turned out to be what Nathan needed, no matter the amount of gene splicing that helped form his genetics. Psion DNA was difficult to work with and the results were unpredictable. Lucas was born a triad psion instead of a microtelekinetic, and he'd been living with that failure all his life.

"Can you be certain?" Gideon asked. "How could Lucas have known about this? About any of it?"

"Only Lucas can answer that question. This"—Nathan gestured at the feed, which was repeating itself—"is Lucas's doing. Everything from here on out will be Lucas's doing, and countering it is going to be difficult. Some of the public will believe this information, and there are those who will not. Who *cannot*. Regardless, preparing for the launch just got more complicated."

"What do you need from me?"

"I want Jason Garret," Nathan said flatly. "I want his power for use on

Mars Colony. You will track him down and retrieve him. Which means a visit to the Strykers Syndicate is in order, since Lucas has proven impossible to pin down. They'll have better records than we do on their missing Strykers. Also, I want you to determine whether or not they are dealing under the table with Lucas."

"If I do this for you, will you finally trust me?"

Nathan's gaze cut into Gideon. "That has no bearing on what I require from you right now."

"I think it does."

"Considering the results I've wanted for the past two years, and which neither you nor your sister could provide, you aren't in any position to demand anything from me. If Lucas was dead, things would most certainly be different, and you wouldn't be living in his shadow."

Gideon straightened in his seat. "Then perhaps you should have done it yourself."

"You place a lot of faith in the idea that I won't kill you," Nathan said, sliding behind Gideon's mental shields with a dexterity that belied his age.

"You need me," Gideon said, flinching against the pain in his head, but he didn't look away from his father's face. "You've got no one else to succeed you. I'm all you have left."

"You are not what I require."

"None of us ever were. Now there's a psion out in the world who is, and it's your choice not to hunt him down directly. You want us to use back channels, and I don't know if that will be enough." Gideon lifted his chin, defiance in every line of his body. "I think you could find him, if you really wanted to. But it would cost you, wouldn't it, Nathan? It would cost you in effort and in power and in years. You're too close to your promised land to risk it, so you risk us instead."

Nathan studied his third child, telepathy sliding through thoughts that Gideon didn't bother to hide. "The arrogance of youth has always been annoying. You can't kill me, Gideon."

"I don't want to."

"Yet." The look that settled on Nathan's face could almost be described as pride. "I think you're worth it after all."

Gideon's smile was all teeth. "Thank you."

"Now show me you deserve it and bring back that Stryker."

The pressure of Nathan in Gideon's mind leveled off. "Will anyone in the Strykers Syndicate be expecting us?"

"No."

"I'll need a telepath," Gideon said, wishing he didn't. Working with someone who wasn't his twin was going to be strange.

"Warrick is being briefed."

"I need someone stronger than a Class IV."

"He'll have others in merge with him if things turn out messy." Nathan glanced at the chrono ticking away on the vidscreen. "I have a meeting in two hours and need to prep for it. Keep me updated. You're dismissed."

Gideon left, teleporting to the private levels of the city tower that housed the Serca Syndicate. A faint twinge of pain blossomed in the back of his head at the use of his power, a reminder that he wasn't completely healed yet. If he could have taken another few days to recuperate, he would have. Except Nathan needed him and that need came before Gideon's health.

Gideon stepped off the arrival platform. He headed for a briefing room down the hall and found Warrick Sinclair finishing up with an operations officer. The Class IV telepath was with two other telepaths, Mercedes Vargas and James Olsen, Class VII and Class V respectively. Their lower rankings would bolster Warrick's in the merge. When the operations officer left the room and Gideon stepped inside, Warrick and the other two stood.

"Sir," Warrick said. "Good to have you back."

Gideon nodded at the acknowledgment. "You know we're switching targets. Looking for this Stryker is going to be as difficult as looking for Lucas. Maybe worse. Were you ever assigned to track Lucas?"

"Once. Nothing came of it."

"I've got some defensive tricks we were both taught as high-Classed psions, and I know how Samantha looked for him during her missions. I'll give them to you. We're assuming Lucas shared them with the Strykers he's allied with."

"This Stryker we're after. Is he the one who fucked up the mental grid?"

"That's the working theory. Were you in Buffalo?"

"No, I stayed behind in Toronto until I got called back here. Mercedes was there."

Gideon turned his attention on the slight young woman standing beside Warrick. "Do you have the target's psi signature?"

"No, sir," Mercedes said. "When that power hit the mental grid, it didn't stay static. It changed and kept changing until it was cut off."

"We've got his original psi signature in our files," Gideon said. "And I've got memories of the feel of them from Samantha in my head. See if you can't meld the two with the one that appeared after the fight in Buffalo."

Mercedes pressed her mind against Gideon's shields, her power completely alien to the feel of Samantha's telepathy. With vicious force, Gideon shoved his thoughts and memories of his twin to the back of his mind, compartmentalizing the loss. Regret had no room in war.

He had natal shields? Mercedes asked, surprised. Swiftly, she shared the information with the other two telepaths.

Gideon thought about what Nathan had said, why they'd been assigned this mission, and reached his own conclusion. *Not anymore.*

Warrick stayed linked with Mercedes. *Combining the two will be difficult.*

"We'll have some time to work on that in Toronto before we drop in on the Strykers," Gideon said as Warrick left Gideon's mind. "Get your gear and meet back here in fifteen minutes."

The three telepaths left. Gideon looked down at his hands and only then noticed that both were shaking. It took effort to make them stop.

Samantha was no longer there to remind him. He needed to remember to do it for himself.

[TWENTY]

The meeting of the Serca Syndicate's subsidiaries started precisely at noon. The agenda, however, had changed. Sydney Athe, the patriarch of the Athe Syndicate and family, looked Nathan straight in the eye. Beyond him, the pirate stream played on the vidscreen embedded in the wall.

"Who leaked those shots?" Sydney demanded, not caring that he was nothing more than Nathan's subordinate now and not someone to be wooed.

"It doesn't matter," Nathan said, voice cool. "They were given to the public. The fallout of this will be dealt with by the World Court. I'm sure Travis can handle it."

Anger flashed over Sydney's face at the mention of his son. "It will become our problem once people discover that it was my company which enabled our return to space."

"Your company is owned by mine now. I'll deal with the problem." Nathan smiled tightly. "You're here to be introduced as the newest member and to affirm the schedule that the World Court has laid down. Due to the unfortunate revelation of the Paris Basin, this meeting is now about protecting our investments."

"You promised us berths on that colony ship," a woman halfway down the long table said.

"And those berths remain. Unless, of course, the World Court's requirements force me to pare down my lists." Nathan shrugged. "The launch date currently stands at the end of September and running into October. It was moved up almost a month by order of the World Court. I would be surprised if they don't move it again considering the latest development. Right now, authorized registered citizens are being moved to transport points."

"Do they know why?" Sydney said. His gaze flickered over to the vidfeed of the stream in question.

"No, but they'll figure it out. The average citizen can't reach Paris. That entire country is a deadzone. Physical proof of what's going on will be hard to come by, but it will be found. As much as we would like for the government to keep this and other information hidden, that won't happen."

Of those sitting at the table, only Sydney knew Nathan's true genetic identity. He also knew that Nathan's heir was no longer Lucas, something Nathan hadn't yet publically confirmed. Right now, Nathan didn't need his son to take center stage on any issue, and for all that he was a reluctant supporter of Nathan's goals, Sydney knew better than to threaten with the truth.

"I want all of you to start winding down your individual companies immediately. Try to keep your efforts out of the media," Nathan said, gaze sweeping across the table. He thought about how much easier it would be if he could simply mindwipe everyone into obedience. Unfortunately, all those seated at the conference table with him had a bioware net grafted to their brain, which meant it would take daylong individual meetings with each to perform the necessary psi surgery on them. That was time he no longer had.

"That's going to be difficult given the current crisis," someone said from the far end of the table.

"That is not my problem," Nathan said. "I want it done. Make sure you remind the people cleared for the transport points that if they speak about the launch, they lose their place on the shuttles."

"We'll remind them," Sydney said.

"Good. Let's move on to the next issue."

The meeting should have taken hours. It didn't. They weren't forty minutes into their agenda, the tea and coffee barely lukewarm, when a sharp knock on the conference room door interrupted the conversation.

"Sir," Nathan's secretary said as she stepped inside. "You have an uplink."

"I'm busy," Nathan said. "It can wait."

"Sir, it's from The Hague."

Which could only mean one person. Nathan refused to let emotion show on his face as he excused himself from the proceedings.

"It's a secure uplink on their end," the woman said.

"I'll take it in my office."

It took roughly five minutes for him to make it to his private office, going by lift. He couldn't teleport, not with so many people around. When Nathan finally arrived, he opened the uplink on his desk terminal and then Erik's face was filling the vidscreen.

"To what do I owe this meeting?" Nathan asked.

"We have a problem," Erik said flatly.

"Yes, I've seen the pirate stream. There is—"

"That's not what I'm talking about. The quads up north missed their designated check-in two days ago."

Nathan kept the annoyance out of his voice through long practice. "Why am I only being notified of this now?"

"The World Court doesn't bow to you, Nathan," Erik said, voice cold and vicious. "This didn't become your problem until we had solid evidence that the seed bank was broken into. Half the supplies are gone. *That* is why I am calling you."

For a second, Nathan couldn't breathe. Surprise did not come naturally, as Nathan prided himself on knowing the world's secrets. How he had missed seeing this, knowing this, was beyond him. His team of Warhounds situated in Longyearbyen should have warned him.

Lucas.

Every time his son had infiltrated Serca Syndicate branches and subsidiary companies over the past two years, stealing disparate amounts of information that never added up, Nathan had been left wondering why. Nathan mentally ripped through everything he knew about Lucas's actions during his time on the run. Just a vast sleight of hand when the real goal was so much bigger—a psion with a coveted power and supplies to feed a world. If Lucas wanted to buy his way into power, that would be enough incentive to make anyone agree.

Lucas never had any intention of leaving Earth. He wasn't planning an insurrection on Mars. Nathan could see that now, could see what his son was striving for. The release of evidence about the Paris Basin was merely a distraction. The World Court would have to deal with the fallout of that before pursuing the robbery of the one thing left in the world that was absolutely priceless. The seeds weren't scheduled to be moved until the week of the actual launch to alleviate the risks of transfer from the environment they'd been stored in for so long.

"What do you want from me?" Nathan said after a few seconds of silence.

Erik let out a harsh laugh. "I'm going into closed session with the rest of the World Court to hammer out a new timeline for the launch. We're pushing it up again and it's going to be brutal. *You* are going to Spitsbergen to help Elion with the transfer of everything left up there. I'm sending a small contingent of Strykers as security."

Nathan thought about how easy it would be to end Erik's life. Unfortunately, murder wasn't always the best course of action. Getting rid of Erik now would only bring more chaos, and Nathan had enough problems to deal with already. Later, he could weigh the risk of the president's early death.

"When did you mobilize the Strykers?" Nathan said.

"An hour ago."

"I'm in the middle of a meeting that I can cut short, but the world press has been requesting a statement since the pirate stream showed up. I need to make one."

"Don't," Erik said. "I've already ordered most Syndicates to keep silent on the matter. When the World Court finally comes to a decision on how to handle this fucked-up mess, you'll get your orders."

The uplink cut out, leaving Nathan no option but to play by human rules.

[TWENTY-ONE]

The room was white.

For a long moment, Ciari thought she was dreaming, that the colorlessness of the place was due to her mind dying. Recognition came slowly to her, of where she was, who she was.

She couldn't remember why that was important.

"You're a mess," a quiet voice said from nearby. "I can't fix you this time around. I'm sorry."

Ciari moved her head a little, just enough to see the person standing next to her bedside. The petite black woman wore white medical scrubs, thin dreads pulled back away from an angular face.

"Jael," Ciari said, the name sliding through her thoughts. Her voice was rough, tongue dry, as if she hadn't moved her mouth in days, which was probably the case.

"Yes," Jael said as she stepped forward. She carried a tiny cup and proceeded to feed Ciari ice chips until the dryness of her throat faded. Eventually, Jael set the cup aside. "How do you feel?"

Ciari watched as Jael crossed her arms over her chest, fingers digging into her uniform. The skin over her knuckles was ashy and drawn, the expression on the other woman's face ruthlessly neutral. Except—Ciari could see the tightness in her jaw, the way her mouth curved ever so slightly upward at one corner, the way her eyes were just a shade too wide. Tiny details that most people would miss, except Ciari had spent her entire life reading the emotionality of the human body.

Only now, she didn't know what it meant.

"I don't know," Ciari said. "How should I feel?"

Jael closed her eyes briefly, expression twisting enough for Ciari to recognize the look for what it was. It was a struggle to define it, to know it, despite the long association with the other woman.

Pain.

It still didn't make sense to her. Which told her, more than anything else, that something was horribly wrong. She waited for the panic to come, the fear, but it never did.

"Do you remember what happened?" Jael asked, moving to drag a chair over to Ciari's bedside.

Ciari scratched at the IV line connected to the back of her left hand. "The World Court," she said slowly as she pressed her hands flat to the bed and tried to sit up. Jael tapped a command into the controls of the bed, raising it so that Ciari wouldn't have to hold herself up. "Erik. I was—"

She remembered the feel of incandescent fire running through her body, scouring every square centimeter of her being. Ciari touched the back of her head, where the neurotracker was located, and realized that her hair was shaved completely off. The soft skin of her scalp felt smooth in areas, faint pricks of hair follicles snagging the edges of her nails in others. Occasionally, her fingers ran across tacky residue left behind by a quick-heal patch. Being bald didn't matter to her. Whatever damage came from it, physically at least, was mostly fixed. She remembered that Jael did good work.

"Erik meant to kill you," Jael said. "According to Keiko, he kept his finger on the trigger of the kill switch for five minutes before Travis came to your defense. We had to cut out a piece of your skull to give your brain room to swell."

Ciari flattened her hand against the back of her skull, let her fingers splay over the curve of skin and bone. "I remember it burned."

Just facts, not emotions. It was all she could articulate.

"It—the damage to your nerves was easier to fix than the damage to your mind."

"What's wrong?" Ciari said, looking over at the CMO. She let her hand drop back down to her lap, gripping the sheet that covered her.

"A lot of things."

"Tell me."

Jael grimaced, her gaze flicking away from Ciari's face. "I held your mind together as best I could, but in order to keep it from slipping away,

I had you turn the pain off on your own. It was too difficult for me to try without risking your life. I don't have that sort of reach, not when a mind is almost dead. You turned off the pain, but it created a domino effect from that internal order. Once the pain turned off, everything else—every other emotion—was switched off as well. I can't—I can't fix that, Ciari. I can't undo what you did."

Ciari was quiet for a long moment before she said, "You're the best psi surgeon this Syndicate has."

"I don't have the power or finesse to take your mind apart and put it back together again. Not this time."

Ciari stared at her, brown eyes now tinged silver near her pupils. There should have been anger in her gaze, at the very least a sense of horror, but when Jael finally looked at her, Ciari's eyes were empty of anything that might have resembled emotion. The lack of accusation in her face was disheartening.

"We need you," Jael said. "I hoped a medically induced coma would help your mind reset itself, except that's not going to happen. So I woke you up."

Ciari nodded. "Who's in charge?"

"Erik appointed Keiko as Acting OIC." Jael hesitated before continuing, "Lucas sent Threnody, Kerr, and Jason to retrieve your daughter. I'm sorry. We couldn't stop them from taking her, but we managed to take Threnody into custody."

Ciari closed her eyes. Opened them again.

"Tell me," Ciari said slowly, struggling to wrap her thoughts around a concept she no longer understood, "why you need me."

Words flowed over her when Jael spoke, sound that told a story Ciari tried hard to feel connected to. Except that she didn't—couldn't.

In the end, when Jael finally left her alone, Ciari was certain of only three things. She was still a Class III empath; that genetic fact could not be changed. She could still use her power, on others and on herself. She simply had no name for the emotions she could play with and no reason to care why, either about the people she would have to apply it to or the people she was required to lead and to protect.

[TWENTY-TWO]

The pain in her head reminded Threnody of when she peeled burned skin off her hands in the Arctic, how it came free one ragged piece at a time. The way Jael sought to flay her mind felt the exact same way.

The Class III telepath had already stripped most of Threnody's mental shields from her mind, her personal defenses broken down to their foundations. Now Jael contended with the safeguards Lucas had left in Threnody's mind, and for all that Jael was a skilled psi surgeon, breaking past a shield erected by a Class I telepath was practically impossible.

Coughing, Threnody spat out saliva mixed with blood, tasting the coppery tang of iron on her tongue. She kept her eyes closed. "Just ask me your questions," she rasped, the words coming out slow.

Strapped to a chair in an empty cell, Threnody's hands and feet were encased in rubber gloves that stretched to her elbows and rubber boots that hit her knees. Around her throat was a heavy metal neurocollar with tiny needles that cut into the skin of her throat and into her spine. The external device acted like a neurotracker, a precaution against her using the power she'd been born with. A dark bruise discolored the right side of her face from where her head had hit the wall when Keiko slammed her into it. Keiko's brutality had been unexpected, and Threnody wondered how badly things had frayed in the Strykers Syndicate since her defection.

"We aren't interested in your lies," Aidan said, voice flat and clinical.

Threnody forced her eyes open, blinking rapidly to clear her vision. She winced as the harsh light in the cell nearly blinded her. "They wouldn't be lies."

She hadn't set foot in the Strykers Syndicate since July, when she was assigned a suicidal mission to track a target that couldn't be caught. The target turned out to be Lucas, and the mission had brought her full circle to the only home she'd ever known before she tasted freedom.

Threnody managed to smile at that delirious thought as she looked at Jael, the black woman swimming in her vision. "I want to speak with Ciari."

Pain. It ripped through her mind like one of Quinton's firestorms, burning her from the inside out. Threnody's head snapped back and she let out a strangled cry. She only had Lucas's singular shield to hide behind and she wondered, distantly, if it would be enough. He didn't answer her. No psi link connected them, just the faint touch of his power.

"Aidan," Jael snapped out. "I already said that isn't going to work."

"Keiko said she wanted answers when she got back. Staying our hand isn't going to get those for her," Aidan said, sounding frustrated.

"I doubt Ciari wants Threnody dead, and the strength required to break through that last shield would probably kill her."

"She isn't a telepath. How the hell is she holding it up?"

Panting heavily, Threnody felt blood pool in her nose and had to let her head fall forward to let it drain out instead of back into her lungs. It dripped onto her thighs, soaking into the patched clothes she still wore.

"You didn't tag me for retrieval," Threnody coughed out, feeling blood slid down the back of her throat. "'S'okay, Lucas is better than Nathan."

The sudden quiet in her cell wasn't comforting. Nothing about her current position was comforting.

"What do you know about retrieval?" Jael said, the words sounding as if they were pulled out of her by force.

Threnody laughed, soft and low. It made her ribs hurt. Keiko hadn't pulled her power when she telekinetically hit her.

"Ask me your fucking questions." Threnody lifted her head, staring at the two Stryker officers who were still beholden to the whims of their human masters by way of the neurotrackers in their heads. "Or ask Ciari. Either way, get on with it."

Telepathy curled through her bruised mind once again, attempting to cut into the last defense she had against people she once trusted.

TWENTY-THREE

Keiko squinted through the lenses of her binoculars, glad for the shade the shuttle wing provided. Her gaze caught on the magnified metal wedge protruding from the mountainside and the road that wound its way up to their eventual destination. The visual was enough for a teleport, but they weren't ready to move yet.

Behind her stood Terrence Finn, a Class V psychometrist. He silently took the binoculars from Keiko when she passed them to him. Born with a power that shared traits from both telepathy and empathy, Terrence could pull memories out of inanimate objects. He'd been on medical leave in Toronto after fighting in Buffalo, making it easy for Keiko to add him to the small team of Strykers assigned this mission.

Only four of them had been ordered out: Keiko, Terrence, a telepath, and a pyrokinetic. They'd flown across the Arctic Ocean to this island on the World Court's orders. Erik had imparted to her the details of the mission and the location of the outpost in person, not trusting an uplink after the current political mess running through the media. Their contact here hadn't bothered to leave his shuttle, and Keiko had stopped trying to get orders out of Elion after the first try.

I wonder if Ciari knew about this place, Keiko thought as she surveyed the dead land that surrounded the abandoned airfield.

They couldn't access the Svalbard Global Seed and Gene Bank yet. Not until the World Court's appointed leader of this mission arrived on a government-charted shuttle. He landed less than an hour later.

We really need to stop meeting like this, Keiko, Nathan said as he stepped off the shuttle. Two Warhounds in the guise of human bodyguards and a quad followed him. Meters away, Elion was disembarking from his own shuttle, coming to join their small group.

Keiko realized right then just how little they knew about Nathan's political maneuverings. Or at least, how little *she* knew. Despite taking over as the Acting OIC, Keiko knew certain details were locked in Ciari's head that could be the difference between living and dying. Keiko wished she knew them. Lifting her chin, Keiko watched the group's approach in silence.

"Strykers," Nathan said when his group got within hearing range, "the World Court has seen fit to give me your contract."

You're enjoying this far too much, Nathan, Keiko said, shoving the words into the public area of her mind.

The expression on his face didn't change. *No, I'm not.*

"Sir," Keiko said, careful not to make the word grate.

"I was told there would be a psychometrist in this group," Nathan said, his eyes resting unerringly on Terrence. "Which one of you is it?"

Terrence took a step forward. "I am."

For Keiko, it was strange to face Nathan with people who knew nothing of his true identity. Nathan lived a brilliant lie, Keiko had to admit. Brilliant and deadly. The Silence Law would dictate their actions here, with she as the psion and Nathan as nothing more than human. It would be a tricky dance.

"I've got a visual on the mountain," Keiko said, looking between Nathan and Elion. "Whenever you're ready, I can teleport us there."

"How many Strykers did you bring?" Elion said, sounding agitated.

"Four, myself included." Keiko tilted her head at the shuttle behind her. "Our telepath and pyrokinetic are monitoring the security grid. We've been waiting for your arrival before we proceeded up the mountain."

"We're here now," Nathan said. He turned his head to stare up at the mountainside. "Teleport us."

Keiko steadied her mind before wrapping her power around everyone. She teleported them up to the road that led to the seed bank's entrance. Elion and the quads stumbled a bit on their arrival; no one else did. People who were used to the quirks of a teleport—where the telekinetics always 'ported a few centimeters or more higher than the ground of their targeted location—didn't stumble.

"The ramp can support our weight," Elion said as quads moved to slide open the doors.

Lights came on, brightening the tunnel in sections. The group moved quickly down its length. When Keiko took her first steps into the long storage vault, all she saw was a mess of scattered boxes holding silver-foil packets and glass vials strewn across shelves and the floor. All she felt was quiet, fragile disbelief.

It was one thing to be told about a place such as this. Actually seeing it in person was almost painful. This place, this vast seed bank, was the whole reason why humanity had survived after the last bomb fell. Keiko knew of the launch; she hadn't known about this.

"We've lost half the inventory," Elion said. "We have everything that we need, just not in the amounts we expected."

"And the terraforming machines?" Nathan asked, dark blue eyes sweeping over the mess before them. He ignored the startled look the rest of the party gave him at that revelation.

Elion's voice was bitter. "A third of those are gone as well. Whoever was behind this didn't seem to care about taking everything, just enough of it."

"Or they simply didn't have the means or the time to finish the job." Nathan turned and headed for the hallway. "Show me the rest of the damage."

Elion led Nathan down the length of each of the three cold-storage vaults, reporting on their losses. Only when Nathan's inspection was complete did he speak again.

"The psychometrist will begin with the main door," Nathan said.

Terrence led them back to the front entrance. The doors were still in their casings, but he wasn't going to work with those yet. Unsealing his left glove, Terrence pulled his hand free. He lost the warmth that the insulation provided, but he ignored the cold. Taking a deep breath, he raised his hand to the cold metal of the control panel and pressed his skin against it. He didn't hesitate, so none of the humans present knew that he feared using his power. The neurotracker in his brain denied him the right to protest, denied him the right to give in to the fear that all psychometrists experienced when using their power.

Terrence dropped his mental shields, pulling memories out of cold metal. Memories that were both old and distant, too faint to catch completely, or shining bright and sharp against the backdrop of the mental grid. Terrence's mind opened wide and swallowed the memories whole, instances, moments, that people unknowingly pressed into the physical world around them.

Tell Nathan he can go to hell, Lucas Serca said into Terrence's mind, the clear message left behind days ago for them to find.

Telepathy that didn't come from the embedded memory slammed through Terrence's mind, meeting zero resistance since his shields were down. The attack happened so quickly that Keiko didn't know Terrence was dead until he hit the ground. She stared at the Stryker in shock, forcing herself to not look at where Nathan stood.

"What happened?" Elion said, pointing at the dead Stryker. "What the *hell* just happened?"

You didn't have to kill him, Keiko said, fury breaking up her thoughts as she dropped to her knees beside Terrence, fingers searching for a pulse that wasn't going to be there.

Nathan's gaze was unapologetic. *I don't have time to deal with a broken Silence Law.*

He didn't know a goddamn thing about the Silence Law. What did he see?

It's not your concern. Out loud, Nathan said, "Yes. Do explain what happened to the Stryker."

Keiko stared at the body beside her. Blood trickled out of Terrence's nose, dripping slowly to the ground.

"I don't know. I'm not a 'path-oriented psion," Keiko said, forcing her voice calm as she pushed herself back to her feet, brushing dirt off her knees. "I'm guessing it must have been a mental trap."

"How is that even possible?" Elion said.

"Please, give me a few minutes to find out." She glanced over at Nathan. *Was it Lucas that he saw?*

Nathan's gaze didn't waver. *Call your telepath, Keiko.*

Keiko shook her head, as if she could shake his mental touch out of her mind. She opened herself up to the psi link someone else had stitched into her mind. *Eva.*

Yes?

I'm bringing you up here. Terrence is dead. Whatever was left in the walls killed him.

Well, shit.

The Class VI telepath gave Keiko a visual of the shuttle for the telekinetic to find her. Keiko reached for the Stryker over the distance between mountain and shuttle, teleporting the telepath to their position. Eva Collingsworth landed lightly on the road beyond the support ramp. She was a petite woman in her midtwenties; dark-haired, dark-eyed, with heavy scarring over the lower half of her face and throat. Her body didn't have the capability to accept biomodifications, and cellular regeneration had never worked for her. Eva had lost her voice when she was twelve. Telepathy was her only means of communication.

I'm not a psychometrist, Keiko, Eva said, eyes narrowing with emotion that showed nowhere else on her face. *And Terrence is dead. What do you expect me to find?*

Pretend you're trying to get something out of the hole in the mental grid, Keiko said. *See if you can't possibly find out what killed him. Let me deal with the humans.*

Eva inclined her head to the people in charge before closing her eyes.

"Eva is looking for answers," Keiko said, turning to face Elion and not Nathan. "Telepaths aren't psychometrists, sir. Whatever was left behind by whatever rogue psion who was here, I don't know if Eva will find it."

Elion glared at her. "We need answers, Stryker."

"We're trying to get that for you," Keiko said, sounding frustrated. "I don't know what killed Terrence, but if whatever it was is still embedded in these walls, then it's not safe."

"I don't care if you think it's not safe. You're not in charge. Your contract was handed over to us and you have an obligation to obey the World Court."

"I mean no disrespect, but the World Court hasn't issued a kill order for any Stryker here. Let us do the job you brought us here to do in order to keep you safe. Sir."

Elion opened his mouth to argue, or perhaps to threaten to activate the neurotracker in her head, but Nathan interrupted whatever tirade the other man was about to indulge in.

"Elion," Nathan said. "Let them do their job."

Keiko kept her gaze trained on Eva. Her thoughts, however, were elsewhere. *Don't expect me to thank you.*

For interceding on your behalf? Ciari was never one to play that sort of groveling game unless she had someone needing to be saved. I miss her begging. Nathan kept his attention on the two Strykers. *Tell me, Keiko, how is Ciari?*

Keiko had to force herself not to think about the changes in Ciari. *Tell me, Nathan, how does it feel to be backed into a corner by your son?*

My family is of no concern to you.

You say that like I don't know Lucas hasn't been on your side for two years and counting, Keiko said, a grim sort of satisfaction creeping through her mind. *You didn't order him to do this. You wouldn't, if this is what will feed you on Mars Colony.*

What do you think you know about what I and the World Court have planned?

Security for the launch is why the government keeps us alive. You? Keiko's mouth thinned into a bloodless line. *I don't read minds, Nathan.*

Nathan's smile was faint and barely there, missed by everyone except Keiko. She saw it only because she was looking for it. Then Eva pulled her into a psi link, the telepath unaware of Nathan's presence, and Keiko had to focus on the mission.

Massive telepathic overload, Eva said. *Memories don't do that. They can't. This feels more like a telepathic strike. The people who broke in might still be on the island.*

Keiko looked over at Elion, weighing her options. She knew that if she attempted to change the playing field, Nathan would kill her. As a Class I triad psion, he could easily do it. The cleanup afterward—of bodies and mindwipes—would take time, but Nathan was a perfectionist and Keiko didn't doubt he'd find excuses to keep himself safe.

"Our telepath can't speak," Keiko said. "And we aren't authorized for telepathic contact with either of you. Eva confirmed Terrence died from a strong telepathic attack."

"What about the perpetrator?" Elion asked sharply.

Keiko didn't look at Nathan. "Unknown. Possibly the same rogue psions that were in Buffalo, but those particular psi signatures haven't shown up since the fight."

"That is unacceptable, Stryker."

"Unfortunately, it's all we have at the moment. Perhaps the security system—"

Elion let out a short, harsh laugh. "Don't you think we tried? That was the first thing we checked after confirming the breach. The security logs are inaccessible. It would take weeks to hack through the new encryption embedded in everything now. We don't have that long."

Keiko looked down at Terrence's body and wrapped her power around his form. She teleported the corpse into their shuttle for transport.

"We should begin a transfer of everything in the seed bank, sir," Keiko said. "We can't guarantee that the people who broke in won't return to take the rest."

"These seeds and embryos and everything else require a specific temperature in order to survive. They can't be risked," Elion said. "Considering it seems psions are responsible for this mess, I don't trust your involvement."

"The World Court assigned them this job, but I agree with your assessment, Elion. We'll bring in as many cold-storage units as we need," Nathan said. "We will physically transport everything to London."

The better for you to keep it away from Lucas? Keiko asked.

Do you honestly think I'll be protecting it from just him?

Images of the *Ark* from the pirate stream ran through Keiko's mind. She knew that society wasn't going to take such deceit lying down. Everyone's view of the world was changing, and change never came easy.

You'll do what the government requires of you and you'll die for it, Nathan said. *But some of your Strykers will live, so keep your mouth shut.*

"Take us back to the shuttle," Nathan said, the look in his dark blue eyes curiously satisfied.

Keiko decided she should have brought an empath after all. Tapping into her power, she pulled everyone into a teleport.

PART FIVE
FLUCTUATE

SESSION DATE: **2128.03.25**
LOCATION: **Institute of Psionics Research**
CLEARANCE ID: **Dr. Amy Bennett**
SUBJECT: **2581**
FILE NUMBER: **270**

Aisling hums again. The sound is an offbeat melody that clashes with the noise the EEG and supporting machines make behind her as she leans over the seat of her chair and stares at the camera. She is alone.

"I can see what it's going to be like and I think that scares them."

Her head hangs down, her hair falling around her face like a curtain. The wires lay heavily across her back.

"It scares me." She kicks her legs a bit, smacking the toes of her shoes against the ground. "Everyone's afraid of me. I don't have any friends here."

Aisling waves one small hand at the camera in a vague gesture before she props herself back up on both hands. Then she sighs and collapses again over the chair. She scratches at a line of electrodes adhered across her forehead and pushes wires out of her face.

"It could have been different, and it is, but then it wouldn't end. Mama said it should end." Aisling glances at the camera, her gaze looking past it. "I don't want Nathan, Marcheline. I need his son."

[TWENTY-FOUR]

Threnody."

She opened her eyes slowly, staring at her knees. She knew that voice.

Slowly, achingly, Threnody lifted her head enough to see the woman standing in front of her. For a moment, Threnody thought she was dreaming. Gone was the dark brown hair, shaved off completely for the surgery the older woman must have gone through. Harsh red lines still laced the skin of her skull, and her eyes were like empty holes in her face. She wore soft-looking black pants and a gray, long-sleeved shirt. She looked as if she had lost weight.

Ciari looked fragile.

Threnody sniffed loudly. Her nose itched from all the dried blood inside it. "Never saw you out of uniform before."

"I've never seen a Stryker without a neurotracker still breathing," Ciari said.

"Liar." Threnody smiled, the corners of her mouth cracking. Her lips were dry.

Someone had brought another chair into Threnody's cell while she was unconscious. Ciari sat down in it and laced her hands together in her lap. She stared at Threnody with a heavy, unblinking gaze that was hard to meet. Something was off about the way the older woman acted, and it made Threnody uneasy.

"I'm not giving you up to the World Court," Ciari said after a moment.

"That's not really a kindness."

"You took my daughter. It's not about kindness."

Threnody rolled her head from side to side, trying to ease the heavy ache in her shoulders. The motion brought a wave of nausea, but she managed to not throw up this time. She stank enough as it was. She hadn't eaten since being teleported in, but she'd been given some sips of water. It wasn't enough to sooth the parchedness in her mouth. Swallowing, Threnody stopped moving so her stomach would settle. The pressure in her head was all mental trauma, but Lucas's shield was still standing. She assumed it was the only reason she was still alive.

"Her father wanted full custody, not visiting rights," Threnody said. "Sorry."

"Lucas is making a mess of things."

"So, no more pretending?" Threnody let out a heavy sigh, flexing her fingers. The rubber gloves made her skin itch. She couldn't stretch her arms, not with her wrists cuffed to the chair, and her joints felt tight. "I would have kept your secret."

"Jael already knows. She was keeping it safe. How did you find out where we were keeping her?"

"The Syndicate trained me as a tactician, remember? I took the details we had and came up with the best possible scenario."

"Was releasing information about the *Ark* your idea?"

"I'm just a soldier, Ciari. All I do is follow orders."

"No, you aren't. And, no, you don't."

Threnody licked her lips and chuckled softly. "Never was very good at lying about how I felt."

Ciari nodded agreement. "It's what got you into this mess in the first place. I never wanted to send you on that mission to the Slums."

"You were just following orders, right?"

"I won't apologize for my actions."

"I know," Threnody said quietly. "You have nothing to apologize for."

"The world knows about the launch now. About the *Ark*. The World Court is pushing up the launch date, which means we Strykers have only got days left to live."

Threnody stared at her, not liking the toneless way Ciari was speaking. Her voice had no emotion, not even the coldness that came with an empath's rigid control. She was just—empty.

"What can I say that will make you believe there's a way out of this?" Threnody said. "That the Strykers don't have to die like animals?"

"Belief requires faith. I have none."

Threnody flinched. "I learned to."

"You aren't the first to make that mistake." Ciari pushed herself to her feet and approached Threnody. "You won't be the last. But mistakes are what make us human."

Ciari unlocked first one cuff, then the other. Threnody stared blankly down at her freed hands.

"Lie down and get some rest, Threnody. We aren't done fighting yet."

Ciari walked out of the cell without looking back. Threnody slowly pulled her arms free of the cuffs and stretched them, groaning as stiff muscles protested the movement. She peeled off the rubber gloves, tossing them away. Then she leaned over to undo the cuffs around her ankles, hissing as the ache in her ribs got sharper. She pulled the rubber boots off her feet before carefully sliding out of the chair. Her aching ribs protested the movement, but Threnody still lay down on the cold metal floor, fingers of one hand curled over the collar wrapped around her throat, the bioware tipped needles digging deep into her skin and vertebrae. She still obeyed the order given to her.

Threnody closed her eyes to block out the light, and slept.

[TWENTY-FIVE]

SEPTEMBER 2379
THE HAGUE, THE NETHERLANDS

Sharra knew what it meant when the pirate stream hit the world press and society was unable to look away. She paused in front of the vidscreen long enough to watch it all the way through once. Then she retreated to the bunker suite she called home and began to pack.

They were on a schedule that Erik had been keeping to over the past few years. It was easy for her to go through that mental list and see exactly where she was in packing up her life.

"Mama, what are these boxes for?" Lillian asked.

Kneeling, surrounded by heavy cargo trunks, Sharra craned her head around to watch as her daughter walked into the bedroom. "They aren't boxes, sweetie. They're for storage."

"What are you storing?"

Her perfectly human daughter climbed onto a trunk, sitting on the lid. She was dressed in her school uniform, the jacket slung over a chair in the kitchen. Sharra had left Lillian there eating cookies under the watchful eye of a soldier while the movers rattled around the suite of rooms.

Sharra tucked a stray strand of blond hair behind her ear before beckoning to Lillian. "Come here, sweetheart."

The little girl hopped off the trunk and walked over to her mother. She didn't protest when Sharra pulled her into her arms, giving Lillian a hug that almost hurt.

"You know how important your father is," Sharra said, stroking Lillian's dark hair. "Sometimes important people need to make very hard decisions, and that's what I'm helping your father with."

"But all our stuff is going away."

"Yes, well. Your father has been working extrahard to make sure you have a wonderful new home. Not everyone is special enough to live there, and we didn't want to make people jealous, so it was a secret. Unfortunately, that secret got out and now we're going to be moving a little earlier than your father thought."

"What about school?"

In that regard, Lillian was her father's child. Sharra had been illiterate until the age of nine, when she found her way into an illegally run school in London. She could read and write, do basic arithmetic, but any sort of desire for education that Lillian had did not come from Sharra.

"There will still be school where we're going," Sharra promised her.

"And my friends?"

"You'll still have your friends. Don't worry, honey. Everything's going to be okay. Right now, I need you to go to your room and pick out only your most favorite toys. Can you do that for me?"

"Why can't I take them all?" Lillian asked, pouting. In this, she was most definitely Sharra's child.

"Because I said so." She gave Lillian another hug before gently pushing her toward the door. "Now go. Do what I say and there might be cake for dessert tonight."

Whatever anger Lillian might have had, it faded in the face of every child's favorite meal. "Chocolate?"

"Perhaps. You won't know until you begin to sort out your room."

"I'll do it, I promise!"

Lillian raced out of the bedroom. Sharra pressed the side of her hand against her mouth, biting down carefully on the skin there to hold back the sick feeling in her stomach. What she wouldn't give for a glass of wine, but even she knew there came a time for sobriety. For her daughter, she would learn it.

Sharra spent the next few hours mindlessly filling the trunks in her room with what would fit from her life, tearing apart a place that had been home for so many years. If she dropped a vase or two because her hands were shaking, no one said a word, and the mess was ignored. It was pointless cleaning a place they were never going to see again.

Sharra was in the middle of closing another trunk when Lillian came skipping back into the room. "Daddy's home!"

Sharra got to her feet and smoothed out the wrinkles in her pale blue dress. She hadn't thought that Erik would be back so soon. "Come along," Sharra said, reaching for her daughter's outstretched hand. "Let's go say hello to your father."

They found Erik in his office, the first place Sharra knew to check whenever he was home. It was of moderate size, lived-in, with antiques cluttering up the corners and holopics of his family on the wall that she hadn't got to packing yet. Sharra had decorated it for him years ago, and nothing within those four walls had ever changed. Erik never really cared about what surrounded him, only who. His desire for power was similar to Sharra's desire for safety, and they were losing both.

"Daddy!" Lillian shrieked, letting go of her mother's hand to fling herself at her father.

Erik embraced her easily enough, but most of his attention was on the vidscreen embedded in the wall. It was separated into four different news streams, and the latest update wasn't pretty.

Sharra came to stand beside her husband, glancing from him to the vidscreen. "What are they saying?"

Erik shook his head, the tight look on his face evidence enough of his answer. If it had been less of a problem, he wouldn't look so exhausted.

"Nothing good," he said, smoothing back Lillian's hair. "I had to sign off on payment for stolen oil with a terrorist group earlier this week, oil which we need on Mars Colony, and some hacker found the trail of funds. That's just the latest bit of proof the media is using to rip us to shreds."

"Hasn't anyone argued on the government's behalf?"

"People have, but no one's listening to our side of the story. Everyone's only interested in what the pirate streams can dig up. Thank God no one has found out about the seed bank yet, but I doubt that ignorance will last. We've already lost half that inventory to a breach."

That news sent a cold chill running down Sharra's spine. She placed a hand on her husband's arm, holding on to him. "Erik?"

"The Strykers couldn't pull anything from the location. A Stryker died doing recon and they think it's the same rogue psion that orchestrated the mess in Buffalo. I don't have any confirmation, but it's the only logical suggestion offered up so far. Nathan Serca is overseeing the transportation of the remaining inventory to his Syndicate's tower for safety reasons before transferring it to Paris. It's going up on the first wave of shuttles."

Sharra swallowed thickly. "Is London safe enough to house the seeds?"

"Nowhere on this planet is safe right now." Erik pressed a kiss to Lillian's cheek and hugged her a little tighter. "I want you to finish packing within the hour, Sharra. I've got to give a press conference soon to try to buy us a little more time. We're moving up the launch to this week."

Erik went quiet, his eyes locked on the vidscreen and the satellite readout of the *Ark*'s design. "We only wanted to save humanity," he said. "We just can't save everyone."

Only the strongest could survive. Sharra knew that rule more intimately than Erik ever would. Sharra let go of her husband's arm and turned to leave. "I'll finish packing."

The bunker still had furniture and art cramming its walls. Wineglasses were still in the kitchen sink, unopened bottles scattered around the suite. She was trying to be prudent with the packing, only taking what they absolutely couldn't leave behind—holopics of their life here, her collection of jewelry, Lillian's handful of stuffed animals.

Their lives would fit into a dozen cargo trunks, and that was all they would take with them into space. Sharra tried not to think about what they were leaving behind.

[TWENTY-SIX]

SEPTEMBER 2379
AMUNDSEN-SCOTT SOUTH POLE STATION, ANTARCTICA

That's a lot of hyposprays," Quinton said. "Are you sure it's going to be enough for everyone?"

Rows of silver hyposprays stretched out down the long table, each calibrated to give twenty doses of the virus-carrying nanites before needing to be discarded. Quinton picked one up, holding the thin object in his hand. It didn't weigh much, didn't look as if it had the power to change a person's life, but that's exactly what Lucas had created. Korman didn't care to see the value in something that would save psions, not at the expense of the human bondworkers he had tested it on. Quinton didn't let himself dwell on the process, just the results. As horrendous as the process was, it was still saving people.

"It'll be enough," Lucas said without looking up as he packed them into carrying cases. "Your job is going to make sure you use them all."

"I thought we were just dropping them off and breaking Threnody out?" Kerr said.

"I would bet my Syndicate's entire bottom line that Erik is pushing up the launch, which means we need to work on convincing your Strykers that they need our help."

"You ask for the impossible a lot of the time," Samantha said as she closed one carrying case and reached for another. "It's very annoying."

"You want to know what I find annoying?" Matron said, glaring at Lucas. "The way you keep killing off my scavengers. Fahad'd been around a long-ass time. He deserved to see the end."

"He wasn't *your* scavenger and he wasn't as loyal as you think. You're lucky it wasn't me who killed him. Kristen was actually quick for once," Lucas said. "Her version of nice."

Matron opened her mouth. Lucas shut it for her, telekinesis wrapped around skin and metal. He stared at her across the worktable in silence. Matron closed her eyes, hunched her shoulders, and got back to work. One packed carrying case later, Lucas retracted his power.

Jason came into the crowded workroom five minutes later, dragging Kristen behind him telekinetically. The younger girl knew better than to fight his hold, but the second he freed her, she invaded his space again.

"You want me to fix your daughter?" Jason snapped at Lucas. "Keep your sister out of my fucking head."

Lucas rolled a hypospray between his fingers, staring at them. "I sent you to get the rest of the hyposprays, Kris. Not to touch things that aren't yours."

"Little, itty-bitty thing is a Serca," Kristen said. "I just wanted to say hello."

Whatever else Kristen might have said, Lucas cut her off before the thought was even half-formed in her mind. The empath's head snapped back from his telepathic blow, mind cracking a little beneath her brother's strength. Lucas let his telepathy drift through the growing stain of insanity that was creeping back into his youngest sister's mind, familiar holes that were beginning to open all over again. He could sense the places that Jason's stolen pattern had once filled and which were slowly dissolving. Kristen's mind wasn't meant to hold sanity.

She couldn't be fixed; he had always known that.

I never blamed you, Kristen said, her voice soft and achingly sweet in the maelstrom that was beginning to churn once again through her mind.

It wouldn't have mattered if she did.

"Keep a closer watch on her," Lucas said to Samantha.

"She seemed fine" was Samantha's irritated reply, not looking up from her current task.

"That's never a guarantee."

Scowling, Samantha left her spot and went to drag Kristen to the far side of the table.

Jason watched them get settled with the last of the hyposprays that needed to be packed and shook his head. "Please tell me she's not coming with us."

"I'm not leaving my sisters here."

"Take Samantha. Leave Kristen. She's insane."

"Everyone always underestimates her because of that." Lucas looked over at him. "You did, remember?"

Jason didn't bother to argue that fact. "Korman doesn't have any hyposprays left. He didn't trust Kristen to tell you that this is everything we've got to do the job."

All of which could be counted up in carrying cases full of a virus and the hope that they wouldn't get shot on sight when they teleported to the Strykers Syndicate. Lucas pushed away from the table, taking in everyone's attire. "Change out of your skinsuits. If things go badly, I don't want them to have a hint of where we've been."

"If things go badly, we're all fucked," Quinton said, leaving the room.

Jason left with Kerr, the two heading for the room on the far end of the station they'd been sharing since their arrival. The pair stripped out of their insulated skinsuits and dragged on a set of mismatched street clothes that left them shivering a bit in the low warmth of the station. Power was gained by way of three old generators, only two of which Matron's scavengers had managed to get up and running. They had heat; it just wasn't enough without skinsuits to stay warm continuously.

"Think Threnody's still alive?" Jason said as he yanked on a shirt.

"Lucas isn't worried," Kerr replied as he laced up a pair of boots. "Which means she can't be dead."

"I'd hate to be in Quinton's shoes right now."

"You hate what we're doing anyway."

"Can you blame me?" Jason looked over at Kerr as he grabbed the jacket hanging off the chair. "I don't care if Lucas thinks he's going to save everyone. I don't trust his methods."

Kerr leaned forward on the bed where he was sitting, resting his elbows on his knees. "Maybe you should try. He's got a way to save us, Jays."

"At too high of a price." Jason tapped the side of his head. "You're not in my head anymore. Feels fucking weird."

"It's worth it. You know that."

Worth it to not have his shields skidding out from beneath his control, to not be at risk of an insanity driven by a storm of the world's thoughts. Telepaths were born to read minds, but they craved a silence they would never get. Kerr had only ever found silence behind Jason's natal shields, and now those, too, were gone. Both of them were exactly what they were supposed to be, but that didn't make their lives any easier.

"All the times when you were in my mind, did you ever know what I really was?" Jason asked.

"No," Kerr said with a shake of his head. "I couldn't get very far past your shields. I only got far enough to readjust my own and hold them to the pattern that you had. I never knew you were a microtelekinetic, the same way I never knew I had an empathic power. Hell, I never knew your kind of power even existed."

"You and me both."

The two looked at each other, separated now by so much more than the space between them. The severing of their bond was still a wound in both their minds. For Kerr, it was the constant reach for something that was no longer there. For Jason, it was the emptiness in the back of his mind that used to be filled with the hum of someone else's thoughts. He never felt that anymore unless Kerr produced a psi link, but the connection would never again be the same.

"I never said thank you," Kerr said, looking Jason in the eye. "For how you kept me safe and sane."

"Yeah, you did." Jason gave him a faint, bittersweet smile. "Too many times to count."

"Sometimes I never meant it."

"The times you were screaming in my head and wanted me to kill you before you went crazy? I know, Kerr. And I don't blame you for giving the bond up. You didn't need it anymore. You got your mind fixed. That's all you ever wanted, and I'm not a shitty enough person to hold that against you."

"I never wanted to leave you like this."

"Fuck that, man. You can't get rid of family."

Jason had been the volatile one growing up, always ready to defend Kerr in the face of derogatory comments and dismissive attitudes from their fellow Strykers. Jason didn't care that his shields made him an anomaly back then, and he counted the black marks in his old record for fighting for Kerr like honor badges.

A knock on the door brought Kerr to his feet. The door opened and Quinton leaned into the room. "Hey. You two ready?"

"We're ready," Jason said.

The three of them headed back to the workroom, finding Lucas and his sisters already there. Matron was leaning against the table, having sorted the carrying cases into five stacks. Kristen pouted when she wasn't handed any.

"What about you?" Quinton asked the scavenger. "You've been with us since Buffalo. Aren't you coming?"

"Been with Lucas longer than that and I ain't always with him when he goes running off," Matron said.

"You make it seem like I'm the reckless one," Lucas said as he tossed an apple from one hand to the other.

Matron shrugged, rubbing at one shoulder where the metal cybernetics of her arm attached to flesh and bone. The cold made the connecting points ache. "You've always been reckless with everyone else's life."

Lucas only smiled at her. Matron bared her metal teeth in a responding grin. It wasn't the first time that Matron wondered about the faith she was putting in him that wasn't going to her God, but she wasn't going to stop now. "I pray to God you're doing the right thing here, Lucas."

"Your God isn't why I'm doing this. Remember what I told you when I pulled you from the swamps of Chicago?"

Matron snorted. "You think I forgot that? You promised me a garden if I did your dirty work."

Lucas tossed her the apple. Matron caught it easily in one hand. "Keep sorting the seeds."

"I know how to do my job," Matron said, dark eyes wide and opaque, face full of a belief that wasn't for Lucas, but for what he had the chance to make. "Don't forget about us down here."

"Never," Lucas promised. He almost sounded as if he meant it.

Lucas wrapped his telekinesis tightly around his sisters and the other three. He kept the visual in his mind of a white room as he teleported them all across the world in a single 'port. Their feet hit the platform in the arrival room with a heavy sound. This time it was guarded, but Lucas wasn't concerned about that. Beside him, Samantha let out a soft gasp as she recognized a familiar presence that had been missing from her mind since Buffalo.

Lucas slammed his telepathy up through half a dozen levels filled with psions and humans alike, leaving a burning path of pain on the mental grid in his wake. He slid into a cracked mind that was no longer familiar and looked through Ciari's eyes.

[TWENTY-SEVEN]

SEPTEMBER 2379
TORONTO, CANADA

Gideon stared out the window of the suite, squinting through the polluted haze that lingered over everything. He was in a private level that the Serca Syndicate owned in one of Toronto's city towers. It came with a perfect view of the city tower that housed the Strykers Syndicate, its top floors a government-owned prison on the outskirts of the main cluster. Beyond it, Lake Ontario was a dark swath of water against the landscape.

Toronto was nothing like Buffalo. The slums surrounding the city towers were mostly aboveground and sprawled over land that hadn't suffered as badly as other cities during the Border Wars. Buffalo existed mostly belowground, in sealed bunkers and tunnels. That city's towers were far fewer than the count here, limited in numbers because of the deadzone that took up most of New York State.

Gideon was glad for the differences. It made being in this part of the world bearable.

"Have you matched the psi signature yet?" he said. He could see the reflection in the plasglass of the three telepaths who were seated at the conference table, surrounded by datapads.

"No," Warrick said, rubbing at his temple. "We have nothing in our database on who that psion might be."

"There's no match with our target's records or the psi signature from Buffalo either," Mercedes said. "I'm still willing to say it's Jason Garret. It certainly wasn't Lucas, and the way it registered off the scale? Lucas is strong, but this power tops his strength in a very specific way."

One of the Warhound teams on surveillance duty in Toronto had tagged a strong, abnormal psi signature two days earlier on the mental grid. It originated from the Strykers Syndicate, and Gideon refused to believe it could be anyone else.

"I'm not hearing any answers," Gideon said.

"Because there aren't any, sir," Warrick said. "Not with the information we have. The Strykers would have more than we do, especially since that psion was in their Syndicate."

They should have initiated their visit yesterday, but Nathan had informed Gideon about the breach in the seed bank before they left for the Strykers Syndicate, which had delayed the visit by twenty-four hours. Gideon adjusted the tie knotted around his throat. He was wearing a suit for this endeavor. He would have preferred a field uniform.

"Feels like Kristen is in this city," James said.

Gideon turned to give the telepath a sharp look. "I doubt Lucas would make it that easy to find him again."

"It's not your sister, sir. It's her dysfunction that feels similar on the mental grid. Insanity has a particular spike to it."

"Strykers rarely keep dysfunctional psions. The government usually orders their termination at a young age. Most likely it's someone injured from the fight in Buffalo." Gideon walked over to the chair where his suit jacket was hanging and put it on. "Let's go."

They were doing this the human way, restricted from using Gideon's ability to teleport. He knew what the Strykers Syndicate looked like; specifically, their arrival rooms for psions, but Nathan wasn't quite at the point where he could risk their family's secret coming out.

They left the suite of rooms for a shuttle that was locked into one of the landing docks that stuck out like spokes down the side of the city tower, just one of many used by the registered elite. The walk there took them down to a public level, past brightly lit department stores and restaurants, the hologrids that lined every wall showing news streams and not the usual adverts. Residential routes cut away from the public space, leading off to the lifts that would carry people to their homes.

The atmosphere was muted and tense. People walked by with their heads down, looking at no one as they went about their business. The group made it to their assigned shuttle walkway and entered the short, enclosed tube that extended to the shuttle's hatch. Minutes after they strapped in, the pilot disengaged the anchor locks once given the all clear.

The flight to the other city tower and the Strykers Syndicate was short. Gideon had the pilot dock the shuttle on a lower level and the four disembarked, heading for a lift that would take them right to the top. A security system had already scanned their eyes and faces for identities, so when the lift came to a stop and the doors opened onto a sleek lobby, Gideon was greeted by a familiar woman.

"Keiko," he said, stepping out of the lift and into the Strykers Syndicate.

"Sir," she said evenly. "This is unexpected."

"We have business to discuss."

Despite being surrounded by psions and humans, only four people in this Syndicate knew the truth about the Sercas. Keiko wasn't about to break the Silence Law. She didn't argue Gideon's order and simply led him to a lift farther inside that had access to the rest of the Strykers Syndicate's levels.

Keiko took him to the administrative level. She took him to Ciari.

Gideon was surprised to see the other woman conscious. Considering the trauma that Erik had inflicted on her at The Hague, Gideon expected her to be well on her way to dying. Instead, Ciari looked decently recovered. She had Aidan and Jael with her, and while those two acknowledged his arrival, Ciari continued watching a news stream.

The World Court was standing before the cameras again, on trial themselves before public opinion in the face of irrefutable evidence that they still categorically denied.

"This should be interesting," Jael said. It was anyone's guess if she meant the current company or the current news as Gideon crossed Ciari's office to take a seat before her desk.

"I've never cared for your interests," Keiko said.

On the vidscreen, Erik was arguing his case, backed by the other fourteen judges that made up the World Court. Between the judges and the reporters was a line of quads with pulse-rifles, which said more about the situation than anything else.

"We who have held the title of judge on the World Court, all of the previous men and women who have presided here over the past two hundred and fifty years, have only had the world's best interests at heart," Erik said, his voice filling the office. "The Border Wars nearly destroyed Earth, making it impossible to live in all but the most desperate of places. Even now, we are a desperate people, but we have not lost the greatest part of our humanity. We have not lost our capacity to hope for a better life, for a better world.

"The Fifth Generation Act was just one of many plans implemented in order to help society distance itself from its horrific past. Five generations to cleanse our DNA, with the Registry securing the identities of those who succeeded. It had to be done, if only to separate us from the psions that the Border Wars created. The psions threatened and still threaten our own existence to this day, their disease a reminder of what is still at stake—our survival as a people, as humans."

He paused for a moment before the cameras, taking in a deep breath. "Fewer of us are born every year with the ability to live healthy lives. Too many of us are born with genetic defects, caused from leftover radiation

taint. Too many of us die young from disease. It is difficult, almost impossible, to heal everyone in the population. It takes time, but we have
been *trying*."

Someone shouted a vicious dissent from offscreen, but Erik didn't react.

"Since the end of the Border Wars, the government has been trying to
make this world a better place. It's a seemingly impossible task, but we
have done the best job we could over the years. Yes, there have been dra-
conian measures taken to ensure humanity's survival, but that's the cost
we pay to live. We have come so far since the collapse of the old world
and we aren't prepared to stop now. These lies that unregistered dissidents spread are abhorrent and insulting."

"Lies," Ciari echoed. "We could teach him something about that."

On-screen, the crowd of reporters was being jostled by a ruckus out of
view of the cameras. More shouting ripped through the audio, and the
quads leveled their guns at a crowd that was starting to get unruly. It was
mere seconds from becoming a massacre when everyone went suddenly
quiet and still. People froze where they stood, the silence in the room difficult to comprehend after that sudden fit of fury.

"Empath," Jael said, arms crossed stiffly over her chest. "Who's on
guard duty?"

"Three teams," Keiko said. "The World Court is protected. They authorized psionic interference if necessary."

"You seem to have everything under control," Gideon said. "It's a far
cry from the government."

Ciari finally turned her head to look at him, and the deadness in her eyes
was shocking. Gideon studied her face and noted the lack of expression.

"Our orders stand," Ciari said. "We've been tasked with protecting
the registered elite in the city towers during their transfer to the Paris
Basin. We have no choice."

"You always have a choice with us." Gideon offered her a careful
smile. "Let's discuss those choices, shall we?"

"I was under the assumption that Nathan wasn't extending us help.
As he pointed out, it's too late for retrievals."

"We said we'd take your high-Classed psions and bring them with us into space, but as of right now, we'll only do that if you give us the one we really want."

"We haven't been hiding Lucas from you."

"We don't want Lucas any way but dead." Gideon shrugged. "We want Jason Garret."

He didn't miss the way everyone but Ciari went tense at his demand. Gideon studied Ciari intently. He was not a 'path-oriented psion, but he'd lived eighteen years with one digging through his mind. Something was wrong with the Strykers' OIC.

"That's a bit of a problem, considering he defected," Ciari said slowly.

"He was here during the fight in Buffalo. The Warhounds in this city felt his presence. Don't lie to me."

"I'm not."

Gideon leaned back in his chair. "So you'll risk all your people for the sake of one psion?"

"We can't risk anyone when we don't have the person you're looking for," Jael said. "Jason Garret has been targeted for kill on sight by the World Court since he managed to escape. Do you think we could keep him here when we're scrutinized so closely?"

"The fact that we're having this conversation in your office proves you wrong."

"No, it simply proves we can circumvent the system, but not for long and not frequently," Aidan said. "With what's going on, the World Court has more important things to worry about than watching our every move so long as we obey orders."

"Considering how badly they need you for security right now, I doubt that."

Ciari tapped at the controls on her desk, turning off the vidscreen. "At some point, even we won't be enough. I'm sorry, Gideon. I can't accept your bargain. I don't have who you want."

Gideon looked her in the eye, searching for something he couldn't find, because all he saw was a faint glint of silver in brown depths. "Does Erik know you're awake?"

"Yes."

"Does he know you're going insane?"

The question hit home hard, none of the officers standing around Ciari's desk able to hide their surprise quick enough at his assessment of the situation. Ciari, on the other hand, couldn't care that he knew what was wrong with her.

"Is that a threat?" Ciari asked.

"Can you even tell?"

"Damn you," Jael said, slamming her hand down near the corner of Ciari's desk. "We can't give you what you want, Gideon."

"Prove it," Gideon said, still refusing to look away from Ciari. "Let Warrick here link me to you, Ciari. You can't lie mind to mind, not in the state you're in."

"Absolutely not."

"I wasn't talking to you, Jael."

Ciari slowly tilted her head to the side, studying Gideon. "You remind me so much of Nathan right now. He should have chosen you sooner."

Gideon had to fight back the scowl. "You don't know what you're talking about."

"And you don't know what you're asking for." Ciari flicked her fingers at him. "Do it."

She was still the OIC, even in the wrecked state she was in. Her officers couldn't counter her order, even though they wanted to. Warrick, telepathically merged with Mercedes and James, pulled Gideon into a psi link and reached for Ciari's damaged mind.

[TWENTY-EIGHT]

Gideon was on his feet when the crack of displaced air exploded in the room. Bodies dropped out of a teleport, but he was already stumbling away from Ciari's desk, information cutting through his mind from what Warrick and the other two were able to discover for him. The echoes of Lucas's thoughts in Ciari's mind were like a telepathic punch he had no defenses against.

"You have a *daughter*?" Gideon exclaimed.

You never could learn to leave things well enough alone, Lucas said into his mind.

Then suddenly he was there, in a way Nathan had never been, cutting so deep through Gideon's thoughts that the younger man didn't have a chance at surviving. Not on his own. Gideon had an image of a room burned into his mind, of an escape all Warhound telekinetics never forgot, except he couldn't reach it. His telekinesis couldn't make that final jump into a teleport, and the panic at that realization nearly drowned out the agony from Lucas's attack. Gideon fell to his knees while around him chaos erupted.

The three Warhounds who'd come with Gideon were doing their level best to block some of Lucas's attack against Gideon, but they weren't strong enough to win against a Class I, even in merge. Faced with the daunting odds in Ciari's office, they fought to save their own skins for as long as they could. Their efforts were joined by the Stryker officers, who didn't take kindly to being ambushed.

Kristen was slammed against the far wall by Keiko's initial telekinetic punch. The Japanese woman knew how devastating Kristen's mind could be and needed to preemptively take her out. Kristen would have been severely injured if Jason didn't cushion her landing, ripping Keiko's power off the teenager. Keiko retaliated against Jason even as she shielded Ciari and her fellow officers.

"Shit—we didn't come here to fight this time!" Jason yelled at her.

The three Warhounds were bearing down on Lucas's mind with telepathic strikes, and Jael added her own attack to the mix. She found it deflected not by Lucas, but by Kerr. Her mind, still bruised from the last blow he'd leveled through her thoughts, flinched against the pressure of his touch.

Jael, we mean it, Kerr said. *Don't fight us.*

But both sides knew that they couldn't give any ground, not with everything that was happening in the world. Jael's duty right now was to protect Ciari's mind. She might only be a Class III telepath, but she'd spent her entire life putting minds back together. She knew how to take them apart. Kerr may finally have gained solid shielding, but Jael knew where weakness once resided in his mind, and she attacked those areas with her telepathy. Jael managed to stop Kerr's next strike before it even touched her mind by aiming hard and fast for the bottom of his shields.

A psion mind never forgot, and Kerr instinctively flinched against her attack. His shields held, but Jael managed to bruise his mind. Training demanded retaliation, but Kerr came up short. Jael was the Strykers Syndicate's CMO and they weren't here to murder their former officers.

Fire erupted in Ciari's office, controlled by Quinton as he targeted the Warhounds. Skin burned just as easily as anything else, and the horrific screams of the two men being engulfed in flames rang in everyone's ears. The stench of burning bodies filled the air, making everyone gag. Jason wrapped the Warhounds in a telekinetic shield, limiting the damage Quinton's fire could do to the floor and ceiling. The woman the other Warhounds had come with managed a mercy killing for the two before Samantha broke her mind so thoroughly that she was dead before she hit the floor.

Then it was just Strykers and Sercas, the lines of loyalty blurred beyond all belief. With a sinking sense of anguish, Samantha focused all of her power on her brothers—and stopped Lucas from killing her twin.

The mental grid reverberated with her attack, the backlash slamming against everyone else's shields. Lucas doubled over from the white-hot pain in his mind, swearing loudly, unprepared for her sudden betrayal.

Gideon knelt on the floor, hands clawing at his head. His mouth was open in a soundless scream, agony written in every line of his rigid body, and all Samantha could see was her other half.

I'm sorry, she whispered into the fractured remains of Gideon's mind. Lucas had torn apart every memory that held the information about his daughter and damaged even more than that. Samantha could see what Lucas had done, could see the insidious corruption that was already snaking through Gideon's mind like acid, eating away at everything that made him who he was. The torturous mindwipe could only result in death.

But Gideon still had his power. And, for just right now, he had her.

Go, Samantha said into her twin's mind, pieces of who she was imprinting onto him. She gave him enough balance and clarity to finish the teleport he still struggled to form, a last attempt at an apology he would never accept.

Gideon disappeared.

When Lucas slammed his mind into hers, Samantha wished she could as well.

Why? Lucas demanded.

He's my brother, Samantha said, struggling to hold up her shields. *Same as you.*

Except Gideon was her twin and she owed him more than Lucas. That debt was paid now. Lucas peeled her shields apart and Samantha let him, knowing she couldn't stop him if he wanted to kill her.

"Stop."

Ciari's voice cut through the melee like nothing else could. Everyone obeyed, ingrained training impossible to ignore when the OIC spoke, no matter how long some of them had been gone from the fold. With one final, vicious wrench of his telepathy, Lucas let his sister go and didn't bother catching her when she fell to her knees, forehead pressed to the floor. Samantha laced her hands over the back of her head, as if she were trying to keep her skull from breaking into pieces.

Around them, the mental grid was layered with the minds of those Strykers still within the confines of the city tower, Lucas and Kerr merged and working to hold off their attacks.

Ciari was on her feet, hands flat on her desk. "This gets us nowhere."

Lucas met her gaze evenly. "Is your security loop still running?"

"Since Gideon walked through the door. We have ten more minutes on the clock." She pointed at the three dead Warhounds. "Get rid of those."

Jason teleported the bodies away, dumping them from a distance into Lake Ontario. Quinton doused what was left of his fire, but the smell of smoke and burned human flesh still filled everyone's lungs when Jason collapsed his telekinetic shields. Too many minds in close proximity on the mental grid had Ciari pressing the palm of one hand to her forehead.

"Jael, tell everyone to stand down," she said.

Jael hesitated, but she didn't argue, which was probably why Ciari asked her and not Aidan. *Stand down.*

The Strykers were reluctant, but they listened. With the pressure gone, Ciari straightened up, staring at Lucas. "It's been a while."

Lucas stared at her, dark blue eyes unblinking as he assessed her mental state. "I can't fix what's wrong with you."

"I don't recall asking. Pick your sister off the floor."

Lucas didn't move. Samantha got to her feet with Kristen's help.

Keiko watched them warily, both hands pressed to the sides of her head. The pressure didn't help clear her mind of the pain. "Why are you here? Did Nathan send you?"

"Lucas." Kerr jerked his thumb at the other man. "It was his idea."

"He figured you wouldn't want to die," Jason said.

"As if he has the capacity to care," Keiko said.

"Considering I've gone out of my way to ensure your survival, kindly shut your mouth," Lucas told her as he set about divesting himself of the carrying cases he still held. He tossed one telekinetically to Keiko, and she had to catch it or risk it slamming into her chest. "You're going to need that."

"What is it?"

"A virus capable of reprogramming the neurotrackers. Every last one embedded in your Strykers."

"*What?*" Keiko said, her eyes riveted on the case in her hands. "That's suicide. Attempting to access the neurotrackers on that scale will get us all killed quicker than if Erik decided to flip every kill switch by himself."

"I see he's already started with Ciari."

"Leave her out of this," Jael said, voice hard.

"She agreed to it," Lucas said, glancing at Ciari. "There's no backing out now."

"You didn't give her a choice."

Ciari tipped her head to the side, face disturbingly blank. "He didn't need to. It was either take this chance and find a way out, or do nothing and die when the government is done using us up. We psions don't live long, Jael. Twenty-five at the most, thirty years if we're lucky. Longer than that if the government deems us useful, but not by much. How many times did you wish you were born free? I want that for my daughter."

"Wait," Keiko said weakly. "Ciari—what are you talking about?"

"The newest Serca," Kristen answered from where she stood beside Samantha. "But Ciari hasn't named her yet."

Aidan's and Keiko's shock was hard to miss, but they'd spent a good chunk of their lives playing with secrets no one else knew about. They took the news in stride, even if it didn't make them happy.

"I really want you to be lying," Aidan said. "But I know you aren't."

Jael took the case Keiko was holding and opened it, staring down at the secured hyposprays. "Nanites. You know this is dangerous. We only ever use them in a biotank and only within strict medical parameters. How do we know you're not trying to kill us all before the launch to get us out of the way?"

"Unlike Nathan, I never had any intention of leaving Earth," Lucas said.

Jael huffed out an angry little laugh. "Of course you didn't."

"Look, I've been the least agreeable since Lucas took us out of the Slums," Jason said, glancing from one group to another. "I don't like Lucas, and he knows it, but I've seen the source code for this virus and it's good. Better than good. While it won't be able to turn off the tracking signal, it will be able to turn off the kill switch without alerting the World Court. It will save us."

"We're scattered all over the planet," Keiko said. "The Strykers are all working to transport registered humans to the Paris Basin as well as fight off attacks by unregistered humans. It's becoming difficult to do both. Everyone wants a spot on those shuttles and a berth on the *Ark*."

Lucas shook his head. "The logistics will be worked out."

"Really? Thought of everything, have you?" Jael said. "I'm not buying it."

"Then read our minds," Kerr told her. "We aren't lying about any of this."

Jael looked from face to face, seeing only determination in their expressions. "Drop your shields."

First Kerr, then Jason and Quinton, dropped their shields and power washed through the mental grid. Jael wasn't going to risk her sanity by trying to read the minds of Nathan's children, so she settled with the soldiers who had once been under her medical authority. Sliding into their thoughts, she came across psychic wounds that were half-healed and deeper ones that might not ever heal. When you lived with something for so long, you got used to its being there, even after it was gone.

Like the spark right before an inferno, she didn't realize what she was falling into until Jason's mind seemed to swallow her whole. Even with his shields down, Jason's power was difficult to quantify. It filled the mental grid around them, his psi signature an imprint Jael had never experienced before.

Oh, Jael said into Jason's mind, her thoughts colored with awe. *No wonder the mental grid almost broke.*

She sifted through their thoughts and memories, skimming over the conscious and subconscious areas of their minds. Jael struggled to stay focused, the vast power that Jason harbored now difficult to work through. She sent her mind twisting down the anchoring bond that tied him to Quinton, letting her telepathy pool in the back of Quinton's mind, feeling the emptiness in Kerr's.

I can't undo this, Jael said almost apologetically to the three of them.

No, you can't, Quinton agreed, sounding resigned. *We're not asking you to.*

It will kill you eventually. I can see what Lucas did, but you don't have the space in both your minds to hold your power in check, Jason.

There's enough, Kerr said. *It's why Lucas used Quinton and not me.*

They still weren't comfortable with the change, she could read that easily enough. It was permanent, a by-product of a fight that wasn't over yet.

Jael retreated from their minds, but she kept her attention on Jason. "What are you?"

"A microtelekinetic." Jason offered her a crooked little smile. "Anyone want to trade places with me?"

In the silence that followed his words, almost no one knew what to say. Quinton, however, had only one concern. "Where's Threnody?"

Jael pushed a few thin dreads behind her ear, getting her hair out of her face. "Alive."

Quinton headed for the door without another word.

"Where are you going?" Ciari said.

"To get my partner. I doubt you've changed the cells in this place since we left."

He was gone before anyone could stop him. Lucas looked over at Jason. "Go with him."

"If her wounds are extensive enough that she needs my help again, we'd be better off with sticking her into a biotank," Jason warned before hurrying after Quinton.

Jason found the other man about to run down a team of Strykers standing guard outside Ciari's office. They were refusing to let him pass. Before things got ugly, Jael came out and joined them, her presence alone guaranteeing their safety.

"I'll take you to Threnody," Jael said. "Follow me."

It didn't take that long to get to where they were holding Threnody, and the Strykers who saw them could only stare. Strangely, they didn't pass any humans. Even Jael seemed surprised until Lucas's telepathy crawled through their minds. *I'm not risking our presence here. The Strykers*

will do what Ciari says regarding us. The humans assigned here only obey the
government. They're guards as much as they are employees of this Syndicate.

What about the bioware nets? Jael asked.

I didn't touch their minds. Your Strykers are keeping them occupied else-
where.

Lucas disengaged his telepathy, leaving them alone. When they finally
reached Threnody's cell, Quinton wished Lucas hadn't left so quickly.
He'd have asked the other man to show the same sort of care Threnody
had received to Jael.

Quinton stared through the two-way viewing window at where his
partner lay, trying to control his temper. "Open it."

"What happened here was protocol," Jael said unapologetically. "We
did what we had to do in order to protect ourselves."

Quinton shot her a murderous glare and shoved past her once she
tapped in the code to open the door. Threnody was lying on her back,
the clothes she wore filthy with vomit and bloodstains, an external neurocollar locked around her throat. Blood was dried on her face and in
her hair, but Quinton didn't hesitate when he touched a hand to her
shoulder.

"Thren."

"Took you long enough," she croaked out, but no heat was in her tone.

Jason knelt down on her other side as Threnody opened her eyes.
"Thought I told you not to undo all my hard work?"

She managed a tight smile. "Couldn't help it."

Jael leaned over and pressed her thumb to the sensor lock on Threnody's
neurocollar. The biometrics read her print and it unlocked. Jael got out
of the way so Quinton could carefully pry the restraint off, pulling the
bioware-tipped needles out of Threnody's skin and spine as carefully as
he could. He tossed the neurocollar aside, hearing it clatter against the
floor somewhere behind him.

Jason rested his fingers against the back of Threnody's hand and let
his power sink into her body. His vision layered itself to countless degrees
of magnification, creating a kind of vertigo that made his stomach heave
as he felt the damage in Threnody's body along his own nerves.

"Ribs," he said clinically. "They're bruised and cracked, but not broken. Nothing that would account for the blood."

"You'll need Lucas for that." Threnody coughed. "They broke all my shields. His is the only one I've got left."

"Bastards. All right, hold still. You're lucky I got all that practice working on Quinton's face and arms."

Jason knit bone back together quicker than he had with Quinton. Practice and use was going a long way to showing him how this was supposed to work. It was like building something tangible with his hands, only he was using his mind to reshape cells. Jason didn't have any nanites this time to guide him, but he was beginning to realize he didn't need them.

Threnody finally took in a deep, unlabored breath and turned her hand over to squeeze Jason's. "Thanks."

"Don't mention it."

Quinton helped Threnody to a sitting position, supporting most of her weight. "You need a shower and some rest."

"I *want* a shower and some rest. I *need* to know what's happening." Threnody rubbed carefully at her throat and the small holes leaking blood there. "Get me up, Quin."

Between Jason and Quinton, they got Threnody to her feet. Threnody bared her teeth at Jael in a smile when she saw the other woman. Jael didn't seem bothered by the animosity.

"You should have asked," Threnody said. "I would have told you the truth."

"Maybe you should have let me into your mind," Jael retorted.

Threnody turned her head to look at Quinton. "Take me to Lucas."

[TWENTY-NINE]

Nathan stared down at the limp form of his son on the medical bed, studying the stress and agony lines that ravaged Gideon's young face. His mind wasn't much better, a jagged mess of broken thoughts and missing memory. When Gideon had teleported into the Warhound arrival room, Nathan was forced to abandon his job overseeing the last of the seed bank transfers from his Syndicate in London to Paris and help save his only remaining child.

The damage Lucas had done to Gideon's mind was uniquely twisted, but had echoes of Nathan all throughout. Nathan had trained Lucas extensively in the capabilities of a Class I power and he had learned those lessons well. This torture went deep, seemingly cutting out the most recent memories stored in the short term before widening out for days, sometimes weeks past. Nathan wondered about that. Wondered just what his oldest son was trying to hide that Gideon had found out—and now no longer knew.

No answers were to be found in Gideon's mind. Nathan stopped the mindwipe from doing any more damage, but he couldn't fix what was already torn apart. Lucas knew the value in total eradication, and that's what he'd attempted here. It was sheer luck that Gideon managed to make it back to London, luck that had a name: Samantha. Her act of guilty compassion stood out in bright relief in Gideon's mind, the thing he'd clung to in order to escape. It didn't absolve her.

Nathan stood with his hands in the pockets of his suit jacket and closed his eyes, thinking about his options and how little time he had left. The Genome Privacy Act he'd lobbied for weeks ago merely legalized actions taken by his family over decades at the behest of the World Court.

It enabled him to search out unregistered humans without needing to hide his actions anymore.

Nathan was supposed to have weeks left to seed the Registry with targeted, unregistered humans who had unclean DNA. They were essential to his plans for Mars Colony, because high-Classed psions only came from the dregs of humanity. He'd been planning to have Gideon help him coordinate the movements of all those people and the Warhounds to the launch site, but now it fell on him alone, as it always did.

I wonder, Marcheline, Nathan thought, thinking of his long-deceased mother, *if you realized you were throwing everything away when you demanded I breed four children instead of just one.*

She'd forced him to break with tradition, ignoring the personal bylaws that the Serca family ran on. It didn't matter, not anymore. Marcheline died years ago and Nathan was left dealing with the fallout of her orders—three lost children and one damaged heir.

Nathan opened his eyes and dipped his mind into Gideon's to wake him. *I need you to focus, Gideon.*

Dark blue eyes opened slowly, a faint glint of silver staining their depths. Nathan had seen that gleam before, in Kristen, a warning sign of impending insanity. "Father?"

More a question, not really recognition. Nathan grimaced. "On your feet."

Gideon slowly pushed himself to a sitting position before swinging his legs over the edge of the bed. "What happened?"

He didn't know, his mind a jumbled mess of fractured memories. Nathan didn't have the time to help Gideon sort it all out. The blank spots Nathan could feel in Gideon's mind were hard to accept, but he couldn't replace what had forcibly been lost.

"The details are in there," Nathan said, removing a hand from his pocket to point at the datapad sitting on the nearby table. "You can review it later. Right now, we need to move."

Gideon stood up on shaky legs, squeezing his eyes shut as a headache jolted through his skull. He blindly reached for the datapad. "I can't—where's Samantha? I can't feel her."

Confusion filled his voice, but no panic. No sense of the permeating ache Nathan had felt in Gideon's mind since Samantha's defection.

"I'm not concerned about your twin." Nathan looked over Gideon's shoulder at his new CMO, Hu Yin. The Class IV telepath stepped forward and firmly took hold of Gideon's arm, giving him support.

"I have his mind shielded," Hu said, his telepathic presence in Gideon's mind hard to miss. Hu carried a heavy medical trauma kit in his other hand. Trunks were stacked behind him, some bearing the international symbol of the Red Cross, still used by those who worked in the medical field, be they human or psion.

Nathan closed his eyes, blocking out everything.

Sharra, Nathan said, reaching for Erik's wife through an increasingly volatile mental grid. *Open your eyes to me.*

The psi link they shared, thin and tenuous and part of her registered baseline, pulled stronger. Nathan saw the inside of a private waiting room that lacked any adornments and housed only chairs. He sensed people around her, just a few political aides and technicians. More than that, he sensed Dalia, his human spy.

Visual established, Nathan teleported himself, Gideon, and Hu into the room Sharra waited in at the Command Center above the flood of wastewater in Paris. The humans weren't expecting his arrival, but it didn't matter. Nathan telepathically put them to sleep where they sat, Dalia catching the only one who was standing. She dragged the heavier man over to a rickety chair.

"Nathan," Sharra said in a shaky voice as she held Lillian tighter, her daughter suddenly dead weight in her arms. Her blue eyes skated past him, taking in the sight of Gideon and Hu. She'd seen enough wounded psions in her life to know that Gideon was hurting.

"Dalia, lock the door," Nathan ordered.

"Are things that bad out there?" Sharra said as Nathan gestured Hu to take care of Gideon.

"The fact that you don't know means that you simply don't care."

Sharra swallowed and moved to lay Lillian down on the floor, on top of a small blanket that looked as if it came from the child's bed. She smoothed back some of her daughter's hair before straightening up again.

Nathan watched her, the look in his eyes flat. "When is Erik joining you?"

"I don't know. He and the rest of the justices are still at The Hague." Sharra tugged at the collar of her blouse, biting her lip. "The transfers are picking up, but they're still far under the numbers the World Court hoped to move. The launch was supposed to take weeks, not days. They're working to ensure enough of us get out before the riots get out of hand."

"So he's still trying to position himself as the savior of the world," Nathan said contemptuously.

"We wouldn't be in this situation if you had controlled your children."

Nathan reached for her, not with his hands, but with his mind. *I'm of the opinion that this insolence in our children comes from your side of the family.*

He telekinetically slammed her down into the nearest chair with enough force to bruise her tailbone. Biting back a cry of pain, Sharra held herself still. She knew better than to fight, not here.

I got what I bargained for, Sharra thought bitterly as Nathan approached. A bargain between a psion and a human was never really a bargain. She had learned that lesson late in life, but she still learned it.

"Yes, you did," Nathan said, reading her thoughts. "Survival. I know the new timeline for the launch. I was notified when Erik authorized the changes. That infiltration program you set up on my orders proved useful, like yourself."

"What do you want?"

Nathan tilted her chin up with his hand, releasing his power. She could move, but Sharra didn't dare. "You'll be taking Gideon with you on your assigned space shuttle. Remove someone else if you have to, but he is going with you."

Terror filled her mind, worry for her daughter an almost overriding partner to it. Sharra glanced down at where Lillian lay on the ground. She was a small thing, skinny, like her mother. Lillian was going to grow up beautiful, if she grew up at all.

"I wanted a life for her on Mars Colony," Sharra said desperately. "That's all I ever wanted."

"A mother's instinct and a mother's love. I can honestly say I've never felt either."

"That's because your mother was a monster."

Sharra remembered Marcheline only too well, remembered the paralyzing fear that always wracked her whenever the woman entered her prison cell in the Serca Syndicate all those years ago. Freedom from the streets meant wearing a golden collar in a gilded cage. City towers weren't all that much better than the gutter. Mars Colony was supposed to be the answer. Maybe it wasn't.

Gideon had never cared for the human side of his genes. It stood to reason he wouldn't care about his half sister. Sharra didn't want to lose Lillian.

"One of the few things we'll ever agree on," Nathan said. "I don't expect you to care about Gideon, but I know you'll care about your own life. Keep Gideon with your retinue until I get up there. Don't let anyone put you or him into cryo sleep."

"I wasn't planning on going through the procedure until Erik arrived on the *Ark*."

Nathan's smile was slight and condescending. "Keep being that dutiful wife, Sharra."

She jerked her chin up, finding a sense of defiance from somewhere. "I never regretted becoming this."

"No, you just regretted never knowing if Erik loved you. Would you like to find out?"

"Damn you."

She had always wondered—would always wonder—if it was Erik's own feelings or Nathan's psionic interference that existed in their marriage. The kind of courage it took to claw her way out of the streets of London was different from the strength it took to tear apart her carefully crafted second life.

Sharra was brave, but she wasn't stupid.

"Live with what you've made," Nathan said, taking a step back. "And get my son off this planet."

All Sharra could do was obey.

"Dalia," Nathan said. "Make sure they get on the next space shuttle."

The uniformed woman with an unremarkable face only nodded. "Of course, sir."

Nathan teleported out, the only one to leave. Those people rendered unconscious during Nathan's arrival snapped back to awareness, none the wiser of their brief blackout. Neither did they ask questions of the two newest faces in the room, Nathan having erased their curiosity and implanted new memories. Lillian stirred at Sharra's feet, and Sharra bent to pick up her daughter and pull the girl onto her lap.

"I fell asleep?" Lillian asked, yawning through the question. She rubbed at her face with one small hand, looking and sounding grumpy. All her toys were packed away and she was bored.

Sharra tucked Lillian's head under her chin and closed her eyes. "Just for a little while."

She rocked her daughter in her arms, thinking about what it took for her to reach this moment. From the streets of London to the isolated glitter of The Hague. From the launch out of Paris, then the flight to the moon and the colony ship there by way of space shuttles painstakingly reverse engineered from those left behind after the burgeoning age of space was destroyed by bombs.

For far longer than the length of Sharra's life, the government had been making careful forays into space to hone the skills needed for this venture and to bring the *Ark* back online for their escape. So much effort, so much deceit, so much hope placed over the decades for the safety and survival of the human race onto the shoulders of the men and women who ascended to the World Court.

All of it useless in the face of the Serca family's machinations and desire for the same freedom Sharra and those like her wanted.

"Sharra."

She grimaced at her name coming from her son's mouth. "What?"

"I'm not going with you."

She opened her eyes and lifted her head in shock. "But Nathan—"

Sharra never finished her sentence, much less her thought. A foreign telepathic touch invaded her mind, ignoring the risk of being discovered by the bioware net. It didn't matter anymore. Her orders didn't matter because she no longer remembered Nathan delivering them.

Sharra blinked, staring dazedly around the room, wincing against the tension headache that pounded through her head. The woman charged by Nathan to look after them approached and nodded down at Sharra and Lillian. Dalia looked how Sharra felt. "Let's get you on a space shuttle, Mrs. Gervais."

Sharra nodded and stood with Lillian in her arms. It took several minutes for everyone to get organized and leave the room. The small group was met in the hallway by a scientist who took them to the ready room being used for the more important transfers. They were helped into space suits by a dozen workers, bodies wrapped in an enclosed environment that made Sharra feel claustrophobic. She held Lillian's hand tightly in hers and followed every order given to her.

Dalia walked them to the small dock shuttle and helped them get settled before letting the pilot know they were ready. The jaunt to their assigned space shuttle was short. The dock shuttle locked into place against a shielded transport tube and the hatch opened. Sharra took in a heavy breath and undid her harness, then Lillian's. One step, then another, took her closer and closer to an escape she wasn't sure would save them.

"Mama?" Lillian said as they were escorted into the space shuttle by its crew. "I'm scared."

Sharra knelt in front of her daughter and framed the child-size helmet with her hands. She managed to dredge up a smile from somewhere. "I know. But everything's going to be fine. Be my brave little girl, darling. I'll be right here with you."

"Promise?"

"Always."

They were strapped into their assigned seats so tightly it hurt to breathe. Sharra held Lillian's hand in her own as hard as she could and didn't let go.

Erik, she thought. *I'll see you soon.*

Sharra would remember leaving Earth in flashes, not whole memories. How the space shuttle's engines roared in her ears and shook her bones. How the g-forces flattened her body against the curve of her seat. The way her breath was forced out of her lungs as the pressure got worse down the two-kilometer-long, curved launch ramp before they were flung into the sky. The sharp pop of her ears over and over as the space shuttle gained altitude, struggling to break orbit on a one-way trip to a new life. The way she never let go of her daughter's hand.

Left behind on the ground, Gideon watched the space shuttle until he couldn't see even the spark of it anymore. Beside him in the viewing room, Hu watched Gideon with a frown on his face. "You should have been on that shuttle."

Gideon pressed the heel of his palm against his forehead. "I don't need you questioning my actions."

"I shouldn't be doing this, Gideon. Nathan wanted you on the *Ark*."

"Nathan needs to learn I'm the only one he's got to rely on. He can't do that with me in space."

Hu let out a heavy sigh. "Then let's find a private room to wait. It'll give me time to sort out your mind."

Gideon turned away from the window and the view stretched out beyond it, no longer interested in what it had to offer.

PART SIX
SALVATION

SESSION DATE: 2128.04.09

LOCATION: Institute of Psionics Research

CLEARANCE ID: Dr. Amy Bennett

SUBJECT: 2581

FILE NUMBER: 308

"You broke it," Aisling says as she tugs on the short sleeve of her yellow dress. A wire is caught in the fabric and she frees it with careful fingers. She kicks her feet where they dangle in the air.

"We didn't break anything," the doctor replies, not looking up from the datapads on the table.

"Tell that to the people of Río Gallegos."

The doctor's head snaps up, face turned toward the two-way mirror near the door. She makes a gesture with one hand, one she has made before.

"Too late," Aisling sighs. "You're always too late. Bombs away."

The doctor slams her hand against the table, shaking it. "We wouldn't still be in this situation if you helped us!"

"If I could help you, I would, but you would still be in this situation." The girl slides a little in her chair, her small head tilting back. She stares at the ceiling, with its bright lights, and doesn't blink. "Please don't be mad. I'm trying to fix this."

"How? How are you trying? You're not giving us the information we need."

"I'm sorry, but you wouldn't understand."

[THIRTY]

The Strykers Syndicate was pared down to a skeleton crew over the course of hours. Every Stryker was ordered into the field to deal with the escalating riots, including those who were still recovering from wounds incurred in Buffalo or elsewhere. To stay behind meant dereliction of duty and the promise of instant termination. That was the order of the World Court, and Ciari heeded the warning. Their absence meant Lucas's small group had far fewer people to run into and risk tipping off the government.

They gathered in a debriefing room, standing around a large conference table that had the small carrying cases stacked neatly across it. Everyone's attention was on the vidscreen embedded in the wall.

"This isn't going to trip an alarm, is it?" Jael asked.

"I know government code and I learned a few new tricks while on the run," Jason said, never taking his eyes off the vidscreen. "They won't know we're hooked up where we're not supposed to be."

"Will it last?"

"Longer than the measures you've got running in Ciari's office to hide your activities."

The vidscreen showed a view none of them had ever before seen. A hazy, ethereal blue glow seemed to smudge the center, dividing black from a curve of gray-blue. The cloud formations were gray and thin over a murky blue ocean. The darkening shape of a continent moving into night seen from space was unfamiliar. The old satellite they were using didn't have the best focus capabilities after decades of floating through space without upgrades. Still, Lucas knew what was happening when he saw it.

"There," Lucas said, leaning forward, eyes on the grainy picture.

A tiny, brightly glowing dot was lifting off the planet, rising into space. It grew larger, the satellite bringing the shape into focus. It was a space shuttle, the first of many, and no one could look away as it left Earth behind and disappeared offscreen. More space shuttles followed the first.

"That's the start of it," Lucas said. "We'll only have so much time left now. A few days at the most."

"With the amount of people they need to move, I'd think it would be longer," Keiko said.

"The launch site was built to house space shuttles, not people. It's a bottleneck in terms of movement. It's why the government wanted to do this over the course of weeks, not in the middle of a panic. They can't hope to ship thousands and thousands of people into space, then put them all into cryo on the colony ship quickly. Cryo is complicated and there are only so many doctors on board the *Ark* who can oversee the process."

"Which means a lot of people won't make it," Ciari said, staring at the vidscreen.

"If a registered human misses their shuttle to Paris, then there's no chance for them."

"And the ones in space?" Threnody said.

Lucas shrugged. "I've seen the schematics of the *Ark*. It's mostly storage space, bays and bays of cold boxes for cryo sleep and storage units for supplies. Easier to pack bodies in as cargo than as passengers. You use up less space if you don't have to factor in living quarters for anyone but the crew."

"Will that ship make it to Mars in one piece?"

"It's survived over two hundred and fifty years cold-docked in space. It'll survive a few more."

Ciari stared across the table at him. "You don't want it to."

"I thought we could let them go, let them fly to some uncertain future." Lucas ran a hand through his hair, nails scratching against his scalp. "We'd have Earth, which is all I ever wanted, but they would return."

"Are there Warhounds on the space shuttles launching right now?" Quinton wanted to know.

"There will be Warhounds on every single one until Nathan has transferred them all."

It went unsaid that when the *Ark* returned from a failed colonization on another world, it would arrive bearing humans and psions beholden to Nathan, who would fight for his rightful place in society. The world didn't need another war.

"What now?" Kerr said. "You want to stop the launch? How do we do that and save the Strykers as well?"

"Distributing the virus has priority. We're going to need everyone free to help fight, because we won't be enough on our own, even merged," Lucas said.

"Can you be sure they won't run away?" Samantha said, not looking at her brother. She hadn't looked him in the eye since letting Gideon go free. "If I was a Stryker and no longer had a neurotracker in my head, I'd go to ground in an instant."

"When I give an order, Strykers obey," Ciari said. "You weren't trained how we were. Don't believe all of us will abandon our posts. Freedom won't mean anything if we don't have a place to stay and live."

"Speaking of living," Keiko said. "The government only has half the supplies from the seed bank in the Arctic. I helped Nathan organize the transfer of everything left. If that's what they were using to replenish the SkyFarms over the years, we're going to need the rest of it. Where did you take it, Lucas?"

Lucas smiled at the question. "I see someone found my little message in the wall."

"Your damn message got a Stryker killed. Where's the rest of the seed bank?"

"Safe. You don't need to know where."

Keiko opened her mouth to argue, but Ciari interrupted her with "That's all we need to know, Keiko. Leave it be."

Threnody spared a glance at Jael before saying, "If we want the Strykers to believe what we tell them about the virus, they'll need to hear the reason from an officer."

"That's why Keiko will be with Jason and Quinton to administer the virus," Lucas said. He cut off Quinton's protest with a look and a warning touch against the pyrokinetic's mental shields. "I'm sending Threnody and Kerr on a different mission that requires their powers. Aidan will monitor Keiko's progress, and when she returns, I'll teach her the basics of merging."

"What about them?" Aidan said, pointing at Lucas's sisters.

The permanent smile on Kristen's face was half covered by one hand, which she used to prop up her chin. She was seated next to Samantha, tapping her fingers against the edge of the table. "We're going to the City of Lights."

"Where is that?" Jason said. "I've been to almost every city that's left in this world. I've never heard of that one."

"Paris," Samantha answered in a clipped voice. "We're getting Lucas a sitrep on security at the launch site. No one will question us Sercas being there if humans discover our presence."

"Is that safe with the amount of Warhounds that will be around? Not to mention the toxicity of the surrounding area."

"The radiation won't be as high as it was in the past, but it's still intolerable, especially if you're human." Samantha shrugged. "We need to know what's happening in Paris now that we no longer have people providing us inside information."

"It's been so long, you'd think the radiation would fade," Jael said. "But it doesn't. It just gets in your cells and lingers."

"Sounds like everything's been decided," Quinton said, turning his back on the room and the space shuttles on the vidscreen that were still launching. "Come get me when it's time to go into the field."

He left, ignoring Threnody when she called out his name. Sighing in frustration, she shoved away from the conference table, calling over her shoulder to the room at large, "I'll be back."

Jason's careful, meticulous hack of the security system that spanned the Strykers Syndicate had been limited. Quinton couldn't go far. Threnody found him in a room that held rows of empty research terminals, the people who would have manned them currently reassigned. Quinton didn't immediately look up at her arrival.

"Hey," Threnody said, putting her back against the door.

"You could have argued," he said after a moment, letting his hands rest on the edge of a terminal as he glared at her. "You could have done something other than accept everything that comes out of Lucas's mouth."

"Where would that have gotten us? This is the only course of action. If it means we have to work apart, then we work apart."

"You don't know if this is the only way."

"Yes," Threnody said quietly. "I do."

She had faith in a child that no one alive had ever met, that no one ever would except through saved encrypted files. Maybe Threnody didn't trust Lucas, but she trusted in his goal, and Quinton couldn't doubt that, because it meant he'd be doubting her. Quinton shook his head and tried to smile, but it came out wrong, crooked. She saw it for what he meant it to be.

"Damn it," he whispered. "Why can't I ever argue with you?"

Threnody shrugged. "Maybe you should have. I'm the reason why we got sent to the Slums in the first place, remember? Maybe if you reminded me to toe the line growing up, fulfill our contracts without arguing, and do as we were ordered, we wouldn't be here."

"It wasn't my place to tell you how to do your job, Thren. It was my place to follow where you led."

Threnody pushed away from the door and went to his side. She adjusted the flak jacket he wore, settling it more evenly on his broad shoulders. Threnody let her hands rest there, thumbs pressed against the bare skin of his neck. She could feel the electric pulse that ran through his body, a thing she knew just as intimately as she knew her own.

"I'm glad," Threnody said, "that they gave you to me as my partner, Quin. I don't regret that, and I don't regret everything that brought us here to do this. I just hope you won't either."

Quinton splayed one hand against the back of her head, fingers digging through her loose hair. He leaned down to press his forehead to hers, staring into her eyes. Conviction filled Threnody's voice, the same conviction that had gotten them through countless hellish missions over the years. It was a belief that they could survive anything, that they could survive this, and Quinton wondered what he would do without her by his side, shoring him up.

"I don't regret you," he said.

She offered up a tired smile, some of the tension leaving her body. They were family, no matter how hard the government tried to beat that belief out of them. A few years shy of thirty, the two of them, and they had survived so much. Psions had long memories, and forgetting anything that happened in their lives was damn near impossible. The neural pathways linking the intricate relationships of memories meant a lifetime could be recalled with crystal clarity. In that lifetime, they would always have each other.

"Come on," she said, pulling away, eyes clear of everything except determination. "Let's get back to the others."

When they returned to the conference room, they found only Lucas and Kerr waiting for them. The vidscreen was running the satellite feed, but nothing of interest was happening. It seemed the launch was at a lull. Lucas focused his attention on Quinton once the other man stepped inside.

"I don't like disobedience," Lucas said.

"You're going to get a lot of it when you free the Strykers," Quinton said. "If you're hoping to grind us under your heel when this is over, you're not going to like what happens."

Lucas nodded at the door, ignoring the threat. "Go find Jason. He's with Keiko figuring out the best route for teleportation over the continents."

Quinton knew a dismissal when he heard one. He still hesitated, wondering if he could get away with remaining in the room. Threnody shook her head. "Go, Quinton. It'll be all right."

"Watch your back," Quinton said as he left. The door slid shut behind him.

Threnody eyed Lucas. "What now?"

"Everyone has their orders but you two," Lucas said. "I'll explain what needs to be done after we leave tomorrow."

"Why?" Kerr said.

"We need to pick up Novak. You need a hacker and Ciari can't spare one from the Stryker ranks."

"And you can't spare Jason," Threnody said. "When we get Novak tomorrow morning, where are you teleporting us? What do you want us to do?"

Lucas smiled, the expression an echo of Nathan's ruthlessness, Nathan's cruelty. "You're going to steal a bomb."

[THIRTY-ONE]

SEPTEMBER 2379
PARIS, FRANCE

The streets of London echoed with the voices of rioters demanding entry to the restricted area around the city towers. Bodies were strewn in the street near where military defense holed up, but people still struggled forward over the fallen. Segregation based on the cleanliness of a person's DNA had been the norm for centuries, rarely challenged, and always rigidly enforced. Now the government was applying segregation to an extent never before seen in society, and the people who had slipped through the cracks all their lives were refusing to be forgotten.

Unregistered humans weren't the only ones joining the growing worldwide fray. The military, with its scores of quads sent out to police what was left of the world, were made up of a mix of people. Some soldiers came from families that had barely made it into the Registry when the Fifth Generation Act was enacted. Other soldiers called the streets home. City towers refused to have unclean DNA in their midst, and the soldiers who patrolled those areas refused to work in the streets. The military had become as divided as the rest of society. It wasn't any great shock when it began to break apart and soldiers took opposite sides in the fight.

People held their ground in the streets of surviving cities, waves of protesters hitting against the anchor foundations of sealed city towers. In London, it was no different, and in the early light of morning, its streets were crowded.

Lucas's group teleported out of Toronto when it was full dark, arriving in London when the sun was starting to rise over the distant horizon. The air had a faint bite of cold to it, an early warning of the oncoming change of seasons. Dawn filtered through an overcast sky filled with smoke and pollution as their feet hit the roof of a tenement with a hard smack. Lucas was executing this part of the plan through shortened teleports, needing to conserve his strength for the oncoming fights ahead. The brief rest everyone had managed before scattering across the world was only that—brief.

A scan of the tenement proved it was almost empty, the majority of its inhabitants drawn to the riots. Lucas looked out over the city as he sent his mind skimming through the mental grid, tagging the population. People on the streets of London were closer to the foundations of the city towers near the Thames than any other territory. He wondered how long the registered humans would last before security was overwhelmed.

"I really hope they don't burn the city to the ground," Threnody said as she surveyed the area from behind her helmet. "There's less toxicity around here and there's no room in any of the other cities for this population. The bunkers couldn't handle the overflow."

"It will stand for now," Lucas said as he squinted into the dawn. The city tower he once called home was backlit by the rising sun. "Nathan still needs it as a launching point to Paris for his Warhounds. He's not going to risk losing them because of the riots."

All of them wore specialized skinsuits capable of shielding against radiation, with hard helmets instead of skinmasks coverings their heads. The places they needed to go weren't kind to survivors. Samantha adjusted the strap on her shoulder, the metal carrying case also shielded against radiation. It held extra supplies they couldn't risk getting contaminated, items she would need when they got to Paris.

Kristen wandered to the edge of the roof, crouching down beside the crumbling safety wall. "They're all so angry," she said, smiling through the words. She turned her head to glance back at her siblings, the sunlight skating over her gleaming dark blue eyes, turning them silver for an instant. "Are we going to keep it?"

"Don't concern yourself with London, Kris. It's not your problem."

Lucas lifted a hand and gestured at Kristen, telekinetically pulling her back from the ledge. She was deposited back beside Samantha, the older girl looking disdainfully down at her sister.

"I wish you would take her with you," Samantha said, pointing at Kristen. "I can handle Paris on my own."

"Perhaps, but Kris will keep you honest."

Samantha's mouth curled up contemptuously. "Don't trust me?"

They were all three of them Sercas, with complicated blood ties and psi links that bound them together to an impossible degree. Lucas was supposed to one day own their family's Syndicate, and the rest were simply supposed to fall in line and obey. He had learned—eventually—that blind obedience was never useful.

"I trust you more than you could possibly imagine," Lucas said, surprising Samantha with that confession. Then he telekinetically yanked her to his side, Samantha's body cutting through the air until she was eye to eye with him, feet centimeters above the ground. "But don't mistake your freedom for something it isn't."

Samantha stabbed her telepathy into his mind, holding it against his shields, knowing better than to attack any further. That Lucas let her get that far had more to do with his twisted sense of generosity than her skill. Something deep in his mind resonated in her own, and it sparked pain throughout her head.

She closed her eyes for a second or two. "What did you do to me?"

"What had to be done."

He shoved her away, retracting his telekinesis. Samantha couldn't keep her balance and fell, skidding against the grit and old debris on the rooftop. Her teeth bit through the inside of her cheek at the impact. Swearing, she got to her feet, swallowing blood and saliva.

"If this is what having siblings is like, I think I'm glad I never knew mine," Kerr said.

Samantha shot him a dirty look. "A field partner is nothing like a family."

Kerr gave her a pitying look. "Yeah, but I never have to watch my back around them."

Kristen closed the distance between herself and Samantha, wrapping her arms around the other girl's waist and resting her head on Samantha's shoulder. Kristen only had eyes for Lucas. "It hurts here. Can we stay?"

"No," Lucas told her. "We can't."

Samantha extracted herself from Kristen's grip. "She's unstable, Lucas. She's going to make this mission difficult. You really should have left her behind."

"She'll be all right." Lucas glanced in the direction of the city towers before saying, "Hold on everyone."

The next teleport was shorter than the last, taking them to Paris. They arrived on a dilapidated street braced by the gutted remains of buildings survived only by their foundations. Some streets were collapsed into the subways, quarries, and sewers that existed beneath the old city. They could make out a few scraggly trees and bushes nearby, none of which looked healthy.

What they could see of the city around them consisted of hard, discolored dirt in craters that broke up ancient asphalt, and stunted vegetation that crawled over the surrounding ruins. In the distance, a rusted and broken Eiffel Tower clawed for prominence in a sky that was eclipsed by launch platforms built over the dead city. Sunlight was a bit brighter here; they'd lost an hour in that split-second teleport.

Threnody walked a few meters away from the group, slowly turning to take in a rotting city that had been one of the greatest capitals on earth. "Hard to believe millions once lived here. I wonder what it was like?"

"Loud, cramped, and noisy, I would guess," Kerr said. "Like a bunker city, but with sky over your head instead of a metal roof and dirt beyond it."

Samantha looked across the distance that separated them from the launch platforms. Even as they watched, a space shuttle was barreling down the long, curved launch ramp, hurtling itself into the sky. The smoke trails of previous launches left a haze in the air. The hard helmets they wore made it impossible for them to smell the exhaust and stagnant pollution.

Warhounds are scattered all over those platforms, Samantha said at the edge of Lucas's mind. She went to pull Kristen away from a crumbling set of ruins that had caught her attention.

Nathan might be holding them back, Lucas replied. *Probably to coordinate the transfer of their people. I doubt they'll need to get rid of any extrane-*

ous registered humans anytime soon. There's plenty of seats right now for them to take over.

We need to get inside.

I know. I'm looking for the right pair of eyes. Lucas had his own closed in concentration.

Once we have what you need, what then?

I'll bring you back and we stand our ground, so to speak.

Samantha glanced over at him. *You're serious about the Strykers, aren't you?*

Yes. We need them just like we need the humans that are being left behind. More so, since they're going to be our source of power.

You really think they'll bow to you? After so many years dying for the humans, do you honestly think once they've tasted freedom, the Strykers will accept you holding them down again?

I'm the one who made their freedom possible. You'd be surprised what sort of loyalty that can buy.

Samantha's hand tightened on Kristen's shoulder, an involuntary protest to the knowledge that her loyalty hadn't been bought, but forcibly imposed on her.

"Found her," Lucas said, opening his eyes.

"Found who?" Kerr asked.

"Dalia."

Kristen perked up at the name and let out a gleeful little chuckle. "Nathan isn't going to be happy you've touched his toy."

"I'm not going to use her mind. The fact that she's still here means Nathan hasn't arrived yet. She's coordinating shuttle routes."

Lucas didn't use Dalia to get a visual. Instead, he skimmed through the static human minds showing up on the mental grid, dipping in and out of dozens until he found the one he needed. The scientist in question knew the layout of the Command Center, knew the restricted areas that people left vacant for hours. Lucas pried from the man's memory the image of a dimly lit room belowground, surrounded by metal and machines.

It wasn't the best thing to draw from—human memory was so easily broken—but he managed to piece the room together through other people's memories once he knew what to look for. When he finalized the visual, Lucas teleported them into a cramped generator room. They dropped down onto a metal floor, all five of them appearing in the small aisle between machines.

Kerr moved and bumped his shoulder against a safety railing as machines thrummed loudly around them. "Shit, Lucas. Cutting it a little close, aren't you?"

"I know the space I 'port into," Lucas said.

Threnody craned her head around, taking in the loud machinery. "Where are we?" she asked, raising her voice in order to be heard.

"One of the support columns that holds up the Command Center."

"We're surrounded by wastewater? Bloody hell," Samantha said as she undid the helmet of her skinsuit and pulled it off. She scratched around the bioware lining her face to hide her identity. "Is using Dalia an option at all, Lucas?"

He shook his head. "Nathan's been in near constant contact with her. Don't try it."

"She'd be the best source of information on security."

"Which has all been severely altered due to the move-up of the launch. I don't want to gamble on Nathan discovering our presence."

"All right." Samantha dropped her case to the floor. Kneeling, she dug through it for the clothes she and Kristen would wear to disguise themselves and the dark glasses that would hide their distinctive eyes. "Kristen and I will get you what you need. I'll contact you when we're finished for an extraction."

"Don't get caught," Threnody said.

"I know how to do my job," Samantha said without looking up.

Lucas didn't say good luck or good-bye before teleporting out. Samantha didn't expect him to. Their family didn't believe in something as flimsy as luck. Blackmail, torture, and political maneuverings, yes—but not luck.

[THIRTY-TWO]

The drug cartels have overridden the barriers around the city towers in Sapporo, sir," an aide said, looking at a point over Erik's shoulder. "Reports coming in state that four of the thirteen city towers have been destroyed by dissident bombings."

Erik half rose from his desk, hands pressed flat against it. *"What?"*

The aide drew in a shaky breath, sparing a glance down at the datapad he held in his hand. "That's all we have at the moment. We're still trying to get numbers on casualties."

"There shouldn't *be* any goddamn casualties!" Erik snarled. "Where were the Strykers when this happened?"

"In the field, sir. The security grid showed that some died during the collapse."

"They died during a collapse that shouldn't have happened. Where was the military? Where were the rest of the Strykers dispatched to protect registered humans?"

The aide swallowed, glancing over his shoulder at the door he'd come through. "The, ah, the OIC of the Strykers Syndicate is here to address that."

Erik froze where he stood, body going tense. His eyes narrowed at that announcement, fury momentarily twisting his face into something ugly. "Bring her in."

The aide scurried out; Ciari let herself inside. Erik studied the bald woman as she approached his desk, her steps careful. Her punishment had left marks etched into her skin. Erik couldn't recall anyone wearing a more empty expression than Ciari wore on her face right now. It was like seeing a dead soldier walking and it should have brought some measure of comfort to him, but it didn't.

"My aide informed me that we lost city towers in Japan," Erik said through clenched teeth. "Explain yourself."

"The Strykers weren't holding the line" was Ciari's simple, easy answer.

"Come again?" Erik said after a moment, disbelief in his voice.

Rather than repeat herself, Ciari stepped closer and offered up the datapad she carried. Erik took it with surprisingly steady hands, the information on the screen making cold sweat creep down his back. He swiped his thumb over the screen, scrolling through the report, some distant hint of panic rising inside him as he studied the changed placement of Strykers.

"Has this been verified?"

"In Japan and elsewhere, but not across the board." Ciari tilted her head to the side, staring at him with unblinking eyes. The weight of her attention made his skin crawl. "We can't reach some of the teams from our end back in Canada. I came to see if perhaps you were giving out orders I didn't know about. I can't do my job, Erik, if you don't let me."

With a sudden, vicious motion, Erik hurled the datapad at the far wall, a wordless shout ripping from his lungs. His atypical reaction didn't seem to faze Ciari.

"You can't do your *job*?" Erik shouted. "Is that why you're here? Because you can't do your fucking job and you want a reprieve?"

"If I begged, would it make a difference?"

"The Strykers aren't doing their job and people are dying, Ciari. *Good people.* Their lives are worth a hundred times as much as you psion dogs."

Erik stalked out of his office. Black spots danced across his vision as he hurried down the halls of the Peace Palace. The building was mostly empty, the mass evacuation of the world capital and the bunker city beneath it having been well under way for hours. Staying longer was beginning to seem like a fool's choice.

He turned a corner blindly and nearly ran into Anchali, the much smaller and older woman catching her balance between her cane and the wall as she pulled up short. "Erik?" Anchali asked, taking in the fury on his face. Her attention jumped from him to the psion who followed obediently at his heels.

"Anchali," Erik said, hands clenching and unclenching near his thighs. "I'm sorry. If you'll excuse me?"

She caught him by the arm before he could walk past, her wrinkled face tilting up to look at him. "No, I will not. What is going on, Erik?"

He didn't turn to look at Ciari, but he could sense her presence. Erik was struck, rather viscerally, by how useless the layers of security that surrounded the Peace Palace were in the face of losing the upper hand. The military wouldn't be enough against Strykers who might have slipped their leash.

"I'm heading for the command information center." He was so careful to keep the fear out of his voice, to look only at Anchali. "Come with me."

Anchali didn't like what she saw in his face, but she wasn't going to leave him. She followed him to the center of the Peace Palace and the lift that would take them below to the barricaded and burrowed heart of the world's military.

Once there in those steel corridors, Erik headed for the area that handled communications with the Strykers Syndicate, to the officers whose sole job was to monitor and control the psions through technology. The Strykers Syndicate in Toronto was saturated with spyware and monitoring equipment, as well as formal programs for government communications. Through the world's security grid, the military could monitor every single Stryker baseline and their location through the neurotrackers in their brains.

"Show me Japan," Erik ordered as he strode into the operations hub.

Soldiers rushed to obey. Despite the world's fracturing, it was nice to know that military discipline was still intact. The vidscreens that circled the walls and terminals soon showcased the pulsing dots of nearly a hundred Strykers scattered across the map of the only inhabited island of Japan. The unique neural pattern of a psion's brain was fed through nerves into bioware, which then translated the information into a signal. The output of that signal was fed into the security grid by the neurotrackers. It was those signals that cut across the screens, solid placement of psion baselines pinpointing locations through satellite connections and bioscans in the security grid.

"Bring up the locations of all Strykers on a world map," Erik said, voice carrying through the buzz of conversation. "Priority given to my order."

His order was executed immediately, the data scrolling across the main command screen.

"Erik," Anchali said in a low voice, "what are you doing?"

"Laying to rest a problem."

It took five minutes to bring up and verify all Stryker positions across the globe, the government's security grid showing up in tiny patches across too-empty continents.

"Positions confirmed," a woman said.

Erik stepped to the nearest terminal, hand hovering over the controls. He turned, just enough that he could see Ciari and the blank expression on her face, but he couldn't find any emotion in her eyes.

"Will you beg now?" he asked, biting out the words. Her silence was answer enough, and Erik pressed his hand down against the sensor. "Initiate full termination sequence."

The soldiers overseeing the security grid obeyed instantly, activating the kill switch in every neurotracker the system was linked to. Anchali watched the vidscreens and the data while Erik refused to look away from Ciari.

"You're wiping them all out," Anchali said, her gaze sweeping across the storm of red that ripped across the map. Solid confirmation of roughly twelve hundred lives snuffed out in an instant.

Only the Stryker with them was still breathing and the signals on the screen were still showing up as active.

Erik staggered against the terminal, legs gone suddenly weak. He pressed his hand against the sensor a second, third, fourth time, but the results didn't change.

Ciari still lived.

"You—," Erik choked out.

Anchali heard fear in his voice for the first time in her life. She turned to see what could cause the president of the World Court to sound like that.

Erik knew that Ciari was only an empath. He had preferred dealing with that kind of psion over one who could read his thoughts. He had never felt that he constantly needed his hand on the kill switch when facing down an empath over contract issues and Stryker transgressions through the years. It struck him suddenly that he only knew the names of maybe a dozen psions in the entire Strykers Syndicate. The rest had always been nameless numbers on the company's bottom line.

They were never people to him. Never human. Erik had trusted blindly in the chains that science had built to contain the disease psions lived with, but technology could always be subverted. Diseases could evolve.

"We were informed of the World Court's decision regarding Strykers and the launch," Ciari said into the sudden silence. "We couldn't fight the orders when you told us to protect you."

The quads scattered throughout the room sensed the threat and moved, aiming their weapons at the enemy. They put themselves between the government and the lone woman who was still perfectly cognizant and alive in the face of people who had only ever used her kind.

Erik stared past the quads at her, voice coming out ragged and harsh. "And now?"

"We won't fight you." Ciari smiled slightly, the expression eerie and wrong on her face. "And we won't beg anymore."

"We *own* you," Anchali snapped out, wrinkled face ashen from shock.

Ciari pressed her fingers against a small, circular bruise that stood out on the side of her throat, the only evidence of Lucas's deceit, even if the humans didn't know it. "We own ourselves now."

"Ciari," Erik said. He thought of the eleven years he'd ordered her to live by his rules and all the rest before that when she'd fought in the hardscrabble streets of the world on orders from the government. Loyalty wasn't found in slavery.

"Stay on Earth, Erik," Ciari said. "If you stay, we can show you a different way."

"Go to hell."

The quads opened fire, but it was too late. Ciari was gone, teleported out to who knew where by some other newly freed Stryker, taking with her Erik's faith in the way the world worked.

[THIRTY-THREE]

SEPTEMBER 2379
THE SLUMS OF THE ANGELS, USA

Keiko teleported herself, Jason, and Quinton into a safe house buried in the Slums of the Angels. The broken mess of buildings and roads that surrounded the city towers of Los Angeles were where most of the population resided. She stumbled when her feet connected with the ground, and only Quinton's firm grip stopped her from checking out the floor of the arrival area with her face.

"You all right?" Quinton asked.

Keiko straightened up. She swiped at her nose and the faint hint of blood that leaked from it. "Yeah, I'm good."

"I could have pulled this round," Jason said.

"You teleported the last time, and you spent more time in Japan shielding than I did. It was my turn anyway."

They'd been teleporting across continents and oceans during the last sixteen hours without rest. That many teleports, across increasingly longer distances, mixed with the arguments and fights that inevitably broke out with every group of Strykers they met, had exhausted them. Quinton looked marginally better. After the first twelve times, he'd been the one to submit to telepathic verification by other Strykers to confirm the truth of their orders, sparing Keiko and Jason from having someone else mucking around in their minds.

Keiko took a moment to stretch her arms over her head, trying to ease the knotted tension in her body. "At least we've reached North America again. We're almost finished."

They knew they were working under a time limit and had hit the ground running back in Toronto before moving on to Buffalo. They kept going east, teleporting across the Atlantic Ocean to arrive in London and begin the hard task of giving Strykers the virus beneath the heavy presence of the government's security grid.

It had taken long hours to work their way through the Stryker ranks in Europe under the pretense of Keiko checking on their status as the world rioted. They couldn't reach their people in The Hague. Africa had been easier, with less than a dozen surviving cities across the entire continent. They bypassed the Middle East, which, like most of Russia and nearly all of Asia, was full of deadzones. They'd skipped from Africa to Asia's ravaged coastlines along the tip of India and the southeastern swatch of land appropriated by China. Australia was nothing but desert and firestorms, and they'd just come from Japan.

They still had two continents to work their way through, with at least 250 Strykers left that they needed to reach.

"Here's hoping this group doesn't argue like the last one," Quinton said tiredly as he touched the bruise on his face.

Jason snorted. "I can't believe you let her get past your defenses."

"I wasn't going to burn a fellow Stryker. I figured she'd accept Keiko's authority as chief operating officer after picking through my memories. How was I supposed to know she'd have an emotional breakdown?" Quinton shrugged uncomfortably. "She still believed us and didn't question Ciari's orders."

"Telepaths tend to believe more quickly than anyone else," Keiko said as she stepped off the arrival dais in the corner of the large garage. "So let's find one."

They didn't even reach the door before a short, young man was palming it open. Telekinesis slid against their own shields, a heavy weight that made Keiko's headache worse. "Daeng," she said. "We're here on the OIC's order."

Daeng pointed at Keiko's companions. "Sir, you know we've got kill orders for those two."

Keiko managed to dredge up a smile from somewhere. "Orders have changed. We're here to save your life and that of every other Stryker in the Slums."

He hesitated, not quite believing her, but they didn't have time to deal with wasted moments.

"You got a telepath on-site?" Jason said.

"Yes," Daeng said. "Tanya is our senior telepath right now. She's up-stairs."

"Call her down here so she can verify our actions and that we're not trying to kill any of you."

Daeng looked at Keiko for confirmation; she gave it. His eyes lost focus for a second or two as he tapped into the psi link he shared with his team. "Tanya's coming."

A minute later, a thin Mexican stepped into the arrival room, wariness in her gaze. "Sir?"

"Link with Quinton," Keiko said. "Ciari's orders."

Strykers knew better than to disobey their Syndicate's officers, especially the OIC. Tanya pulled Quinton into a psi link, taking the memories that he shoved into the forefront of his mind and reviewing them.

"You're kidding," Tanya said, staring at them in disbelief. "That should kill us."

"Hasn't killed anyone we've dosed so far," Quinton said.

"Ciari wants her Strykers to live," Keiko said, her voice cracking from exhaustion. "You will accept her orders and recall in shifts every Stryker in the Slums. We don't have time to waste on petty arguing."

"No," Tanya said after a moment. "I suppose we don't."

"Tanya?" Daeng said warily.

She gave the younger Stryker a lopsided smile, eyes bright. "It's fine, Daeng. We're going to follow their orders."

It took ten minutes for Tanya to telepathically contact all the Strykers assigned to the Slums and coordinate teleportation for everyone. Keiko, Jason, and Quinton left her to deal with the transfer while they went to set everything up.

The Slums were filled with rioters, the buffer zone around the city towers a veritable bloodbath between the military and assigned Strykers holding back the deluge of people hoping to reach a transfer shuttle. The safe house had been ignored only due to psionic interference. The World Court had tasked those Strykers in the Slums to keep everyone down on the ground and out of the city towers. Not that it mattered any longer, with most of the registered humans leaving, but the Strykers still had a job to do and they were going to do it to the bitter end.

That maybe the end wouldn't be so bitter was why no one really fought this procedure. The virus could save them, and no one living with a kill switch in his or her head was going to say no.

Jason rubbed a hand over his burning eyes as he gestured at the first few Strykers who had arrived. "Find a place to sit or lie down. It can't be administered standing up."

Daeng was the first to pick a spot, sliding to the floor with his back against the wall. "What exactly does it do?"

"Turns off the kill switch so the government can't fry your brain. The virus reprograms it around the internal security system. We can't turn off the tracking signal yet. If Strykers started going missing on the security grid in large numbers, the World Court would just fry everyone before we got to them," Jason said as he prepped the dosage. "Took the doctor who wrote the code months to get it right."

"What happened to the doctor?"

"He's still alive." Jason knelt down and pressed the tip of the hypospray against Daeng's throat. "Hold still. This is going to hurt."

"The government won't know?"

That was the fear and the choke hold that all Strykers lived with, the knowledge that if the neurotracker processed even a glitch in its programming, they would die. Jason tapped the hypospray gently against skin.

"It's bioware the code is targeting and nanites are machines." Jason smiled, but it was more teeth than anything else. "We're nothing more than biological machines, when you get right down to it. The virus is going to create a backdoor through our wetware. It'll take a few minutes to complete."

Jason stabbed his thumb against the hypospray button. The soft shushing sound the thin cylinder made as it pressed a dozen tiny needles into skin was echoed by air sucked through Daeng's teeth. Jason moved back and switched the hypospray to his other hand, lifting his free hand to scrape his teeth over the small bruise on his thumb.

He'd pressed that button hundreds of times since leaving Toronto. Those that received the shot came away with a perfect circular bruise on their throat, right over their carotid artery. The rest of the procedure was just as painful, as if the kill switch itself had been flipped.

The nanites, already activated within the hyposprays, followed their programmed orders. Even as Keiko, Jason, and Quinton urged the other Strykers to relax, the nanites were already moving through the internal carotid to where it joined with the arterial circle of Willis. From there, the nanites disseminated through the smaller capillaries and reached the areas where bioware filaments connected to the nerves and brain.

The neurotrackers, when the bioware died, felt as if they took their bodies with them, the way the Strykers thrashed against the agony, nervous systems out of whack and bodies suffering through an unwanted machine's death throes. When it was over, the Strykers remained unconscious for a minute or two as their bodies and brains adjusted to the absence of something they had lived with for most of their lives.

"Breathe," Keiko was saying to another Stryker. The recipient shoved herself up straight in her chair, face pale and bleeding from the nose. "Take a deep breath, it's going to hurt for about an hour."

The Stryker ran her fingers over the back of her head, where the neurotracker sat beneath skin and bone. "Hurt doesn't really cover it." She opened her mouth wide, trying to ease some of the pressure in her skull. "Fuck, that burns."

"You sure it's off? That it can't kill us?" Daeng said from where he sat. His breath was coming quick and fast through his mouth.

"We're sure. Ciari would never risk her people on something that wouldn't work," Keiko said. "The signal is still going strong. Take a minute to catch your breath, then get back to your posts."

Keiko, Jason, and Quinton managed to get through five more shifts of Strykers before the clock ran out. Their luck couldn't last, but that didn't stop Keiko from reaching desperately for the Stryker beneath her hands, who suddenly reared backward, clutching at his head. He started screaming and wasn't the only one. Other Strykers they had yet to dose keeled over screaming, clutching at the back of their necks and heads.

Keiko yelled wordless protests as bodies convulsed around her. She'd seen too many Strykers die like this over the years to not know what was happening. The mass termination was quick, but it was brutally painful to watch, made worse because they could do nothing. They had no way to save the Strykers writhing on the floor as their entire central nervous systems were fried from the inside out.

Keiko didn't know she was crying until she couldn't even see through the tears in her eyes.

"Fuck," Jason yelled, slamming his fist against the wall. *"Fuck."*

"We weren't finished," Keiko said, voice breaking as she stared at the bodies strewn around her. Reflexively, she clenched her hand around the hypospray she carried.

It wasn't just the Slums. They still had cities to pass through, Strykers to dose in the Latin Corridor and South America where they were embedded in cartel territories or the few actual cities that had survived below the equator. Only it didn't matter anymore, because they were too late, and all the remaining doses of the virus-carrying nanites were worthless.

Quinton carefully pried the hypospray out of her hand, wrapping his fingers around hers. "Keiko," he said, voice raw. "Take us back to Toronto."

He was asking her to focus when all she wanted to do was fall apart. Keiko swallowed thickly. "Such a fucking waste."

"I know. But our job isn't finished."

Keiko ran the back of her hand across her nose and took in a deep breath. "Tanya, deal with the bodies. We need to keep a presence in this city and that order comes directly from Ciari."

"We don't have to stay," Tanya said.

"Where will you go?" Keiko asked in a brutally hard voice. "That's what we asked everyone else we've dosed. Where will you be safe in a world that would rather see you dead if not leashed? That's a mentality we need to change, and it won't happen if we go running off to save our own asses or for revenge. It will get us nowhere."

Tanya ducked her head a bit, expression twisting as she stared down at the bodies of her fellow Strykers. "Do you care about the registered humans?"

"Not as much as the people on the street," Jason said, rubbing at his face. "We psions need them to survive, and anyone in the city towers who's not in a shuttle right now is shit out of luck. The World Court has to see the tracking signals are going strong, which means they've got to know most of us aren't dead. They'll push the launch even harder now."

"All right," Tanya said. "We'll hold the line for those on the street and help them fight off the military. We'll wait for Ciari's orders."

"Try to keep the city towers intact," Keiko said. "We're going to need something to live in when this is all over."

Keiko teleported the three of them back to where they started, arriving in Ciari's office back in Toronto. She looked around, realizing that everything in the office but the lights and a single vidscreen showing a map of the world was switched off. The only one to greet them was Jael.

The Strykers CMO's eyes were red. "You're back early."

"We didn't make it in time," Jason said, choking on the words.

"I saw." Jael tilted her head at the vidscreen. "On the monitoring system."

Keiko sucked in a deep breath and turned around to face Jael. "Where's Ciari?"

"She's gone. Left with Lucas for The Hague."

"Just now?"

"About an hour ago." Jael let her attention focus on Jason and Quinton. "Who is Aisling?"

"Fucking hell," Jason said. "What did they say?"

"Only that this is what Aisling wanted. Ciari's words, not Lucas's."

"Aisling," Quinton said, "is who Lucas has been taking his orders from, near as we can tell."

"Where is she? Can you bring her here?"

Jason and Quinton shared an uncomfortable look. "We've never met her," Jason said.

"Are you telling me that Lucas has been following orders from someone that you've never seen or spoken to? And you just blindly trusted in Lucas's word for this?"

"No, we don't blindly trust him. But he's been right every single time, and what he wants—" Quinton broke off to take a deep breath. "What Lucas wants is better for everyone in the long run."

"If I didn't know how many Stryker lives the Serca family has saved for us over the years, I'd be disgusted to know that you believe in their propaganda."

"We weren't scheduled for retrieval."

"Not by us," Jael agreed, a sharp look in her hazel eyes. "I'm thinking Ciari had her own agenda."

"You think?" Keiko said. "Aren't you in her mind?"

Jael sighed and shook her head. "Ciari ordered me to sever the psi link."

"What the hell is wrong with her?" Quinton said.

"You know Erik fried her brain," Keiko said. "She almost died. What you don't know is that the psi surgery went wrong and she lost control of her empathy."

"She turned off part of her own mind," Jael said quietly, looking down at her hands. "I told her to. It was the only way to save her."

The silence that followed that remark was uncomfortable and difficult to fill. Keiko chewed on her bottom lip before asking, "Can we kill the signals in the neurotrackers now that we no longer need to hide our freedom? We don't need the government knowing where we are anymore."

"There's a way," Jason said. "I need access to the government's working satellites, though."

"I can get you that. We should do it now before they try to cut us off." Keiko waved a hand at Jason and Quinton, beckoning them to follow her out of the office. "We'll be on the command level, Jael."

The door slid shut behind them, their footsteps fading away. Jael looked around at an office she had wandered in and out of for years. She wondered what the walls remembered of her, if the history embedded in this place would paint her as something other than a desperate woman trying to survive.

"Computer, activate. Chief medical officer override," Jael said, digging her fingers into her thighs, nails scratching at her uniform. The terminal behind her switched on.

"Receiving," the disembodied voice said. "Voice identification confirmed. Command required."

"Pull up the Registry records. Locate the listing for Lucas Serca and backdate."

"Acknowledged."

The Registry had been put into effect to support the Fifth Generation Act. Every family listed in the Registry was required to submit an intact genealogy that stretched back to the Border Wars. It was viewable to the public, an issue of transparency the burgeoning World Court back then had required. Truth, in that instant, couldn't be locked away. Jael closed her eyes, hoping she was wrong as the computer began to spit out names, dates of births and deaths, the years spinning backward.

[THIRTY-FOUR]

SEPTEMBER 2379
KRASNOYARSK, KRASNOYARSK KRAI, RUSSIA

Threnody's fingers were cold, even through her heavily shielded and insulated skinsuit, but they still found a handhold along the rock face. She hauled herself up, feet scraping against the rough stone, breathing quickly through her nose. One wrong move, one wrong grip, would mean her death. She wasn't afraid of heights, but this place could make her learn to be.

"You know what? Screw Lucas. He couldn't spare us a damn telekinetic from the rank and file once the Strykers were dosed?" She gasped as she pulled herself over onto the flat ledge of rock. "Or do this himself?"

Kerr, already crouched on the ledge, shook his head and helped her the rest of the way up. "He has other things to worry about."

"I don't give a fuck." Threnody moved until she had her back pressed against the rock, careful of her oxygen tank. She was on her second set and they didn't have a third. "He could have at least teleported us up here. I realize he couldn't get us into the holding site, but damn it, we've been trekking through this area for hours."

"Have you seen the security around this place?" Novak said from where he sat nearby. "Even with the codes Lucas gave me, it's difficult as hell to hack. If he dropped us on their doorstep, we'd have been shot before we took a single step. Trying to hack it from anywhere but the system's perimeter would have triggered an alert, no matter how good my skills are. Maybe Jason could have done it, but he ain't available."

Threnody felt sweat slide down the back of her neck and face, but she couldn't wipe it away. Squinting up the last curve of the path before them, she sighed heavily. "We're almost to the top. The sooner we leave, the sooner I'll feel like we're not walking over bones anymore."

"Not like we haven't been doing that since we got dropped off," Kerr pointed out.

Stretched before them lay a vast, empty vista. Not even nature had fully reclaimed the shattered remains of the ruined city they could see, but the glistening ribbon of the Yenisei River still flowed across the land. Krasnoyarsk was an abandoned city, capital to a deadzone, and a place few in their right mind would venture. Radiation still tainted everything, and while no bones or bodies were left, everywhere they walked seemed to have the black, ashy imprint of the dead.

Mountains rose into the sky in the northwest, ruins to the northeast. No sound but the wind existed as it blew across barren plains and the steep mountainsides. It whistled through the countless fingers of rock that surrounded them, the stone thrust up from the ground like ancient pillars. They had pushed through this forgotten reserve for over half a day already, and the bleakness of the scenery wasn't changing.

Threnody got to her feet, brushing off dirt and tiny bits of rock. "Are we still off the security grid, Novak?"

The hacker glanced down at the tiny datapad hooked into the neuroport on his left wrist. "So far. The loop must be holding because I haven't gotten a blip."

"Then let's finish this."

Her sense of time was off and hadn't resettled through four teleports and as many continents. Threnody understood Lucas was delegating more than he liked, that he needed to save his strength for the final push, but she knew he was uneasy giving up control. Regardless, she could have used more people for this mission. Shaking her head, Threnody led the way down a rocky patch to a tiny, lead-lined bunker half-built into rock. They had to pass through a cleared landing area that looked just big enough for a small shuttle to land in.

This was government-owned property, built in the middle of a dead-zone to keep watch over a weapon everyone in his or her right mind feared. Novak kept his attention on his hack and the security loop, walking steadily toward the heavy door bolted into rock and metal.

I'm sensing four people inside, Kerr said into Threnody's mind. *Three are human. One is a Warhound.*

Class?

He's a dual psion. Class IV telekinetic and Class VII telepath.

Threnody frowned as she approached the control panel, pulling out the gun on her hip. *Lucas did say that Nathan always had some of his people on duty here along with the government's. We were hoping they'd all be recalled for the launch, but maybe not. It's possible this one has orders like ours. Can you keep him from teleporting out?*

Kerr nodded. *Yes, but I'll have to stay behind you. I'll block whatever psi link he has in his mind so he can't get a warning out and then immobilize him. I don't want to make myself a target any more than I need to.*

Understood.

Threnody entered code after access code, each one accepted as she went through the entire list Lucas had given her. Since few people knew about this outpost, the codes didn't change that often. He'd stolen this set last spring, and she breathed more easily after the last code processed and the thick, heavy doors slid open.

She went in shooting, feeling the recoil in her wrist as she picked out her targets and kept her finger on the trigger. The first room in the bunker seemed to be the common area, and two men were sitting at a table playing cards. Both were halfway out of their seats when they each took a bullet to the chest, blood spraying out over the scattered cards and credit chips. They fell to the floor, twitching and gasping for breath as they drowned in their own blood. Threnody stepped closer and put a bullet in each of their heads.

She chanced a look through the inner door that led to a short hallway, not seeing anyone. Behind her Kerr came inside the bunker. The heavily shielded door slid closed on his heels. He nodded at her, gaze distant, and she trusted in Kerr to handle the Warhound, which meant the only one left to deal with was human. Moving down the hallway, Threnody reached another door, this one closed and locked. She took up position beside it.

"Here," Novak said as he edged around her, carrying his own gun. "Took a security card from one of the others."

The security card was bloody, but the lock scanned it just fine. The door slid open and Threnody immediately went to her knees as shots were fired chaotically through the open doorway. Novak hit the ground at the same time she did.

"Amateurs," he muttered. "I hate them more than crack shots."

Threnody nodded, shifting her weight and angling her body so she could shoot into the room when the bullets stopped. It was a risk to put herself out in the open like that, but necessary. She saw a woman frantically trying to reload her gun, shaking hands making it impossible to slide the magazine home. A man was sprawled at her feet, blood leaking from his nose and the corners of his half-opened eyes. He wasn't breathing.

Threnody aimed, fired again, and put a bullet into the woman's chest, straight through the lungs. Her second shot missed, but the third clipped the woman in the arm. Threnody took in a steadying breath, aimed one more time, and hit the woman's gut. She collapsed to the floor and didn't move. Threnody got to her feet, approached the bodies, and put a bullet through their brains just to be sure.

Clear, Threnody said through the psi link to Kerr.

He met them at the far end of the main hallway, at a door that looked stronger and heavier than all the rest. "Door is sealed up front," Kerr said as he undid the hard helmet locked around his throat. He pulled it free of his skinsuit. "Air's clean. The environmental system here is built along the lines of a city tower. Place is tightly sealed, filters are working, and my tank is running low."

"Mine, too," Threnody admitted, unlocking her own helmet and pulling it off.

Novak removed his as well. With Lucas's codes having reached their limit of usefulness, Novak began a hack on the door. An hour later found them walking into a high-tech laboratory built around a single object. Sitting behind a thick partition of lead, metal walls, and specially treated plasglass, and perched on top of a work terminal whose base was drilled into rock, was a single weapon. When Novak finally got a good look at it, all the blood drained out of his face. The tattoos inked into the skin of his skull stood out sharply.

"That's—," he choked out hoarsely.

"Yes," Threnody said as she approached the secured casement of something that could, and had, caused so much destruction. "Lucas said Nathan probably wouldn't have removed it yet, or even planned to. What use would he have for something like this on Mars Colony?"

"This is crazy."

Threnody shrugged. "This is our mission. The access codes change every week and Lucas said he was months behind the cycles."

Novak's hands shook as he smoothed them over his face and the curve of his sweaty, tattooed head. "You couldn't just pull the codes out of their minds before you killed them?"

"The scientists didn't know the removal codes," Kerr said. "I pulled that from the Warhound's mind. Only high-ranking government officials have the ability to unlock this system."

"Novak." Threnody tilted her head in the direction of the intricate terminal with its complicated-looking control panel. "You need to get us in."

"What? No. This is anathema to the very way we *live*," Novak said, eyes wide and frantic in his face. "You can't be serious."

"This made the way we live," Threnody said fiercely, glaring at him. "And we suffer for it endlessly. I may not like it or agree with Lucas's methods, but this is the only way we're going to secure our safety."

"Are you even listening to yourself?" Novak pointed at the terminal, eyes wide with terror. "That's a *nuclear bomb* in there."

"Novak," Kerr said, his telepathy pressing down hard on the other man's static human mind. "You don't have a choice. Neither do we. Now get started."

Novak swallowed thickly, shoulders slumping. "This system is going to be difficult to hack."

"Remember what Lucas said? You'll hack it or die trying." Kerr grimaced, not liking the order at all. "You better hope you die after, because right now you're the only one who can do this."

"Why didn't Lucas just get a damn telekinetic to teleport the thing out of here?"

"Pressure plates," Threnody said, pointing at the platform through the view window. "If they're removed without the codes being entered, an alarm is triggered. Lucas said there's always a team of Warhounds on standby ready to teleport in. Considering the state of the world right now, we don't know if they actually would, but we can't risk it. Nathan can't know we're stealing the bomb."

"Great." Novak unsealed his gloves and freed his hands. "Never thought we'd be repeating history."

"For a hacker, you lack imagination," Kerr said. "Lucas is making history, not repeating it."

"Says you." Novak stared bleakly at his task. "This ain't right."

"Stop arguing and get to work. We don't have much time left. We aren't teleporting out and we need to be finished before our pickup arrives."

Novak reached for the controls attached to the work terminal. He pulled out a hard wire and attached it to the neuroport in his left wrist. Taking a deep breath, he opened himself up to the inevitable, inspecs flickering in the back of his eyes as code flowed through his brain.

PART SEVEN
TEMPORAL

SESSION DATE: 2128.07.10

LOCATION: Institute of Psionics Research

CLEARANCE ID: Dr. Amy Bennett

SUBJECT: 2581

FILE NUMBER: 627

When the doctor enters, Aisling is standing in front of the machines, staring at the monitors and the data that moves across them in sharp lines; high peaks and deep valleys dictate who she is. She has one hand pressed against a vidscreen that shows her baseline, the graph far more skewed than a human's.

"Aisling, please step away from there," the doctor says.

"Don't worry. My power isn't the kind that affects machines." Aisling slides her fingers over the baseline reading. "That one isn't born yet."

The doctor takes her seat at the table, and Aisling calmly returns to her own. The wires trail behind her and brush along the ground. She climbs onto her chair and looks at the camera instead of the doctor.

"You know I'm right, Ciari."

"Please focus, Aisling," the doctor says. "Let's stick to what's important."

"She *is* important. They all are down the years, so long as they listen."

The doctor glances up at her. "Will it change anything, these people you dream about?"

"They aren't dreams," Aisling says, scowling. "They're real. And things will change if they listen."

"What if they don't?"

Aisling shrugs. "There are lots of ways this could end, but I chose to only see one."

THIRTY-FIVE

SEPTEMBER 2379
LONDON, UNITED KINGDOM

D *id Gideon make it onto the space shuttle?*

Nathan felt Dalia wince at his telepathic demand, the psi link in her mind an overused ache that she couldn't block or ignore. *Sharra's space shuttle launched hours ago with all passengers accounted for, according to the manifest. By tomorrow morning, they'll have reached the Ark.*

You're certain?

Yes. We've been launching space shuttles all day, but we only have one ramp and only so much space to house people, even if it is temporary. I've transferred all the Warhounds you've sent me into priority boarding, but that's all I can do right now. How many more should I expect?

Half of my Warhounds haven't even left their posts yet. There are supplies and other things that are important to gaining control of Mars Colony that we can't leave without. By tomorrow, you should have close to a quarter of those left behind.

Are you sure that's safe? Dalia's thoughts shook with exhaustion and fear. Nathan clamped down tighter on her mind.

As you said, the government has only one launch ramp and little safe space in Paris for everyone. The launch is going to take days and it's going to be messy. There will be space shuttles still available.

Of course, sir.

Nathan cut the connection, his attention refocusing on the half dozen uplinks spread across his work terminal's vidscreen. Human field controllers loyal to the Serca Syndicate by deep mindwipes and Warhounds whose duties weren't quite done yet waited patiently for his commands.

"Where were we?" he said, bringing the meeting back on track.

It didn't take long. Twenty minutes later, he was cutting the uplinks, the vidscreen going blank. Nathan got to his feet and paced over to the window wall behind his desk, looking out at the dark London skyline. The view was familiar, committed to memory long ago. Back when he was a child, he thought London would remain his home. That he would die here, young and seemingly human, but that was no longer the case. London would only exist in his memories and Nathan found he wouldn't mind forgetting it.

Rioters still fought on the streets surrounding the city towers. Their attacks against the government and registered humans hadn't abated, were in fact becoming more violent with every hour that passed. Shuttle launches to Paris were scheduled to continue for the next few days. It was enough time for everyone not on the colony list to come together and fight for rights long denied them, but it was a fight they would lose.

The world population of highly educated people was dwindling at an alarming rate, with registered humans fleeing Earth for a tenuous promise in the stars. The remains of society would struggle to pick itself up, if anything was left after the first year of abandonment. The brain drain the World Court had engineered would cripple those left behind. Perhaps not into extinction, but close enough that the rot in the world would win. The rioters were protesting their oncoming deaths. Nathan thought it a futile action.

The computer chimed, alerting him to an incoming uplink. Nathan turned around to see that it was tagged with an emergency code. He went over to his desk to accept it. Erik's face filled the vidscreen, pale and frantic.

"Nathan," Erik said. "The neurotrackers failed."

The words froze Nathan, disbelief twisting through his thoughts. It was swiftly followed by a rage that tunneled his vision, and Nathan had to work at showing fear instead of fury. That's what Erik would expect from him, in the guise Nathan lived with. "Did you use the master override?"

"Do you think I don't know how to put down a dog? We can still track some of their positions, but they aren't all *dead*."

"Explain yourself."

"Ciari was here." The woman's name fell from Erik's lips like a curse. "She had some asinine offer that they could save us if we stayed. She didn't die when I issued the mass termination order and was teleported out before we could shoot her. We know that a few hundred Strykers died in the Americas and some here in The Hague, but all the rest were showing live signals on the security grid before we lost contact. I doubt any of those Strykers are dead."

Nathan felt his fingernails bite into the palms of his hands. "I'm to assume your version of using a panic switch is to uplink with me? What do you think I can do about this problem?"

"Your family created this damn technology and sold it to the world when psions were first discovered. I'm hoping you have an override that can fix this problem. You Sercas don't give up anything for free."

It was a rather astute assumption, even if Nathan couldn't outright acknowledge the underhanded way his family functioned. Moving to his seat, Nathan kept his attention on the uplink.

"What are your plans right now, Erik?"

"If you can't give us a way to kill the Strykers, then the World Court is leaving tonight for Paris. We aren't safe anymore if the Strykers decide to rebel and come after us."

"Like the rest of the world?"

"Don't act like you won't be joining us on that shuttle, Nathan." Erik frowned, weariness pulling at his mouth. "Why are you still in London anyway?"

"My Syndicate requires a firm hand to wind it down on such short notice. I'm waiting to hear from the Athes."

"You'll be waiting a long time," Erik said flatly. "The city towers in Sapporo fell. Sydney is dead."

Nathan tapped his fingers against his desk. He'd been so focused on transferring the contents of the seed bank and his Warhounds that he missed the news coming out of Japan. "When did this happen?"

"Within the last few hours."

"I hadn't heard. What about Elion?"

"He's still in Paris. I don't know if anyone's informed him of his grandfather's death. If they haven't, Travis will when we arrive."

"When do you expect to leave?"

"Right now, if you have nothing to give us."

Nathan stared at Erik in silence for a long moment, weighing his options. "I may have something."

Erik let out a deep breath, mouth twisting, despite the relief seeping into his eyes. "Why am I not surprised?"

"My family guards its secrets the same way the World Court guards theirs. We're just better at it. I'll take a shuttle and be at The Hague soon to see what can be done."

"We'll await your arrival."

The uplink cut off and Nathan leaned back in his seat, grinding his teeth, free now to let his true emotions show. He had no doubt that Lucas was behind the failure of the neurotrackers. His son knew the intricacies of the technology, both its strengths and carefully guarded weaknesses, just as well as he did. Releasing the Strykers from the chains that had bound them since their emergence after the Border Wars meant the Silence Law was void. His family's genetic secret was fair game now, and if Ciari was in The Hague, Nathan only had one option left to him regarding the World Court.

He had no qualms about taking it.

Again, Nathan found that the hard decisions were left to him. He didn't regret the decisions that had let him live this long, to see this happen. The only thing he regretted was his family and the way he couldn't use his children to further his own life. Being born a Class I triad psion meant his body was just looking for a way to kill his mind. Dying was slower for him than for most psions because of his social status, but he could no longer expect that to hold true.

Gideon was on his way to the *Ark,* safe from Lucas's machinations, but also out of reach of Nathan. Lucas, Samantha, and Kristen were hidden somewhere on Earth, fighting for a goal that Nathan didn't understand. The one thing Nathan wanted, he could no longer bargain for, not with the neurotrackers disabled and the Silence Law broken. Jason Garret was out of reach now unless Nathan opened his own mind and used his powers to their absolute limits to find the Stryker. The effort would surely kill him.

Nathan wasn't that desperate.

He reached for the controls on his desk, fingers skating over the touch panel. The uplink came through in an instant. "Ready my shuttle."

[THIRTY-SIX]

Erik stared at the security feed monitoring the defenses surrounding the Peace Palace. He couldn't see the streets beyond the wall, they were so crowded with people. Quads on the perimeter were all that existed between them and the fury of a people that the government hadn't deigned to save.

The Strykers were gone, the World Court's dogs having fully slipped their collars for the first time in 250 years. The bitterness, the fear, was difficult to cope with. The only people left to protect them were human, and there was no guarantee how long the military would continue to believe the lie that they would have a place on the *Ark* to guard the new world on Mars Colony.

"I think it's time we leave," Travis said, eyeing the vidscreen from where he stood with a cluster of other judges. "Enough of those chosen have heeded the transfer orders. If any are left behind, then their failure to keep to the schedule is on them. We gave enough warning for people to muster out. It's not in our best interest to remain any longer."

"I'm inclined to agree," Nathan said. He stood beside Erik in the courtroom before the judicial bench, both men focused on the security feed. "There is nothing I can do about the neurotrackers, not after what failsafes my Syndicate had didn't work. The last of the inventory from the seed bank is being put on a shuttle right now for a launch. The entirety of the supplies left to us will be safely out of reach. The most essential part of this plan is safe."

"They can't be safe if we're missing half of what we were charged with keeping track of," Erik said. "It makes me wonder what happened to those missing supplies. It makes me wonder who betrayed us. The Strykers shouldn't have been able to get free."

"I did warn you, Erik. Our attempts at ownership weren't enough over the years if this is the result," Anchali said from where she sat on a chair, both hands resting on top of her cane. "They bypassed our control and this is the result of our failure to keep them leashed."

"We had humans working all throughout the Strykers Syndicate. We had monitoring systems in place that infiltrated not only every psion office but their own bodies. This should have been impossible."

"Impossible or not, why haven't they tried to kill us?" Cherise Molyneux demanded. "Reports have come in from all over the world that Strykers left their posts guarding the city towers and retreated to the streets, taking half the military with them. They haven't murdered the people who held their contracts."

"Yet" was Anchali's sharp retort. "Their timing, I must say, was perfect. Unfortunately, we don't have the time or the means to track them down and kill them, and thus our only option is retreat."

"This is no retreat, this was planned," Erik said, voice cold.

"Plans never go accordingly." Anchali shook her head, gray hair swaying around her thin face. "We are done here, Erik. We are *done*. Let us go while there is a window of opportunity left and soldiers still loyal to the cause to fly us out of here."

Erik pressed his thumb over the biometric key on the remote he held, dragging it down the sensor. No confirmation of termination came from the hub of soldiers charged with administering termination. Anchali was right. They had done their part, played their roles as saviors. If they stayed any longer, they would play a role of martyr that none of them desired.

Gripping the remote, Erik spun and threw the device with all the strength he had at the ancient, stained-glass windows that spanned the wall over the dais. It slammed through the fragile glass and shattered part of a pane. Tiny shards fell to the ground, thin cracks spiderwebbing across the rest of the picture.

"Does that make you feel better, Erik?" Nathan said.

Erik turned to give the other man a sharp look. "If anyone is to share blame, Nathan, it is you and your family."

"I find that you have little ground on which to blame us for your mistakes." Nathan gave him a cool look. "My family offered up the science to keep humans safe from psions. We offered a way to alter human DNA and clean it up. We lobbied for segregation with the World Court's support for the greater good. You owe me your rank by virtue of the knowledge my ancestors shared."

"Like hell."

"I'm inclined to agree with Nathan," Travis said, gesturing at the other man. "But it doesn't matter anymore who's to blame. Are the shuttles at the airfield ready for us to board?"

"Yes," Anchali said. "Save your male posturing for when we arrive on the *Ark*. We have better things to do than argue which family is more human than the rest."

"A difficult decision amongst you fifteen, perhaps," a familiar voice announced. "Not, I think, for the Sercas."

The door to the courtroom was pushed open, a slim figure stepping inside. Erik choked down his fear as he recognized the uniformed woman striding down the aisle between the rows of seats.

"Someone call the quads," Anchali said, clutching at her cane.

"They are occupied elsewhere," Ciari said calmly.

The last time the World Court had seen her, she'd been writhing in agony and bleeding on the carpeted floor of this courtroom. She had changed, the expression on her face remote. She no longer had a collar to hold her in check. Her gaze swept over the group, judging them as they once judged her.

"We offered you another way and you refused it," Ciari said. "Abandoning this world isn't the answer. Do you really think you'll find a better life on Mars Colony?"

"You don't know what you're talking about," Erik spat out. He stepped backward, away from her.

Ciari touched her neck, fingers sliding over the circular bruise that stood out in stark relief against her pale skin. "I know what I've lost and what I've gained, Erik. Do you?"

"You have gained nothing," Travis said as he pulled an antique gun from a shoulder holster beneath his robes. He aimed at Ciari's head. "I made a mistake when I voted to spare your life if this is how you repay our generosity."

He pulled the trigger, the crack of the gun loud in the courtroom. Travis's aim was true and Ciari stared at the bullet as it spun in place directly in front of her nose. She carefully touched the bullet with one finger. It fell to the floor.

"There are more with her," Anchali said in warning, her voice high with fear.

"Of Strykers, there's just me," Ciari corrected. "Rogue psions? You have only one other here."

"Along with one lost cause at that," a tenor voice said from up in the balcony. "Though, really, you lot are worse off than I could ever hope to be even if I tried."

Everyone's attention was drawn upward, Nathan's head immediately snapping up at the familiar voice that greeted everyone. Lucas stood above them, arms braced against the wooden railing of the balcony. Wearing a black-on-black Strykers BDU and carrying no weapons, he only had eyes for one person in the room.

"Hello, Nathan," Lucas said. "Do you like what I've done with the world?"

It had been two years since father and son last stood face-to-face. Two years of sabotage, of hunting and being hunted. The lies and deceit the two men shared were family secrets that should never have seen the light of day. Yet here they were, stripping themselves bare as they clawed their way to a future that each saw differently, that each believed in differently.

"Lucas," Nathan said, the name falling from his lips in a sharp hiss. "And so the prodigal son returns. What—inconvenient timing."

Lucas offered up a thin-lipped smile. "Am I disappointing you again? I'm not really sorry about that."

"*What* is going on here?" Erik demanded, staring in pale-faced shock up at Lucas. "Nathan, why is your son wearing a *Stryker* uniform?"

"We haven't seen your son in two years, Nathan," Anchali said, rising to her feet shakily. "You will tell us what is going on."

"It's family business that doesn't concern you," Nathan said.

Erik turned angrily to face Nathan. "You don't give the orders here. Tell us what the hell—"

The garbled scream that came out of Erik's mouth was issued around a broken jaw, the sound of bone cracking loud enough to startle everyone. Cupping his face in both hands, Erik screamed and gasped for breath through a mouth that wouldn't close, his lower jaw hanging at an awkward angle from his skull.

"Shut your mouth" came Nathan's icy order. He hadn't moved.

"Mon Dieu," Cherise yelled at Ciari. "What have you done?"

"Nothing. I'm an empath," Ciari said.

"Don't you hate it when they give credit for your work to someone else, Nathan?" Lucas asked, voice calculatingly cheerful. "The seed bank, the space shuttles, the program to bring the colony ship back online. Everything our family has ever done for the humans and they pass most of it off as their own."

"Do you really want to do this now?" Nathan said flatly, refusing to look away from his son.

"When will we have the chance if I don't?"

In the blink of an eye, Lucas teleported down to the courtroom floor. The judges collectively stepped back, fear replacing shock on their faces, none of them capable of speech.

Nathan faced his son, cold anger filling his dark blue eyes. "I will kill you."

"You'll certainly try," Lucas said.

Travis, like most of the rest of the judges, looked from Lucas to Nathan with a growing sense of horror. He was the first to speak. "Did the Strykers buy you off, Nathan? Is that why the neurotrackers don't work?"

Lucas's laughter made their skin crawl. "Buy us off? Hardly. We were their salvation."

"What are you talking about?" Anchali asked, voice strained. "Lucas, what have they done to you?"

"Did you honestly think the Strykers would simply let you slaughter and discard us, over and over again?" Ciari asked. "You had to know we'd find a way to save some of our people, even if it meant giving up control to someone else. We gave up high-Classed psions that were scheduled for termination to the Sercas. The Serca family's Warhounds were always a better option than death, no matter the violations to our minds once the kill switch was removed."

"Warhounds," Cherise said, the word coming out mangled. "Nathan, what is she talking about?"

They were all looking at the owner of the Serca Syndicate, disbelief and horror in their eyes, on their faces, desperately hoping for an answer that would keep their world on an even keel.

Your inability to see things for what they really are is staggering, Lucas said into everyone's mind. *Did you really think you could leave all the psions behind to die? Your entire dream was shored up by my family, and we happen to be some of the strongest psions on this planet.*

Lucas didn't bother to hold back, shoving his power into their static human minds without care. The fifteen judges were unable to handle the intrusion and several of the older ones collapsed.

If this was the point you wanted to make, it won't do you any good, Nathan said, a riot of power surging beyond his words.

Lucas readied his telekinesis for a teleport and felt his shields almost buckle beneath Nathan's powerful telekinetic blow. He stumbled forward a few steps, balance thrown off by the strength of the attack. Lucas lifted his head, glaring at Nathan, hating to reveal even a shred of weakness before his father.

You never did learn to obey your betters, Nathan said. *I blame Marcheline for that.*

The combined telekinetic and telepathic strikes against Lucas's shields were expected. He held up beneath the attack, mind still reaching for the teleport. Lucas could see his destination in his mind, had strength to get there, even through Nathan's power—except it was only enough to carry himself out of The Hague. If he was going to be at all ready to fight later on when his power would be needed, he couldn't fight for anyone's life save his own. Neither could he remain here much longer.

Lucas felt too-warm fingers touch his cheek, sliding down the curve of his jaw. Felt lips brush against his ear. "Save my Strykers," Ciari said, her voice soft. "You owe me that."

He owed her everything. They both knew it.

"Good-bye," Lucas said.

He slammed his power against Nathan's defenses, putting every bit of strength into that one blow. It bought him seconds, enough time to teleport out of Nathan's reach, physically leaving Ciari behind. She briefly closed her eyes, feeling an echo of Lucas in her mind.

Nathan stared at the empty spot where his son once stood, trying to find some reason behind Lucas's actions.

"You can't be a psion," Travis whispered, begging for it to not be true. "Nathan—you *can't*."

"He is," Ciari said, gaze locked on Nathan's face. "Every Serca has been. You've all wondered over the years about who controlled the rogue psions of the world and allowed them to thrive. The Warhounds have been the Sercas' private army since the beginning."

"And for all the psions we saved at your behest and those who held your rank in the past, this is how you repay my family." Nathan gave Ciari a faint, mocking bow. "So glad to know where your loyalties lie."

"With my people" was her answer. "Always with them."

"You'll certainly die with them."

If the World Court thought they could beg, barter, or bargain their way out this time, they were in denial. Nathan heard their pleas, their willingness to do whatever he wanted, pay whatever he asked, if he would only spare them.

Like you spared all the psions you and your predecessors enslaved and killed? Nathan asked, his power fluctuating across the mental grid with deadly force. *I have no use for most of the humans who belong to the Registry. This was planned over generations, over centuries. There is nothing you have to offer me, for I already own everything you thought you would keep.*

For all the arrogance of the World Court, for all the pride that collective government body took in saving the human race, their discriminatory practices destroyed them in the end. Knowledge of what they had unknowingly harbored in the pristine halls of government since the end of the Border Wars—diseased psion DNA in a family that looked so human—left them reeling.

They died, one by one, minds burning out beneath the onslaught of a telepathic strike that had no boundaries. Human minds weren't capable of handling psionic interference. Nathan took them apart, unraveling their lives until nothing was left except empty minds and empty eyes; just bodies with hearts that beat, and then, just corpses.

Ciari watched them die and felt nothing. She raised her eyes to Nathan as he turned to look at her, neither of them bound anymore by the conventions of a life they were born into.

"My son should have saved you," Nathan said as he skimmed his power over Ciari's fragile, broken mind. "His loyalty has always been questionable."

"He didn't come to say good-bye to you."

Ciari smiled as Nathan's mind slid into hers, breaking through mental shields tainted with insanity. Her smile was small, just the faint quirk of her mouth, but it held so much emotion. A lifetime of wanting, of hoping, brought Ciari to her knees, the schemes of a child laying waste to her memories as Nathan cut into her mind. He ripped apart the foundations of her shields, baring her mind to the cacophony of the world's thoughts and emotions, but he hesitated when faced with the irrefutable presence of growing insanity. The hesitation lasted only a moment before Nathan continued his onslaught.

A second telepathic touch flowed through Ciari's thoughts—familiar, cool. She sucked in a quiet breath even as pain began to override her body. She thought she understood it now.

Close your eyes, Lucas said, telepathic fingers sliding over everything that she was, everything that she had lost, hiding all that she knew from Nathan. *I'll take you away from here.*

She did as he asked, his telepathy a barrier that Nathan couldn't cross, no matter how hard his father fought. Ciari's mind was a battlefield between a pair of Class I triad psions, and she didn't have the capacity to survive it. Lucas knew that, had always known that. Somewhere in Ciari's mind, she knew it, too.

This isn't what Aisling promised me, Ciari said as she opened her eyes and looked around at the familiar, twisted landscape of her birth city, Buffalo a tangled mess of forgotten dreams and living nightmares spread out before her. The Hague and the Peace Palace seemed like a lifetime ago. She thought she could still feel the carpet beneath her cheek.

I know, Lucas said, standing by Ciari's side in the street he built in her mind.

Clouds were in the makeshift sky, and a breeze touched Ciari's skin, freezing her by centimeters. Somewhere in the distance, there was thunder, growing fainter with every breath she took.

We tried, Ciari said, tipping her head back to stare at the sky and the storm that was leaving her. *That has to count for something, doesn't it?*

Lucas touched his hand to hers, but she didn't feel the pressure. *It does.*

The air smelled wet, felt shock-edged with potential. Lucas's hand fell away. When Ciari turned to look at him, only emptiness was beside her, around her.

The rain, when it came, fell soft and clean down on a memory blowing through a world that was crumbling away.

Lucas let her go.

[THIRTY-SEVEN]

SEPTEMBER 2379
TORONTO, CANADA

Matron picked them up, flying a familiar shuttle through the gray Russian sky to retrieve them from the rocky outpost. The scavenger took one look at where the three stood at the bottom of the cargo ramp, heavy, hard-backed metal carrying case resting between Threnody and Kerr, and shook her head.

"Just tell me it ain't gonna blow us out of the sky," Matron said.

"So long as you don't roll the damn shuttle, it'll be fine," Novak said in a ragged voice. "Tell me you got painkillers on this piece of junk."

"Stop whining and go dose yourself."

The hacker staggered up the cargo ramp, every step looking as if it hurt. He headed for the med-kit bolted to the deck near the front hatch. Matron watched him go with a frown on her face. "What's wrong with him?"

"He fried half his brain getting us the bomb," Kerr said as he reached down to grab the handle on his side of the carrying case. "You should take him to Korman after you drop us off in Paris."

Matron swore. "Goddamn that boy. Lucas is gonna kill all my scavengers and what the fuck am I supposed to do then?"

"I wouldn't recommend asking."

"Go scrub off in the decontamination tent once you get that thing inside. It's set up in the corner."

Threnody and Kerr carefully hauled the carrying case up the cargo ramp. Matron made sure to keep several meters' worth of distance away from them as the two secured the bomb in the cargo bay. The scavenger was already in the pilot's seat, readying for launch, when Threnody made it to the flight deck. She'd stripped out of her skinsuit and gone through decontamination. The clothes she wore now were from Matron's stores. Threnody sat down in the navigator's seat, strapped herself into the harness, and started pulling up information.

"Didn't know you could fly," Matron said as she put on a pair of reflective dark glasses.

"Most Strykers can pilot a shuttle," Threnody said. "I prefer not to, but you need a navigator and I'm leading this mission."

"With your power, I can't imagine why you'd want to fly."

"It's why I have Quinton." Threnody reached over to toggle some of the controls between them. "Lucas wants us back in Toronto."

"Why didn't he teleport you?"

"Didn't want to risk the bomb."

Matron glanced reflexively over her shoulder, but all she saw was the closed hatch. "Nice how he don't care about our asses."

"Let's get in the air. We need to stay clear of government flight paths."

"I know. Military is shooting down anyone who gets close and don't squawk proper ident. We'll go north, over the Arctic Ocean."

"Again?"

"No one's gonna be flying our route. Everyone's heading for Paris."

They were as safe as they could get with a nuclear bomb strapped in the belly of their shuttle, and that wasn't saying much. But Matron knew the uncharted routes between government security grids better than most people. They made the long, uneasy flight back to Canada beneath a cloudy sky all over again.

Hours later, they pinged against the security grid that surrounded Toronto, but no one on the government channels initiated an uplink. Someone in the Strykers Syndicate did.

"It better be you in that shuttle, Thren, do you copy, over," Quinton said.

Threnody jammed her finger down on the audio control, opening up the line. "Good to hear your voice. We're carrying precious cargo that needs delicate handling, over."

"You're clear for the rooftop landing pad, out."

The uplink cut off and Threnody let out a deep sigh, some sense of calm trickling through her now that she knew Quinton had made it back from his mission alive. Slouching in the navigator's seat, Threnody rubbed hard at her burning eyes. Teleporting across time zones, fighting to complete their mission, then flying back to Toronto had screwed with her inner clock. The chrono on the flight controls said one thing, her body was saying another. The headache pounding through her skull wasn't going to go away anytime soon, and her eyes burned with the need to sleep.

Matron made a soft noise in the back of her throat and Threnody looked over at the other woman. "What?"

"Never been to a city tower before."

"Really?"

"Government don't care for my kind. Not how they cared for yours."

"Given the choice, I would have preferred your freedom."

"It wasn't all that great."

Matron was a good pilot, years spent crisscrossing countries around deadzones and security grids forcing her to be. She landed the shuttle on the rooftop with precision. A small group of people waited for them beyond the illuminated safety lines. Threnody recognized them all.

She got out of her seat and palmed open the hatch. The cargo ramp was already opening, and Kerr was busy undoing the restraints that secured the carrying case in place. Novak was passed out on a row of seats from exhaustion. Threnody left him for Matron to take care of and went to help Kerr with the bomb.

"You got it," Lucas said as he strode up the cargo ramp.

"Yeah, we got it," Kerr said as he kicked the anchor straps aside. "Was like a nightmare flying back with it."

"What did they get?" Jason asked as he came jogging up the ramp, Quinton hot on his heels.

Lucas waved off the question, attention focused on the cargo. "Let's get it somewhere secure first before we talk about what we're doing next."

"You got medical personnel in this place?" Matron said as she helped Novak to his feet.

"Got a whole level," Threnody said with a grunt as she finally pushed the release lever all the way down. The metal clamps used to keep the case in one place released.

"Good. They better work on Novak without complaint."

Jael? Lucas said, linking with the Strykers Syndicate's CMO. *I'm sending someone down for your people to fix. Get him sorted, then come meet us in the command briefing room.*

Give me ten minutes and I'll be there came Jael's response.

Lucas teleported Matron and Novak to the medical level's arrival room before focusing his attention on the Strykers. "Let's get below. We've got decisions to make."

Instead of teleporting, Lucas headed for the stairs. If anyone thought it strange, no one said a word. Threnody and Kerr handled the carrying case with a careful wariness that told Quinton and Jason the cargo wasn't ordinary.

The Strykers Syndicate was filled with a new sense of urgency, with fewer humans manning posts than ever before. On their way through the command level, Threnody noticed the empty terminals first and the Strykers second.

"The virus worked?" she asked as they passed by half-empty monitoring rooms.

"We didn't get everyone," Quinton said tightly.

She heard the guilt in his voice. Threnody tilted her head in his direction as they walked. "Did you get most of them?"

"As many as we could."

"If you're going to dwell on numbers, then focus on the positives, not the negatives."

Easier said than done, and they both knew it.

The command briefing room was as streamlined as every other room in the Strykers Syndicate. The company wasn't about comfort, but about security and making money. Threnody wondered if that would change when this was all over.

Keiko and Aidan were already waiting for them. The two officers were studying a command window of information, the touch screen that filled the entire length of the table filled with a grid map of the world. Threnody didn't know enough to make sense of what she was seeing without being briefed, but she could guess.

"What is that?" Aidan asked suspiciously as Kerr and Threnody carefully placed the carrying case onto the table. Threnody touched the control panel nearby, freezing the local screen and shuffling the data around the carrying case.

"A difficult answer to a difficult problem," Lucas said as he pulled a seat out and sat down. "We'll start when Jael gets here."

Nine minutes later, Jael arrived. "Your hacker is going to need brain surgery, Lucas. What the hell did you have him do?"

"He helped get that." Lucas pointed at the carrying case sitting on the table between Threnody and Kerr. "Sit down, Jael."

She took the seat farthest from Lucas. "Where's Ciari?"

"She's not coming," Lucas said.

"Why not?"

"Because Ciari is dead. So is the World Court. Nathan killed them all in the Peace Palace."

Keiko's telekinesis slammed against Lucas's shields with enough strength to rattle the conference table. Threnody and Kerr both reached for the carrying case, holding on with white-knuckled grips to keep it steady.

"Stop!" they both yelled, the fear in their voices causing Keiko to pull up short.

The Japanese woman was half out of her seat in a rage. Lucas slammed her all the way back into it, leaning forward in his own. "Ciari went to The Hague to die," he said. "She went while she still understood the choice she could make."

"You fucking bastard," Jael said harshly. "You took Ciari there to kill her, didn't you? To get her out of the way so you can take control of the Strykers Syndicate."

"As always, your imagination is impeccable, Jael. But, no, I took Ciari there so she could offer Erik a way out of this mess. He vehemently declined." Lucas pinned Jael with an angry look. "You know her mind was breaking. What you did to save her from that aborted termination broke her. She wasn't going to last much longer, not as the Ciari you knew anyway. She was too old to survive something like that."

"So you put her out of her misery, is that what you're saying?" Quinton said.

"I'm saying I let her die how she wanted to."

"But not how Aisling wanted?" was Jason's sharp question.

Lucas pressed both hands flat against the table, data streaming away from his fingertips. "Aisling doesn't concern you."

"Like hell."

Lucas ignored him. "Ciari knew what was at stake. Why do you think she did all this? Why do you think she gave me the four Strykers I needed in order to break the government's hold on you? Ciari knew exactly what she was doing when she was sane."

"What about when she wasn't?" Keiko demanded.

"You have Jael to thank for that, not me."

The Strykers Syndicate's CMO flinched with her entire body, but Jael didn't protest his accusation.

"Ciari set all of you free," Lucas said, gaze sweeping over everyone. "She made it possible to get the neurotrackers taken out of your heads. She made it possible for me to have a child not beholden to the rules that run my family. Be grateful for that. I know I am."

"So is that it?" Aidan asked. "We're free and we let the registered humans leave without a fight?"

"No," Threnody said. "We're not letting them leave."

"Why not?" Keiko asked. "Let them have Mars Colony. They can't touch us anymore."

"Maybe they can't, but their descendants might."

"You're seriously going to force a fight over something that might happen?"

"Lucas isn't working on a timeline beholden to *might*," Jael said, speaking up. Her hazel eyes were steady as she stared at Lucas. "Are you?"

Lucas ran a hand through his pale blond hair, shaking his head. "I should have known you couldn't kill your curiosity."

"It's my job to look after the collective health of Strykers."

"I am not a Stryker."

"No, you're simply taking over for Ciari, whether we like it or not."

"I'm not going to live long enough to rule you people."

"So you're leaving it to your daughter?" Jael frowned in his direction. "How can you be sure she'll be strong enough for the job? She won't be a high-Classed psion. We breed low on the scale when psions breed at all. We need corrupted human DNA to build off of."

"It's rare, but it happens." Lucas pointed across the table at Jason. "My genes are stronger than most. My daughter will be a Class I triad psion, she just won't have my exact attributes. Jason is changing her Class and her telekinetic power."

"Into what?"

"Into a more stable version of what I am," Jason said. "I'm a microtelekinetic, remember? I can manipulate cellular structure on the atomic level. Do you know what that means?"

Jael didn't have to think too hard on the answer. Her words came out in a raw whisper. "We could live a human lifetime."

"If we find psions before they're born, then yes. Not only that, but we can work on cleaning up this planet," Lucas said. "It might take a few thousand years, but we have the means to do it now, both in technology and genetics. The humans left behind will need guidance. We're losing so many people who had knowledge on how this world works that we psions will have to pick up the slack. The registered humans who didn't make the launch won't take kindly to psions taking over, so what better way to prove our right to lead than to show them what we're capable of?"

"They used us without a second thought," Quinton said. "They can work with us to rebuild or find a bunker near a deadzone to live in for all I care. We don't need to prove anything to them."

"Hating them isn't going to help us," Threnody said.

"Then let it benefit the next generation of psions. I don't give a damn about those people. I'd rather worry about the ones in the street."

"They aren't the only ones you have to worry about," Lucas said. "What we're planning won't last if we let Nathan leave with everyone on those shuttles."

Jael tapped her fingers slowly against the table. "Aisling told you that, didn't she?"

"No," Threnody said. "She told me."

Quinton jerked his head around to stare at his partner. "Come again?"

"Aisling said if we let them leave, they would come back, and we wouldn't win that fight. Nathan's Warhounds have more higher-Classed psions than we do, courtesy of the Silence Law. Even if we give it a decade and they return, we'll still be at a disadvantage. Nathan is filling half those shuttles with people not in the Registry. He'll have the means to breed psions on the *Ark*, if not Mars Colony."

"Are you certain?" Keiko said.

"Aisling is a precog," Threnody said slowly. "I believe in what she said."

"So she's alive?"

"No," Jael said with a sigh as she folded her hands together on the tabletop. "Aisling Serca died during the Border Wars. Her death is in the Registry, ancestral genetic proof that the Serca family's DNA was supposedly clean. They wiped most of the psion markers from her genome, but a few remained for me to note the distinction between Aisling and her older brother."

"Matthew Serca wasn't a psion," Lucas said with a sharp smile. "He only carried the genetic capability for it, and that capability showed up in his descendants as triad psions. Matthew followed his sister's orders and hacked her medical records when she was committed for therapy and experimentation by her government at the time. Aisling was the first psion and Matthew made sure we wouldn't forget her."

Jason rubbed hard at his face. "Fuck. Are you serious?"

"Serious enough to believe in what Aisling says. Mars Colony isn't the answer." Lucas closed his eyes, an unreadable expression crossing his face. "It never was, at least not for us. I was willing to let the government leave Earth, but that won't solve our problems. They'll only return somewhere down the line, and I needed Threnody to see that. Stopping the launch is our only option."

"How?" Aidan said. "Shuttles are still flying to Paris, and the military is still patrolling the skies over that country. How are we going to stop it?"

Threnody carefully pressed her hand against the case. The thick metal was cool to the touch. "With this."

"Do I even want to know?" Keiko asked.

"It's a nuclear bomb," Lucas said, opening his eyes. "Hard to believe our ancestors could make them so small, but they seemed to excel at destruction on many different levels."

Everyone except Lucas, Threnody, and Kerr shoved themselves away from the table and put their backs against the wall.

"Holy shit, are you *insane*?" Jason snarled.

Threnody dropped her hand away from the case and looked over her shoulder at Quinton. "Sit down. It hasn't been activated yet."

"We wouldn't be alive if it were activated," Quinton felt the need to point out.

"Do you think I would have agreed to this if I thought there was any other way?"

The two stared at each other, becoming the center of everyone's attention. Quinton shook his head in denial, a pleading look filling his face. "Thren, this is—we can't do this. It makes us no better than the people who started the Border Wars."

"How is that any different than the one we'd be heading into if Nathan gets all his Warhounds into space?" Threnody asked quietly. "Nathan's people will return wanting what we're trying to rebuild and we'll be left repeating history. The old countries fought for their fair share, so how is this different?"

"Because it's *wrong*."

"And I'm not saying it's right. I'm saying it's our only option."

For a moment, no one moved. Then Quinton took a step forward, heels dragging against the floor. With jerky motions, he pushed his chair closer to the table and sat back down.

Slowly, everyone else did the same.

[THIRTY-EIGHT]

SEPTEMBER 2379
TORONTO, CANADA

Samantha's feet hit the floor of the Strykers' arrival room in the medical level with a heavy thud, Kristen landing right beside her out of the teleport. The empath smiled widely at her brother.

"It's a madhouse back there," Kristen reported cheerfully.

"I know," Lucas said. "It's almost as bad here."

Samantha dropped the bag she carried on the arrival platform before stepping off, eyeing her brother. "Why are you wearing that?"

Lucas tugged at the collar of the Stryker uniform he wore over his insulated skinsuit. "Easier to tell Strykers apart from Warhounds and humans if we're wearing a uniform. I doubt Nathan is going to have his people in field uniforms when they board those space shuttles."

"Which means they'll just find it easier to target us."

"The Strykers are used to the risks that come with this uniform. What Warhounds remain on Earth will stand their ground. Nathan won't back down from this fight."

Samantha curled her lip at his attire. "I suppose you'll want us to wear it as well."

"You aren't an exception anymore, Sam." Lucas gestured at them to follow him. "Let's go."

He led them to a decontamination room, where he waited while they washed off any lingering taint of radiation. They had ditched the skinsuits in the generator room back in Paris, but this was standard protocol when returning from a deadzone.

When they were clean and wearing a new set of skinsuits and uniforms, Samantha and Kristen met with Lucas out in the busy hallway. Samantha tapped a finger to her temple, damp blond hair sticking to her skin. "I've got what you need for Paris."

Lucas pulled her into a psi link and let Samantha dump the information straight into his mind. It was already mentally sorted, information practically choking his thoughts. Grimacing, Lucas pressed a hand to his forehead. "Nathan isn't in Paris yet?"

"He's scheduled to arrive tomorrow," Samantha said. "He's busy hailing himself as the only one who can replace the World Court, and people are listening, judging by the conversations we overheard. Did you kill them?"

"No. He did."

"The world press is blaming psions for their murders."

"Of course they would. Better the monsters they know than the ones they don't."

Samantha covered her mouth, yawning. "You have the security information. What else do you want from me and Kristen?"

"For you to get some rest," Lucas said. "I'll find you in a few hours. I need both of you clearheaded for what's going to happen next."

"I don't know the layout of this Syndicate. Where are we sleeping?"

The two were abruptly teleported into a room that looked to house four people at a time, but was currently unoccupied. The beds looked as if no one had slept in them in a while.

Sleep, Lucas said into their minds. *When you wake up, I'll brief you.*

Samantha didn't feel like arguing, even if Kristen did. She pushed the younger girl to the lower bunk on one side of the room. "Listen to him," Samantha said firmly. "Close your eyes and sleep."

Kristen shrugged and curled up in a ball on the bed, promptly dozing off. Samantha didn't remember her head touching the pillow. She knew she must have slept, but the hand on her shoulder that pulled her back to consciousness sometime later was unwelcome.

"I could still sleep," Samantha grumbled.

"We all could," Lucas said. "Get up. Your shuttle is scheduled to depart soon."

Samantha sat up slowly, careful not to knock her head on the bunk above. Kristen was already awake and seated cross-legged on the other bed, eating her way through a ration bar. Samantha took the handful that Lucas offered her, all of them already torn open. She ate them mindlessly.

What's the plan? she asked.

I'm sending you and Kris to London. Lucas bent his head so he could look her in the eye. *Not to the Serca Syndicate, but to the outer city zones. You'll be traveling with most of the telepaths here, and others will meet with you in London. Jael is already there, getting things sorted.*

Samantha kept chewing. *Why am I not going with you to Paris?*

Because London is closer than Toronto for what I need from you and the Strykers. They don't know how to merge, Sam. Keiko is the only one I had the time to teach, and her understanding of it is shaky at best, but I need her in Paris with the telekinetics.

I'm perfectly capable of watching my own back in the field.

I know you are, but the merge I'm asking you to help hold together is too massive for you to concentrate on anything else. You'll be a liability in the field.

If that's the case, why are you leaving Kristen with me?

She won't be in the merge. Lucas nodded in Kristen's direction. *Her job is different.*

If I'm handling the merge, then what is she doing?

"I'm making sure Lucas doesn't feel a thing," Kristen said, her manic glee tempered by her brother's desire to see this through to the end.

Samantha cleared her throat. "I hope you know what you're doing, Lucas."

"This isn't how I thought we'd finish it, but I'm not going to argue how we're choosing to fight. It's something Nathan never understood," Lucas said.

"What? How you saw the world?"

Lucas shook his head. "Choice. Marcheline showed me that, Sam. I didn't care for her programming or Nathan's, but at least she showed me what it meant to control my own mind."

"What about my choice?"

"Do you really need one?"

She didn't have to think about her answer. "No."

Lucas smoothed back her hair with one hand. His mind tangled against the edge of hers and something resonated deep in her thoughts. She couldn't find its origins, but a part of her would always wonder if the answer came from herself or from Lucas's subtle, subversive mindwipe. Samantha supposed she would never know.

"Nathan never believed in humanity. Humans make their own mistakes and he despised them for that. Like everyone else in our family, he felt he was above them. That he deserved better," Lucas said. "We can't blame humanity for their errors when they made us through their faults."

"Is this how you save them? Through some preemptive strike?"

"It doesn't matter how I save them, just that I do."

Samantha leaned away from his touch, picking up her last ration bar. She didn't look at him when she said, "You told me to trust you. To follow you. I should hate you, but I don't. I think that's all you, but I'll follow your orders if that's what you need from me."

"It is." Lucas straightened up. "Your shuttle is getting prepped. Let's get you to it."

They walked instead of teleporting, needing to conserve their strength. Lucas led them to a lift that took them four levels down to one of the enclosed walkways. It connected to the landing docks, which protruded from the sides of the city tower. A large group of Strykers was already boarding. Most of them looked back warily at the three Serca siblings who approached. The only ones who didn't were Threnody and Kerr.

"You're flying with us dressed like that?" Samantha asked them.

Both Threnody and Kerr wore expensive outfits over skinsuits. They looked strange out of uniform or the grimy clothes of the street that they'd worn all their lives.

"We're being dropped off at one of the city towers in London," Threnody said. "Jason hacked our names into a passenger manifest using the information you brought back from the Command Center. We'll be flying into Paris with registered humans, so we need to look the part."

Between Threnody and Kerr sat a heavy-looking carrying case and two bags that looked as if they held clothes. Kerr leaned down to grab the handle on his side of their cargo. "See you on board."

The two followed the rest of the Strykers onto the shuttle. A quick scan showed Samantha that the majority of the Strykers traveling with them were telepaths, but quite a few telekinetics, pyrokinetics, and electrokinetics were in the mix as well.

Psychometrists and most of the empaths won't be accessing the mental grid, Lucas said. *We've ordered them into field positions to coordinate Stryker movements across the continents. I've allocated some 'kinetic-oriented psions for defense, so you'll be protected.*

You're putting a lot of trust in psions who hate us.

They know what's at risk. Now do your job.

Lucas walked away, leaving Samantha and Kristen alone to face down people who were once their enemies. The two boarded the shuttle last, strapping into seats near the front next to Threnody and Kerr. The shuttle wasn't built with luxury in mind, geared more toward transporting large groups of people. The seats weren't all that comfortable, but they settled as best they could. Samantha wrapped her hand around Kristen's wrist and closed her eyes as the shuttle unlocked from the anchoring arms of the docking cradle.

Close your eyes, Samantha told her sister. *Rest your mind.*

They slept on the flight to London, only waking when the pilot announced over the comm system that they were descending into a city tower. Samantha opened her eyes and yawned, trying to wake up. Kristen hadn't changed position at all during the flight over, though she was no longer sleeping, even if her eyes were closed.

Samantha turned her head to look at Kerr. "See if you can't mindwipe your pilot into landing in the rear of the launch area, behind the Command Center. It's the area with the least amount of security feeds, though that's not saying much."

Kerr nodded as the shuttle locked into a docking cradle with a heavy shudder. "We'll take that under consideration."

He and Threnody were the only ones to disembark, leaving the confines of the shuttle with the carrying case held between them. Samantha watched them leave until they were out of sight. The hatch closed again and ten minutes later the shuttle got the all clear to depart.

Whatever hack Jason was able to perform, it must have been good. They weren't challenged at any point during their flight across London. When the shuttle finally landed with a heavy shake on the cleared street, everyone undid their harnesses and got to their feet. The group disembarked in an orderly fashion, with Samantha pulling Kristen after her. Jael greeted them outside in the street.

"Can't say I'm happy about this," Jael said as the pair stepped off the shuttle.

"Considering what's going to happen, no one really should be," Samantha said as she studied their location.

The Strykers had taken over a single block of tenements in an outer city zone. It was night and the streets weren't lit. The building they were working out of had light escaping around the edges of badly boarded-up windows. A quick scan of the place told Samantha no humans were in the area. A lot of psions were, however, and she frowned at the way all those Stryker minds pinged on the mental grid.

"Right, first thing I'm doing is teaching you lot how to read like humans on the mental grid," Samantha said. "We don't need to be advertising our presence to the Warhounds still here."

"Lucas said all the telepaths involved in this merging venture aren't to exhaust themselves," Jael said as she gestured for the two younger girls to follow her.

"This trick of the mind is fairly simple and needs to be done if we're to stay safe."

"We're using the street as an arrival area for those telekinetics in Paris and the ones nearby to pull the wounded out of the way. We've got 'kinetic-oriented psions guarding the area along with empaths and psychometrists. We'll be safe."

"Against a city dead set on burning itself to the ground?" Samantha shook her head as they walked into a musty-smelling building. "No, we can't take any chances."

"The riots won't reach here. We won't let them."

Samantha still retained her uneasiness. Blinking her eyes to adjust to the bright interior, she took in the space that was their safe house for the time being. Strykers wearing the white scrubs of doctors and psi surgeons milled around inside, handing out bunks for the telepaths assigned to London. Samantha declined a bed or couch, not liking the looks of the ones she passed, and instead took up position in the kitchen. She and Kristen claimed a small table with four chairs. Kristen immediately folded her arms over the tabletop and rested her head on them, body canted at a sharp angle.

She gave her sister a sharp smile before closing her eyes. "It'll be brilliant, Sammy-girl."

Samantha sat down under Jael's watchful eye, not protesting when a nurse started to hook her up to a monitoring machine. "Remember your orders, Kristen."

"Don't worry. Lucas won't feel a thing."

PART EIGHT
ASCENSION

SESSION DATE: 2128.02.17
LOCATION: Institute of Psionics Research
CLEARANCE ID: Dr. Amy Bennett
SUBJECT: 2581
FILE NUMBER: 160

"Should we fear you?" the doctor asks.

The child shrugs and picks at the lace on her white sock. She is kneeling on the chair and hooks a finger beneath the strap of one shiny black shoe as she stares around the room. "I think you already do."

"This is only a precaution. Do you consider yourself dangerous, Aisling?"

She wrinkles her nose at the doctor. "I'm four."

"You don't act it sometimes."

Aisling shrugs again and settles more comfortably on the chair, her feet swinging freely through the air after she shifts position. "I can't help that. I can't help what I see."

The woman settles a hand over her datapad, leans forward, and offers up a smile. It doesn't reach her eyes, barely curls her lips. "You're the first person we've found who has a one hundred percent accuracy rating. We need that. We need you."

Aisling tilts her head to the side, the way any inquisitive child would. "You don't need me, you need my dreams. But they aren't for you."

[THIRTY-NINE]

Nathan was in the launch command room, in the middle of a conversation with the head of operations, when the security grid around Paris pinged with numerous threats. The chatter in the command room picked up, growing louder with every second that passed.

"Those aren't confirmed routes."

"Sir, no one is answering our hails."

"Someone get those jets scrambled!"

Nathan took one look at the targeted mass of dots drifting closer to the ruined city on the hologrid map before abruptly turning on his feet and leaving the room. The hallway that separated the command room from the rest of the boarding facilities of the building was filled only with scattered government employees. It wasn't private, but it was empty enough for what he needed to do.

The four Warhounds masquerading as soldiers in a quad followed him out and stood guard when Nathan put his back against the wall. He closed his eyes and sent his mind skimming across the mental grid, picking up Warhound telepaths and dragging them into a merge. Bolstered by external power, Nathan allowed himself to reach for the cluster of buzzing thoughts that were getting closer with every second that passed. A morass of psi signatures hit his leading mental shields, and Nathan abruptly pulled back, retreating in a way that snapped pain through his head when he opened his eyes.

"Sir?" the Warhound to his left asked. "What's wrong?"

"Confirm the numbers we have on-site for Warhounds," Nathan said in a low voice.

"The last groups are still flying in. They number a little over one hundred. On-site? We've got two hundred Warhounds still waiting to board and about fifty already on their assigned space shuttles. Everyone else is already en route to the *Ark* or on board the colony ship."

Nathan calculated the odds. Three hundred of his Warhounds, half of them higher-Classed psions, were already in space and unavailable for this fight. Nathan had staggered the exits of Warhound teams, knowing that things would be going to hell during such a shortened transfer time frame. He ground his teeth, exhaling sharply through his nose as he picked through his options.

"Get them off those space shuttles and out of this building. I want them on the streets and ready to fight *right now*. That's Lucas flying in with Strykers and we need to be ready." Nathan gestured at the hallway they were in. "Send me all the Class VI and higher telepaths and empaths we have on-site. Tell them to prepare for merging."

One of the Warhounds nodded sharply at the order, and Nathan headed for the command room. He pulled his suit jacket straight as he walked back into chaos. The grating static of human thoughts beat against his mental shields as he took up his post next to the command terminal manned by the head of operations.

"Jets are confirming no response from those shuttles, sir," someone told the man in charge. "We're starting to lose uplinks with the jets as they approach the targets."

"What do you mean we're losing uplinks?" the government officer demanded.

"They're disappearing from the security grid."

"Do we have a visual?"

"Negative."

"Why the hell not? Get me that goddamn visual!" The assistant ran off to obey and Nathan took his place. The officer didn't look up from his terminal. "You shouldn't be here, sir. Grab a quad and have them take you to the space shuttle we're readying for launch. We need to get you off this planet."

"I can't leave just yet," Nathan said.

"If I have to haul you onto that space shuttle in cuffs, I'll do it. We need you alive, sir."

"Yes, but that won't happen if those incoming shuttles aren't stopped. You have no clue who you're dealing with."

The officer scowled and waved over a quad. "I don't have time to listen to politicians. They're taking you to a shielded transport shuttle and putting your ass on the next space shuttle in the launch queue."

The first soldier to lay a hand on Nathan got his arm broken, and the breaking didn't stop until the screaming man was a mutilated mass of pulpy flesh and shattered bone lying on the floor. It took only a minute for the man to die, but it seemed like eternity to those watching. Nathan stared disdainfully at the dead man and tugged his suit sleeve straight.

"Don't presume to tell me what to do," Nathan said, raising his eyes to meet the officer's shocked and uncertain gaze. "I don't take orders from humans. Not anymore."

Words died on the man's lips as Nathan telekinetically broke his neck. Another body hit the floor and Nathan tossed it aside, clearing the way for him to take control of the command room. He could feel the rising panic in the large room, fear meshing into a ragged mob mentality that would have left him short of needed people for the controls.

The Warhound telepaths and empaths that entered the command room took care of that for him, brutally mindwiping the humans of their fear and panic. The mindwipe kept the basic pattern of human thoughts intact, leaving them with the ability to still function and do their duty. They were essentially puppets now, with bodies going through directed motions, all except Dalia.

She rose from her seat and crossed the room to take the second-in-command position one terminal down from Nathan. "Bringing up the visual you wanted, sir," she said crisply, hands flying over the controls in front of her.

Nathan nodded, hands resting on the edge of the command terminal as his eyes flicked across the vidscreens and hologrid. The Warhounds settled themselves where they could, minds sliding into a pulsating merge that hovered near the back of Nathan's mind.

A visual finally came up, taken from a security feed two kilometers away. The remains of fighter jets burned in the broken streets of Paris, smoke curling black and ugly into the sky. Strykers were already on the ground, moving around the wreckage. Nathan licked sweat off his upper lip before merging with the waiting Warhounds, taking the apex position in that grouping of minds and power.

Don't let them near the launch area, he said. The order burned across the mental grid, reverberating and branding itself into every Warhound mind he could reach. *Our priority is protecting the space shuttles. We can't let them gain access to even a single one.*

"Dalia," Nathan said. He stared through the information scrolling across his terminal, feeling sweat sliding down the back of his neck, following the curve of his spine. "Keep the launches going. I want—"

He broke off as a familiar mind spiked on the mental grid, the psi signature one he didn't think he'd ever feel on this planet again. Nathan jerked his head around, staring in anger and shock as Gideon leaned against the side of the command terminal, face calm.

"Nathan," Gideon said.

"Why the *hell* aren't you on the *Ark*?" Nathan demanded. "I need you off this goddamn planet, Gideon."

"I have what you need."

Nathan stared at him in disbelief, noting the soft silver gleam that stained his son's dark blue eyes. "Lucas nearly burned out your mind. You've got holes in your memory. You don't even know what to look for."

"Lucas didn't destroy everything." Gideon slid a hand through his hair and pulled, the action one of Kristen's habits. "There's an echo in my head. Where Samantha used to be."

Nathan didn't ask for permission before entering his son's mind, sifting carefully through broken thoughts for the scar that was left of the psi link Gideon once shared with his twin. Tangled through its raw layers were pieces of memory, transferred from Samantha in that moment when she saved Gideon at the Strykers Syndicate. Nathan saw it and carefully mapped out a large fragment of a psi signature that didn't belong to either of his children.

"How did I miss this?" Nathan said.

"We're twins. We can't remain apart forever." Gideon smiled slowly, the curve of his mouth tight and forced. "You always did fear insanity, but it's all that's left for you now."

Nathan couldn't deny that fact. "Suit up, Gideon. You're right. I'm going to need your help to stop Lucas."

[FORTY]

SEPTEMBER 2379
PARIS, FRANCE

The shuttles landed in the streets of Paris, between the remains of bombed-out buildings and away from the wastewater that flowed through the Seine. It was as close as the Strykers could get to the launch area without running up against Warhound telekinetic shields. If the Strykers didn't land, they risked ending up like the military jets, blown to pieces after hitting a barrier their instruments couldn't pick up.

The rest of the fighting was taking place on the ground, in the middle of a deadzone with toxicity levels that were still dangerous, even to psions. The two-pronged push came from the west and the north, both Stryker groups filled with telekinetics, pyrokinetics, and a few dozen telepaths not drafted into the Stryker merge.

They outnumbered the Warhounds by a decent margin, but that didn't mean anything. Most of the Warhounds were higher-Classed psions than the Strykers, and all of them knew how to merge. The crushing telekinetic blow that slammed into the Stryker ranks coming from the west tore through weaker shields, throwing people to the ground with bone-breaking force.

Jason anchored his telekinetic shield with all his Class 0 strength against the Warhound merge. His shield wavered beneath the heavy weight of foreign power, but didn't break. Swearing, Jason shoved his power forward at breakneck speed to clear the street ahead of them. Beside him, Quinton had a fireball formed, the crackling flame joined by dozens of others as pyrokinetics prepared to attack.

"Dropping shields," Jason shouted. *"Go!"*

A firestorm ripped down the street, riding gas and burning through debris to add fuel to the fire. The pyrokinetics forced the fire to burn white-hot on its way to their targets. They came up short against telekinetic shields, but the fire served as a needed distraction. The Strykers had numbers on their side, and the hundreds of mental strikes started to slowly bog down the merged Warhound telekinetics. Some shields caved, sending Warhounds to their knees on the street, screaming from severe psionic overload in their minds.

The Strykers kept searching for weak spots, struggling to find a way into the center core of that power. They found some with Lucas's help, his guidance enabling them to shatter pieces of the merge and, with it, some of the Warhounds' concentration. The telekinetic shields in their immediate area disappeared and the fire consumed Warhounds.

Screams echoed in the air, along with the stench of burning human flesh, but the Strykers ignored both on their push forward. Quinton looked over his shoulder to where Lucas ran, dark blue eyes like holes in his face behind the helmet of his skinsuit. Blood slid out of his nose in a thin trickle. He was skirting a line of mental damage far beyond psi shock by being here on the ground, but he had no choice. Lucas was commanding this battle, and if he was on the field, Nathan wouldn't be looking for an attack anywhere else.

"Can you handle this?" Quinton asked as he adjusted the grip on his pulse-rifle. The strap was slung across his chest; he'd let the rifle go in order to use his power.

"Don't question my judgment," Lucas said.

"I'm not. You got us this far, but if you're dead, we're fucked."

Lucas waved at Quinton. "We have to keep moving."

Quinton took him at his word and lengthened his stride as Jason picked up the pace, pulse-rifle gripped in both hands. Everyone was loaded down with weapons for this fight, but half the Strykers on the field treated them as an afterthought. Telekinetics were guilty of that mind-set more than others, used to relying on the physical force of their power over the guns in their hands.

The sun beat down on them through a partially cloudy sky, smoke warping their line of sight. Telekinetics wrapped layered shields around everyone as they double-timed it down the street. The mental grid was like a warzone beyond every Stryker and Warhound shield, telepathic and empathic strikes ripping against hundreds of minds. The constant mental attacks wore down everyone's defenses, with shields slipping beneath the weight of focused power. Once those shields slipped, the minds behind them were torn to pieces. Lucas's merge of telepaths was holding off a good many Warhound strikes, but the distance between London and Paris put them at a disadvantage.

You should have let us onto the field, Samantha said through the psi link that tied her to Lucas. *Here, catch the next layer.*

Power slid through his mind, bolstering his Class I strength, burning against the edges of his shields. The faint hint of pain was caught by Kristen and locked down somewhere that Lucas couldn't reach. His sisters were like twin spots of brightness buried in his mind. Kristen's presence was chaotic and distracting, her empathy pulling at his mind in ways it didn't want to bend, but had no choice but to accept. Samantha was a mental bridge between Lucas and the Strykers in London, linked beyond that to other Strykers across the planet. A web of psionic power spanned the world, and she was slowly spinning it all together, feeding him the power. Her own Class II strength was barely enough to guide the Strykers into the merge and help Lucas hold it together.

Lucas was the apex of that merge, the only one who could have carried the load and survived. Nathan made it a point to target him first.

The next telepathic strike caused Lucas to stumble in midstride. Jason caught him with one hand, keeping Lucas upright as they ran. Jason didn't look at him, all his attention focused on the street ahead. "Lucas?"

The crushing pressure of merged minds weighed down on Lucas's shields, echoed in the drag of his feet against the ground. He blinked black dots from his vision. "Let's start teleporting."

Telekinesis wrapped around everyone, dozens of Strykers picking up their fellow teammates and teleporting across the distance ahead in short-distance 'ports. They judged the distance as best they could using binoculars to get a visual, putting kilometers behind them in seconds rather than minutes or even hours. The Strykers came out of the last teleport into a hail of enemy gunfire, energy darts and bullets slamming into telekinetic shields and Warhound telepaths struggling to break their minds as their feet hit the ground.

The Strykers in the scattered group spread farther out. Some telekinetic shields fell beneath Warhound attacks, forcing Strykers to find physical cover behind broken cement foundations. Some weren't quick enough and took bullets in the back, collapsing to the ground. They didn't remain out in the open for long. Telekinetics pulled the wounded out of fire range, teleporting them back to London with the help of telepaths who provided up-to-date visuals.

Quinton dragged Lucas down behind a crumbling wall with Jason's help, watching Lucas's back while he watched over their minds. Lucas let his head fall back, helmet scraping against a cracked cement wall. His breath came rapidly, the oxygen coming out of his tanks clean, even if it tasted like copper on his tongue.

The sound of gunfire filled the air, screams echoing every once in a while over the shouted orders coming from both sides of the fight. Voices echoed down dozens of psi links, the mental chatter buzzing in the back of everyone's mind. Beyond the Warhounds and conscripted human soldiers, the launch platforms were visible with their space shuttles, sunlight glinting off fuselages.

"They've got a space shuttle on the launch ramp," Quinton said as he ducked down to reload.

"Lucas, who's on it?" Jason asked.

"Unregistered humans," Lucas said after a moment, the telepaths in his merge bringing him the information. "Some Warhounds."

"What about Nathan?"

"No. He's still on the ground." Lucas coughed, trying to catch his breath. "We can't let that space shuttle launch."

"Then we won't."

Quinton looked over Lucas's head at Jason. "You pulling back your cover?"

"No other choice," Jason said grimly. He handed Quinton his gun. The Strykers ranged around them moved to compensate for his loss. Jason slid down beside Lucas and put his back against the wall, closing his eyes. "Can't let the Warhounds have a gene pool to breed from. Besides, this will buy Threnody and Kerr some more time."

Lucas nodded tightly. "They're almost in position."

"Good to know," Quinton said as he focused on the enemy. "We'll watch your backs."

Lucas pulled Jason into the merge, reaching through him for Keiko. She was on the other side of the city, having come in from the north, her group of Strykers closing in on the launch area. Lucas's mind pressed against Keiko's shields and she dropped them.

The merge had mostly been filled by telepaths. Samantha anchored the 'path-oriented psions as Lucas rolled through Keiko's mind, pulling the telekinetic into a secondary merge that began to meld with the first. Keiko knew every last Stryker in the Syndicate, both those in Paris and the ones left scattered across the world. She gave up those psi signatures to Lucas, their locations sparking across the mental grid for Lucas to see.

He reached for them, searching out the psions that read to his touch as telekinetic, and pulled the ones he could spare from the fighting into the merge. It was difficult for the Strykers to give up control, to cede their power to someone else completely. In the face of a changing world, they succumbed to Lucas's mental order reluctantly, and he felt the merge strain beneath hundreds of psion minds. This merge held more power and more minds than any other Lucas had ever created, and its strength scorched through his own power, nearly shattering his concentration. Pain crept through his awareness, pricking at his thoughts.

That's not for you to feel, Kristen said, his sister suddenly there in the center of his mind.

She turned off the pain, the safety function that enabled a person to know when something was dangerously wrong going dormant. The body needed pain, needed to know what was wrong with itself, as did the mind. Lucas couldn't know, not for this. Kristen locked down all the pain synapses in his head and body, her empathic manipulation a mental block not even Lucas could break down.

Through the jumbled eyes of too many people, the Strykers in merge saw the space shuttle launch, saw it streak down the long length of the curved ramp as it was propelled into the sky. Engines fired with a roar, the vapor trail streaming behind the space shuttle, thick and impossible to miss in the late-summer sky as it fought gravity to leave the planet.

Jason, Lucas said, his thought echoed by hundreds of others. *Take point.*

The bottom seemed to drop out of the merge, every single one of Jason's shields falling. His power exploded on the mental grid as a novalike burn, channeling into the merge. Through Lucas, Jason linked to every telekinetic in the Stryker ranks they could spare from defense on the field, drawing on their strength to bolster his own as he telekinetically reached for the space shuttle with a crushing mental grip.

Lucas nearly lost Jason in that rush of power, struggling to hold on to the other man's mind in the sheer massiveness of the merge. It took Quinton to find him, the bond between the two stretched taut, but it held. The backlash rolled through Quinton's mind, springing back down the bond in a never-ending loop that threatened the pyrokinetic's sanity. Lucas threw up a telepathic shield around Quinton's mind, struggling to keep the other man from succumbing to madness. Quinton's thanks was wordless and desperate.

In the sky, the space shuttle hit the upper atmosphere. In Lucas's mind, the merge was a glimmering monstrosity. Jason was somewhere in the thick of things, his Class 0 strength straining everyone's connection. Despite the Warhound merge striking against their minds, driven by Nathan's angry desperation, the Stryker telekinetics still managed to grab the space shuttle and wrench it off course. The broken angle of ascent was helped along by way of merged telekinesis. The space shuttle shredded apart as it fell back to earth.

NO!

Dozens of Warhounds minds screamed the word through the mental grid as the aborted launch—so close to its goal of escape—ended in hundreds of fiery fragments that streaked across the sky like meteorites. Silence stretched across the mental grid where the space shuttle fell, the static of human minds diminishing. They died in Earth's atmosphere, burning up as gravity pulled them home.

Nathan's merge ripped through the frayed mess on the mental grid, aiming for Lucas's merge. The mental grid tore beneath the clash of so many minds slamming together, so many minds breaking apart and dying, threatening to take neighboring minds with them. Then Samantha was there, cutting and tearing the Stryker merge apart from the inside out. She reassembled it into something that would hold, struggling to keep it stable.

Lucas's mind momentarily blanked out beneath the weight of the merge, thoughts and power twisting with something he couldn't identify, some emotion that Kristen refused to let him experience. In that moment where it seemed his mind would tear out of his body, Nathan slammed through his thoughts, fracturing everything.

Lucas's mind didn't break, though it took every bit of skill he had to force it to remain together. He borrowed strength from the merge itself, taking power pulled out of the willing minds of hundreds of Strykers. Aisling had seen this symbiosis years ago, lifetimes ago, in a white room bombed to ashes during the Border Wars. The disparate pieces of a world struggling to realign themselves into something new.

Somewhere, in the space that existed between two heartbeats, in the possibilities that festered in the human mind, Lucas saw it all. In the bottom of his mind, in memories too numerous to count, Lucas thought he could hear her.

Tell me that they're worth it, Lucas remembered saying once as a child as he gripped his future in his hands, knowing even then that it was too late to back out. Too late to give up. *Tell me that what's left of humanity is worth the future you're trying to give them.*

Silence was his only answer then, same as it was now. He'd heard all her excuses before anyway.

He was the means. His daughter was the end.

In the here and now, none of that mattered, not when the only thing that everyone was striving for was survival.

The sound of a gunshot, too close for comfort and too loud to ignore, jerked Lucas's attention out of the merge, instinct pulling up a telekinetic shield around himself. The split-second distraction lasted long enough for him to recognize the voice that started screaming, to feel Jason wrench himself free of the merge. Jason's abrupt exit ripped too many minds apart in the process, ruining the network Samantha had built through Lucas's mind.

Lucas opened his eyes, the world gone bright and liquid as his mind overloaded. He saw a familiar figure standing in front of them, gun leveled at someone else. Lucas watched Gideon smile.

"You couldn't hide Jason forever, Lucas," his younger brother said. "You didn't mindwipe me deep enough. I still had his psi signature in my memories."

The crack of displaced air from a teleport broke his tenuous concentration, and Lucas spiraled downward into a fraying merge that Nathan was taking apart one mind at a time with lethal, focused intent.

At the bottom of that tangled mess, Lucas found a way out.

[FORTY-ONE]

SEPTEMBER 2379
PARIS, FRANCE

With the help of a telepath, Gideon used the eyes of a dying Stryker for his visual and teleported in behind the Strykers' defensive line. Quinton never saw him arrive, but he felt it when Jason got shot. The crack of the gun going off drowned out the sound of the teleport. The bullet slammed into Jason's chest at close range with telekinetic help. The sudden agony was shared between them. Quinton doubled over screaming as Jason's mind exploded through his own, the trauma nearly incapacitating him.

Jason, tied deeply in the merge, was forcibly yanked out of that connection, his mind ripped away from the collective whole. His eyes snapped open, the world spinning around him with a suddenness that made him sick. He choked back the bile that crawled up his throat, not wanting to vomit inside his helmet. He thought he heard Quinton yell a name, maybe his, as he struggled to breathe.

Blood bubbled past his lips. The hand that suddenly pressed down on his chest pulled a scream out of him that showed up in sound waves and light, in the blood that rushed through Quinton's face and veins and skin. Jason blinked, his power fluctuating in ways it wasn't supposed to—or maybe it was. Around him, he could see a glittering blanket of light, of energy, that flowed back in a connecting line to a body of cells and bones and breath. The connection hummed in his ears, against his skin.

Is this what our powers look like? Jason thought in some distant corner of his mind. *Do we all burn like this?*

His telekinetic shields went down beneath his shattered concentration. Everything hurt, the pain worse than when Kristen ripped open his natal shields. The world was shifting, Quinton pulling him back into the spectrum that they lived in, his mind impossible to ignore through the bond. Jason blinked, and blinked some more, until he was looking up into Quinton's pale face behind his helmet. Quinton's eyes were wide from shock and fear, blood leaking from his nose and ears. The pyrokinetic was leaning over Lucas in order to reach Jason.

"Jason," Quinton said, voice breaking on the name. "Damn it, Jason. You need to hold on."

"I am," Jason gasped out. He lifted a hand to Quinton's shoulder, fingers skittering over rough synthfabric. Jason left streaks of blood behind where he touched, the shape of hemoglobin in his sight swallowing him whole. "I am."

Jason felt the tug of foreign telekinesis pull at his body, like the shock of a defib machine on a heart. Gideon was trying to teleport him off the field. Jason closed his eyes and anchored his power in the only thing that mattered if he was going to survive—Quinton. Jason held on to the pyrokinetic through the teleport, forcing Gideon to bear the extra weight.

They landed hard on a cold metal floor, in a room filled with shouting voices and the steady hum of machines. Jason choked on blood, Quinton's hands yanking at the flak jacket strapped over his uniform to get to the wound beneath. Neither man cared about the guns trained on their bodies; Quinton only cared about Jason, because if Jason died, then so would he, along with the rest of the world. With shaking fingers, Quinton undid the helmet of Jason's skinsuit, pulling it off.

He fumbled at his own, communication lost with the comm link wired into the helmets. He tossed both aside, pressing his hands down harder over the sucking wound in Jason's chest, fingers digging against synthfabric and torn flesh, blood slicking his own skin.

"I wanted him alive, Gideon," Nathan said from somewhere behind them.

With Jason slipping away beneath his hands, Quinton ignored everyone. "Don't do this, Jays," Quinton said raggedly as he leaned his weight against the wound, eyes riveted on Jason's bloodless face. "Don't you fucking die on me. Threnody and Kerr would never forgive you."

Lashes flickered over Jason's eyes.

"That's it. Come on, do what you did for Threnody. Fix yourself."

"No nanites" came the near voiceless reply.

Quinton shook his head fiercely, one hand moving to slap Jason's face lightly to keep him awake. "You don't need it. You never needed it. They were just a goddamn crutch. Now fucking *look* at me and fix yourself."

Jason's protest was soundless, blood bubbling bright and red from his lips. The bubbles popped on a wet breath, and Jason jerked beneath Quinton's hands, still drowning.

"Please," Quinton begged, feeling the bond begin to fray in the back of his mind, starting to give way. He could feel cracks in his own mind at that anchor point, the painful stretch of his thoughts beginning to unravel. "*Please*. Goddamn it, don't do this."

Jason forced his eyes open, black pupils having swallowed the hazel of his irises. He struggled to bring the face above him into focus, Quinton's expression frantic.

"Okay," Jason said, lips barely moving.

He closed his eyes, forced his power to sink into his own body. Down, down, until he saw his own cellular makeup against the back of his eyelids, all the possibility of life held in the double-helix coil of a DNA strand. No need for nanites and a biotank, just the code that defined his body. Just the power found in the genetic makeup of a Class 0 psion.

Jason dragged his power through his veins, through muscle and tissue, the fragile sponginess of his lungs, looking for what needed to be fixed. Tear by tear he healed himself from the inside out, fixing the hole the bullet had torn through him. The blood loss was something he would have to fix later. He didn't have time to remake pints of the stuff by coaxing at

his bone marrow, not when Warhounds wanted to peel him off the
ground and take him into space.

Jason hacked up sticky globules of blood, spitting until nothing was
left in his lungs but air. A metallic taste saturated his mouth as he
gripped Quinton's arms, needing an anchor. The bond between them
shuddered in their minds. It couldn't block the headache pounding
through Jason's head or the shaky weakness in his limbs. Pain burned
through his nerves, impossible to ignore.

"Oh, man," he gasped. "I feel like shit."

Quinton was abruptly wrenched away, the pyrokinetic slammed down
to the floor beside him. Jason felt that same telekinesis pin his own body to
the floor. Weakly, he tried to fight it, but his mind hadn't stabilized yet,
even if his body mostly had. He needed time to focus.

Nathan wasn't going to give him that.

Kerr did.

The telepath slid into Jason's mind with an ease that came from a lifetime of living in each other's head. Jason didn't fight him as Kerr focused
through his eyes. Kerr soaked up the details of the room and used that
visual to teleport in by way of merged Stryker telekinetics, mind cutting
through Jason's bruised and battered thoughts without apology.

Jason—shield!

[FORTY-TWO]

SEPTEMBER 2379
PARIS, FRANCE

The pilot landed the shuttle hard, one of the last civilian shuttles
allowed to come to ground. The Command Center had ordered
everyone else to stay clear of Paris until the current problem was
dealt with.

"Could he not get us killed prematurely?" Threnody said as she glanced at Kerr. "That's the worst landing I've gone through in months. Matron is a better pilot than he is."

Kerr undid his harness before grabbing his helmet and putting it on. "Let's just be happy we got here at all and get the hell off this shuttle."

Threnody stood up. "Couldn't agree more."

The fifty-person shuttle was packed to the bulkheads, the pilot having ignored weight restrictions. They didn't have enough fuel to make it back to London, which was the only reason the Command Center allowed them to land. Kerr mindwiped every passenger and crew member on their way out, erasing their memories of himself and Threnody.

"Maintenance hatch is in the galley," Kerr said. "Let's get below."

They reached the galley and knelt on the floor. The latch was embedded in the decking; Kerr undid it and the hatch dropped down. First Threnody, then Kerr slid into the cargo bay of the shuttle. He locked the hatch behind them.

The space was full of cargo trunks. Heavy-duty straps kept everything held down, with a small aisle between the two sides of the cargo bay. They found the carrying case still secured where they'd left it with their bags. They freed their bags first and stripped out of their clothes in favor of the nondescript workers' uniforms and tool belts Samantha had stolen for them. Then they freed the carrying case from the anchor straps.

"Two options," Kerr said, pointing at the dimly glowing signs bolted to the side of the shuttle at the rear from where they stood and farther ahead. "Loading hatches, or another maintenance hatch."

"Where's the maintenance hatch down here?"

"Decking."

"We'll come out beneath the shuttle?"

"Yes."

"Then we want that one."

It took them five minutes to find it. The wide floor hatch was cordoned off near the rear of the shuttle. They got it open and found themselves staring at the smooth metal launchpad. It was a good four-meter drop, an impossible descent with what they carried.

Threnody lifted her head and looked at Kerr. "Trunks?"

He nodded. "Trunks."

They worked quickly to undo the safety harnesses and ropes that kept the nearest cargo trunks in place, pushing several onto the platform. The noise the trunks made was drowned out by the noise of dozens of transport shuttles sitting with their engines running.

Kerr jumped down to stack the trunks, arms straining to move them. Once they were stable, he climbed on top and waited as Threnody carefully pushed the carrying case over the edge. She grunted as the weight swung from the end of her arms, joints aching, but she didn't let go. She saw Kerr get his shoulders beneath it and some of the tension eased in her arms as he took most of the weight. Threnody quickly pitched herself out of the shuttle and onto the platform.

She landed loosely, letting her body absorb the impact, and steadied herself with her hands. Then she moved to help Kerr. From beneath the body of the transport shuttle, they could see the rear of the Command Center, the squat building taking up most of the view. Technicians raced about, most heading for an emergency exit. Whatever their orders, Threnody and Kerr couldn't hear them. They weren't tapped into the comm channel being used, so they couldn't eavesdrop on the chatter.

"Shit," Threnody said as she stared out at the launch area. "This place is bigger than I thought."

"Let's head for those doors."

They ran as fast as they could, trying not to jostle the dangerous contents of the carrying case. A brief touch of telepathic power on unsuspecting human minds caused the workers to ignore them. They couldn't do anything about the security feed, but hopefully the bioware on the recognition points of their faces would trip up the computers long enough for them to get inside.

The supervisor on duty let workers through the emergency exit in small groups. Threnody and Kerr made it inside within five minutes, the door closing behind them. They waited impatiently inside a small decontamination chamber, the process agonizingly slow to them. Once they were cleared to proceed, a second door slid open and they walked into a hallway crowded with workers. Threnody and Kerr paused only long enough to unlock their helmets and take them off. They breathed in recycled air that stung their noses. The emergency alarm going off hurt their ears; the strobe lights nearly blinded them.

Best place to put it would be on one of the upper levels, Threnody said as they pushed their way through the crowd. *Setting it up in one of the support columns would effectively put it belowground, and that's not going to help us.*

The further up we go, the more Warhounds we're going to encounter, Kerr warned. *I can feel them on the mental grid. They're merged with Nathan and it's not pretty. Their attention might be outside this place, but I can guarantee you that if we're spotted, they'll turn all that power on this building to try to find us.*

We need to stay aboveground.

Then let's find somewhere on the next level. It's the safest place we can use.

They took an access stairwell up, and appropriated the first empty room they came across. The pair set the heavy carrying case down once inside. After locking the door, they tossed their helmets aside. Threnody looked around the storage room at the half-empty shelves and dented walls.

"Let's figure out where to put the bomb," she said.

They wrestled the carrying case to the rear of the storage room before opening it. Strapped securely inside was a second, smaller case that, when opened, revealed the components of a nuclear bomb. Wires protruded from it, connecting to an external receiver, the remote detonator strapped securely beside it. Threnody pried the remote detonator free and set it down on a nearby metal shelf.

"Okay," she said, letting Kerr take her spot. "Let's hope Novak did this right."

Kerr removed the flashlight hanging from his tool belt and propped it up at an angle on the open carrying case to get more light. He then carefully slipped the receiver out of the case and set it down on a shelf. Having grown up with a hacker for a partner, he knew what to do better than Threnody, but that didn't mean he was an expert. Halfway through the setup, Kerr let out a sharp gasp.

"Tell me you didn't just set the timer," Threnody said, trying to keep the fear out of her voice. "We're not ready, Kerr. Everyone's not off the field yet."

Kerr looked over his shoulder at her, face gone gray beneath the harsh lights. "No. Lucas just ripped apart a space shuttle with Jason's help."

Threnody curled her hand around his forearm. "Focus on the bomb."

They wanted to be out on the field with their partners, but instead they were here, finishing what Lucas had started. The two former team leaders of the Strykers Syndicate understood that failure wasn't an option, even if the plan was built through the shady gray areas of morality.

Kerr was plugging in the command codes that Novak said would connect the remote detonator with the receiver when agony exploded through his mind. He bent double beneath the pain, stumbling away from the shelves. Threnody grabbed him, giving Kerr support before he collapsed. He leaned heavily against her, forehead pressed into the curve of her neck as he bit down on his bottom lip against the scream wanting to leave his lungs. She felt something wet slide between the collar of her skinsuit and her throat: Kerr's blood.

"Kerr," Threnody said, voice tight. "*Kerr.* I need you to focus."

Jason's been shot, came the shaky words. *Feels like he's dying.*

They didn't share a bond anymore, but Threnody would never believe that meant Kerr gave up crawling into Jason's mind whenever he felt like it. Shoving the taller man upright, Threnody forced Kerr to look at her. The haunted look in his eyes made her stomach knot.

"Go save him," she said fiercely. "I'll give you five minutes to distract the Warhounds. You better make damn sure Jason has you shielded from anything metal. Understand? I don't care if you have to hold his mind together to do it, you make sure he shields you."

Kerr stared at her. "You're not coming."

"One of us has to finish this. Now go."

"I'll find Lucas," Kerr said as he pulled away from her and ran for the door. "I'll let him know we're almost ready."

She felt Kerr dig his power into her mind so hard and deep that for a moment all she saw was brightly colored spots. *I'll keep you hidden,* Kerr said, and then he was gone.

Kerr hit the hallway running, telepathy spanning the damaged mental grid for the only minds that mattered to him. He found Jason and Quinton first, their tangled thoughts weak and getting weaker. He couldn't find Lucas, but the Stryker merge still held against Nathan's focused attacks. Lucas was alive—somewhere—and all Kerr had to do was find him. But with all the telepathic power in the world tangled up in everyone's mind, Kerr only had one chance.

Using his empathy, he skimmed through the ravaged and dying minds around him, fighting the overwhelming urge to vomit in midstep as the horrendous feeling of hundreds of people dying overwhelmed him. He had to fight to regain his balance and continued running down the lower-level hallway, his footsteps echoing against the metal walls.

He felt Kristen first, her dysfunctional power like a hole in the mental grid that threatened to swallow Kerr's sanity. Keeping his distance would have been the smart thing to do, but he didn't have time to think about his safety, only about what needed to be done. Kerr snapped a telepathic psi link between them, Kristen's thoughts swirling through his mind.

I need Lucas, Kerr said.

He can't hear you, Kristen told him, the usual manic cheer gone from her mental voice. In its place was some emotion he couldn't identify, not in the context of her power. Kristen wasn't the sort to feel fear.

Then find me a telepath who can link with me.

Kristen gave him to Samantha, and Kerr almost lost himself to the merge. He had to claw his way back to a balanced mind, with Samantha dragging Kerr behind his shields to keep him from getting sucked into the pulsating mass of power that was the merge. Samantha was barely managing to hold it together, and he could sense the brittleness in her mind.

Make it quick, came Samantha's strained voice. It echoed, as if she was speaking from far away.

We're almost ready. Start clearing the field.

Understood.

He could feel her pulling away, layers of his shields peeling off as the magnitude of power bruised his mind. Kerr still reached for her. *Wait! I need a teleport.*

Visual?

It wasn't her voice alone this time, but dozens. Stryker telekinetics reached for him with their power through the psi link while others sought to hold off the Warhound merge. Through them, Kerr felt the strikes that

Nathan was orchestrating against the apex, Lucas succumbing to agony, even if he could no longer feel it. Samantha was a conduit between the Strykers and her brother, with the Strykers giving Lucas their powers while still struggling to understand how it all worked. Their lack of knowledge was crippling him.

We need a visual, the voices said again.

Kerr struggled to come back to himself, to keep his focus, reaching for the familiarity of a mind he would know anywhere. Years spent hiding behind Jason's mental shields meant it was simple for him to slide into the microtelekinetic's thoughts, to look through someone else's eyes and see where he needed to go.

Samantha's telekinetics saw through Kerr's mind and out through Jason's eyes, their resolve coalescing into a teleport that broke through the telekinetic shields surrounding the Command Center. Kerr arrived in the command room with a heavy stumble, nearly falling to his knees, surprising everyone. Kerr tightened the psi link between himself and Jason, calling out a warning.

Jason—shield!

Kerr got his balance back and slammed his fist straight into Nathan's face, even as Lucas struck at his father's mind. The physical attack briefly broke Nathan's concentration, head snapping back from the blow. It was enough of a distraction for Jason to slide his telekinesis around them in the strongest shield he could create. He was just in time.

The sudden tearing shock that ripped through the command room rode the back of an electrical storm. It exploded out of every terminal, ripping through the metal structure of the building itself, burning through everything it could. Half the Warhounds in the command room died, burned beyond recognition by electricity surging under psion control.

[FORTY-THREE]

SEPTEMBER 2379
PARIS, FRANCE

Threnody descended into the depths of the Command Center. She wasn't the telepath and Kerr wouldn't remain undiscovered for long, not with the core of the Warhound merge in the levels high above them. They both knew it, Lucas had known it.

You'll only get one chance, he'd said back in Toronto. *Make it count.*

She planned to.

Threnody ran down the hallway, counting down the seconds in her head. She held a gun in one hand and the remote detonator in the other. She kept her weapon out of sight when passing people. Most were talking frantically into personal comms, too focused on the emergency to pay her any attention. Psionic interference, she thought. She could distantly feel Kerr through the psi link, his concentration a pressure in the back of her skull that faded in and out. It made her ears ring. She swallowed to make them pop as she dodged into an access stairwell.

Threnody's knees started to ache with every impact her feet took on the way down to the bottom level. The schematics Samantha had stolen were downloaded into the datapad hanging from Threnody's tool belt. Threnody had them memorized, the layout pressed indelibly into her mind. She had one goal and it lay at the very bottom of a support pillar—where the generator room Lucas had teleported them into on their way to pick up Novak in Antarctica was located.

She slammed her way out of the access stairwell, stumbling into a short hallway. The alarm seemed louder down here, the flashing emergency lights hard on her eyes. Threnody looked up and came face-to-face with a pair of soldiers blocking her way. She didn't think the soldiers were a quad since there were only two of them. The door she needed was located right behind them. Threnody headed for it, acting as if she had every right to be there, but one of the soldiers grabbed her arm.

"What do you think you're doing?" the man snapped.

"Do you hear that alarm? Do you know what's happening out there?" Threnody said. "I've been ordered to do a manual check of the generators."

"A manual check was done an hour ago."

"Now the brass wants another one. You can help me with it."

She spun, lightning quick, slamming her elbow into the man's throat hard enough to crush his trachea. She dropped the remote detonator and shoved him against the wall, one hand pressed over his mouth and nose, cutting off his air as she shoved her electrokinesis into his body. With her other arm, Threnody aimed her gun and fired twice, one of her bullets finding its mark in the other soldier's face. Quinton was a brilliant teacher. She would never reach his level of expertise with firearms, but he had ensured she would survive a gunfight.

Breathing heavily, Threnody bent to pick up the remote detonator and headed for the door that led to the generator room below. She stepped on blood, feet skidding on slick wetness. When she reached the door, she discovered it was locked. Threnody smacked one hand against the control panel, frying the system. The door shuddered in its casing and she had to wrench it open, muscles straining against the weight. Her goal was within reach, the one place in the heavily shielded structure where she could start a chain reaction and guarantee it would affect the entire Command Center.

Threnody squeezed through the opening and stumbled onto a cramped landing. Several flights of stairs led down to the confines of the generator room. She started down them and was two steps up from the generator-room floor when she caught movement out of the corner of her eye. A lifetime of training saved her from getting killed, but not from getting shot. Pitching herself over the metal railing, Threnody took the bullet high in her right thigh instead of in the chest.

Threnody landed hard, heartbeat pounding loudly in her ears. She managed to keep her grip on the remote detonator. Adrenaline masked the agony in her body, long enough for her to get a shot off at the two soldiers advancing on her position. One soldier took her bullet in the shoulder.

"Wasn't fucking thinking," Threnody gasped. "Two soldiers don't make a goddamn quad."

She smacked her bare hand down on the floor and called up her power. Bright blue electricity erupted from her skin, the metal the perfect conductor. The two soldiers died almost instantly, their nervous systems overloading. They collapsed as the alarm changed pitch. For one frantic moment, Threnody thought the Warhounds had located her.

A merged telepathic strike exploded on the mental grid. Her shields nearly didn't hold. Only Kerr's telepathic maneuvering saved her. He shoved her thoughts further beneath static human minds so hard that her vision swam, or maybe it was the blood loss. She could sense the rest of the Stryker merge behind Kerr's mind, the power crackling across the mental grid. Threnody rolled onto her back, gasping from shock and pain. She pressed one hand over the wound in her leg, blood flowing over her fingers.

"Fuck," she breathed. "*Fuck,* that hurts."

Numb fingers fumbled at her tool belt. She unclipped all her tools and yanked the belt free. Methodically, Threnody wrapped it high around her thigh. She pulled the belt as tight as she could to form a tourniquet, choking back the yell that threatened to rip out of her lungs. Teeth tore through the thin skin of her bottom lip, slicing it open. Blood filled her mouth. She swallowed it, gagging on the taste. Lying there, the metal floor electric-warm beneath her, Threnody tried to breathe.

"You can do this," she told herself, voice raspy and hitching from pain. "You have to."

Threnody rolled to her good side and reached for the handheld laser saw nearby. Gripping it, she got her left knee under her and shoved herself to her feet, using the railing to take her weight when she stumbled. Putting weight on her right leg almost caused her to vomit.

"I fucking hate getting shot."

She hobbled forward. It was hot down here, despite the specialized shielding in place to keep out the radiation taint in the ground. Sweat trickled down her back and neck. She looked around, seeing only machinery beyond the walkway railings. She limped down the length of one generator, looking for the control panel.

When she found it, Threnody set the remote detonator on the floor and gripped the laser saw in shaky hands. She used it to cut through the metal paneling and let it clatter to the floor. She pressed a hand to the side of her head as pain throbbed through her temple. Kerr must have sensed her discomfort because he strengthened her shields with his telepathy. Threnody let him do whatever he needed to keep her under everyone's radar. Taking a deep breath, Threnody stared at the interior of the control panel.

For the first time in years, she thought of Atlanta. Of the scorching summer heat and the muggy feel of the air. Of the acid storms and the churning hurricane that came to shore when she was only three years old. She remembered the night when her natal shields broke in the middle of that screaming storm of wind and rain and ocean salt. How she accidentally fried the generator that supported environmental controls for two blocks of slum tenements, too young to comprehend the damage she had inflicted. Her first use of electrokinesis forced dozens of families out into that raging storm when air no longer flowed through the packed rooms.

Threnody remembered how everyone else in that storm died and how she didn't—saved by the Strykers Syndicate and destined for a life of slavery.

Except Lucas had shown her another way, and maybe it wasn't the best way or the right way, but it was better than how she'd lived under the government's control. Freedom always came with a price. This was hers, and she would pay it.

Panting, Threnody stuck her hands into the cavity before her, wires and motherboards scraping against her bare fingers. She was elbow deep in a piece of the sealed Command Center's complicated wired interior, fingers wrapped around what was, essentially, a computerized nervous system.

It could die.

"One chance," she whispered.

Threnody hoped she had given Kerr enough time to do what needed to be done. She hoped he had saved Jason and Quinton. Closing her eyes, Threnody tapped into her electrokinesis.

Electricity exploded from her nerves with no restriction, bursting through the Command Center. Threnody poured everything she had into the overload she was desperately trying to create. She didn't have lightning this time to fall back on, just sheer desperation.

A deep, cracking groan echoed through the structure, the generators shuddering as they overloaded and died. Electricity burned through the wiring embedded in the walls and floor of the Command Center. Threnody's electrokinesis pushed the damage further, tearing through circuitry until it found the command room itself with explosive, deadly results.

[FORTY-FOUR]

SEPTEMBER 2379
PARIS, FRANCE

Kerr stared through the too-bright electric power as it crawled over Jason's telekinetic shield. Nathan's rapidly swelling face stared back at him from behind Gideon's own telekinetic shield. Around them, humans, telepaths, and empaths fell over, bodies jerking through electrocution. Kerr could sense both Sercas trying to restructure the Warhound merge through those deaths.

"Kerr," Jason said weakly as Quinton helped him sit up. A thick red stain was spread across his chest, tiny bone shards sticking to his torn skinsuit.

For a second, Kerr ignored him, reaching through a different psi link for Threnody. He shoved aside the pain, whispering apologies into her mind even as he pulled a visual for teleportation through her eyes.

'Port here, Jays, Kerr said as he pulled Jason into the psi link and shared the visual, then added a second one of the storage room below. *Don't worry about me, I'll be all right.*

You lying son of a bitch, do you really expect me to leave you behind?

You don't have a choice. You've only got enough strength left for two teleports, three if two of those are short, and one of those 'ports has to get you and Quinton to London.

Kerr—

Jason. Kerr drowned out his partner's thoughts with desperate words, seconds ticking away as the spark of Threnody's power faded. *I knew*

when Kristen broke your shields Quinton would come first from here on out.
He has to if you're going to live.

Kerr could feel Lucas and the merge at the far reaches of his mind, the mental grid lighting up with the thoughts of those who had survived the battle so far.

A hand grabbed at Kerr's leg, fingers twisting around his uniform. He knelt down, prying Jason's hand free and gripping it hard in his own.

You don't have much time. Kerr looked over at Jason, at the blood on his face and the panic in his partner's eyes, and smiled gently. *You'll have to learn to follow someone else after this, Jays. Don't hate them because they're not me. Now go.*

I could stay, Jason said. *I'm the one Nathan wants.*

That's not how this works. You know that.

Slowly, Jason nodded, eyes filled with pain and regret, his mind brimming with countless thoughts and emotion that washed over Kerr. Jason never looked away as he teleported out, taking Quinton with him, his hand disappearing from Kerr's clenched fingers. His telekinetic shield stayed standing.

Kerr turned and pressed his hand flat against the invisible power of Jason's telekinesis, the hard, layered shield all he had left now. The psi link that connected him with Jason was a faint spark at the bottom of his mind.

Nathan's diminished merge was already regrouping and stabilizing. Those dark blue eyes didn't look away from Kerr's face as clarity returned to them.

This ends here, Nathan said, his words riding a wave of desperate power.

Of course it does, Lucas said, slamming into and *through* Kerr's mind with enough force to black out the world. *But you'll never see the* Ark, *Nathan. You'll never see Mars Colony.*

Kerr's strength flowed through the Stryker merge, filling the cracks and smoothing out the jagged edges that had been torn into it. Lucas let him mend what Samantha couldn't, giving up more and more space as other minds extracted themselves from the merge. First one, then two, then a dozen psi signatures disappeared—not dead, but teleported out, carrying Strykers who weren't kinetic-oriented with them. Kerr kept his hand pressed hard against Jason's shield, the support grounding him as Warhound telepaths dug hooks into the merge and his own mental shields.

The Stryker merge kept growing smaller, seemingly beaten into submission by Nathan's. Warhounds started to outnumber Strykers on the mental grid. Kerr felt the strain of the merge start to build up in his own mind as Lucas transferred more and more control over to him. The weight was something he could handle better than Lucas at this point, having been inactive during the majority of the battle. Out of every 'path-oriented psion in the Stryker ranks, Kerr was the only one left who could take Lucas's place.

I thought I could pull you out, Lucas said.

I know, Kerr said. *But the future always changes.*

It's not supposed to.

Maybe. But you did. And I don't blame you for that.

It was Kerr's job now to keep Nathan's merge anchored in this moment and to Kerr's mind. If those connections broke, they would lose this fight and all the rest waiting to start in the coming years.

Kerr held up as best he could, but against a Class I triad psion with years of practice under his belt, it was only a matter of time before Kerr started to buckle. He struggled to shore up all the Strykers' shields until those, too, started to disappear.

I can't hold it any longer, Lucas said, thoughts a fractured, broken mess. Kerr could barely sense Samantha or Kristen in the maelstrom that was Lucas's mind.

Kerr did what he was trained to do, what he had promised to do. He stood his ground.

Let me have the rest of the merge. Jason's telekinetic shield was still solid beneath his touch. Gideon kept hitting it with merged telekinesis, but couldn't break through. *Don't worry about me, Lucas.*

Lucas exited Kerr's mind, leaving behind a gaping hole in Kerr's thoughts that was filled with a myriad of minds from Nathan's merge. Kerr held on to the Stryker merge for a few moments longer, holding up the façade, until everyone else let go and all he could feel were two last people lingering in his mind.

Jason and Threnody.

For a second—Kerr lived a lifetime.

Jason's shield disappeared. Kerr cut the psi link between them. Merged Warhound telekinesis, once held at bay, now slammed into Kerr. He was thrown back by the force, the punch a harder hit than anything he'd ever before experienced. He crashed to the floor, felt his bones shatter from the inside out, felt the deep ache of organs tearing apart. All he tasted now was blood.

Merged telepathy curled deeper into his mind, stripping his shields down to their last layer, down to where his Class IX empathy mingled with his Class II telepathy. It wasn't enough to save him. Not this time.

Kerr blinked, struggling to breathe. Emptiness clawed at the edge of his mind and brightness interfered with his vision. He could see sunlight glinting off the space shuttles through the plasglass observation windows of the command room, everything shining with false halos.

He felt Nathan digging through his mind and Kerr couldn't stop him, didn't even try as the Warhound merge got lost in the maze of his psyche. He let all those minds find anchor points in his own thoughts, tying them down. Blood and clear fluid slid out of his nose and ears, pouring out of his mouth, choking him. He sensed Threnody's determination through the tenuous psi link that still ran between them. Kerr closed his eyes, feeling some distant sort of satisfaction as Nathan found, too late, what was hiding in his mind.

No, Nathan said, his telepathy a ragged, bright line of thought knotted deep in Kerr's mind. *You Strykers would never do this. It goes against everything you are.*

That's why you never saw it coming, Kerr said, thinking of Lucas.

With the last of his strength and every mental trick Lucas had taught him, Kerr held tight to the faded imprint of the merge, trapping Nathan and the merged telepaths and telekinetics there with him on the ground. The Warhounds struggled to get free of the deep holes in Kerr's mind, and maybe some did, but Kerr didn't know how many of them survived. All he knew was the shock that colored everyone's thoughts, their shared horrified, frantic disbelief. In that last hectic instant, Kerr heard them, heard them all as they died screaming.

[FORTY-FIVE]

Threnody felt, distantly, when the last motherboard burned out, the spark of exploding circuits cascading through her brain. Or maybe it was something else, something more immediate. Threnody didn't know, couldn't care, as she collapsed to the floor, struggling to stay conscious.

Everything seemed distant until Kerr's voice whispered through her mind. Threnody could barely understand his words, but it didn't matter. All he needed were her eyes, so she focused on the generator room, everything blurry to her sight. Then it sharpened, brought into perfect clarity not by her, but by someone else. The connection overwhelmed her traumatized system and she passed out for a few seconds. She came back to herself slowly, hearing someone calling her name.

"Thren, please. Wake up," Quinton said, his voice a ragged, painful plea in her ear.

It took effort to open her eyes. She was barely aware of her surroundings, of the person holding her up so she could breathe. She coughed, her lungs burning. She tried to move, but the agony in her body made her choke out a cry.

"It's okay, it's okay," Quinton said, sounding desperate. He shifted her in his arms, one hand resting above the bullet wound in her thigh. "I know it hurts, but we'll fix you up in no time. I promise."

Only one emergency light was still working, whatever power source it ran on spared from the damage she'd caused. It cast an eerie glow over the two men gathered around her. Threnody opened her mouth to speak, but no words came out.

Quinton's shaking hand touched her face. "Jason, get us out of here."

Threnody blinked, the room changing shape with a crack of displaced air as Jason teleported them not to safety, but to the storage room she had left behind for the generator room. A single emergency light burned over by the door. The Command Center must have had a separate emergency backup system that she hadn't been connected to. There still wasn't enough light to see by.

"Flashlight," Threnody rasped out. "Near the case."

"Jason, we don't have time for this shit," Quinton snarled. He still grabbed the flashlight and turned it on. The bright light hurt Threnody's eyes.

Threnody coughed and looked down at herself. Her arms were black husks streaked through with scorched red, her uniform and the skinsuit burned off. Pieces still remained, melted into muscle, mixing with plasma. She could move her fingers, barely, but she couldn't feel a damn thing. Her head felt strangely weighted down.

"The case?" she managed to ask.

"Bomb's still active. The insulation in the carrying case protected it," Jason said in a hollow voice. "The shelves were metal. Receiver is nothing but slag. I can't find the remote detonator."

Threnody let out a choked little laugh. "Had it with me. Left it on the lower level."

She could hear Jason swallow. "Then it's probably slagged as well."

Something wet hit her face; tears, maybe. Or blood. She couldn't smell the difference, couldn't smell anything. Threnody focused on hands that she couldn't feel anymore, muscle memory ingrained in a way the brain couldn't forget. Quinton always said that even after he'd lost his arms or hands to his power, somehow he always thought his limbs were still there. Phantom sensations that his nerves remembered, would always remember.

Hers remembered.

"How much time?" she said.

Quinton's arms tightened around her. The pressure nearly sent Threnody spiraling back into unconsciousness, and she let out a pained noise. Quinton loosened his grip. She squeezed her eyes shut.

"Kerr and Lucas can't hold Nathan back for much longer," Jason said. "Three, maybe four minutes. Everyone else has teleported out. It's just us."

Threnody opened her eyes. The darkness seemed strangely bright to her. "Leave me."

"No."

Quinton ground out the word. Threnody felt his entire body jerk in protest at what she was telling him to do. She struggled to lift an arm, bumping a ruined hand against the line of his jaw, refusing to let the pain pull her under. A roaring sound filled her ears, but she didn't know what it was and couldn't care.

"No choice." She smiled, struggling to form it. "Bomb needs to go off."

"I'll do it," Quinton said, burying his face against the top of her head, his teeth catching on her hair. "Jason can teleport you to London, then come back for me."

She caught sight of Jason's face and the bitter regret in his eyes. "I've only got enough strength left for one more teleport," Jason said. "I can't—"

Save you. The same way he couldn't save Kerr. She didn't need to be a telepath to hear those unspoken words.

Threnody drew in a short breath, finding it hard to breathe. She felt cold. "The world needs Jason. He needs you, Quinton. There's no one left to do this. Just me."

Quinton clutched wordlessly at her uniform, pulling at it.

Threnody felt Jason's hand on her shoulder, his grip shaky. His voice wasn't much better. "We're running out of time."

Quinton picked her up with arms that shook, but his hands were gentle as he cradled her close for the last time. He sat her up against the back wall of the storage room, Jason dragging the black case within easy reach. The glow from the flashlight showed Threnody everything around her, everything that mattered.

Quinton framed her face with his hands, fingers warm against her skin as he looked at her, his eyes searching hers out in the dark as they'd done countless times before.

"Hi," Quinton said, voice breaking.

"Hi." Threnody leaned forward, pressing her forehead against his. "I wanted to see it."

"I know."

"Live it for me. As long as you can." He tried to say her name, but nothing came out, just the shape of it on his lips. Threnody smiled, refusing to look away. "It's okay, Quin. Don't be afraid."

Jason teleported them out in a crack of displaced air and Threnody was left alone, the ghost of Quinton's touch on her face. The flashlight was angled to spotlight the open black case and the shape of the nuclear bomb that rested inside.

Threnody reached out with a shaking hand, ignoring the pain that came with movement, until her ruined fingers hovered over the arming switch near the base of the warhead. The tattered psi link between her and Kerr was held together by mental whispers, and then not even that.

She sobbed out a breath, biting down hard on her torn bottom lip until blood flowed over her tongue. She still couldn't taste it, but she remembered the metallic flavor, and her life, and all the decisions that had brought her to this moment.

Threnody flipped the switch.

The world burned hot and white for an instant. The mental grid dipped. Pulsed. Flattened.

In her mind and Kerr's, everything was quiet.

[FORTY-SIX]

SEPTEMBER 2379
LONDON, UNITED KINGDOM

Telepaths were dying beneath her hands, beneath her power, and Jael could only let them slide away as the merge ate through their minds. Nothing she could do would keep them alive long enough for her to stabilize their minds. She couldn't save most of them, so Jael settled for a few, two of them being Lucas's sisters. She kept a careful mental touch on Samantha and Kristen as she worked on the Strykers she could help. Jael judged the state of the fight by the state of those two Sercas and how damaged their minds were becoming.

Only when telekinetics started teleporting into the street in droves did Jael realize how many Strykers they were going to lose. She was inundated by the spiraling death throes of too many minds, and they threatened to take her down with them. Even her shields weren't enough, the mental shrieks of the dying clawing at her mind. For the first time since she'd dipped into a person's mind for psi surgery, Jael closed herself off to their thoughts and pain, trying to find her balance again.

The telepaths who were purposefully held back from the merge to be available for the fallout couldn't have known what was coming. They couldn't have foreseen that Strykers would be dying in the streets, slumped over one another, bleeding in the gutter, minds tangled together in a knot that no one could undo.

Then the cause of the whole damn mess teleported into the street, legs crumpling beneath him as he appeared. Someone screamed for Jael, but she was already running, stumbling over bodies to reach Lucas. The Stryker merge that had hung over the mental grid for so long finally broke down completely, the Serca siblings losing the viselike grip they had on everyone's minds. Lucas, for all his immense power, was so far gone, wrapped so tight and stretched so thin, that he never even felt it when his mind broke.

Samantha did, but she could do nothing, had nothing left to reach for him with that could help. Her telepathy was as shattered as the merge, and Kristen was no longer present to help pull Lucas out of the mental abyss that threatened his sanity. Kristen was already gone, mind broken beyond repair and shutting down, one dying spark in a wave of many. Try as she might, Samantha couldn't find Lucas in the mess that was the mental grid, and Jael felt the girl slip away somewhere deep inside herself.

Jael crashed to her knees beside Lucas's body, yanking at the lock of his skinsuit helmet and prying it off. She cushioned his head with one hand, letting her fingers catch the weight of it rather than the street. At the touch of her mind to his, Lucas's eyes snapped open, pupils tiny black pinpricks in a sea of dark blue, blood leaking out of the corners like tears.

"Lucas," Jael said, heart pounding in her chest. *Stay with me.*

He focused on her, or seemed to. Recognition was there, but Jael knew, somehow, that it wasn't of her. She would never know what he saw in that moment.

He opened his mouth and choked on words. "I—"

Breath stuttered in his chest. Jael felt his mind fall through the mental grid.

She couldn't catch him.

Jael felt the massive, gaping hole in Lucas's ravaged mind—all that was left of him after the merge—swallow everything in the wake of the trauma he'd inflicted on himself. Jael was effectively shut out, clawing at his mind and not even touching shields, just empty space.

"Lucas," she whispered, staring blankly down at his unconscious form and the slow rise and fall of his chest. Jael needed to transport him to the Strykers Syndicate immediately, but she wasn't sure if any telekinetics were left who had the strength to teleport.

A shadow drifted over her and Jael looked up, staring at Jason and Quinton. Jason had his arm slung over Quinton's shoulder, letting the other man take most of his weight. An ugly rip was torn through his uniform and skinsuit, blood having saturated the area, but his chest seemed whole. The grief they exhibited rubbed against the raw places in her own mind. Quinton was staring down the street with a dead look in his eyes, seemingly unaware of his surroundings.

"It's over," Jason said, eyes bloodshot, voice raw and wounded. "Threnody detonated the bomb. Kerr made sure Nathan and his Warhounds couldn't leave the explosion radius before everyone else teleported out of range."

Jael closed her eyes, her mind still searching for Lucas's. "And the people already in space?"

Quinton spoke, but he didn't sound like the man Jael knew. "Let them die out there."

PART NINE
TABULA RASA

SESSION DATE: **2128.09.28**
LOCATION: **Institute of Psionics Research**
CLEARANCE ID: **Dr. Amy Bennett**
SUBJECT: **2581**
FILE NUMBER: **881**

The doctor kneels before the girl, one hand gripping the cascade of wires that hangs from bruised skin. Those bleached-out violet eyes seem sunken and they no longer look at the camera. They look elsewhere.

"Aisling," the doctor pleads. "We can't survive like this."

The girl is still and quiet, one hand clutching a white card. After a long moment, she unclenches her hand and lets the card fall to the floor. "Thank you," she whispers.

The doctor picks the card up, turns it around to see the shape on the underside. "We don't want your thanks."

"I know." The girl smiles and leans forward, the effort making her gasp. She presses a kiss to the woman's forehead, like a benediction when it isn't, not in her prison cell. "I wasn't thanking you."

The doctor drops the card to the floor and reaches out to help the child lean back in her seat. Behind them, the machines click and hum and whine, a nonstop sound that has been a constant companion to them both.

"What do we do?" the doctor whispers. "What do we do next?"

"Anything you want, Lucas." Aisling smiles, eyes wide and glazed and looking at things no one else can see. "Anything at all."

[FORTY-SEVEN]

OCTOBER 2379
TORONTO, CANADA

It never changed.

Jael wondered about that, the first time she went down into the static of Lucas's mind to try to anchor a psi link. She gave up analyzing it on the tenth try. The vibrancy was gone, the brightness normally there on the mental grid missing. Nothing remained but an echo, a negative imprint that she couldn't hold on to.

Not a memory, exactly. Not really a dream. Just the seam of his mind and the spaces in between that he'd fallen through. Just that last, drawn-out moment before the permanent end he hovered over, unable to let go, because psions were incapable of forgetting. Dying quick was always preferable to dying slow. Bleeding out in the mind happened like this, in increments. Searching for Lucas was like trying to find one clean drop of water in an ocean of toxic mistakes. Impossible without belief, without help.

Jael stared across the medical bed where Lucas lay, at a hollow-eyed Samantha, who swayed on weak legs, Marguerite standing worriedly behind her.

You won't find him, you know, Samantha said, the psi link between them quivering on her end as she struggled to hold on to something that only Jael was generating. *Not how he was. I don't know why you brought me in here.*

I'm not expecting to find sanity in his thoughts, Jael said as she curled a hand around Lucas's lax one. *I'm only interested in what's left behind. We need your brother.*

Samantha hunched her shoulders, the rigid line of her body bending into a brittle curve. *Do you, Jael? You need something he no longer is.*

Samantha could feel him, here in his mind, damaged as they both were, when all the times that Jael had tried before she only felt that vast,

echoing emptiness; only seen a flatline on the EEG and supporting machines, despite the heart beating in his chest. Jael had been in and out of
both their minds for weeks on end, struggling to find the pieces of two
shattered personalities and coming up achingly, bitterly short.

Jael was a Class III telepath. She would never be able to reach far
enough to find Lucas, but Samantha *could*. She could find him, when no
one else had the ability to, because Lucas always led her to him. It took
nearly a month for Jael to realize why, of days spent holding Samantha's
thoughts together while the telepath screamed her throat bloody and raw
beneath makeshift mental shields that wouldn't hold. Permanent shields
weren't an option, not yet, not until they found Lucas.

Samantha was as whole as Jael could make her, something far less
than what the girl had been born to be. Jael could see the fragility in the
blonde, in the tiny mental threads that held her together. All Jael's work
and all for nothing, the Stryker thought tiredly.

Jael pressed her telepathy against the edge of Samantha's mind and the
old scar of the mindwipe that had Lucas's touch all over it. All over his sister. Samantha's mind had never been her own. It had horrified Jael when
she'd figured out what the scars pressed into Samantha's thoughts meant,
yet it also relieved her. Here was the shape of Lucas, in Samantha's mind,
the mold he needed to fill. Here was their salvation, as fractured as it was.

Jael stared at Samantha as their minds plunged deeper into the void
that was seemingly all that remained of Lucas. Then she closed her eyes
and Jael dug her telepathy into Samantha's battered thoughts with precise pressure.

I'm sorry, Jael said, *for what they did to you. For what I need to do.*

Samantha's screams echoed in the room, in their thoughts, bouncing
off the jagged edges of a broken mind and against her shields, as Jael
stripped Samantha of the mindwipe. The last piece of who she was—torn
from everything that had made her into what Nathan and Lucas forced
her to be. Jael cut the psi link between them, and Samantha, no longer
anchored, slipped away, collapsing unconscious in Marguerite's arms.

Jael wondered who Samantha would be, if she would be anything at
all, when she woke up.

The pattern was in Jael's thoughts now, a delicate thing that only a higher-Classed psion could possibly create. Borrowed, for now, as she spread the mindwipe through Lucas's mind, the mental grid humming around her.

We need you, she thought fiercely as that pattern of himself Lucas gave up so long ago seeped back into his thoughts. Some errant shard of a forgotten whole sparked and sputtered in her power, forming into a knotted, twisted psi signature she didn't recognize.

It always came back to that simple, selfish demand that drove humanity forward.

Need. Want. Some distant, half-formed idea of world integration beneath a clear blue sky.

Just some child's impossible dream.

Lucas, please.

. . . Jael.

What seemed like hours later, when she opened her eyes and came back to herself in a medical room at the top of a city tower, Jael was greeted by the soft, rhythmic noise from monitors tracking the synaptic pulse of Lucas's damaged mind, his hand weakly squeezing hers.

[FORTY-EIGHT]

NOVEMBER 2379
TORONTO, CANADA

Here's your weekly update," Jason said as he handed over a datapad to Jael before easing himself into a chair. "The major fallout from Paris stayed inside that country's borders. Winter winds will spread the radiation particles, but whatever damage it might do where it falls won't rate much. The radiation is mostly going to hit deadzones."

"I could wish that was the last time a nuclear bomb is detonated on this planet," Jael said as she scrolled through the report. "Somehow, I doubt it."

"If it happens again, we won't be around to see it."

But they were seeing the political fallout and it wasn't going to be easy to navigate a world where fear of psions might never fade.

"Oh, before I forget." Jason pulled a small fruit out of his jacket pocket and set it on Jael's desk. "That's for you. Courtesy of Matron. Carried it with me when I brought in the latest shipment of seedlings."

Jael looked up from the datapad in her hand and eyed the orange fruit as if it were something dangerous. "You sure she didn't poison it?"

"That woman barely lets people near her garden. You think she'd knowingly allow poison?" Jason shook his head. "Try it. She said it's called a kumquat."

Jael stared at the tiny, bite-size fruit before her with the healthy hesitation that a lifetime of wariness had gifted her. Eventually, she picked up the fruit and popped it in her mouth. The skin was sweet; biting into it was a different story. The taste shifted from sweet to sour on her tongue, the flavor shocking her taste buds.

She made a face and swallowed the pulp as fast as she could, spitting out the seed. "I don't know about that one. You sure you didn't mess up the seed growth somehow?"

Jason scratched the back of his neck, shrugging. "Maybe? Thought I had this tree down. I guess Matron will have to wait on her pears."

"What in the world is a pear?"

"It's another fruit. I think."

Jael set aside her work, wishing she had a glass of water to wash away the taste. "Where is she putting that bush?"

"Tree. Pears grow on trees, and she's thinking of putting some greenery into Kensington Gardens."

"Kensington Gardens is full of transients. What's she going to do? Order them to move?"

"If she wants us to clear it out, we'll clear it out." Jason slouched a little in his seat. "She's just taking what's owed to her. I'm willing to let her experiment, but winter's coming soon and nothing grows in the cold."

"Maybe wait until spring."

"Maybe," Jason echoed, tipping his head back to stare at the ceiling.

The silence in the office was heavy, but neither of them felt the need to break it. Nearly two and a half months since the world almost ended again, and things were still changing. There was an orchard in St. James's Park that people visited, or talked about visiting. It was overseen by Matron and her scavengers, the group having appropriated a building abandoned during the riots. No one in London fought her on her claim that she owned that bit of land, not even the drug cartels. Matron was only human, but she had psions on her side, and that was enough to make anyone pause these days.

Jael ran a fingertip over the line of her teeth, the tartness from the fruit still stinging her tongue. The amount of new food that was growing in Toronto's SkyFarms and others across the world was heartening, even if their stomachs couldn't handle it yet. A lifetime of bland GMO food had prepared no one for the shock that came with taste. Adjusting to the new diet was going to take time. Her people had enough of it for now.

"Does it ever feel weird?" Jason said, his voice jerking Jael from her thoughts. "Sitting in this office?"

"Always," Jael replied, trying not to hunch her shoulders. Leadership was always so much easier when someone else was doing it.

The door to Jael's office slid open, causing Jason to twist around in his chair to see who it was. He stood up as Samantha's thin figure stepped inside. The young woman crossed the office with measured strides, holding herself rigidly, as if she were afraid she would take one wrong step and break.

Samantha wore the soft, comfortable clothes those in recovery were given, though she no longer had a room in the medical level to call her own. Jael had upgraded her physical condition weeks ago to discharge, though Samantha's mental state was still in doubt—she was still at risk for suicide. Jael thought a change of scenery would be helpful; better than being sequestered in a white medical room with machines that constantly showed what she was missing, even if her new room came with twenty-four-hour surveillance.

Psions didn't mutate postnatal. Their Classification, however, could change. Samantha's telepathy was, for the most part, nonexistent now. The merge and Jael's psionic interference had broken her mind down to a Class IX, more human than psion, her telepathic reach no stronger than the softest whisper within her own thoughts. Samantha never used her power anymore, too aware and too prideful of what she had once been to accept what she had become.

Maybe it would have been better, more merciful, if she had died like Kristen. Jael hadn't been able to save Samantha's sister. If she was honest with herself, she hadn't tried very hard. Kristen's mind had torn itself apart during the merge, pain finally overcoming the empath's power. There hadn't been much left for Jael to save, and she didn't regret letting the teenager die. Keeping Samantha from doing the same was a full-time job on some days.

Samantha flicked Jason a wary look. Jason, for his part, made sure his shields were locked down tight. "If you need to speak with Jael in private, I can leave."

"No," Samantha said, her voice raspy. The weeks she'd spent screaming in the medical level during her recovery had permanently ruined her once-pretty soprano voice. "I need the latest report on survivors. There's a press conference tomorrow and I'm better at writing speeches than the people you've assigned to public relations."

Jael picked up a datapad from the pile on her desk and pushed it toward the edge. "It's right here."

Jason took a careful step back, giving Samantha room to take the datapad and not feel as if he was invading her personal space. She took it and hugged it to her chest.

"Latest world population count puts us at over a million by about fifty thousand," Jael said quietly. "Give or take a few hundred. The Registry only told us who was going into space, not who was left behind, and we lost tens of thousands in the riots. The census will take maybe another year or so to complete, but you can report on the rough findings. I think that will satisfy the public."

"And the count for psions?" Samantha said, sounding as if the question was difficult to ask.

"Around six hundred or so, if we're being generous. There's talk of a child or two in the Americas that show signs of being psions." Jael hesitated before saying, "Telepaths, according to the bioscanners. I'm sending out a team for retrieval."

Samantha's entire body flinched. She bit her lip, looking away from Jael and out at the view of Toronto instead. "We need those. There are so few telepaths and telekinetics left."

"I know."

This is all we've got, Jael thought as she watched Samantha turn around and head for the door. *Just the remains and nothing more. We've got to make it worth something.*

Keiko and Aidan were dead, as were nearly 85 percent of the Strykers' telepaths and 50 percent of their telekinetics. The worldwide merge Lucas had led in the assault on Paris had decimated the Strykers Syndicate's ranks. Empaths, pyrokinetics, electrokinetics, and psychometrists outnumbered the other two kinds of psions now, those that survived the riots at least. Prior to that, they had lost roughly 250 psions through the World Court's mass termination. Whoever was brought back from the retrieval mission would never know the feel of a neurotracker in his or her head.

It was a start.

The door slid shut behind Samantha. Jason was kind enough to wait until she was gone before tipping his head in Jael's direction as a silent good-bye and teleporting out. Jael sighed and leaned back in her chair, rubbing wearily at one shoulder. She ached in a way she never had before, body running through the last dregs of life in her cells. Jael knew the signs better than most; she just didn't know how long she had left. Maybe a year, maybe less, maybe more.

"So much to do, so little time," Jael murmured to herself as she got to her feet.

She was never much good at leading beyond the confines of the medical level. Whoever succeeded her would have to be. The Strykers Syndicate couldn't show weakness to the world, but neither could it show the same rigidity the old government had ruled with. It was a delicate balancing act, and she thought only one family could actually pull it all off. Pity the one they all needed wasn't even born yet.

Jael left the office, nodding at the handful of aides working in the area beyond her doors. "I'll be on the medical level if anyone needs me."

She headed for the lift, rubbing at her temple, wishing the headache she had would go away.

[FORTY-NINE]

NOVEMBER 2379
LONDON, UNITED KINGDOM

Jason crossed two continents and an ocean, arriving in London after two days' worth of work back west. His feet hit the floor of the small arrival room with a dull thump. Toronto was five hours behind and still working through its late afternoon. It was evening here. Sighing, Jason stepped off the wooden arrival platform. The room was painted white, but even the paint job couldn't hide how worn-out the place looked.

The door opened manually and he left the room behind, heading for the faint sound of people on the ground level. Matron and some of her scavengers were finishing their evening meal when Jason walked into the communal kitchen. The rest of her crew were still down in the southern hemisphere, cataloguing the seed bank on Antarctica. The shift change wouldn't happen for another week.

Matron looked up from the conversation she was having with Zahara in between bites of stir-fry. "You're back early. Jael like the fruit?"

"No," Jason said.

"She just don't know what tastes good." Matron jerked her thumb in the direction of the tenement's entrance. "If you're looking for Quinton, he's outside."

Matron only meant one place when she said outside. Jason nodded and headed out into the chilly, late-autumn night. He was glad for the warmth of his coat, but the wind still found places to blow through, making him shiver. He crossed the cracked street for the dry expanse of St. James's Park, ducking his head against the wind. The park was a fallow patch of earth that once provided homes for transients, but not anymore. The squalor had forcibly been removed, leaving behind swathes of hard dirt and a barren lake bottom.

Jason cut west across the area. He didn't join the crowd that always gathered around the motley growth of trees and bushes that hugged one small, raised plot of dirt within the perimeter of the lake bed. Glancing over his shoulder, Jason could see the light that played across the tree branches with their brittle red-gold leaves. People were more interested in what Matron was growing with his help than the news streams that slid over the hologrids surrounding the park area, lighting up the night with neon.

Jason wasn't interested in anything except the person sitting on the worn-out cement steps surrounding a cement pillar at the other end of the park. A statue had sat on top of it once, according to records, but it was lost to history now. Jason climbed the steps at an angle, moving around the people gathered there. Everyone ignored him, which Jason appreciated as he went to sit beside Quinton. The older man nodded faintly, the only greeting Quinton gave. Jason got comfortable, watching the crowds pass them by on the street, quads mingling to try to keep the peace on the Strykers Syndicate's orders.

They didn't speak right away. They didn't need to. The bond that linked them had been cut even deeper into their minds during the fight in Paris, a casualty of the merge. It had strengthened the psi link to such a degree that not even a Class I telepath would be able to sever it now. Jason's power hummed down the length of the bond when he used his microtelekinesis, needing Quinton's mind as a stabilizing anchor.

It wasn't going to be enough in the long run; they both knew it. The stronger the psion, the shorter the psion's life, and Jason knew he had only a couple years left if he was lucky. It was the trade-off for what he could do—reconstruct everyone else's life at the cost of his own.

Despite the bond, the two couldn't read each other's mind or emotions, but they understood each other better now because of it. The antagonism that had been there months ago upon joining up for that fateful mission in the Slums of the Angels was gone, buried beneath shared experiences and shared grief.

"You have a headache," Quinton said after a while, staring at the low skyline of London beyond the razed area where a palace once stood. It got turned into a night market over a century ago, and the cacophony of people coming out for an evening of street entertainment reached their ears.

"Same one from this morning," Jason said. "I don't know how to block you from getting feedback."

"It's fine."

Gas hissed as it was released from the biotubes in Quinton's arms. He snapped his fingers, lighting it, letting the ball of fire grow to a decent size as it hovered in the air between them above their knees. The heat made the chill bearable, even if it made everyone else around them draw away out of fear, giving them space. Jason pulled a pack of cigarettes from his pocket and pried one out, lighting it off Quinton's fire.

People around them weren't discreet in the way they gave ground to the pair of psions sitting on the steps. Without uniforms anymore to distinguish psions from the rest of the population, everyone looked human. It was hard to see the differences now that the old laws no longer applied.

Quinton tilted his head back, staring up at the cloudy sky. Jason followed his gaze, blowing smoke up into the air. "Think any of them made it?"

"I don't know," Quinton said, mouth thinning into a flat line. "I hope not."

In the weeks since the nuclear destruction in Paris, the Strykers Syndicate had been focused on Earth, not the stars. If any of the space shuttles made it to the *Ark,* if the *Ark* made it out of cold-dock, maybe the people who fled had survived and were headed to Mars Colony. Maybe not. The Strykers Syndicate only had access to a few working satellites, and even those could only tell them so much. Most of the government's codes and knowledge had been lost when The Hague was half-destroyed and the Peace Palace burned to the ground.

Popular opinion leaned toward abandoning The Hague. Too many memories were left behind in that city, memories no one wanted. The psychometrists who scoured the rubble there said the memories were too corrosive, too strong, to ever really fade. It wasn't worth rebuilding over the lies buried there. But the bunkers and tunnels below were still viable for people to call home. Even if the government left that city behind, civilians wouldn't.

The Strykers Syndicate was still functioning. Most of the Strykers who survived had opted to stay and work rather than leave. Despite their newfound freedom, they had nowhere else to go. Some still left once they recovered from wounds incurred in Paris or in any number of riots that filled the world's streets during that time. Problems were reported from time to time of psion attacks against people, sometimes by ex-Strykers, sometimes by Warhounds. Not all of Nathan's people had died in Paris; they just didn't know how many survived.

Security was an issue that Strykers excelled at, but they weren't doing it for free. If the world wanted stability, it would have to pay for it. The cost seemed high to the registered humans still living—psions wanted equal decision-making authority with whatever government was being cobbled together in London—but most people in the streets weren't as discriminatory, despite the Strykers' use of a nuclear bomb. It hadn't been directed at them, but the registered elite.

"Hell of a way to go, dying on some other planet." Jason took another drag on his cigarette. "I hope they die slow."

Quinton barked out a laugh, the smile on his face humorless and all teeth. "You and me both."

The sound of London at night filtered through the air, the city towers only half-lit. For all that the city towers were open to everyone now, people on the street were still hesitant to enter them. They weren't abandoned, not how some city towers had been in other parts of the world. No one was certain of the whereabouts of those registered humans and probably never would be, even with the oncoming census set to document everyone's identities to create a Registry of humans and psions alike. The old government didn't exist anymore to deny people access based on damaged genetics. That didn't mean old habits were easy to let go.

"We should leave soon," Jason finally said as he stubbed out his cigarette. "Lucas is expecting us."

Quinton didn't move. "I hate Toronto."

"I know."

It was why they lived here now, in London, with Matron and her scavengers. Maybe things would be easier if they moved back to the city tower they'd spent most of their lives working out of, but other Strykers kept wanting to pull them back into a fold they'd left months ago in a broken-down cathedral on America's western shore. While survivor's guilt was shared by all of them, almost every Stryker back in Toronto and those residing in outposts in various cities hadn't experienced what they had.

The loss might be similar, but it wasn't the same.

"I miss her," Quinton said quietly.

Jason's mouth twisted, grief a bitter taste on his tongue, even after all these weeks. He pressed one hand against the edge of the cement step, thinking he could still feel Kerr's hand in his. Thinking maybe, if they'd had just a little more time, he could have saved them. Both of them.

"I'm sorry," Jason whispered.

Neither knew whom he was apologizing to.

Quinton let his hand hover over the fire, his power slowly fading. When the fire was gone, he got to his feet and Jason did the same. Taking a breath in London, they let it out in Toronto, Jason's teleport bringing them to the arrival room on the medical level.

They stepped off the platform, nodding at the Stryker on duty before heading into the hallway. They made their way to Jael's private lab in silence. The door was locked, but Jason had the override. Lucas knew better than to keep them out of the lab. When they walked inside, they could see Lucas standing before the gestational unit, one hand resting against the warm side of the machine that held his daughter. Jael stood beside Lucas, watching him.

"Lucas," Jason said in greeting as he and Quinton crossed the lab space. "Jael."

"Didn't expect you back so soon," Jael said, lifting her hand in a half wave. "Hello, Quinton. Haven't seen you in a while."

"There's a reason for that," Quinton said.

"I know." Jael didn't bother to hide the sadness in her voice. "But you're always welcome here. You know that."

Quinton ignored her words. Jason shrugged at Jael, not willing to apologize for their choice of distance over reunification. "How's the kid?"

"Doing exceptionally well," Jael said as she picked up a datapad and handed it to Jason. "She's got the genetic markers of a triad psion, but I think we can conclusively say her telekinesis is going to be like yours."

"I should hope so. After all the effort I put in to make her into what we needed, she better be like me."

They all knew that the power Jason had engineered Lucas's daughter into having would change the course of history as surely as nuclear war had. Jael no longer hated Ciari for the closely held orders that woman had given, at Lucas's urging, that set them all on this road. She regretted, uncomfortably so, that she never told Ciari that while she still lived. Not forgiveness, nor regret, but a thank-you. Jael liked to think Ciari would have accepted it.

"We'll have to figure out a way to keep engineering this power," Jael said, gazing at the monitors, voice thoughtful. "It's going to take so long to fix this world, even with the terraforming machines, that we can't let this power die out."

"What about when the world is fixed?" Quinton asked as he braced himself against a nearby lab table. "What then? What happens to our kind?"

"If we're going by rates of half-life, psions are going to be around for the next several thousand years, no worries," Jason said, studying the medical information on the datapad. "Maybe by the time we shrink some of the deadzones, what we can do won't be considered a disease. Maybe we'll all be human, able to live an entire human lifetime, but still have these abilities. Maybe it won't take bad genetics to give birth to a psion."

"That's a lot of maybes."

Jason shrugged. "Who knows? It might happen."

"Let's just stick with what we do know," Jael said. "Someone else can figure out the future."

"Someone already did," Jason reminded her, glancing at Quinton. "Aside from not having a death switch in my head, I'm still not sure I like it."

Empty spaces existed in their lives now, silence where another person once lived. The two still grieved the losses of Threnody and Kerr, and always would, no matter how many years they had left to live. They still kept looking over their shoulders for two people who were no longer there, who would never again be there.

Jael tilted her head in acknowledgment of their unsaid words. "That's your prerogative. I'm heading out. Don't keep Lucas in here for too much longer. We need him to get better, not backslide."

"Do you?" Lucas said, his voice quiet, empty.

She'd only allowed him out of his recovery room this week, and he had spent every waking hour in this lab, watching his daughter's heartbeat on the cardiac monitor. Jael stared at his profile, at the bruises still marring the skin beneath his dark blue eyes; those would fade. The bruising in his mind would be with him until death.

Genetically, Lucas would always be a triad psion, but his telepathy wasn't much stronger than Samantha's now, and his telekinesis was completely broken. He couldn't teleport at all. The mess of his emotions, of his pain, was Kristen's legacy. The ruination of his mind was self-inflicted. He would have to live with it, for however long he had left.

"I'm not made to rule," Jael reminded him after a brief pause. "I'm a Stryker, not a Serca."

"You're the OIC."

"I was the last possible choice and you know it. You and Ciari both did."

Jael left the lab on quiet feet, the door sliding shut with a soft hiss. Jason set the datapad down on the table Quinton was leaning against and drifted over to Lucas's side. Jason pressed his hand against the gestational unit, let his power drag him down into amniotic fluid that washed the world out in a sea of proteins, lipids, and other nutrient structures that kept the baby growing. Jason followed the coils of her DNA in his mind, assuring himself that the genes that would make her a microtelekinetic were still holding up strong.

Jason blinked rapidly when he came back to himself, the world solidifying into hard lines with Quinton's distant help through their bond. "Have you chosen a name yet?"

"No," Lucas said.

"You've got a few months until she's born. There's still time."

Lucas splayed one hand over the top of the machine. "Will she have it?"

"I'm not a doctor, Lucas. I wasn't taught medicine. I followed what Korman and Jael showed me would be the best genetic course, but genes don't always stay true to DNA. I think she'll live longer than you or I will. How much longer, I don't know."

"Your daughter's survival for the sake of humanity doesn't absolve you of your actions, you know that, right?" Quinton said, coming to stand by Jason.

"You mean *you* won't," Lucas said, not looking up.

Quinton rubbed his fingers together, the sound of metal on metal grating on their ears. "You didn't need Threnody to change your mind about the launch, to keep everyone on Earth instead of letting them go into space. You could have figured that out on your own."

"No," Lucas said. "I don't think I could have. I needed someone to believe in. Threnody showed me how."

"You had Aisling for that."

"I simply followed orders where she was concerned and Aisling is dead. Threnody wasn't." Lucas lifted his head, meeting Quinton's gaze, seeing the sharp grief that still existed in the other man's eyes. "Your partner helped me see what needed to be done. I couldn't do that on my own. I wasn't raised with the ability to believe in someone other than myself. It's why Aisling told me to find her."

"Threnody wasn't a precog."

"The thing about precogs is that they see so many futures. They have to choose the best end result they can find. In order to do that, they have to build the future that will become our history. That takes a lot of steps, a lot of people, and a lot of time. One wrong move, one wrong choice by any single person, disrupts that goal and forms a new future." Lucas smiled bitterly. "There are linchpins that precogs find who need support, places where the future turns. Threnody was mine. You were Jason's."

"And Kerr?" Jason asked sharply. "What about him?"

"Kerr did what he was supposed to do. He made sure Threnody had time to do her job." Lucas looked away from them, back at the machine that housed his unborn daughter. "We all did what we had to do."

Quinton shook his head. "I don't count this as a win."

Lucas choked on a hollow laugh. "It's never been about winning."

"What if we made a wrong choice?" Jason said. "Somewhere in all this mess that happened, what if we didn't do something right? How do we know?"

Lucas didn't answer, only stared straight ahead.

"We don't," Quinton said as he walked to the door. "That's the problem."

Jason followed Quinton out of the lab, locking the door behind them. Alone, Lucas mentally reached with everything he had for the datapad that sat on the other work counter, mind stretched to its limits, struggling to locate a power that was nothing more than the ghost of a memory.

The datapad did not move.

Lucas stayed where he was, counting heartbeats.

PART TEN
EPITAPH

SESSION DATE: 2128.01.30
LOCATION: Institute of Psionics Research
CLEARANCE ID: Dr. Amy Bennett
SUBJECT: 2581
FILE NUMBER: 99

The doctor holds up the card, the back of it smooth and white where it faces the girl, the side facing her holding a single shape. The child knows this game. It bores her, and it shows. The electrodes attached to her skull and chest and arms itch, the machines she is connected to beeping a familiar cadence into the quiet, white room.

"Let's try again," the doctor says, a strained expression on her face. "What do you see, Aisling?"

She blinks bleached-out violet eyes slowly, a child playing at a grown-up game.

"What do I see?" The smile she offers is more than enough to make the doctor flinch as pupils contract to pinpricks in a sea of bleached-out violet. "I see—"

The machines behind her scream.

"There is a child, a girl, tiny against the backdrop of a ruined city, of a broken world. She wears a jumpsuit, durable little boots that carry her over a cracked street that stretches out before her, green grass shoving up through the dusty ground here and there and there. Her hair is honey brown, her eyes so dark a blue they're almost black. Her mind is wide and open, power burning hotly through the synapses of a triad psion's brain."

A breath. Then another. The cadence of her singsong words never wavers, sounding so much older than the handful of years she has lived.

"A voice calls out to her from behind. Deep. Exasperated. Not her mother, because her mother is dead. Not her father, because he cannot teach her what she needs to learn. But one of the two men behind her are important to her life. The little girl who does and does not listen to her minders skips farther away with a teasing laugh, flowers blooming bright and colorful and alive in the footsteps she leaves behind."

Aisling convulses on her seat, bitten-down nails digging scratches into her skin.

"The world is waking up. Or she is waking the world."